To Terry a
 I hope your journey in to
the Crying House will be a
fun, new ~~expierie~~ expierience
and a journey to something
different.
    Love you both,
    Jillian Osborn

The Crying House

Jillian Osborn

iUniverse, Inc.
Bloomington

The Crying House

Copyright © 2011 Jillian Osborn

All rights reserved. No part of this book may be used or reproduced by any means, graphic, electronic, or mechanical, including photocopying, recording, taping or by any information storage retrieval system without the written permission of the publisher except in the case of brief quotations embodied in critical articles and reviews.

This is a work of fiction. All of the characters, names, incidents, organizations, and dialogue in this novel are either the products of the author's imagination or are used fictitiously.

iUniverse books may be ordered through booksellers or by contacting:

iUniverse
1663 Liberty Drive
Bloomington, IN 47403
www.iuniverse.com
1-800-Authors (1-800-288-4677)

Because of the dynamic nature of the Internet, any Web addresses or links contained in this book may have changed since publication and may no longer be valid. The views expressed in this work are solely those of the author and do not necessarily reflect the views of the publisher, and the publisher hereby disclaims any responsibility for them.

Any people depicted in stock imagery provided by Thinkstock are models, and such images are being used for illustrative purposes only.

Certain stock imagery © Thinkstock.

ISBN: 978-1-4620-0003-6 (pbk)
ISBN: 978-1-4620-0005-0 (cloth)
ISBN: 978-1-4620-0004-3 (ebk)

Printed in the United States of America

iUniverse rev. date: 2/25/2011

For my mom, who's been my inspiration and a guiding light through my many dark paths. I hope others will come to love this book as much as you. I love you always, Mom, forever and a day.

PROLOGUE ◆

Love, an emotion which obtains placement within the hearts of two people. A personal attachment accompanied by passionate affection and deep desire for another person. If this absorbing fondness strongly persists within the hearts of one and the other, then the decision to live as husband and wife will be considered.

Accepting the submission to marriage is a celebration of love and commitment. It's one of God's holiest bonds. A union in heart, body and soul, between a man and woman as they're joined together in holy matrimony.

A commitment in that of marriage is to embrace dreams, realize hopes, face disappointments, and accept when a partner's failed. In saying that, this brings us to reality. Life with a spouse may not always bring sunshine, and it may not always birth gloom, but instead create an order of balance. In an existing world, how things are supply true facts. No one lives the wedded fairytale bliss they dreamt about. Whether it's good days or bad days, feuding or peace, resentment or contentment, these effects will always generate within the foundations of every married couple, from their beginning in time, to the end of their days.

The unfortunate circumstance to those who deem their marriage damaged, and are in pursuit of divorce, usually have an appropriate reason to reflect that matter. Insufficiency to provide love, infidelity, or abuse.

For those that lack strength to break from their marriage, they'll continue a life of misery and a cycle of afflicting events. With an absence of substance we can consider a fact, it's most likely fear as being the object which rules them.

As in the case of one couple who lived long ago, the sad reality to the wife's tragic end might doom her forever, forcing her to repeat grievous encounters she's already endured.

Marriage is an act of faith, and sometimes you'll see commitments get tested.

CHAPTER ONE

Roscrea, Ireland, the 9th of July, 1900.

Nighttide shade had fallen upon the ancestry town of Roscrea. The air was fresh and the breeze was pleasant. But not a single soul had been out to adore the splendid weather. All the folks were comfortably tucked within their beds and sleeping soundly. It was a peaceful hush that rest within the streets of this sleepy town.

Upon the breath of drafting air way in the sky, soared a solo bird of ebon quills and copper eyes. It descended lower upon the homes in soaring flight, then found its placement within a tree and peered its eyes.

Across its way, the feathered flyer spied a window illumed with light. As it sat upon its restful limb of embellished leaves, the stationed creature found itself within the view of a verbal fight.

It was then Aidan's eyes glared as he raged forth in anger. "Ciara, ye never do anything right. You always mess things up. Look at the bed. I've told ye before. I want those sheets tucked in and me pillows fluffed. I don't know why I ever married you. Ye can't follow directions. You belong outside like a dog, ye stupid wench." His voice carried through the house.

"I'm sorry. Please, Aidan. Please stop your yelling," his frightened wife cried.

"Did I tell you to talk? You're pathetic. Look at you. If ye wanted to cry, I'd give ye something to cry about." Aidan put his hands upon

Ciara's shoulders and began shaking her violently. Trying to look away, Ciara continued to squall. "Louder, you wench. I want to hear ye scream. Look at me. Damn it. I said look at me." The fear in her eyes excited him more. "Oh, what? Are ye frightened?"

Tears streamed down Ciara's face as she wailed uncontrollably. Aidan violently slammed his frightened wife against a wall, then leaned into her and began laughing. "You're good for nothing. You'd be better off dead, ye God damn bitch," he roared to her face.

"Please, Aidan, stop," she begged of him.

"What is it? Ye can't handle the truth?" He shoved her, and Ciara tumbled in sluggard motion. Catching her by the back of the head, he jerked her toward him.

"You're hurting me," she cried in pain.

Aidan snickered at her remark. "Oh, come now. Ye didn't feel a thing. But know best. I'll make you." Aidan slapped her forcefully upon the jaw, her cheek now stained within the print of his hand.

An unpleasant squawk arose from outside the window, followed by a violent session of lengthened rappings, as though something impatiently awaited entrance. The squawking continued as it grew louder and louder.

"Damn raven," Aidan yelled in violent anger. He'd thrown Ciara into the corner of a dresser where she'd fallen limply to the floor. Walking over to the window, Aidan shouted at the bird, "Get out of here, damn you." Aidan threw his hands up to scare the bird away, but the raven just sat there tapping at the glass. Aidan continued to shout, "Go on, shoo." He raised the window as the raven flew to a nearby tree.

Its eyes glowed in the dark like burning flames. Looking in on Aidan, the raven continued to squawk. A heavy fog filled the air, accompanied by a rainy mist, and in the distance Aidan heard a woman singing a mournful song. The haunting melody came from the sky and seemed to float on air. Goosebumps covered Aidan's body as shivers ran down his spine, forcing his hairs to stand tall.

The raven squawked, then took off from the tree limb toward the house. Aidan hurried to close the window as the bird yet again began to rap. "Go away," he shouted. The raven beckoned him, but Aidan backed away. Looking down, Aidan saw Ciara unconscious on the floor. Turning her over, he saw the small scratch upon her forehead encased in a large bump. "Wake up. Damn it. Wake up," Aidan shouted, all the while shaking her repeatedly.

He gazed around the room quickly when spotting the small pearl of blood tainting their dresser. Looking back upon his wife, he saw her head continued to swell. At the window the raven still sat rapping. Fear overtook Aidan as he frightfully stared in its eyes. Alongside, a ghostly candle floated in air with its bright flame piercing in through the window.

Aidan laid Ciara upon the bed, then hurried to the window in desperation. In his promptness to close the curtains, Aidan became horrified by the lingering bird and eerie candle that awaited him. In the midst he heard the haunting melody of a ghostly tune refrained within the saddened aria of a lone violin. Sensing it, Aidan began to shake within his skin. Reaching forth his hands quickly, he tugged back the curtains. He then retreated to the bed where his injured wife reposed in sleep.

Ciara was still unconscious, but breathing. Shaken, Aidan balled up within a chair where he sat staring at Ciara until falling asleep. A few hours later Aidan awoke. Glancing at his pocket watch, he noticed it was two-twenty. The room seemed quiet and still. Rising from his seat, Aidan walked steadily toward the window. Peering out from behind the security of the curtains, Aidan no longer perceived the bird nor ghostly candle which had once hovered there. He'd taken a quick sigh of relief just before an unknown sighting would catch the full awareness of his wandering eye.

Drifting through the darkened sky, a strange object glided throughout the fog while shifting in and out of perception. As the unseen object grew closer, a rush of unyielding cries emanated through the air. Aidan looked on, horrified by what he was now seeing.

A creepy black carriage sailed through the night sky with its ghostly master, led loyally by a pair of shadowy horses. Two candles floated away from the carriage, lighting the way. Aidan realized it was a death omen, rightfully acknowledged in Irish lore as the banshee. As with all fatalities, she'd been called upon for collection. Her mournful singing sonorously increased as her carriage approached the dead house.

Floored with shock, Aidan fell to his knees in flabbergasted disbelief while attentively watching his wife's resurrection. Ciara's translucent soul pulled slowly from its quiescent body, detaching itself from Ciara's lifeless shell. Sitting poised within the bed, Ciara quietly floated away from the room and into an adjacent hallway. Guided by the banshee's tune, Ciara followed the haunting melody into the stairwell where she was hypnotically lured toward her home's fore door.

Racing to the bedroom window, Aidan rushed to peer into the fog and mist. There he beheld the banshee's carriage in full sight as it patiently awaited Ciara's arrival. Floating through the corridor, out into the dampened lawn, Ciara roamed the sunless night. Awaiting her entrance, the carriage door creaked open like a rusted gate. And from within its murky depths, a frail, aged, hag-like matron dismounted slowly as she descended disclosure.

Standing beneath the blowing rain, her grey cloak blustered against the swaggered winds, unveiling the gothic dress her body was fashioned within. Her clothes were seemingly tarnished like vintage rags through decades of wear, while musty odors filled and escaped into the stagnant atmosphere. Her long hair was thick, straight, and silver. Her eyes captured the alabaster nakedness of a blanketed snow. And among her hands were elongated nails stretching afar from ossified fingers. Perched atop her left shoulder sat the raven in silent observation.

Extending her right hand, the banshee softly summoned Ciara. "Come, my child. We must go," she had spoken.

Looking up through the window, Ciara grew concerned. "And what shall become of him?" she asked with sincerity.

"He is not your worry. Fate will handle him," the banshee then answered.

Knowing she had nothing to fear, Ciara trustingly took the old woman's hand and climbed through the carriage door. With a light pull, the door creaked shut; then, rising into the fog, the carriage vanished.

CHAPTER TWO

Day 1, the 6th of July, 1950.

"Tristian. Tristian, please. You really must do something about that bird in the cellar. I don't know how it keeps getting in. You know I'm superstitious, dear." The young woman shrugged. "Blackbirds make me uncomfortable."

"Josette, I told you yesterday. I didn't find any bird in that cellar. I've searched high and low. I found nothing," he explained. "There's no way a bird could get in. No evidence anyway."

"But I've heard it today."

"Might you be hearing things?"

"But I've seen it, Tristian. I know it's there. Why would I lie?"

"Josie, I assure you. There's no bird in that cellar. I'll take you down myself so you'll see."

"Forget it. Like always, you never believe me," she replied, shaking her head. "I'm just seeing things. That's what you say." Josie frowned. "I'm going to the living room to nurse my cup of tea," she disclosed as she scooted from the kitchen.

Footing through the living room, she retreated to her favorite chair. A small coffee table stood aside her. On top of the table Josie lit a white candle. Hypnotized by its light, she'd watched the flame dance and shimmer. Josie took a moment before gaining her thoughts. Picking up the book she'd been previously reading, she cracked open its pages and sipped at her tea.

As she sat alone, engaged in retrospection, the soft scent of flowering tea rose mysteriously occupied the entire range of the room. Josie glimpsed upward and in sudden disbelief saw the ghostly image of a young woman staring upon her.

The spectre wore a pretentious lavender dress with white slippers on scanty feet. Fashioned within a loosely fitted bun, solitary, brown, spirals passed below the length of her bantam neck. The woman's concentration was then quickly diverted when abruptly shifting her head. It was as though she was looking upon somebody else, an unknown visitor whom only the ghostly woman could see.

Standing quietly a moment, she then disclosed an answer. "It's upon the top shelf," she voiced through shaken speech.

Josie watched as the woman was immediately taken over with intense fright. Backing up slowly, the woman divulged a second answer. "I promise I haven't touched it … no, please, I beg you." Her face swelled, and she began to cry.

An invisible force spasmodically gained hold of the woman's wrist as she sobbed even harder. "Please stop this. You're hurting me."

The response elicited further rage to stir within the attacker as an indomitable eruption forced upon violent blows. Blood spilt from the victim's nose, bleeding down into the fabric of her once stainless dress. The woman continued to cry in tremendous pain and horrified fear. But her hopeful pleading went unheard as her abuser carried out such fits of turbulent incursion.

Horrified, Josie continued to watch the struggle, all the while hearing each powerful blast crumble the delicate bones in the woman's face.

Screaming again, the battered woman cried for release. "Please stop." In her attempt to break free of the struggle, she was knocked backward by the dominate force. Crawling desperately along the floor like an injured dog, she tried fiercely to wiggle away with resilience. But in her hopeless efforts toward freedom, she found the authoritative force catching the rim of her dress and dragging her toward itself. The woman screamed as she was being turned over. Her head then raised and slammed to the ground as her crying continued.

Josie heard the fear in the woman's voice as she pled for her life, yet the hostile presence failed her request. Within an instant the force gripped the battered woman's throat within the clutch of its hand as

Josie ogled in fear. It was then the frightened woman was carelessly slid through the floor. Her cranium met the wall where she suffered the final blow to the top of her head. Curling into a fetal position, she shook endlessly in fright.

The candle burning beside Josie suddenly imploded. Hot wax coated the wall and covered the wooden floor as it hardened. The angry force had marked its departure. Josie peered upon the crying woman with tears. It was then the ghostly image had grown faint, disappearing slowly from Josie's sight.

Removing herself from the comfort of her seat, Josie rushed to the kitchen, screaming hysterically. "Tristian! Tristian," she cried. Approaching the door, she saw her husband standing upon the countertop, unsteadily swaying through air.

"Watch out. It's up here."

Josie looked toward him in puzzlement. "What on earth are you talking about?" she gave question.

"There was a bird in the cellar. You'd been right," Tristian said, looking over each corner of the room. "It's a raven. But, Jos, I don't understand. How'd the darn thing get in?"

"It's up here?"

"In that corner. See it?"

Josie looked where Tristian pointed. The bird hovered in the corner and began squawking as it peered down upon her. Taking off, it soared across the stretch of kitchen, disappearing into an upcoming wall.

"Impossible. Where'd it go?" Triatian wondered. "That bird disappeared."

"How'd it get in?"

"I'd been reading the paper when I heard a scratch at the cellar. I went to look. When I opened it, that massive bird flew at me. It circled the kitchen a few times, then you came in. You did see it, didn't you? You saw that bird disappear?" Tristian inquired with wide eyes. "Josie?"

"Yes, Tristian. I saw that phantom bird. I've been telling you it was here, but you never believed me." Josie took a deep breath. "I saw something a short while ago that frightened me. I've never been so afraid in my life, Tristian, really." Josie started shaking as a tear fell from her eye.

"Honey? Honey, what's wrong? What is it?" her husband questioned.

"How did you not hear her crying? Something was hurting her. Before my very eyes, Tristian, I watched it abuse her. Her fear. She was filled with such fear," Josie cried.

"Who? Who was?" he asked, rubbing the small of her back. "Josie, what?" He then became diverted. "What's this?" Tristian took his hand away. "Feels waxy."

"The candle ... the candle, Tristian. It blew up. Then, then everything ceased."

"Well? Well, what ... can you tell me what happened?"

"Out of nowhere a sweet odor arose. When I looked up, I became startled by the young woman before me. Her face was embraced in a gentle gaze, so I didn't feel threatened." Josie paused briefly and took a deep breath. "Within seconds someone else had entered the room. But, Tristian, you couldn't see them. The woman then spoke. Her voice was quite shaken, and she was certainly frightened. The force, it grabbed her, squeezing her tightly. As she started to cry, it became ever the more violent, striking her upon the face. She begged it to stop. But it continued to harm her, pushing her down as she tried to escape. Her terror, Tristian. She was scared to death. She was still on the ground when the candle erupted. There's wax all over the floor and wall. When I looked down, the woman had faded. Tristian. Tristian, I don't understand. What's going on in our house? Nothing strange ever happened these five years we've been here. Why ... why would it now?"

"I haven't a clue. I really don't. Forgive me if I don't know what to say."

"You believe me, don't you? I'm certain of what I've seen. It was real, Tristian."

"I'm sure that it was. Jos, I should have credited you about that bird. After seeing the raven, then it disappear, I'll believe what you say."

"What must we do if these occurrences continue?"

Tristian pondered a moment. "What do we know about any previous owners?"

"Nothing, Tristian. We know nothing."

"Then we'll start questioning some of these folks round here. Some good soul's bound to have stories."

"You want to go door-to-door like some salesman and query our neighbors? Surely there's a better way, Tristian."

"What about Mrs. O'Toole? She's lived across the street the better half of her life. She could probably tell us about any previous occupants," Tristian suggested.

"I'll have to go. You'll be at work." Josie thought for a second. "Well, maybe I could drop in a visit tomorrow afternoon?"

Tristian shook his head. "You could tell me about the conversation when I get home. Say, why don't you take a hot bath? You look worn. Go on, relax. I'll clean that mess in the living room."

"I can clean it. It's no bother."

"Go on. Go."

"Are you sure?"

"I'm positive. You've had a long day. Let me do something. I'll be up after I've finished." He then kissed his wife upon the cheek and motioned her on.

Tristian soon found himself upon his knees with a paint scraper in hand trying to clean wax. The mess had considerably melted onto the floor so greatly that the puddle was too thickset to scour. Tristian remembered an old folk remedy using a hot iron. Knowing it was his only relief, he then prayed the resolution not fail him. He moseyed on into the laundry room to retrieve the iron, then foraged through the kitchen, searching for a newspaper and towel. Tristian trailed back toward the living room as he mumbled aloud. "This better work. Lord knows, I don't have the money to lay new wood." As he approached the waxy mess, Tristian stopped suddenly when taken by shock. "What? What's this jumble?" He stood above the hardened glob while peering upon it. Bending down, he dusted his hand across the top to clear away the fresh shavings which now lay before him. As he brushed aside the fragments, Tristian came across an unsettling message etched within wax, *Where's the wench?* Tristian pulled back in alarm. "What the hell's this? Josie? Josie, is this some sort of joke?" He spoke aloud.

Tristian's shock soon turned to dumbfounded horror as he witnessed the once hardened wax mysteriously ooze and expand its way across the wooden floor. "I don't believe my eyes. What's going on?"

Violent rappings began to beat within the house like one-thousand fists harassing the walls. Tristian stood to his feet and turned around slowly. He inspected each of the room's corners, expecting to see a frightful surprise. But the room stood bare to his observance. The rappings were exceedingly intense that Tristian began to experience an onset of panic. Fear crawled up and down his spine like unknown fingers caressing one's back. Tristian's breathing increased, growing deeper and deeper. His heart now racing, pounding quicker and quicker. "For Christ's sake, stop!" he ejected. "Stop. Stop it, I say!" He'd given one final shout.

The rappings then ceased as the room fell to silence. Taking in a deep breath, Tristian sighed while tasseling his hair. He looked down at the wax puddle which seemed to have unnaturally dwindled during an absence of sight. The incorporated droplets were now smooth and ostensibly diminutive by way of impression. The obvious message which had once tainted the mound somehow dematerialized to Tristian's unknown astoundment.

Bending to his knees, Tristian kneeled to the floor. He placed a square of newspaper over the deceptive wax, then covered it with the use of a towel. He ran the iron up and down, then side to side with hope of removing the accumulative deposits. After a good minute of ironing, Tristian set the press upright upon the floor. He set the towel aside, then lightly proceeded to tug at the paper.

Liquified wax had fastened to the exterior of the Gazette, defacing each layer from the top of the landing. Tristian peered down in short-lived relief. His once-gathered easement had now been arrested by repugnance. Deep red droplets had unknowingly supplied the small stretch of floorboard. Thinking quickly, Tristian felt beneath his nose, considering it had bled, then checked his hands and fingers before concluding no scraps. "Where the hell ... where'd this come from?" He pushed aside his confusion as he retrieved a towel and proceeded to clean, yet it'd only taken seconds for Tristian's confusion to baffle him more. With each whisk he brushed the towel stayed clean. Tristian implausibly surveyed each dissipated stroke which unsoiled the boards. To Tristian's judgment, the grounds were now clean as was the appearance of his towel.

CHAPTER THREE

Josie ventured through the bedroom to retrieve her lace gown and night robe. Slipping into her house shoes, she proceeded down the hallway and toward the washroom. Laying her garments across a chair, she then trotted to an off white cabinet and grasped a green bottle. After loosening the cork from its harness, she was presented with the heavenly scent of an ambrosial garden. Josie walked to the claw foot tub, then turned on the water. Allowing it to rush across her hand several seconds, she proceeded to dribble in her gel.

An intoxicating bouquet of flowers encapsulated the room as bubbles rose. Josie inhaled deeply to savor the floral aroma as she became spellbound with enticement. The captive scents gave calming ease as she acquired each cherished breath. Josie disrobed, then carefully draped a single foot into water, making certain it wasn't too hot. She then slipped the other leg over and slowly sank into the depth of her alluring tub. Steam rose off, dampening Josie's face. She laid her head upon the porcelain barrier and closed her eyes. Enjoying the comforting heat, she sank farther into the welcoming waters that submerged her.

Josie lay, relaxing within the warmth of her bath. Wetting her rag, she moistened water droplets upon her neck. As she dabbed her face, the bathroom door was swung open by an invisible intruder, and this was followed by shrieks of painful cries. The door violently slammed as the lock slid shut.

Horrified by the intrusion, Josie watched as the silhouette of a woman came to form. The apparition ran to the corner of the room and bent to the floor, crying. Josie reached from within the tub to comfort the lady. "Who's hurting you?" she asked.

The woman looked to Josie through a flow of tears and faded slowly.

"Wait. Please," Josie shouted. "I want to help you. Come back." She wrapped a towel around herself and quickly climbed outside her bath.

She raced to dry off, then slipped the gown over her head. Josie sped from the bathroom and scurried downstairs. "Tristian! Tristian, the woman, I saw her."

"I suspect bad thoughts, Jos. She may have been murdered."

"Murdered?" she pondered. "What brings you to that?"

"It's just a feeling. A bad feeling."

"You're bound to have seen something to make you think that."

"I can't know for certain, Jos. It's just speculation."

"Then what's brung you speculation?"

"A message."

"What message?"

"Scraped in wax. Said where's the wench?"

"Wench? How more demeaning can one be?" Josie stated, shaking her head. "You saw this yourself?"

"Absolutely."

"What do you suppose had happened to her?"

"That's an impossible question I can't answer. From your perception and my encounter, I'm aware of this sinister presence in our home. By your words it abuses the female spirit. Why haven't you seen it, though, Jos? The evil force? You've seen her, so why not it?"

"I really don't know." She gave thought and tried to explain. "Maybe it doesn't want to be seen? It's no lie, Tristian. This thing's here."

"We need to know who or what we're dealing with and why. Hopefully things will come together soon as you talk with Mrs. O'Toole." Tristian bent to the ground, then handed something to Josie. "Do you see anything on this?"

"What am I looking for?"

"Anything."

"What do you want me to see? It's a clean towel, Tristian."

"Just as suspected."

Josie's eyebrows narrowed. "I'll take it to the kitchen."

"No, wait."

"Wait? Why? Tristian?"

"I had good reason for asking."

"What?"

"I had a bizarre happening with that towel."

"You care to explain?"

"It's mind-boggling really. That towel in your hand. Josie, I used it to clean blood."

"Blood?"

"Yes, blood. You know, the dark red stuff one's body ejects once cut?"

"But there are no stains, Tristian."

"Exactly."

"Exactly what? If you cleaned blood, there'd be stains on this towel."

"I cleaned blood, yet that towel failed to absorb any. The darn thing's clean as a whistle."

"Was it yours?"

"Not at all. I'm unsure where it came from."

"Where did you clean?"

"Right here on the floor. Heavy knocks pounded upon the walls nearly scaring me to death." Tristian pondered for a second. "Maybe we have an angry poltergeist?"

"But why's all this happening now? Why didn't it start when we first moved in?"

"Beats the hell out of me. I'm trying to make sense myself. Well, it's getting late, Jos. We need to get some rest. We'll talk more in the morning. Go on. I'll be at your side shortly."

As the couple proceeded up the stairs, they parted ways at the top. Josie ventured into the bedroom while Tristian moseyed toward the bathroom door. Reaching for a bar of soap, Tristian then sudsed up. He cupped his hands beneath the cascading water, then splashed at his forehead. Ringing out a rag, he then padded off any moistened drops that dampened his face. As he did, Tristian caught the glimpse of a young man staring steadily upon him from behind the mirror. The fellow had piercing pearl-blue eyes while pale blond hair rested upon his head. A disfiguring scar raised beneath his right eye with a jagged grin crinkling his lips.

An uneasiness swept through Tristian's body as the man continued to glare. "This is my house," the man spoke with authority. "No outsiders welcome." He punched the glass while Tristian pulled back in horror. Cracks splintered the mirror, shattering certain areas of reflection. The man looked to his target and sinisterly howled.

Tristian stood to the mirror. "You're not going to scare me. I won't have it," he told the man. "If this be anyone's house, it's mine."

"Fabricator. Ye lie," the man enraged. "Noting terror, something I generate, know best that I will," he said before vanishing.

Tristian tried to calm himself as he took deep breaths. He then footed from the bathroom trying to disregard what had happened.

Josie watched him through the corridor. "What was that loud noise? You break something?"

"The mirror broke," he answered.

"Were you beating it up?" Josie laughed. "I've told you, reflections don't lie. We are what we see," she kidded.

"He punched it."

Josie's joking nature then turned serious. "He? He who?"

"The man."

"What man?"

"He was in the mirror."

"What man in the mirror? Tristian?"

"His eyes were cold as ice, Jos. And he had this scar upon his face." Tristian remembered, lost in thought. "That voice of his … unhuman when he spoke. It brought a chill to my spine."

"He spoke to you? Tell me, Tristian, what'd he say?"

"He made it clear. This is his house. He's the one who broke the mirror."

"You don't suppose he'd harm us? Do you, Tristian?"

"Maybe if he really wanted. He's angry, Jos. The man's clearly hostile. I see why he frightens that woman so. Just having him look at you's frightful enough."

"This really has you shaken. Come closer. I'll rub your back, help you relax."

Tristian smiled briefly. "It should be me comforting you. Jos, you've seen stranger things. I know they've upset you." Tristian turned to his wife and wrapped her in arm.

Josie's eyes swelled while watery streams passed down her face. "I can't help but worry about that woman, Tristian. She looked so helpless. If only you had seen her. Every tear she cried; it broke my heart. I wish there were something I could have done. Hearing the pain in her cries each time he'd hurt her just plagued me to no end. There must be something we could do? Something to release her from this hell she's repeating."

"Like what? I don't know much about crossing spirits, Josie. Do you?" Tristian questioned.

"I don't know, but there's bound to be something. We need to get rid of him. He's no good. No good for her or this house."

"We can't just tell him to leave, Jos. I don't think he'd be willing to listen. We'll anger him," Tristian remarked.

Josie didn't say a thing as she sat and wondered.

"Sweetie? Sweetie, it's late. We really should retire." Tristian kissed Josie upon the forehead, then laid into bed. He reached over and turned off his lamp. Soon after he'd fallen into sleep.

Josie had trouble acquiring slumber. She laid in bed alert and awake as she gazed through the barrier of the bedroom window.

A pale moon glowed high in the sky as dark clouds gathered, then shifted by. A light breeze blew into the screen, carrying in dampened air. Swaying within the current, the curtains danced as each gust brushed against them. Lightning crippled and blazed in the sky with crackling thunder back-riding the night, commanded by its phantom drifter.

The fresh scent of rain carried on air. While minding the small droplets, Josie felt ease as each tear exceeded the Heavens. Looking to Tristian, she found him still taken with sleep. Sitting off the bed, she moused to the window. Watching the rain shower the grounds, Josie leaned into the wall continuing to peer among the darkened sky. The lightning upheld several bolts while the falling rain became heavier. After several minutes Josie turned and trotted toward bed.

Thirty minutes had passed as Josie lay still and awake within the warmth of her covers. Beginning to feel restless, she once again emerged from her side of the mattress. She wandered into the hallway, leisurely pacing through the house. Walking into the bathroom, she turned on the light. Her throat yearned for moisture as she picked up a glass. Filling it to the rim, she ran in cold water. Acquiring a few swigs, she soon quenched her thirst-stricken throat.

As she rested the glass upon the sink, a loud shatter arose from the parlor. Josie stood in stillness to devour further commotion. It was then the violent shout of an angry man echoed upstairs. "Damn you! Get over here, ye filthy wench," the man blared.

Josie crept to the banister and peered down with ease. A broken plate lay shattered just aside the bottom stair. Josie then witnessed a thrown bowl impact the wall, then break into pieces.

"Look at this. You're good for nothing. Absolutely nothing. Why I ought to…" the voice shouted.

Josie heard heavy footsteps carry on the stairs as though someone were running. A cool breeze brushed against Josie's arm as an unseen visitor traveled by.

"Where'd ye think you're going? Filthy wench, get back here. Damn it. God damn it! Don't ye make me come after you."

Josie stood frozen with fear. Unable to move, she frightfully observed a ghostly male appear upon steps. He walked with heavy feet, becoming more clear with each stride that he took. Midway through the staircase he had taken the credible resemblance of a factual person. Beating his hand against the wall repeatedly, he shouted, "Ye better come out of your hiding place, ye petrified cat. Ye wouldn't want me finding you, now would ye?" He continued up the steps.

Josie felt the cool breeze once more as it brushed beside her. The man reached forth his hand trying desperately to grasp that which had been retained out of sight. Suddenly Josie heard a loud bang followed by resounding thuds as a body hit the stairs. Looking on, she viewed the tempered soul transporting an undisclosed torso along the steps behind him. The man grew faint as he approached the last tier. As quickly as he came, the man had disappeared.

By that point Josie was strained by oppression, now left alone to recount her shock. Reoccurred images of the incidents she'd seen and heard plagued her troublesome mind. Wishing it were all just a horrible nightmare, Josie pled to awaken. But actuality stirred on a conscious note. She knew what was witnessed had been very real. In her rationalization, Josie knew no evident doubts proceeded.

Journeying down the stairs, she decided to straighten up the broken mess. But approaching the end land, Josie noticed there were no longer signs of shattered glass. Due to a mysterious instance, the fragmented clutter had vanished.

The Crying House

Returning quietly to her bed, Josie speechlessly prayed that no further developments would happen. Not making any sudden movements, Josie crept slowly onto the mattress as not to awaken Tristian. "At least one of us is getting some rest," she stated meekly.

The rain still beat against the house, and small cracks of thunder were heard in the distance. Josie laid in bed for awhile till her eyes felt heavy, and she drifted to sleep.

Awakening a short while later, Josie heard an odd tapping clatter the window. She opened her eyes to a stygian bird ogling through the impediment. The raven took its beak and ungraciously scraped it against glass as it made a horrible racket. Its fixated eyes radiated beyond the dark like sweltering embers. Turning to Tristian, Josie snuggled within the crook of his back, seeking security. Finally she was able to find sleep in his comfort.

CHAPTER FOUR

Day 2, the 7th of July, 1950.

The warm rays of the sun shone through the window like burning cinders. Tristian inhaled the scent of bacon and eggs being cooked in the kitchen. His stomach soon growled when hunger attacked. Squinting beneath the lustrous sting, Tristian's opticals fluttered to open. He then rose from bed, thereon following his nose to the heavenly aroma awaiting him. "Something sure smells good," he said, complimenting Josie.

"Aw, Tristian, you're up. I wasn't expecting you for another ten minutes. Have a seat. Your breakfast will be on the table shortly. I'll pour you a glass of juice. Will orange be okay?"

"Only if you'll have some with me," Tristian replied, kissing his wife's forehead.

Josie blushed mildly. "Did you sleep well?" she asked.

"Like a cradled baby."

"I take it you didn't hear the storm?"

"No," he said, shaking his head. "Didn't hear a thing."

"It began to thunder and rain last night. I watched from the window awhile. Too bad you weren't up. The fresh air was invigorating." Josie set Tristian's plate upon the table. "Wait just a second. Your toast is about to spring. Strawberry jam?" she added as she opened the fridge door.

"What would I do without you?" Tristian smiled.

Josie snickered. "Your own cooking, my dear. Here's your jam.

The Crying House

Now let me grab that toast." Josie started toward the counter when suddenly, grasping her stomach, she moaned in pain. "Oh. Oh God."

"Josette? Josette, what is it?" Tristian stood from his chair, then rushed to her side. "Sweetheart? Sweetheart, are you all right?"

"The pang … oh God, Tristian. I can't straighten up."

"I've got you, Jos. I've got you. Take baby steps. I'll get you to the table."

"Oh my. I'm breaking sweat. Quick, Tristian. I need a cold rag."

"Okay. Okay, sure."

"Cold, Tristian. Real cold."

"Here. It's brisk as ice."

"Please rest it upon my neck."

"Josie, what's going on? What just happened to you?"

"It's nothing. A minor pain at most." Moments later Josie swallowed her sentence while doubling in agony. "Oh, have mercy. Tristian, help," she cried.

"You need a physician. I'm calling off work and taking you to Dr. Emerson," he told her.

"No-no. I'll be fine. I'm certain. Go on. Finish your breakfast."

"Jos, if this happens again…"

She agreed, "Fine. All right. If it happens again, I'll go." She sat quietly within her thoughts. "What about Mrs. O'Toole? I told you I'd see her today."

"You don't worry about that now. You're ill."

"I feel fine." Josie sighed, then picked her food.

"At least try to eat," Tristian finished, then placed his dishes in the sink. "Could I get you anything perchance? Perhaps more juice?"

"No, dear, no. I'm good. Go on to work. I'll be fine. All right?"

"Josie, don't lie. You haven't experienced more pains, have you?"

She lightly nodded no. "Go on, go. Get ready for work. I'm fine, see here?" She got up, then trotted toward the sink to clean the dishes.

"Well, then, if you need me, I'll be upstairs." Tristian moseyed to their room and sorted his clothes while Josie was finishing dishes.

She walked out to the corner of the staircase. Standing there, she peered to the top. "I ironed your shirts yesterday. They're in the closet."

"Yes, I see them."

"There's fresh socks in your drawer."

"Yes, Jos. Thank you."

"Oh, uh, Tristian."

"Yes?"

"I put your loafers in the chair."

"Anything else?"

"You'll find a new tie on the dresser." Josie then started into the living room. She noticed the thin layer of dust on the highboy. Grabbing a rag, she started to wipe down the furniture.

The air soon filled with a familiar scent. Josie whisked around to see the young woman sitting among the couch. She looked at Josie with a warm smile, then got up and walked into an adjacent room.

Josie followed behind, but could not find the previously viewed specter. She walked back into the living room as another pain struck without warning. Doubled in cramps, she fell to the floor. The agony intensified as she pulled toward a chair.

Tristian was treading down the stairs when he saw his wife propped against the settee. He quickly rushed beside her. "This is it, Jos. I'm taking you to the doctor."

"It's winding down. I'll be all right."

"I'm calling the bank. You can't go through another second of this, so don't even fight me."

"But, Tristian."

"It's settled. I've made up my mind. Mr. Ashford should understand." Tristian dialed the number. "Good morning, Mr. Ashford. This is Tristian O'Brien."

"Oh, good morning, Tristian. What can I do for you?"

"Well, sir. I'm afraid my wife's fallen ill. I need to see her to a doctor. Could I have permission to take this day off?"

"By all means, son. Take as long as you need. Tell your sweet wife I hope she feels better."

"I greatly appreciate it, Mr. Ashford. I'll be sure to. Bye now." Tristian helped Josie into the chair. "Mr. Ashford sends you his blessings."

"Such kindness he gives," she stated.

"Come, I need to see you to the car." Tristian opened the door and helped his wife to the seat.

CHAPTER FIVE

Dr. Emerson's office wasn't far from the house. Inside, Tristian found a nurse and quickly informed her of Josie's ordeal. The assistant immediately led them into an open room where they awaited Dr. Emerson's arrival.

The door swung open awhile later as the squatty, undersized doctor strolled in. He favored the part of a little, ole, cheery elf. Blanched hair matured atop his head consistent to the timeworn intelligence obtained from decades of precedent years. He wore a round face with fat little cheeks which flushed within a russet glow. His onyx spectacles perched upon a button nose as his green eyes beamed within the spangle of a glimmering star. "Hello, Mr. and Mrs. O'Brien. I might say, I haven't received the pleasure from a visit in awhile."

"Good day, Dr. Emerson," the O'Briens replied.

"So what brings you kind folks my way? Nothing too serious, I hope."

"Josie's not well. Might be a flu bug, I'm guessing."

"I feel fine, Dr. Emerson. But obviously Tristian sees otherwise. It was his beliefs that have brung me to see you."

"At a good thing that be. Several bouts of the flu have infested some people. You feeling sick, dizzy, or light-headed?"

"No, doctor. Just a few pains along my side here." She showed him.

"Could you describe the affliction?"

"Sort of striking, I'd say. It merely lasts a few seconds."

"And when did this start?"

"This morning. We were getting ready for breakfast," Josie stated, while Dr. Emerson started his exam.

"You don't have a fever. That's a fine sign. You're looking a bit worn, however. Are you experiencing any stresses?"

"Here and there. But honestly, sir, who doesn't? Life's a stress in itself."

"Any good soul suffering from stress may fall sick, including graces as fair as you."

"So stress is my ailment?"

"I'll proceed with a couple tests to see what I find." Dr. Emerson pushed on Josie's stomach. "Some discomfort I see."

"Is that at all normal? Am I all right?"

"How are your menses?"

"Sometimes heavy, other times light. Every month my flows are different."

"Have you had one this month?"

"Not of yet. I'm running late. Come to think, I'm not certain the last time I've had one."

"Is that regular for you?"

"Not at all. My menses have always been exact."

"In that case, I'd like to perform a pelvic exam. You might have something going on internally that needs my attention. Place your feet in the stirrups and rest your legs to the side."

"Please, no bad news, doctor. Just tell us everything's fine."

"Well, Josie, I'm not feeling any abnormalities, masses or ill-favored growths."

"Then there's nothing wrong with me?"

"You're completely healthy internally. That's a reasonable indication for the development of your baby."

"Baby? Are you saying I'm pregnant?"

"It appears so. Congratulations."

"Tristian. Tristian, you hear that? We're going to be parents!" she exclaimed with a smile.

"Oh, Josie. Josie, this is wonderful! God, I'm so proud. I know this is something we've both wanted." Tristian took his wife in his arms, then held her tight. "We're finally starting a family. Oh, sweetheart. I love you so much. Congratulations, mum," he whispered softly.

"I'm proud for you both," Dr. Emerson remarked.

"But, doctor. Doctor, what about the pain? Is it normal I be experiencing it?" Josie asked with concern.

"It's completely normal for one to experience abdominal pain during pregnancy. This is usually caused by the stretching of ligaments as the uterus grows. In other cases some women experience pain when the egg has carried to the fallopian tubes rather than traveling to the uterus. But that isn't a dilemma for you to worry about, Josie. However, if by any means you should experience severe pain that lasts several minutes or begin spotting, you'll need to come back and see me at once. Even if you begin to run a fever, I think it'd be in your best interest to return. For now I want you off your feet the rest of the day. Try to take it easy."

"Thank you, doctor. You've been more than helpful," said Josie.

"I'll make sure she stays off those feet," added Tristian.

"I want to take a few vials of blood before you leave."

"Certainly, doctor. Will there be anything else?"

"Just the blood, Josie. Then you can be on your way. I'll have a nurse sent in shortly."

"All right then."

"Do call if any problems arise," Dr. Emerson said as he walked to the door.

"Now you heard Dr. Emerson, Jos. You're to stay off those feet. We need to keep the baby healthy."

"I'll rest, Tristian. Don't you be worrying."

CHAPTER SIX

Tristian pulled to their house, then helped Josie to the door. "Now, I'm putting you to bed. No if's, and's or but's."

"Stay with me at least."

"Of course. We both know you need to stay well."

Josie peered upward to her husband. "Would you mind grabbing a pillow and blanket? I feel like resting on the couch."

"I'll help you up the stairs, Jos."

"I'd rather be in the living room." Josie then trotted to the sofa and gently sat down.

"I'll be back then." Tristian went upstairs and retrieved a pillow and blanket from their room. "Here, Jos. Nice and fluffy. Are you comfortable enough?"

"This should make do."

"Is there anything more I could get?"

"Could you fix me a cup of tea? I have chamomile flowers. They're in a caddy on the counter. Just steam them for me."

He nodded. "I'll be back in a couple minutes."

"Tristian, there's a bucket of wild strawberries in the fridge. Would you bring me a bowl?"

Tristian walked into the kitchen and began boiling water. He soon spotted the caddy upon the counter. Spooning out a mound of tops, he transferred the steady portion into a pouch. The kettle began to whistle as steam rose away from the spout. Tristian turned off the burner, then seized the feverish vessel. He channeled hot water into Josie's mug before infusing the dry bag.

The Crying House

Within the refrigerator Tristian sought the fresh berries. He trotted to the sink with a handful in palm, then rinsed them beneath the flow of cold water.

As he turned to walk away, a sudden movement surrendered his step and kept him in place. Just behind him a kitchen chair slid beyond the floor, then smacked against the wall where it trembled and quaked.

A young woman appeared across the way, holding her face within her hands as she broke down to cry. "Why does he do this?" she wept aloud. "Again and again I've tried not to fail, but yet he still scathes me. His evil deeds yield no evasion. *Guaire*, guardian God, encase me in your protective hand, I pray thee."

Tristian watched as the woman shifted her hands from her face, exposing a puffy lip and bleeding gash. Heavy footsteps filled the room when the chair that seated her began to shake even more. It was then her hair was violently tugged above her as strands were coercively stripped from her head. The woman cried and fought to break free. "Please, leave me. I've done nothing wrong. I've done nothing wrong." She pled while fiercely slapping her hands.

Tristian stood watching, trying to figure out how to help. "Leave her alone. Damn you. Leave her alone! Can't you see what you do's hurting her?"

The angry force rapidly unleashed the woman's hair as its heavy footsteps made way toward Tristian. A whirlwind of cool air blasted his face, then an invisible hand reached forth, gaining grip of Tristian's collar. Lifting him into the air, Tristian felt its icy breath breathe upon him.

Condensation began to form where the person's mouth would have been. "I'll tend to me pig the way I see fit," a voice spoke. "Don't ye interfere. That pig's me business. Not yours." The man then loosened his grip, releasing Mr. O'Brien to the floor.

Tristian felt light-headed and dizzy while choking in a breath of air. The icy, cool, chill that previously surrounded him had subsequently disappeared. Tristian then struggled to shake off the incident as he gathered Josie's tea. "Here you go," he muttered lightly.

"Tristian, what's happened to your face? You're all red."

"It's nothing, Jos. Don't you be worrying." Tristian knew if he told his wife what had happened, it'd steer her to far greater upset; a risk he knew wisely to avoid.

"Well, all right," Josie stated. "Would you like a seat beside me?"

"I have several things I should tend to round here."

"You going to fix dinner?" Josie laughed. "That is ... if you're aware what to do."

"Oh?" He grinned. "You don't think I could fix it? Well, you'll see. My skills shall prove your doubtfulness wrong. Just you wait."

"Self-assured, are we? Well, while you're at it, there's laundry needing tending to. You don't mind, do you?"

"Laundry, too, huh?"

"I planned to bake a cured ham today. You'll find a bowl of juniper berries soaking on the counter. Tristian, make sure they're soft. Don't forget to score the ham. In a bowl you'll need to combine one and a half cups of mustard and a cup of brown sugar. Coat the ham with the blended mixture, then put it in the stove. I have soda bread from yesterday. I set it in the pantry. Tristian, if you need me to cook, I will. It's my place, not yours."

"Not a chance, Jos. Your job's to lie here and rest. Don't worry about a thing. I'll handle it." Tristian returned to the kitchen. Looking alertly to each corner, he made sure the room had been absent of souls. He pulled a Dutch oven from the cabinet, then placed it amongst the counter. Picking up the ham, he then laid it within the cooker. He scored the top with a sharp knife, then inserted the soft berries. *I can do this*, he thought.

Next he dumped a combination of mustard and brown sugar into a bowl and proceeded to mix. Once blended to a paste, Tristian covered the ham, then slid it into the stove for cooking.

Meanwhile, Josie had fallen asleep on the couch trying to recover the needed rest from the night before. But unbeknownst as she slept, a dark stain bled through the ceiling.

It gathered, then wept teary drops to her face. Following its long stride, the first struck her forehead while the last downgraded as it spilt to her lips. Within that moment Josie was surely roused by surprise. Distracted, she quickly uncovered her eyes.

Above, on the ceiling, she'd witnessed the splotch bleeding down. Josie screamed with terrified panic as she brushed at her face. Blood smeared across her lips like liquefied rouge as she bellowed in craze with redundant horror.

Tristian heard her cries as he came running in. "Josie. Josie!"

"Make it stop," she wailed.

Looking up, the unnerving sight stalled Tristian's movement as it rendered him speechless. He paused, eyeing the seepage drip steadily from the ceiling where it pass to the couch. "Move, Josie. Move!"

"It's coming from the bathroom," she cried.

"Wait here, Jos. I'm going up."

"Tristian, no. Please don't. Don't leave me," she begged.

"I'll be back," he said, running off.

Josie shouted, "Tristian. Tristian, no!"

Racing up the flight of stairs, he darted to the bathroom. Inside, he found a rejecting sight that would horrify even the most bravest of souls. The room looked like an overwhelming gore den with large amounts of blood splattered onto the walls while puddles of coagulated secretion coated the floor. "Oh, Christ, son of God. What corruptions have occurred?" Tristian closed his eyes tightly while taking in a buried breath. "I view no further maligns before me as the sins of this room now become pure," he recurrently affirmed, requesting it away. Tristian opened his eyes to find the lavatory flawlessly unsoiled.

Approaching the steps, Josie saw her husband reach the first stair. "Well? Did you see anything?" she asked, trembling.

"Blood, Jos. So much blood," Tristian stated.

"Blood? But how? Did you clean it?"

"No, thank the good Lord."

"You can't just leave it there, Tristian. It must be cleaned."

"No need you worry. It's no longer there."

"You said you didn't clean it. How can it not be there?"

"I willed it away."

"You're telling me that worked? Come on, Tristian."

"I'm not lying to you, Jos. The bathroom's clean. No mess."

"Where did it come from?"

"I think the better question's who'd it come from?"

"Tristian, this frightens me. What should we do?"

"Let me clean those smears from your face." Tristian returned to the room and wiped the dried spots from his wife.

"Tristian, I don't know how much I can take. I don't feel safe," she uttered.

"Would you rather us move? Maybe start a new life elsewhere?" he asked, taking a seat beside her.

"I don't want that at all. I love this house. Tristian, we have memories here. And now with a baby on the way, I want us to have more."

"We can't live with this violence, Jos. What if we become victims?"

"Then we need a priest. Maybe an exorcism on this house? At least a blessing of prayers. Something to help us," Josie suggested.

"What if the ceremony fails? We'd be stuck with that wretched sinner. This house would be hell."

"He's a resentful spectre, Tristian. Not some inhuman soul breeding havoc among us. At some period he was mortal. A priest shouldn't find it hard to exterminate him. Just a few words here and there would drive him off."

"Any man who acts on beating his wife's inhuman enough. He's a demon, Jos. He's ruled by the devil."

"Have faith, Tristian. If you believe something will work, then it can."

"He'll put up more fight than you know."

"Then we'll get two priests, three priests, or four."

Tristian stared into Josie's eyes. "I'm glad determination has principled your core. Least one of us is touched by sound guidance as rule. Call me bullheaded, stubborn, and fixed. I just think this spirit's an unyielding attempt."

"I may not be able to reason with you, Tristian. But I stand firm to my beliefs as you with yours. I have faith in the sect. I know the divine cleric shall deliver this sin."

"I support you, Josie. Don't feel that I don't. My faith's just a wee less stinted than yours. How's your stomach? Anymore pains?"

"I feel fine, Tristian. I'm just tired. I was awake most of the night. This house gets to me. Maybe I just don't feel comfortable to sleep."

Tristian sighed. "You know you need the rest, Jos. You won't function without it. If not for yourself, then think of our baby."

"I'm aware of that, Tristian. Our son or daughter deserves to be safe."

"It won't do the baby good when you're avoiding all slumber. I'm telling you to lie back down. If you don't, I'm calling the doctor."

"Will you check me at least?"

"I'll break regularly for scouting. Now, I've got these dishes to do, then tend to the laundry. In the meantime, you rest."

He went to the kitchen, then washed up the dishes. Afterward, he gathered the laundry and proceeded to the washboard. He later checked in on Josie as she slept on the couch. The instant he found her resting, Tristian advanced outdoors where he moseyed to the shed. Searching for a pair of trimmers, he decided to snip and shorten the shrubbery.

It was mid-afternoon. The sun brightly shined with a handful of clouds scattered stagnant in the sky. A warm, gentle breeze carried through the air as Tristian began trimming and shaping the hedges.

He would later water the flower bed and shear down the grasses. Then, wiping his hand across his forehead, Tristian brushed away an accumulation of sweat. His persistent sweep stunned the droplets from tainting his eyes. Then, through an innocent peer toward a window, he witnessed her standing.

Just behind his bedchamber's shrouds, the woman stood poised, gazing through glass. She hovered in place for eight solid seconds, then floated away and vanished from sight.

In a rush Tristian relocated his trimmers to the shed, then, with haste, he tread toward the house. Upon the couch he found Josie still sleeping. So he proceeded to the kitchen and checked the baked ham. Afterward, he returned to the living room with a newspaper in hand. Taking the seat nearest Josie, he relaxed in his chair.

The room was quiet except for the light respiration of Josie's breath. Tristian watched as she soundly slept, bundled within the security of her sheltering blanket. The silence in the room was soon interrupted as loud noises were heard thwacking within the barrier. The vibrations prompted thoughts of something arduously disassociating the interior.

Tristian observed in disbelief as a pair of hands reached forth through the wall. Following that, a body stretched onward, removing itself from the chambered enclosure. Delivering further, trailed the torso of a man crawling the surface akin to a fly traipsing one's screen. Then, much like a spider, he scurried the wall, ready and willing to ensnarl its snack. Racing to the ceiling, he clung with no effort.

Slanted upon Tristian, fervid hate sweltered the visitant's eyes while locking intently upon his receiver. "Where's that wench, ye piece of filth?" the demented being mouthed. He scuttled back down the impediment, then melted into it like hot, boiling wax. Before Tristian's eyes the eerie spectre then vanished, leaving behind no attesting trace of his presence.

Tristian darted his eyes toward Josie and, thankfully enough, detected her still taken with sleep. Getting up quietly, he stepped to the kitchen. Withdrawing the ham, he removed it to cool, then cancelled the heat which emit from the stove. He went on to gather the soddened laundry and placed it in a basket. Afterward, Tristian shuffled to the back yard with his bushel in hand. Hanging the muggy clothes upon lines, he granted the sun the extraction of moisture.

Gazing around, Tristian ogled a raised rose which had bloomed in his yard. As a sweet gesture, he snipped the rosette in hope of fancying and marveling his wife.

Retreating to the rear entrance, Tristian propped his empty basket to the side of the house. Sneaking in lightly, Josie took him by surprise. She stood patiently waiting while he proceeded with entrance. Tristian took the rose and whisked it to his back with hope of withholding its sight from her eyes. "Hi, beautiful. How was your nap?"

Josie stretched. "I'm gratefully rested. Oh me, look at that ham. My, what a marvelous job you've done."

"You think so?" Tristian beamed.

"I do. Absolutely."

"I had fun, Jos. I really did."

"You had fun? Cooking? Tristian, is that possible?" she joked.

"Well, I didn't expect it to be as messy as it was. That's for certain. Tell you what, Jos. I couldn't have done it without my brilliant instructor as my guide."

"But how does it taste?" Josie kidded. "Will you earn your satisfactory applause?"

"I guess I'll find out." Tristian poked the ham. "It's baked all the way, right?"

"Are you panicking that it's not?"

"I want to make certain we won't be eating any under-cooked meat. That's how you get worms."

"It's fully cooked, Tristian. I honestly assure you."

"Say, what would you think of me becoming a chef?"

"In a poplin hat, wearing your cuffed jacket?"

"With a cruet in one hand and tongs in the other?"

"Pursue culinary training first, dear."

"Hey now. I've had my beginners day of practice. So, how many sessions before I'm called chef?"

"Well, mister. If you plan to be an executive, I'd say three years, no less," his wife affirmed, tasseling his hair.

"But I don't have that kind of time on my hands."

Josie smiled. "Now you know why you work at the bank."

"Well, my lady, I do what I can."

She then kissed his forehead. "And that's enough to keep me happy."

Tristian reached forth his hand with means to stroke his sweet love's face. "My fair Josette. A delicate gift for the likeness of you." Tristian unearthed the rose he had hid at his back. "Here's to my beautiful wife and sweet child inside you."

Before her, a single rosette stood poised in his hand. Josie's eyes suddenly watered as two streaming tears passed down her face. "It's beautiful, Tristian." She sniffled lightly. "Your kindness is touching, and it's making me cry."

"I love you, Jos, and I'll love our baby," he said, rubbing her stomach. "Come on, my sweetheart. Let's get ready to eat."

Tristian carved the ham, then placed slices onto plates while Josie gathered glasses from the counter to fill with tea. "Hey, now. Jos, what do you think you're doing?"

"I'm filling our glasses."

"Ah ugh, no. I want you sitting down. I'm tending to everything."

"You are? Well, what a cheery surprise."

"Go on now. Take your seat."

"I'm sitting. I'm sitting."

"Okay, here comes your plate. Watch your head."

"You know, waiter? I could get used to this pampering."

"Well, certainly. Eat it while you can."

"I certainly will."

"Declared like a pro."

"Uh, waiter? More ice to my glass."

"But of course, my sweet. Anything more, my fair, lady?"

"Bread's in the pantry. The crock of butter's in the fridge."

"And the silverware and napkins. We'll surely need them."

"Not bad, Tristian."

"See? I'm catching on."

Josie pulled the soda bread into separate halves, placing one on Tristian's plate and the second upon her own. Tristian got the silverware from a drawer, then set them upon the table.

Prior to their meal, they said a short prayer, then proceeded to eat.

"So? What do you think?" Tristian asked.

"You've done a wonderful job. Thank you for filling my shoes today, Tristian. I appreciate all your work here."

"Your health's important, Jos. Rest whenever you can. I'll be here to help. Your pains, dear. How have they been? No more, I hope."

"Not since this morning."

"I pray you no more. I don't like seeing you hurt," Tristian said, with care.

"So far I'm feeling good. Maybe those pains have finally ceased." Josie got up from her chair and carried the dirty dishes to the sink when the lights began to flicker as they went on and off. "Tristian, what's happening?"

"Must be a fuse." The lights then expired, leaving them cast to the dark. Tristian stepped from his seat. "I hardly see a thing. Jos, just stay where you are." He paced slowly through the room. Suddenly the lights flickered and came back on. To the O'Briens' amazement, a hot spread now sat upon their table, passing off steam.

"Tristian, where'd that food..."

The chairs began to move. Within Tristian's, the phantom image of a man took form. He was slouched over, drunk in his seat with a bottle of ale fit loosely in hand. In Josie's appeared the faint outline of a woman. She sat poised, unlike the crouched man.

"What ye be waiting for? Fix thy plate, wench," the man snarled.

The woman hurried to his demand. She piled food onto his plate, then set it before him while patiently awaiting his grateful approval. "It's your favorite," she said softly.

He stabbed at his plate, then took the first bite. A look of disgust crept upon him as he hawked the food onto his wife. "This lamb tastes awful. What were ye thinking? You can't even cook me a decent meal, ye blasted idiot." He pitched his plate to the floor where it had broken to pieces. "Come here," the man demanded. "Are ye deaf?" he shouted. "I said come here!" He quickly removed himself from his chair and struck the woman's face. "Ye can't do anything, ye stupid, lazy, wench."

"I try," she cried. "But everything I do's never good enough."

"Never good enough? Never good enough?" he shouted loudly. The man's face emerged a bright red shade. His eyes became buggy, protruding from sockets. Then, as large veins thrust down his throat, it was beneath skin they began to pulsate.

He pushed the woman's chair into the wall just behind her. Then, screaming with fright, the man struck her again. "Keep up ye balling. Ain't gonna do ye no good. Nobody cares. You're nothing more than a thorn in me side. Look at you. Pathetic sitting here crying like that. Why, I haven't hurt you. Clean those tears from your eyes. They make you look ridiculous."

"I beg you. Stop yelling. My head aches."

"My head's aching. My head's aching! Please stop the yelling," he raged sarcastically, mimicking her. "Your stupid head's always banging. Die already, so I don't have to deal with you."

The woman leaned over and cried in her lap. "Have you no decency? How could you be so callous and cruel?"

"Because I hate you. That's why."

"I'm your wife. If you despise me so, then why are we married?"

"This marriage is amiss. Just like you. Get out of me sight. Ye sicken me."

The images of the man and woman suddenly vanished. The lights stopped flickering as the room fell to silence.

"I can't take this, Tristian. I have to get out. I'll be on the porch. Come sit with me?" Josie asked.

"Certainly. We're in need of fresh air," Tristian added.

They walked to the porch and sat on the swing.

"It's more calming here," stated Josie while enjoying the breeze. "At least I feel safe, Tristian. I don't in that house. I don't want to live watching each corner and checking my back."

"Then we'll lie here awhile."

"I never thought I'd have to live like this, Tristian. It's not right. We shouldn't live with fear in our house."

"I don't like it either, Jos."

"This is it, Tristian. I'm going to Mrs. O'Toole's tomorrow. Let's hope she can help. We need answers. We need them now."

The sun began to go down as the sky was soon painted in shades of pink and gold. Josie laid her head upon her husband's shoulder. "I wish things could be this peaceful more often," she spoke softly.

Grasshoppers began to sing as the sky became dim. And all the sounds of the night had slowly stepped in. The light scent of rain floated in the air while clouds took the sky above. Light showers sprinkled the streets and sidewalks, veiling the earth with a damp, glossy, sheen. The streetlights shined luridly, reflecting the night. And a pale moon arose through scattered clouds, indicating an observable arrival.

Josie peered up to Tristian. "I wish we could just sleep here, don't you? It's more peaceful where we're at."

"We're bound to get drenched once those rains settle in. I don't think you'd want cold showers blowing upon you while you slept."

"I don't care, Tristian. As long as I didn't have to go back in that house and face its terrors."

"What if you fall ill, Jos? Not just you, but the baby? You'd never forgive yourself. I'm sorry, sweetheart. I won't let you stay here. I'll make sure you're safe. Nothing will happen," Tristian said, stretching his hand. "Please say you'll come in."

Josie nodded, then took her husband's hand. He helped her from the swing and walked to the door. "Allow me," he said.

"Leave those dishes, Tristian. I'll finish them."

"You don't have to. Just leave them till morning."

"I'd rather not. I just want them out of the way."

"Okay. Well, I'll be upstairs then. If you need me, yell."

Josie finished the dishes, dried them off, and returned them to the shelves. In the distance she perceived something startling. It was much like wings heavily flapping through air. She turned, looking desperately for the sound. Growing closer, it progressed to the kitchen. Loud squawks soon followed, all the while echoing throughout the room.

Josie glanced in a circle when suddenly the bird appeared. It soared about, periodically drifting in and out of sight. Finally it flew to the refrigerator where it made easy landing.

The raven picked its jet feathers and loosened one free. The detached quill then glided toward the ground as it dangled in the air. As the bird's eyes sailed across the stretch of room, they then fell upon Josie. Staring intensely onto her, it marked no movement. Josie looked into its blazing eyes and soon found herself hypnotized within their dancing embers. It wasn't long before she was taken by its trance.

Josie was overwhelmed with calmness as her breathing became shallow, as though the bird was convincing her to not be afraid. It blinked before soaring off the fridge, then disappearing into thin air, the raven had vanished. The magnetic hold influencing Josie had weakened. Gaining composure, she snapped away from the transfixed state.

Walking to the refrigerator, she grasped at the feather. Had the bird intentionally left it behind? she wondered. Holding the quill, she examined its colors. The feather was mostly black, but with closer inspection Josie detected hints of deep purple and tinges of blue. It was remarkably smooth and silky to touch. Holding it tightly, Josie shut out the lights, then trudged from the kitchen.

In the living room she closed all the windows and positioned the curtains. Locking out the lights, she stepped from the room. Josie had then made her way toward the stairwell. Undesirably recalling what she'd seen the night before brought shivering quivers to race down her spine.

Rushing to the second floor hallway, Josie stood under dusk. Her vision had been obscured from luster, except for a faint light which glowed from her room. She walked down the gallery surpassing the guest bunker. Before the entry barrier Josie discerned whispered cries. Curious, she stalled by the doorway and there listened quietly. Taking deep breaths, she carefully accessed through the door. Josie peered through the shadows, inquisitively searching the dark. Reaching her hand along the wall, she felt for a light. Then, flipping a switch, she still found the room fixed to darkness.

Beyond the room, Josie overheard a haunted tune. It had discharged through a music box while saddening the air. The weeping melody carried forth, discoursing the night. It was soon Josie spotted the bashful woman upon the bed. She appeared dimly beneath the lackluster room, faintly glowing enough to make out her sight. Tipped forward with tears, the woman sobbed in her hands, then, using a hanky, dabbed the moist specks from her face.

"Miss? Miss, are you okay?" Josie asked.

The woman turned easily and stared toward the door. "Do you be the visiting spirit which haunts me?" the woman asked mildly.

"Spirit?" Josie remarked.

"I've seen you before, haunting my home." The handkerchief fell from her hand, then dangled to the bed as she faded from sight.

"Miss, wait. Don't go." Josie paced through the room as the jewelry box prolonged its play near the bed. Picking up the hanky, Josie held it in hand. It was still moistened with the tears the woman had cried.

Walking into the hallway, Josie proceeded toward the bathroom. Turning on the light, she examined the handkerchief more clearly. It was the color of cream with tiny pink flowers embroidered upon the edges. Patterned along the right corner were three calligraphic initials. *C, A, O.*

While returning to her room, Josie encountered Tristian.

"I was ready to send a search party after you."

"Sorry, dear. I got caught up."

"Anything important?"

"This handkerchief," Josie explained. "I'm certain it's that woman's. These must be her initials, Tristian. I'm pretty sure."

"How would you know for exact?"

"I found her in the guest room crying."

"How do you know that's hers? She give it to you?"

"It fell to the bed before she faded." Josie grew quiet for a moment, then softly spoke her husband's name. "Tristian."

"What is it, sweet pea? Something wrong?"

"Tristian, she ... she thinks I'm haunting *her*."

"She talked to you?"

"She thinks I'm a spirit."

"She *what*?"

"I could hardly believe it."

"Did you ask her name?"

Josie shook her head. "She was gone before I could."

"Well."

"Well, what?"

"Be thankful you have her initials. Look at it as a start, Jos."

"It's strange, though."

"What's that?"

"It didn't disappear."

"You were meant to have it then."

"I saw the raven, Tristian. It returned to the kitchen."

"You saw it again?"

"And for once I felt no fright," Josie explained. "I don't believe it's here to harm us. I suspect it has something to do with our house. Maybe even those spirits nonetheless."

"They could be separate hauntings, Jos."

"Perhaps. But somehow I feel it's interrelated."

"We can't know for certain."

"Well, I have my hunches, along with this feather. Here."

"How? How'd you get this?"

"The raven left it. Seems strange. Within an eight minute span I get a feather and hanky. I'm beginning to think I'm blessed."

Tristian laughed lightly. "Maybe they're gifts."

"How about clues? An indication to the woman's identity and, and a suggestive token to the raven's existence?"

"You sound like a detective piecing leads. Well, whatever it is, it's unreal. I can't say I've ever heard anything matching our ordeal. It's definitely unique."

"I'm going to find my way to Mrs. O'Toole's come noontide. If she's unaware, maybe she could direct me someplace else," Josie relayed as she climbed into bed.

"All we have's hope. And with the right individual, we'll probably be able to put part of this perplexity behind us."

"I'll pray to that." Josie laid her head upon the pillow and closed her eyes. "Good night," she said softly.

Josie had fallen into a deep sleep while Tristian snored lightly, restlessly tossing and turning in sheets.

The moonlight sent a veil of beams through the window, leaking in its azured shine. Then, approaching through shadows, lurked a dark mass. Its impression was exceedingly unholier than night. It came from the corner slowly, then with unsound stride crept toward the bed. The air became icy-cold as the phantom grew closer. Goosebumps promptly secured to Tristian's body as he reached toward the sheets. He stuffed the quilt beneath his chin only to have it furiously stripped from its place.

Opening his eyes, Tristian gawked upon the onyx entity perching below him. While Tristian gasped in sudden fear, the obsidian figure rose forth, closing in. Tristian lay stiffened in sheets. His heart raced rapidly as the dusky intruder stared down his face. A breath of cold air stunned Tristian's flesh while gusting forth its misting flurry. Sleet passed upon him and froze Tristian's skin. His lips turned cerulean, corresponding to the colorations of beryl asters. His brows now thickset within the stirred snows projected from the wrathful specter.

Passing through the enclosing wall, the looming mass disappeared. Tristian lay frozen, still icebound in chills. It'd taken plenty productive pants of his warming breath to thaw those icy crystals secured to his face. When gaining flexibility, Tristian quickly pulled the covers above his head. There he hid in security until feeling relieved enough to go bed.

CHAPTER SEVEN ◆

Day 3, the 8th of July, 1950.

The sun was rising slow in the sky. And with short time, the first kindled ray alighted Josie's face, soon rousing her stir. Her eyes burned while she struggled to open. Rubbing her lids, she diminished the sting, then laid at her side to peer toward the windows. The heavens were painted in resplendent shades of purple and orange, marking its radiated arrival to birth a fresh day.

Josie innocently drew her eyes to the clock upon her stand. Suddenly withholding discernment, a man's hand materialized in the air, abruptly grasping her face. Josie screamed unexpectedly as Tristian awoke.

Shooting forthright from the bed, he found his wife clutching her face while crying. "Jos? Josie, what's happened?" he asked with concern.

"A hand. A hand! He meant to crack my jaw, Tristian."

"Shh now. Let me take a look," he spoke softly.

"Well?"

Her face was swollen and bruised while finger marks rose from her skin. "My God, Jos. What has he done? Can you move your jowl?"

"It's sore. Tristian, don't push, it's sore."

"Why would he attack you?"

"I don't know. I just saw the hand. Next thing I knew he had my face. It was as quick as that."

"Let me get you a cool rag." Tristian went to the bathroom, then returned seconds later. "I know it's cold, but you have to hold this on you."

"Do I need a doctor?"

"I don't think so. As long as you're able to manage, I'm sure you'll be all right. Do you need me home today?"

"Probably not. You need to work. We need the money."

"I guess I'll take a quick shower then. I have to be in at seven."

"I'll have your breakfast ready once you're out." She slipped into her robe and house shoes, then walked to the kitchen.

Josie took several eggs from the fridge along with some pork links and bacon. Heating the burners, she began cooking. She set an iron kettle upon the stove and prepared hot tea. Pouring the fresh brew into mugs, she then topped them with raw milk before setting the drinking cups aside.

Josie returned to the stove and finished assembling breakfast. As she reduced the burners, she heard her husband upon the stairs. "Tristian, your food's ready. I hope you've brung an appetite." Josie loaded her husband's plate, then, turning toward the table, found his chair empty.

Puzzled, Josie set the plate aside, then moseyed toward the stairwell. Peering up, she saw no one. Seconds later, the bathroom door opened as Tristian emerged.

"I see you there. You spying on me?" He laughed.

"Were you just on the stairs?"

"No. Why?"

"I could have sworn I heard you coming down."

"No, Jos, wasn't me. I've been in the bathroom."

"I see that now. Well, your breakfast is ready. Come on down when you're through."

"All right then. I'll be just a moment."

Josie returned to the kitchen when she noticed something odd. "Now wait a minute," she spoke. Tristian's plate had been dusted clean. Not a single crumb tainted his platter. "I know there was food here. I'm certain." Josie peered into her husband's mug, it, too, empty. She then gazed to hers while witnessing the vanishing steam rise.

Tristian entered the room, then noticed the strange look upon his wife. "What's with the confused stare? Something got you baffled?" he asked.

She shook with bewilderment. "Someone's eaten your food."

"What, Jos?"

"Your plate and cup are empty," she spoke in disbelief. "Here, let me get you more." She put the dishes into the sink, then retrieved a clean platter from the cabinet. Once again she loaded Tristian's plate and, like before, topped his mug with hot tea and milk. Josie rested the plate before him. Then, fixing her own, she joined him for breakfast.

"You're sure you'll be okay on your own? You're not having more pains, are you? Jos, be honest."

"Just a few small ones here and there. Nothing like those yesterday. I'll be fine, Tristian. If anything happens, I promise to call you."

"What if that man should attack you again, Jos? Aren't you afraid? I can't protect you when I'm not here."

"Of course I'm afraid. I'm scared beyond my mind, Tristian. We never know when or where he'll appear. It's a matter we'll learn to cope with rather we like to or not. We live here, you and me. That man needs to understand and move on. You can't be removing yourself from work because our house is suddenly haunted. You need your job. Our income relies on your payroll, Tristian."

"I can't help but worry about you. Josette, you're my wife. Keeping you safe's part of my creed. You shouldn't be victimized in your own home. This is supposed to be a place of comfort, not some nightmare."

"I understand your concerns, Tristian. But without your job we'll have nothing. How would we support a child with no income? Money doesn't just grow on trees and wait to be picked. Life's not that easy. This isn't heaven. Nothing's free."

"How do you expect to protect yourself? Just answer me that."

"I don't know, Tristian. Prayers, crosses, bible excerpts, possibly even holy water." Josie thought for a moment, then fished through her pocket. "Maybe defunct evil with this feather." She then laughed. "Oh, gosh. I know that sounds silly."

"You really think that raven's feather could shield you from harm? Come to your senses, Jos. That quill has no effect upon corrupt souls. You'd get as much use with that as you would a stone," her husband remarked.

"Call me crazy then, Tristian. There's reason to why I have this. I just know it somehow."

"Have you stopped to think it could bring you ill fate?"

"I don't feel it will. If I did, Tristian, I would have gotten rid of it at once."

"If anything happens. I mean anything, Jos. You're to call me, understood?" he said, glancing at his watch. "Ah, gee, look at the time. I have to get to work before I'm late."

"I'm going to Mrs. O'Toole's come noon. If you should call and can't reach me, I don't want you worried."

"Like I've said, I can't help but worry." Tristian kissed Josie upon the forehead. "I'll see you sometime this evening. I love you, sweetheart. Be safe."

"Love you, too. Bye, dear." Josie washed the dishes and tidied up the kitchen. Afterward, she footed to the second floor and proceeded the bedroom. There she slipped into a tinted peach dress. Following her way toward the bathroom, she promptly stopped to clean up. The familiar image peering behind the mirror clearly showed the deep bruising along her jowl. Josie powdered her face several times to cover the noticeable discolorations. Then, dusting an airy brush of color upon her cheeks, she highlighted her skin with a resplendent glow. Last she added a tinge of rouge to her lips, thereby completing her artistry. She then returned to the kitchen moments later.

She began thinking silently. Mmm, I should probably make something to take to Mrs. O'Toole. It'd be rude if I didn't. Josie pondered on what to bake before deciding upon a traditional tea cake.

She immediately gathered her ingredients; butter, a few eggs, and some milk, which she soured with vinegar. She poured in her dry additives consisting of baking powder, salt, and sugar to a mixing bowl, then, dumping in butter, she proceeded to cream it. After finishing, Josie added the eggs and buttermilk. Lastly, she added vanilla extract and currants to the batter, then folded it under.

Josie greased a nine-inch baking pan and layered in the blend, then placed the prepared batter into the hot stove. She went back toward the refrigerator. Taking out cream cheese, she lapped some to a bowl along with powdered sugar. She juiced a lemon above the confections to add a zestful flare.

Now Josie had a glaze ready to top the cake. She put the combination among the counter and covered the bowl. In the back yard she noticed the forgotten laundry Tristian hung the day before. She got a basket and headed toward the yard.

Stretching forth, she unclipped the clothes from the line. As she did, a minor pain struck her side, forcing her to double and cringe. Josie's distress would then worsen as it extended throughout her abdomen. Soon the agony became severe as Josie was enforced to sit. She sat bent forth, sobbing while clutching her stomach.

A warm breeze picked up, and Josie could smell the familiar scent of flowering tea rose. The sensation of someone's arms embracing her soon furthered her ease. Within moments, the invisible guest had gone, and once again Josie was deserted solely to herself.

She gathered the remaining clothes from the line, then stacked them in her basket. Within that instant, Josie felt a pair of inspecting eyes upon her. Looking toward the doorway, Josie was bemused to see the ghostly woman spying back. Her docile soul expressed a humble smile upon her narrow lips as she slowly budded departure.

Josie felt a sense or tranquility as she strolled to the house. Making her way toward the bedroom, she hung away the tidied clothing. Progressing to the kitchen, Josie gazed upon the tanning pastry. The scullery smelt scrumptious while emanating the native scent of Madagascan vanilla.

Josie pulled the stove door slightly to gain a better view. The cake had risen beautifully, and the color was splendid enough to be perfectly right. At that time Josie felt it was ready to cool. She tugged the loaf from the rack and placed it before a window.

She then fixed herself a cup of warm tea, then proceeded toward the table where she sat with her drink. Blowing away steam, Josie sipped her beverage while opening the day's newspaper.

Josie read silently, unknown that her sink's handle initiated movement by means of twisting mysteriously. It generated slowly, pressuring the warm water to suddenly turn hot. Steam saturated the sink and rose through air. The handle then increased power while furthering on to full blast. Water shot from the faucet like an untamed hose lacking surveillance. Josie was now distracted by the cascading flow. Watching in shock, she witnessed both knobs spinning out of control.

She rushed to the sink without thinking. Grabbing the unhinged latches, she quickly tried to shut them off. But due to her lack of judgment, Josie was suddenly scalded by the extreme heat adhering to both handles. Her encounter caused her to bake the delicate skin overlaying her palms.

Josie screamed in upscaling pain. Suddenly the water stopped even though the handles kept spinning. Then, without warning, a spout of water projected forth with far more heat than before. Grasping towels, Josie cloaked the knobs in hope of ceasing their succession. But soon the water was replaced with hundreds of vexatious flies pouring from the nozzle. Josie fell into panic as she started to scream. A horde of annoyances swarmed around her, engulfing Josie in their embrace.

She fought to rid them, but her profit was shortcoming as they sustained to plague her wherever she moved. Running to the living room, Josie tripped on her dress as she fell to the floor. The unyielding impact caused her to scrape her arms and hands. Josie lay on the ground as the flies swooped forth to flood her.

The high pitch buzzing magnified a hundred times and rang in her ears. Josie huddled into a fetal position and cried for support. Within immediate closeness she heard hostile laughter hover round.

Josie soon experienced frigid, icy hands upon her ankles as she prolonged her screaming even more. She felt her body being violently drug through the room. Opening her eyes, she hunted desperately for her attacker, but was unable to see anyone there. Her body had been yanked toward the stairwell, then furiously jerked above each step. Giving her best, Josie intensely fought for freedom. But the further effort she released, the more angered the entity became.

Josie's back ached as each stair scraped against her tender spine. She cried in severe pain as another struggle emerged. "Let me go. Let me go!"

The man continued to laugh wickedly as she cried. Grabbing a spindle, Josie grasped for dear life. The man tried to tug her the rest of the way, but found he couldn't. Josie's hands were tired and hurting. Blisters rubbed into her palms as they burst and began bleeding.

A loud squawk then rose from the air as the raven appeared. It flew with great speed facing the stairs while directing itself toward the concealed entity. Its talons thrashed out as it landed atop the unobservable head.

The raven reserved its beak into invisible flesh, pecking its prey. Its advancing force impacted the entity with pain and annoyance, all the while lessening its grip on Josie's ankles. Following that, her legs fell to the stairs, and the intense struggle was over. The entity was gone as the raven flew forth, disappearing into the rear bedroom. Josie pulled herself up with the use of the banister. Her back burned intensely like it'd been submerged into sweltering fire. She eased up slowly until being able to stand. Pacing weakly upon the stairs, Josie hobbled to the bathroom.

She stood with her back to the mirror while undoing her dress. Bright welts covered her spine with shaved flesh scaling off. Traces of blood dampened her skin, tainting the once perfect sheath. Josie looked down at her blistered palms, realizing she was barely able to open them.

She filled the sink with cold water and submerged her hands. Her cankered flesh stung as three tears spilt along her face. Josie wrapped her hands within a towel, then searched the bathroom for a salve to cover her painful gashes. She soon spotted a blue tin of ointment. Trying her best to smear the medicine on her back, Josie tried to cover her scrapes and scratches.

Josie returned to the kitchen, then gently laid her fingers upon the cake. Noticing it still needed a little time to cool, she went outside to gather a few bunches of wild flowers. Josie set the cluster atop the table, then walked to the counter to retrieve her glaze. After the pan had cooled enough, Josie carefully flipped the cake onto a platter and drizzled the frosted glaze. As a finishing flare, Josie decorated the cake with all sorts of beautiful flowers to lend forth a colorful touch.

CHAPTER EIGHT ◆

Josie started through the front door with the cake in hand, then walked across the street a ways. As she did, Josie felt the strange sensation of eyes upon her. Turning over her shoulder, she peered at her house. Glaring forth from the door was the man standing silent. Chills ran down Josie's spine as she quickly turned away. She picked up her pace while approaching Mrs. O'Toole's. Trotting beyond the steps, she rang the doorbell when a little old woman answered.

"Good afternoon, Mrs. O'Toole. I hope I'm not bothering you."

"Nonsense, child. What's there to bother? Please, dear, won't you come in?"

"Thank you, Mrs. O'Toole."

"Josette, dear, please call me Agnus. Mrs. O'Toole makes me feel wrinkled." She laughed.

Josie blushed to her remark. "I'll certainly remember that."

"So what's brung the pleasure of this visit?"

"I was hoping I could talk with you. This loaf just came from the stove. It's nice and warm."

"How sweet of you, dear. Please, come to the kitchen. I'll warm us some tea." Agnus walked to the stove and set the kettle on top the fire. "Let me grab us each a plate."

"Are you certain I'm no bother, Agnus?"

"Of course not, sweet girl. I haven't had company as long as a year has days. This is a nice surprise, you coming by. Gives me someone to visit." Agnus hobbled back toward the table. "Here we are, dear. Now doesn't that just smell delicious?"

"I hope you like it." Josie gleamed. "It's one of my favorites."

"A sweet baked by a sweet. I know it'll be pleasant."

"I do try my best."

"That's better than no effort. Well, my dear, shall we savor this snack?"

"I should certainly hope so." Josie laughed.

"So, deary, what's this unease you've brung with you? Something's got you set with distress. It's tugging your soul, I feel."

"You've picked that up?"

"A person's eyes never lie. To see within's a natural gift bestowed upon us who have the vision. You'll, too, be able to spot this, come time."

Josie rubbed her napkin lightly within her fingers. "I was hoping to talk to you about a man and woman I believe used to live in my house."

"Sure, dear. I could help you with that. I've known most every soul who's lived there."

"You wouldn't happen to have known a woman with the initials C, A, O, did you?"

"Let's see. You said C, A, O?"

"Yes, ma'am." Josie pulled out the handkerchief and set it upon the table. "Does this at all seem familiar?"

Agnus picked up the hanky and smiled warmly. "Yes, dear. Oh, yes ... my, how long these years have been."

"I didn't mean for you to cry, Agnus. Are you all right?"

"Her name was Ciara Ann O'Neill. Such a charming, bloomed, youth she was. One of the fairest ladies you'd ever meet in her time. But, oh, how that child lived a mournful life. Such terrible tragedy fell her. Remembering now somehow feels like yesterday."

"Can you tell me about her?"

"Ciara was one of a kind. Truly an admirable soul. Someone who was everything and beyond. Sweet, helpful, and sincere was she. But her husband." Agnus shook her head. "Aidan was violent, and his hatred enraged him. In 1896 the O'Neills moved to your house. The perfect couple at first. He loved his wife dearly, as she did him. He was most respectful and caring when it came to Ciara."

Josie interrupted suddenly, "I don't see that."

"Something unspeakable happened to Aidan which changed him

forever. And that's where their story starts. The beginning of Ciara's sadness would prove tragic. Aidan owned and operated a popular pub in town. Most the time he'd stay till close, minding the business, if not cleaning it. Like always, after leaving his shift, Aidan passed by the old graveyard near Kinley's hill. When returning home, he told Ciara of the mysterious misfortune that befell him that night. He spoke of rolling fog inhabiting the boneyard and the light mist which filled the air. Then in the distance he'd witnessed a creature. It crept forth from a headstone. Convinced the horrid beast was nothing less than a hellion of fairy lore; noted as the infamous phouka. The most feared fairy in all Ireland. A grotesque goblin whose avid capabilities allow alteration. What makes the phouka so dangerous is its mastery of disguise. As a sovereign of forms, the phouka can adopt the semblance of any frightening figure it chooses. The *diabhal sióga*, or devil fairy, is not a tranquil being. It lacks harmony, friendship, and love. If sighted, it's best to stray abroad since the phouka's apt to instant attacks."

"Agnus, what happened to Aidan then? Was he assaulted?"

"That thing stared him down beneath the moonlight gazing through its glossy blue-white eyes, then leaped to the air where it landed on top of a tomb. It sat stilly making irregular noises all the while hissing at Aidan. In fear he stood, standing, watching the *diabhal*. It became angry when he did not leave. Aidan claimed clear as day that grotesque goblin had shape-shifted into a large black dog before his very eyes. It took off through the cemetery dashing toward him. Aidan said its speed was that of a bolting horse, and when it reached him, a foul odor seeped forth from its body. It attacked by clinching teeth into Aidan's ankle and forearm. Once it had its feel, it retreated to its desolate home in a nearby mausoleum."

"Did the attack somehow alter him for the worse? Please, Agnus, you must tell me."

"You must understand that the phouka's saliva tainted Aidan's blood, driving him mad. He attained the vulgar mouth of a sailor, and his appearance had changed in just a short time. His eyes became an unnatural cast of blue, and his skin took on various shades of crimson hues. It wasn't but a day or so after that he initiated Ciara's abuse. His violence was generated verbally and physically through such intense extremes. People said that Aidan became possessed by the phouka and, in fact, became a demon himself. When he wasn't bartending,

Aidan was drinking up most of the ale. He sought fights with anyone who'd challenge him. He was drunk most the time, nevermore to care about any one thing, not even Ciara. When she was twenty-eight Ciara started suffering from intemperate headaches to the point they'd make her black out. She was notified through her doctor that she'd fallen ill. Believing the reason for her headaches was due to induced pressure upon her brain, such as inflammation, Ciara's doctor performed a procedure to decrease the compression. During the operation he was stunned to find his hypothesis had proved him wrong. The matter of the fact as it turned out was the poor dear was suffering from a intracranial tumor. Her doctor was too afraid to remove the cancerous growth due to a sudden risk of death. In the early nineteen-hundreds neurosurgery was a touchy issue when concerning cancer. The doctor told Ciara the possible dangers involving a second operation. There was a ninety percent chance she'd pass during the procedure. So, together, they decided the best means for her was to allow the cancer to run its course. By that she was assured some additional time. Since the tumor was, in fact, inoperable, the doctor openly stated she'd have a few months at most."

Josie sniffled. "Did her husband at least mind her during or after surgery?"

"No, dear, I'm afraid not. Aidan wanted no part of it. His concerns were in his mugs of ale and his faulted hands."

"Then who kept over her? Surely she didn't care for herself?"

"I was with her at surgery, and it was me who nursed her back to health come following weeks. It wasn't till she was back on her feet that she assured me she'd be fine. Aidan didn't seem to care about Ciara's condition before surgery nor further on. He battered her throughout her recovery and far after."

"Didn't you do anything? Agnus? You didn't leave her alone to him? How could you?"

"The beatings she sustained happened when all eyes were absent. Each day brung new bruises, gashes, and scrapes. I told her countless times she had a room with Miles and I. But her response was always the same. I'll come when I can no longer stand it. Sad words indeed. I tried, I did, but she just wouldn't break from him." Mrs. O'Toole's eyes filled with tears. "Poor, Ciara. That poor, poor, child. The things she saw. The things Aidan put her through. No man should treat his wife the way he did her."

Josie wiped the trickles from her eyes. "Did he … did he kill her, Agnus?"

"Some say he did. Others say it was a tragic accident."

"What had been the cause?"

"The night of her death it was thought Ciara and Aidan got into a terrible fight in their room. Some say he pushed her. Others claim she accidently collided with their dresser and hit her head. Sadly, the impact caused the tumor to rupture as it spread on her brain. Aidan claimed his wife fell into a coma that night. She never regained consciousness. She passed away just a short while later. That was the ninth of July, nineteen-hundred."

"Did he admit to pushing her?"

"Course not, that lying brute. He told the constables, doctors, *Gazette*, and town folk she'd woken from sleep and staggered half awake. Supposedly she'd tripped, then fell toward the dresser."

Josie had tears streaming down her face. "I don't believe that. He's horrible. Aidan was capable of killing her, I know it. That just makes me sick. How could someone not care about another person's life?" Josie shook her head and continued to cry softly.

"Here, dear, I think we need some tissues."

"Do you believe her death to have been an accident, Agnus? I'm sure to say I believe it was not."

"I never believed it that first day, nor have I ever. I'm firm on my concept. I say that he did it. I know that low-life being's the reason Ciara's in her grave."

"What about Aidan? Was he arrested? What happened to him?"

"There was never an arrest. He simply got away with it. So he thought. He probably went on to believe he escaped his earthbound imprisonment. But honorably enough, justice had found him in different form. The rule of karma does apply, and it came back on him. As stated in belief, you'll get yours, and he did."

"Did he have a freak accident? Did she come back to kill him? Agnus, what happened?"

"His story, dear, is quite interesting. What happened to Aidan seems an unusual coincidence. It was murdered for murder revenge. It'd been the day of Ciara's funeral. I stood proud to see the show of locals who respected her. And I'm sure to them she smiled. Aidan appeared midway through the service. So shameful of him. He was sloshed beyond his mind, barely able to open his eyes or stand. His behavior was intolerable, and he was escorted outside the church. He later joined the graveside service after sobering. There, Aidan never shed a tear for his wife. He just stood unaffected through a solid face and dead set eyes. Only a few people noticed. In fact, I was one of them. It upset me so seeing her in that casket cold and him not fazed. They were married eight years. Any moral soul who's lost a mate would be deeply affected by their loss. It was as though Aidan was putting an empty coffin to rest. I think in their final moments together Aidan grew to hate Ciara more and more. Even though he mistreated her the way he did, she never had room in her heart for hate. That wasn't her nature. That day after the funeral Aidan returned to the pub to do nothing more but get stewed. During that time Aidan had no knowledge of the concealed intruder hiding within his house. He was waited on until his return. Aidan had been viciously slain in his bathroom. The murderer dissected his throat repeatedly, nearly cleaving it off. The final blow was the four knife wounds to his heart. The vascular organ sustained substantial damage upon all valves. His pulmonary, tricuspid, bicuspid, and aortic semilunar valves had all been split to halves. It was the bloodiest mess to have ever been seen. It was like the walls and floor had been hosed in his discharge. It wasn't a sight for sinless eyes, know that."

"You saw it?"

"I helped clean the mess. It was terribly nauseating."

"So it wasn't you who killed him?"

"Is that what you thought?"

"I don't know who to think. I'm sorry, Agnus. How wrong of me."

"Josette, dear, no need to be sorry. You're freely allowed to speculate."

"If not you, then Ciara? You said it was murdered for *murder* revenge."

"The murderer was not me. As I'm certain to say it wasn't Ciara either. She loved Aidan, possessed or not. If she never harmed him in life, how could she in death? For nearly fifty years that incident's caused mystery. Nobody really knew who Aidan's killer was. Not a single soul had ever been caught or charged for that crime."

"Was there no evidence? Could something have been overlooked?"

"There was nothing recovered, no. The crime was simply flawless. As legends emerged, they all suggested Ciara's spirit to have revenged her death."

"There's no one you could think of?"

"This was a peaceful community. No one I knew was capable of that. I won't lie and say I never gave suspicion. At one point I pondered Ciara's brother Kieran."

"What was your reasoning to suspecting him?"

"He blew up on Aidan outside the church for his disgrace of coming in sloshed and being late for her funeral. The display of words between them was pretty exceeding. Kieran told Aidan he deserved to be buried, not his sister. When Aidan laughed, Kieran said if Constable Crichton didn't cast him to a hole, he would. Kieran was a serene individual, but Ciara's downfall made him despise Aidan."

"So it was possibly her brother?"

"One could only speculate, dear. But as you see, the honest truth is unknown. Henceforth, our considerations lack certainty."

"Was there anything absolute?"

"Ciara dealt with Aidan's possession for about a month and a half before her death. Nothing sunny nor blissful was meant to flourish within those walls after Aidan's change. Their house was sucked of its warmth and love, then replaced with coldness and hate. All eyes may have been absent, but the folks here still had their ears. Strolling by the house, many people heard Ciara cry while Aidan shouted. Disturbances were tumbled upon day and night. Those individuals may not have seen it, but they heard what went on. In public Ciara acted as though her life was fine. But in reality her eyes showed her pain. Not to mention the physical imperfections Aidan had left her. Everything from broken bones to bruised eyes. Word spread, and soon the towns folk called that place the crying house."

"What about children? Did they have any kids?"

"There were no children, no. But I knew Ciara wanted her own."

"Maybe it was best she didn't. Who knows what Aidan would have done to an infant."

"Despite them having any, there was a child, however. He looked upon Ciara as a mother. He'd visit her on the porch when she was out.

Ciara would give him change to buy candy. Feed him if he was hungry. She just did that sort thing because she was nice. Logan ran tasks here and there for the O'Neills. If something were needed from the butcher or general store, he'd be eager to lend help."

"How old was this child?"

Agnus pondered briefly. "Logan was at least eight or nine when he began his visits with Ciara. And I believe he was about twelve or thirteen when she died. His mother had abandoned him as a small boy, so he lived with his father down the way. Shamus was a good man. A working farmer who spent his days sun up to sun down. Because of that, he found it was difficult to make time for his son. With a lacking father and an absent mother, Logan sought Ciara's attention. She listened to the child and took care of him nearly every day. Shamus never minded it. He knew the goodness in Ciara, and that gave him comfort. In a sense, I suppose she adopted Logan as her own. He just didn't live there was the difference."

"What happened to him after her death?"

"He was stricken with grief and severe depression. Ciara was the only mother he'd ever known. After her death, he became deeply withdrawn. About ten years ago Logan suffered a heart attack. He was fifty-three at the time. He now resides in a nursing home, the poor man."

"Sounds like Ciara lived an awful life she didn't deserve," Josie remarked.

"I just hope that poor dear's resting peacefully. I keep a picture of her and Aidan in a hope chest. You care to see?"

"Oh, yes, I certainly would."

"Let me get it for you." Agnus hobbled into her living room. In front of a window stood an old antique chest. Agnus reached inside, then dug through some pictures. She found the frail photo of Ciara and Aidan moments later, then returned to her kitchen. "You know, dear. Looking at this, I see you resemble Ciara in some ways." Agnus handed the photo to Josie.

"She was beautiful, wasn't she?"

"She was a stunning lady indeed. Always poised and proper."

"She seems so happy." Josie studied the picture. "I can't get over that being Aidan beside her. What a difference this photo shows."

"They'd been married three years when that was taken. At the time the world was their oyster. They had so many hopes and dreams, then within a few short years those images shattered." Agnus wiped the tears from her eyes. "My dear, if you don't mind me asking, what's your interest with Ciara and Aidan? You just curious? Might that be it?"

Josie sat quietly a moment. "Mrs. O'Toole ... well, Agnus ... well..."

"What is it, dear? Don't you be frightened. Tell me what's on your mind."

Josie stared Agnus deep in the eyes. "I have reason to believe they're haunting my house. My suspicion's not foolish. I've seen many things which my eyes have beared witness. For my peace of mind, Agnus, I feel I must ask if you credit the existence of an unbodied substance?"

"As an old lady? Indeed, I believe. I'm aways from skepticism, my dear. I like to keep an open mind."

Josie sighed. "I'm relieved to hear that. Knowing makes me feel more stable."

"Do tell, Josette. What might these things be you've seen?"

"Well, you know, Tristian and I've lived here for years. Honestly, Agnus, nothing other worldly's ever happened in our home. Then it just started somehow. And for what reason, I don't know, but I tell you, I'm frightened."

"What started?"

Josie fell into thought as her words were submitted. "Everything had been fine until that raven's arrival," she explained.

"A bird, you say?"

"And not a live one at that. Soon after's when those spirits came. First I thought I was crazy, then Tristian began to see. Agnus ... Agnus, it's horrifying these things we've witnessed." Josie broke down to cry. "It's tearing me apart. I'm afraid I don't have strengths to endure this madness a second longer."

"Don't you be afraid, dear. You can tell me what you've seen."

"Agnus, I've ... I've seen Ciara. I ... it's..." Josie put her face in her hands. "He beats her constantly. Just over and over like a degraded animal. I can hardly bear these situations. There's nothing I can do. Nothing. But I want so to try."

"Tell me, is the air perfumed when she's around?"

"Yes, as a matter of fact. I always smell tea rose. How ... how might you know this?"

The Crying House

"That was one of Ciara's favorite scents. She kept vases throughout her home. What about Aidan? What do you feel when he's there?"

"The air's always frigid. Icy-like. At times he beats her, though I've failed to see him. Other occasions it's him who's seen, never his wife. Just recently they've appeared together." Josie thought over her statement while bowing her head. "How insane these words must sound. You probably think I'm crazy."

"Not in the least, Josette. Many people have seen things they believe to be crazy. But the fact is, there's much more to this world than just the physical aspect. So if you suspect you've seen Ciara and Aidan, chances are you have."

"I know it's them. I can say that and be certain. This photo before me validates my assumption. After supper yesterday they both appeared at my dining table. He was raging on about the meal she'd prepared. Ciara was perched in her chair when he beat her horribly. Sometimes I believe they see us. Other instances are like looking into the past watching them. I suffered my first attack this morning when waking. After Tristian left for work, I was attacked a second time. That encounter proved more violent."

"Are you able to talk about it, dear? What happened, I mean."

"Well, during the first attack my jowl had been squeezed. Because of that I can't open my mouth real far. I was in the kitchen as the second assault emerged. The faucet turned, spraying water. I scalded my palm upon the feverish handle. Soon after, hundreds of flies poured forth and swarmed me. I escaped to the living room where I fell. It was there Aidan's laughter rang throughout the room despite the fact he wasn't seen. Grabbing my ankles, he proceeded to drag me." Josie began to cry. "I tried to fight as he pulled me up the stairs. He delivered bruises and scratches all over my spine." Josie undid her dress and showed Agnus her back. "I hurt terribly, and my hands ... look at my hands."

"Oh, gracious, dear. How'd you acquire those blisters?"

"Grabbing a spindle. I held on for my life."

"You poor child. This is terrible. Just terrible. Might I get you something to treat these wounds?"

"I put salve on after the attack, but I still hurt. I need something to numb these painful aches." Josie shook her head. "Tristian asked me to call if anything happened. I didn't know how I'd tell him. My daily life shouldn't have to interrupt him at work. I don't want him losing his job over this. I'm truly scared, Agnus. I hate to say this, but I'm afraid Aidan might kill me. I don't know what to do, nor where to turn. I shouldn't be frightened in my own home, but I am." Josie squalled.

"Shh. Shh, now, shh. Josette, I want you to know I'm here. My home's open to you and Tristian. If you don't feel you could stay in that house, I have an open guest room. You and your husband would be gladly accepted. You'd be more than welcomed to stay when needed."

"Ah, Agnus, we'd really appreciate that. But."

"But what, dear? What is it?"

"I'm afraid we'd feel like intruders. Your home's not an inn, Agnus. I'm sure you wouldn't want your privacy disturbed by two sophomores." Josie smiled.

Agnus laughed. "I may look old, but I've always been young at heart, my dear. Your youthful infancy doesn't infringe me in the least. Therefore, my offer still stands whenever you're ready. Now you've said this haunting just started?"

"Yes, ma'am, that's correct."

"You might be surprised to know the fiftieth anniversary of Ciara and Aidan's deaths are approaching. That could be the answer to why they're here. Maybe they'll leave once that tribute has found its pass."

"How do you figure exactly?"

"Mystics believe when something violent and tragic happens somewhere, including houses, the energy gets pulled into objects, leaving imprints. Your house, for example, has seen its share of nasty fights and brutal deaths. The energy fields were so strong while those occurrences were happening. For that, the conductivity was pulled into inanimate objects. It left imprints in things such as walls, tables, dressers, and so forth. Mostly what you've seen were things that have happened in the past. Residual imprints that have made their way to the future. For you, it's a proliferation of Ciara and Aidan's fights. Further on, these productions could lead to their deaths. Some people believe these replications happen every day. Others believe it's on the tribute of that person's casualty. They could also return upon the time leading to their deaths. This could very well be the cause since the anniversaries are near."

"You said the haunting's residual, Agnus? But how could these spirits be aware other times?"

"It sounds at separate intervals it becomes what's known as an intelligent haunting."

"Okay. Okay, but what's that?"

"Having the awareness of you being there. They can see you and even interact if they feel. But I must say it's somewhat strange, however. Usually a residual haunting never becomes intelligent. That strikes me as odd. Residual hauntings don't interplay or react to the living, whereas intelligents do. They must be one form or the other, unless ... well, unless you have multiple hauntings, that is."

"I haven't seen anyone else, though. Besides Aidan and Ciara, there's only the bird. As bizarre as it may sound, I'm sure it has something to do with them being there. I know I can't explain how or why, but I feel almost certain." Josie pondered for a second. "Agnus, is it possible spirits don't know they're deceased?" she asked.

"Yes, dear, on occasions. There have been cases where the deceased do not know they're gone. They believe they're still going about with their daily lives. They get mixed into our reality. It's a case of coexistence. To those who see us, they believe they're the ones being haunted. It's hard for spirits to come to terms with death. In reality there are several different reasons for hauntings. Some oversee unfinished business which they feel they must attend. Others haunt places they have ties to or don't want to leave. There are those who are aware their time has passed, but those that don't things are confusing to them. If you try telling them they've departed, they don't want to listen. Mostly they don't understand or can't come to terms. The best way to release someone from this plane of existence is to direct them to the light. Their home exists beyond that brilliance. There, over, is where they belong. Once you tell them it's okay, they'll find rest. Usually they'll leave soon after and don't return. Some, however, are stubborn, set in their ways. They won't leave. For personal reasons they'd rather stay here."

"Why would that be?"

"I suppose it could be the fear of what's waiting for them on the other side. A fear of the unknown. They shouldn't be afraid, though. For most spirits it's a better place awaiting them. Unless hell is their final destination. They'll do everything to avoid having to go. It's all about who you were in life that brings the outcome to where you belong."

"I don't think Ciara knows she's dead. I'm relieved you said sometimes spirits don't know that. I appreciate you sharing this knowledge, Agnus."

"That's what an old lady's for. At my age you've seen everything there is to see."

"But you do suppose they'll leave at some point? I don't mind Ciara being there. In fact, she's welcome to stay, but I want Aidan gone. I won't share my home with him."

"Once the anniversary comes to pass, I believe you'll be free from their intrusion. For now, you'll have to deal as best you can until everything has been played out. I have to be honest now, and you may not like what you hear. But situations will get worse before they become any better. As long as you believe you can make it through all this, you can and you will. You just need to be strong. Having a demonic entity in your home isn't easy, but you can beat it."

"How, though? I'm afraid Aidan will run Tristian and me out if he hasn't yet killed us."

"Don't let him make you weak, Josette. You're in control. Any fear you feed him will only make him stronger. That's why he's been able to attack you. You've allowed him to cross one dimension to another. Don't grant him the strength to do that. Let Aidan remain stuck in the past. That's where he belongs. Once his anniversary occurs, death will take care of him the way it sees fit. He'll get his dues, and trust me, that boy won't be able to hide. It'll come to get him, and it will take him. I can assure you, Aidan won't be willing to go. Once a demon has lived on this earth, it doesn't want to be taken away. In Aidan's case, his existing privileges can no longer support him, and he'll be forced to move on."

"That's the best news I've heard all day. Thank you for listening, Agnus. You've truly been an oracle of knowledge. I feel grateful since I've talked with you."

"You're most welcome, my sweet child. I'm delighted I could help."

Josie smiled as she shook her head. "How is it you know so much, Agnus? You've amazed me."

Agnus smiled at Josie with stars in her eyes. "I've dabbled in my share of things, my dear. Being able to explore the unknown and not be afraid can give you more wisdom than you've ever imagined. That's how I acquired my attribute to knowledge. You just learn to be open and never afraid." She raised her brows.

Josie studied Agnus a moment's time. "Are you a…"

"Yes, dear, I am. As was my mother and my mother's mum."

"I knew there was something amazingly special about you."

"Oh, shucks, dear. You've made this old lady bloom her cheeks." Agnus smiled as Josie laughed modestly. "Could I get you some more tea?"

"That won't be necessary. But, ah. You had said earlier Logan suffered a heart attack and is in a nursing home. Does he ever receive visitors?"

"Well, I do try to see him the days I can. But I'm afraid lately my age has interfered with me getting out. Physically I'm not the young lass I used to be. I'll be eighty-two my next birthday. Sometimes I don't feel it, but when I look in the mirror, I see that old woman staring back. It's never hard to notice that's who I am now. Unfortunately, time can't stand still, so I pursue this seniority. That's the rule of life, though. Some things are just beyond our control, with age being the first of many."

"It's all part of acceptance." Josie paused a moment, then continued. "Might you suppose Logan would mind if I dropped him a visit? I understand he doesn't know me, but I'd be delighted to talk with him. You wouldn't suspect that to be a problem, would you?"

"I wouldn't see why not. I'm sure he'd enjoy the company. I think it'd be nice you going to see him, Josette. He could meet the wonderful lady inhabiting Ciara's home. Logan stays at the nursing residency in town."

"Thanks, Agnus. I'll surely set aside some time to see him," Josie declared as she glanced toward a clock. "Oh, my. I hate to cut this short, Agnus. I do. But Tristian will be home in an hour. Dinner has yet to be arranged." She laughed. "I've undoubtedly enjoyed this time together, but I really must get back."

"It was my pleasure, sweet child. I've fully enjoyed your company. Now. Now, Josette, dear. Remember, if anything happens you and Tristian are most welcomed to stay here."

"I appreciate your kindness, Agnus. I really do. I'll surely keep it to mind." Josie hugged Agnus. "Hopefully we could do this again sometime."

"I'd like that, dear. I really would. Don't be a stranger here. Feel free to drop in when you want." Agnus walked Josie to the front door and waved her goodbye.

CHAPTER NINE ◆

Josie walked slowly toward her house when dread knotted her stomach. Tristian will be home soon. I'll be all right, she'd told herself. Josie dug into her pocket searching for her skeleton key, then unlocked the door. As she traipsed into the hushed house, the front door slammed behind her, locking shut. Looking around, Josie soon found herself unfamiliar with her surroundings. "Surely I'm mistaken," she whispered softly. Josie returned to the door and tried twisting the knob, but nothing happened. "Please open so I can get out of here," she begged. She grasped the handle once more as it stayed rooted in place. "Oh no." If someone finds me here I'll be put away for intrusion. Josie slid her key into the hole and prayed it to work. "Don't do this. Oh, please. I just want out." She continued to fight the handle. Finally Josie was left with no choice than to abandon all effort. Inspecting the dwellings further, Josie realized an eerily, odd, coincidence. Despite the interior being dissimilar, the house somehow seemed her own.

The furniture was unmatched to that which she'd known, while the walls were polished in a citron shade. Disordered by the setting, Josie began to panic as she slowly paced throughout the house. The voice of an angry man transmitted into the hallway of the second floor landing. Josie stopped in her tracks, afraid to move farther. She remained upright and frozen within her steps while the inflamed speech grew ever more spiteful.

"Ye blasted wench. I'll tell ye once more. Bring your filthy ass over here. Damn it, ye lousy dolt. Don't ye make me come hurt you."

It was then a blood-curdling scream stretched through the house.

The Crying House

Josie peered upon the stairs as she eyed Ciara racing forth from a room. Blood poured from a fresh wound sunken into her cheek and splattered the floor.

Aidan came rushing from behind with a pair of scissors in hand. He caught Ciara by the back of her neck, then propelled his helpless wife into a barrier wall. Clutching her hair tightly in hand, he viciously tugged her head backward with might. In a fit of rage Aidan held the scissors to his wife's throat, then began threatening her savagely. "I ought to cut you ear to ear and let ye squill like a slaughtered pig. Ye don't belong here, ye stupid wench," he screamed to her ear. "A burst to your juggler and I'd bleed ye dry."

Ciara constricted her eyes as she shook without yield. "Aidan, don't do this please. Don't do it," she wailed. "I beg you. I beg you. Let me be." He brought the scissors back while his wife squalled with terror. "Aidan. Aidan, no. No, no, please. Aidan, no!"

Aidan drove the scissors into the barrier while Ciara slowly skidded to the floor. He peered down as she cried to the wall. "You're so damn pathetic," he said, spitting into her hair.

Ciara slid across the floor toward the stairs in a desperate attempt.

"Where'd ye think you're going, huh? I didn't say I was finished with you yet." Aidan tread toward Ciara as she urgently crawled the stairs trying to get away. Bending forward, he took hold of her leg, jerking it violently.

Ciara screamed in pain as Aidan disjointed her hip. Disregarding her sufferable whimpers, he continued tugging her limb with all his might. Soon after, he rushed to the stair where he proceeded his wife, and there grabbed a heaping wad of her hair. Dragging her torso the following steps, the sound thudded like an excessive sack of potatoes. He gave one final heave of her head as Ciara tumbled to the floor. "That ought to keep ye taught for the day, ye lousy wuss. I'm marching to the pub. When I get back, ye better be present. And don't ye be running to the neighbors with tears. They won't help you. Those fools could care less," he said, vanishing at the door.

Josie crept forth from the living room where she'd been hiding. She saw Ciara stretched on the floor, then rushed to her aid. "I want to help you. Please let me help you." She cradled Ciara within her arms, hoping to provide comfort.

Looking upon Josie, Ciara held tears in her eyes. "Are you a courier of divine message?" she asked. "Please, gentle spirit, remove me from all this."

Josie gazed upon Ciara as her eyes swelled, then stung with burning tingles. "I wish I could. Oh, how I wish I could." Josie upheld the sorrowed woman as she sighed at her side.

"He'll kill me. I just know it. Is there nothing you can do to save me?"

"I'd take you away if I could. But you and I, we belong to separate worlds. I pray to God for your surety of defense. May he guide and protect you."

"Do I have long, spirit? Just remark to me that. I perceive the rage which pumps through his veins and grows stronger each day. I'm afraid of him. So afraid," Ciara stated before fading in Josie's arms.

Josie rocked herself on the floor in distressing concern. Moments later she gazed throughout the room in disbelief. The walls suddenly painted themselves beige, then, expanding below the wooden border, stretched sheets of floral paper. The furniture seemingly changed before Josie's eyes to that of her own. She rejoined her home as she knew it, recovering accustomed surroundings.

No longer wishing to inhabit her dwellings, Josie got up from the floor. She traipsed on out to the porch and patently awaited her husband's arrival. She set alone for a near half hour before Tristian pulled forth in the car.

"Jos, you look awful, sweetheart. What's happened?" he asked as he sat beside her.

"This house has been hell," she said, frowning. "I know you informed me to call if anything happened. It was for foolish reasons I didn't. I'm sorry, Tristian." Josie took a deep breath.

"Josie, be honest with me. What happened today?"

"That man attacked me again."

"What'd he do? Josie, speak up."

"I was afraid for my life, Tristian. I thought he'd kill me. I was chased by flies. I fell in the living room, he grabbed me, then drug me on the stairs. The raven saved my life. Tristian, if it wasn't for that bird I think Aidan would have surely slain me."

"Aidan? Is that his name?"

"O'Neill. Aidan O'Niell."

The Crying House

"What about the baby, Jos? That bastard didn't harm our child?"

"I don't know, Tristian. I can't say for certain."

"Does your stomach feel all right? Do you hurt?"

"My belly feels fine, Tristian. It's my back that has problems."

"I knew I should have stayed home. I didn't feel right upon leaving. What if he killed you? I couldn't live with that on my mind." Tristian put his hands on his head. "Oh God, Josie. I feel like I've failed you."

"No, Tristian. It's okay. Everything's good. I'm still here. You've done nothing wrong," she assured him.

"But it's my duty to make sure you're safe. Because of my stupidity, I wasn't here to protect you."

"Please stop worrying. I'm safe now, and you're here."

"I'm glad you weren't severely injured. Jos, if he weren't already dead, I'd sure in the hell kill him."

"You're not a murderer, Tristian."

"That doesn't mean I couldn't be. You were able to see Mrs. O'Toole, I take it?"

"Things would still be unknown had she not been acquainted to the O'Neills. Thank God for her undoubted accounts of their existence. Least now we have something to go by."

"You plan to fill me in, or you going to force me to speculation?"

Josie turned toward Tristian. "Aidan's wife's name was Ciara. Mrs. O'Toole confirmed they'd been a fine couple. Said they loved each other very much. Agnus had spoken of Aidan owning a pub. She mentioned one night after his shift he'd been attacked near a graveyard. Apparently his assailant was something called a phouka as she'd said."

"A phouka?" Tristian gasped.

"Agnus acknowledged it to be the most terrifying creature in fairy lore. With that look on your face, Tristian, you must know what I speak of."

"Well, certainly. Of course. Most folks around here do."

"Why haven't I heard of it then? I've lived here and had no knowledge."

"Probably because you're not Irish, dear. Every country has its own lore. Accounted for their placement, mythology and superstitions could be similar or dissimilar. You do understand?"

Josie shook her head. "I see where you're going."

"To see a phouka is known to be rare. But still it's something you don't want to cross paths with. I always believed phoukas to be dark beings from fairy tales to frighten children and cowering adults," Tristian admitted.

"It's no fabrication, I assure you. The phouka that intersected Aidan's path had been real."

"How was he attacked?"

"Since they're known shapeshifters, the being became the embodiment of a dog before the attack. Mrs. O'Toole claimed that Aidan had become possessed by that creature. She verbally verified his change, and how it took place. His appearance had somehow altered into an undeniable form, along with a temperamental replacement which violently developed into a resentful disposition. This was no light matter, Tristian. The issue was serious. Aidan became indignant with Ciara, beating her on a constant basis."

"So it was a possession which led to his indecency? However, prior to that he'd been fine? No wretched acts or lewdest speech?"

"They loved each other. But it was that night near the graveyard which changed him forever. Mrs. O'Toole said when Ciara was twenty-eight she'd been diagnosed with a brain tumor. She didn't have more than a few months. Aidan's transformation forced him to not care about her nor his wife's illness."

Tristian looked on in disgust. "He even beat her once she fell sick?"

"Every day. Men don't do those things; only monsters."

"Men don't do those things, period. Not to his wife, his mother, or even an own child."

"That's what I meant when I said they don't do those things. He became overpowered, even ruled by the evil inside him."

"Now that I know how much of a monstrosity he was, what did he do to kill her?"

"The night of her death, Ciara and Aidan had a terrible fight in their bedroom. It would be the beforehand incidents which led to her death."

"Which was?"

"He threw Ciara into a dresser where she hit her head. She died later that night."

"Just like that it was over for her? What about him? What happened to Aidan?"

"That's where things take an unlikely twist."

Tristian's proclivity changed. "An untoward surprise. My sadness turns to approaching interest. Tell me what doubtful coincidence befell him?"

"Someone murdered him the day of Ciara's funeral."

"Really? How fate-stroked is that? What a shocking truth. I wonder what he thought?"

"It was chance driven, I agree. The person awaited his return home, then killed Aidan in the bathroom."

"Did Agnus tell you how?"

"I believe she said his throat had been slit, and he'd been stabbed four times in his heart."

"Talk about an over kill. Hell, even for him. That's plenty enough for one individual's encounter."

"He may not have deserved it that severe, but, tragically enough, it happened. As Agnus said, he was given one's dues."

"I guess he paid his. But star-crossed enough, Ciara still services her eternal wages. How sad it is she'll never find freedom and, better yet, peace."

"That's what bothers me, Tristian. She doesn't deserve to relive this over and over. That one time had been enough."

"Who killed Aidan? Were you able to find out?"

"Mrs. O'Toole spoke of a legend which spread around town. The public claimed Ciara came back to revenge her death by killing him. This place was labeled the crying house, and I'm afraid it still is."

"So Ciara was the one to kill him?"

"It's not a fact, but it's what the people came to believe."

"There were no living suspects?"

"Not one, but Agnus had her suspicions."

"Who did she think?"

"She wondered about Ciara's brother, Kieran."

"Would he have been capable of doing it?"

"I'm pretty sure. But then again, it's no fact. It may have been her father, for all we know. I imagine at this point we just have to guess."

"What if it were Ciara? You know spirits can get vengeful. Maybe as punishment Aidan brought her back here to repay for her sin? Then again, it's just a theory," Tristian replied, shaking his head. "Did Mrs. O'Toole give you a possible explanation to why they're here?"

"Her suspicions led her to believe it could be due to the fiftieth anniversary of the O'Neills demise. Agnus said that spirits could return to reenact their deaths and the time leading up to it. What happened in this house was dramatic enough that it made imprints. The past has been replaying itself."

"Will they ever leave?"

"Mrs. O'Toole concludes that, once the anniversary comes to pass, they should likely depart. Dear God, I hope she's right. I just want our lives to be normal again."

"You know, Jos, if this haunting continues after their anniversary, we'll have to move. I'm sorry, but I don't want to raise our child in this horror-stricken house."

"For now let's pray they leave and that Ciara may find the peace she deserves. And as for her bruting husband, may the fires of hell reach up to snatch him."

"I agree. May he reside in hell where he belongs and nevermore taint this earth with his presence. Hopefully one day Ciara can finally be free from his hands."

Josie sat quietly for a moment's time as she thought silently. "Mrs. O'Toole was telling me about a child named Logan."

"Who's that exactly? Did the O'Neills have a son or nephew?"

"No. No, not either. He was just a young boy who looked to Ciara as a mother figure. Agnus said he was devastated when learning of her death. As I understand, he was placed in a nursing home sometime back."

"Is he crippled or ailing?"

"What I learned from Agnus, Logan suffered a heart attack some years ago."

"Is he fit to receive visitants?"

"I should suppose so. Agnus mentioned going to see him on occasion. She'd go now, but her health's been shifty. I gave question to rather or not we'd be allowed admission. I'd like very much to visit with Logan and maybe see what he might tell us about Ciara and Aidan."

"Maybe we could go after dinner?" Tristian suggested.

"Oh, shoot."

"Something wrong?"

"I don't have anything made," Josie explained. "How terrible of me. Maybe I could make some quick sandwiches. Would that be okay?"

Tristian nodded. "That's fine. I don't want you overdoing yourself."

"I'm sorry, dear. My time got caught up while visiting Agnus. I should have had dinner ready soon as you came home. What a lousy wife am I? I couldn't even prepare a meal for my husband."

"Jos, cut it out, please. You're not lousy. So you slipped up for a day. Things happen. It's not like you mindfully forgot or didn't want to."

"But I did mindfully forget. When I looked at the clock I realized it was already too late. It was an honest mistake."

"But you had a good time with Agnus, didn't you?"

"Our visit was lovely." She smiled. "It kept me out of this house, which I needed."

"Then that's all that matters. You had a good time, Jos, with some freedom to get away. It's not like you do it that often. Yet you do deserve it now and then."

Josie snickered. "I guess I do."

"Come on now. I'll help you up." Tristian walked his wife into the house, then assisted her to the kitchen.

Josie rummaged through the freezer, searching for something to defrost. "My apologies, Tristian. Dinner's going to be much later than usual. I don't know how long it'll take these filets to thaw."

"Just set them before the window. The warm air should do the trick."

"They're frozen solid." She laughed. "It could take hours."

"Well, maybe you could steep them in warm water?"

"You know what? That gives me an idea. Run some in that crock there."

"This one?"

"Yes, that one. Then take the oven grate and lay it on top. I'll set these packages of filets over the base and cover the crock with another large bowl. Hopefully by doing that, I can steam off some chill."

"That's a brilliant idea, Jos. Why didn't I think of that?"

"Keep check on them, though, Tristian. We don't want that steam cooking the fish. I'll go on and prepare the batter."

"I should flip these packages, shouldn't I?"

"That'd be a good idea, if you don't mind."

"They're starting to loosen up now. You want me to empty this water and fill in fresh?"

"Is it cooling off?"

"Seems to be."

"Leave it for another minute or so, then refill it."

Tristian waited as the time passed. "They're almost ready."

"Okay, refill the crock, then keep it covered another minute or two. After that, remove the top and set out the packages."

"What'd you know? It worked." Tristian smiled. "Here you go, Jos. They're all set."

"Will you rinse them in cold water? I'll start battering them when you're through."

Josie covered both sides of the filets, then cast them to grease. Upon the counter she reached for a loaf of bread, then, cutting it into sections, had Tristian spread mayonnaise over each slice. Once the fish sizzled to golden perfection, she placed the filets between the slices of bread.

Josie set the plates upon the table while Tristian prepared the drinks, then joined his wife in a seat. "I'm sorry we're having to eat light. We'll just have to get by on this. I promise tomorrow I'll have a real dinner prepared," she said.

"This is plenty good enough. I wouldn't expect you to make a full course meal now, Jos. I know you've been sick."

His wife looked upon him and smiled. "You've always been most kind to me, Tristian. I don't know what I'd do if you weren't."

The O'Briens were midway through their meal when out of the living room rose a disturbingly loud noise.

"Stay here, Jos. I'll see what's wrong." As he paced into the living room, Tristian viewed the furniture racing across the floor and crashing into walls. Pillows and other objects soared rapidly through the air, while violent rappings beat within the house.

A large knitting needle stood tall on a table as though someone were holding it. In moments it began spinning and burrowing deeply into wood, leaving a hallowed out hole. Suddenly the needle stopped as it floated in the air. Pointing aligned toward Tristian, it rotated in a circular fashion much like a drill bit ready to hull out an incision. The apex thorn whirled evermore rapidly as Aidan's voice broke air. "Get out of me house, ye piece of filth," his delivery echoed.

The needle took off, racing through air in line to Tristian. The event was so sudden it left him with no act of response. Unable to elude the unblunted peak, the needle dug its way into the shoulder of its selected prey. Tristian ejected in agonizing pain as the thorned-spike burrowed itself within place. Blood surpassed the wound as the needle furthermore pierced his skin.

During Tristian's unpleasant ordeal a sudden development arose. From out of a wall came the raven, flying like a master of the wind with great speed. Its talons thrashed forth while enclosing the needle. Its skill ceased the acute tip from excavating farther into Tristian's flesh. Then, pulling the pin from his arm, the blooded metal transcend the floor.

In hurried movement, the furniture returned to its rightful place as every last suspended object fell to the ground. It was that moment the preposterous activity came to a halt, leaving with it the impression of Aidan's presence.

Tristian's heart was pounding in his chest, his breathing accelerated. Grabbing his shoulder, he made an attempt to suppress the seeping wound. Looking up, he saw one last glimpse of the raven before its disappearance through a window. Walking back to the kitchen, Tristian called out to his wife. "Josie, I need a bandage. That damn Aidan's torn a hole in me." He stopped in his tracks when viewing his wife's abnormal position. Contained against the wall by unseen hands, Josie had been elevated several feet in the air. A profusion of muffled moans escaped her throat as Aidan gripped Josie's windpipe. Tristian dared to inch closer when he was unexpectedly struck in the face. A hand mark proceeded his cheek while the bright red pattern dishonored his skin.

Aidan slid Josie up the wall, moving her within inches of the ceiling. Her face flushed from a depletion of oxygen, and her green eyes raised bulgy from their sockets. Tristian pulled a chair just adjacent to his wife. He scurried into the seat, then stood steadily on foot. Trying to contest with an unseen entity was no use, though he tried. As Tristian desperately endured the struggle, he wrapped his arm around his wife. Through his determined attempts to fetch Josie loose, the chair beneath him was unmistakably kicked, tipping Tristian sideways. But his balance would prove to defend him. An angered bluster filled the room when Aidan realized he didn't fall. While clenching Josie's throat, he slid her head into the ceiling. She battled for breaths, but with every attempt Aidan constrained her esophagus even more. The lack of air in her lungs forced Josie into suffocation. Tristian managed to pull on her waist, hoping he'd be able to glide his wife down. But his furthered attempts would only prove to anger Aidan more.

In an explosive rage, Aidan kicked Tristian's face. The powerful donation overwhelmed him as it propelled Tristian from the chair. The discharged impact bloodied his nose and incredibly left his face tainted with the sole impression of Aidan's boot. Abandoned to the floor, Tristian laid dazed in confusion cupping his gushing snout.

Josie was now left alone with urgent strive to safeguard her life. Her battle with Aidan was nothing less than debilitated. Her shallowed vigor confirmed ineffectual to assisting her fight. Beating her hands against the wall through wearied animation, Josie panicked with dreaded hysteria. It was soon after her dueling struggle to escape was defeated. Josie's arms fell against her, where they rested limply at her sides.

Tristian stood to his feet and rushed below his wife while commanding Aidan. "Let her go, you bastard." Grabbing Josie's legs, he shouted again. "I said let her go!"

Josie fell into Tristian's arms as a sinister laugh inhabited the room. "She's no good to you now," Aidan spoke harshly. "You'd be foolish to help her, ye fumbling twit."

Tristian cradled his wife and screamed. "Why must you do this?"

"Don't ye be grilling me."

"She's done nothing in turn to deserve what you've done," Tristian yelled at the top of his lungs. "Why won't you just let us be?"

Aidan slowly appeared by the wall. "I own this dwelling and all that's inside. Ye don't want to dicker with me, then scuttle your ass out."

"I will not," Tristian objected. "This is my house."

"You were never invited."

"Neither were you."

"Get out," Aidan said in a low voice.

"You can't run us off. No. We won't leave."

Aidan groaned in anger. "Then rest assured, I'll kill you come time."

A loud squawk rose forth from a window followed by the raven. Its fiery eyes were set on Aidan as it raced ahead. Its needle-like talons flared, advancing forward in the air.

Aidan hollered blatantly, "Damn that bird to hell." The raven screeched as it made chase. "One day fowl, I'll roast you like a duck." He delivered before they both disappeared into a wall.

Tristan sat with his wife. "Josette. Josette, wake up. Oh, merciful me. This can't be. Josie. Josie, please," Tristan begged frantically. "Jos. Jos, come on, love, liven up."

Fluttering her eyes, Tristan watched as they retracted into her head. Her gasps were raspy and her breathing shallow. Picking her up, Tristan carried Josie to the comforts of their couch. Then enclosing her hand in his, Tristan laid his head near her heart. "Jos, don't you leave me behind. Don't you do that, you hear? Think of all the more memories we have to share." Tears streamed from Tristan's face as he cried. "You're my one and only. I want no one else. Come on ... come on. You have to wake up. You lying here's harrowing my heart. I know you hear me in there. Josie, please. Won't you squeeze my hand at least?" He mourned, sorrowfully. Yet Josie's hand lay limp to his inquisition. "Mighty God, giver of life, secure her breath to make her all better," he prayed aloud. Tristan held his wife within his arms while tears showered his face.

Josie's throat was swelling where Aidan had forced his grip. Thinking quickly, Tristan ran to the kitchen to retrieve some ice, which he wrapped in a tattered scrap of cloth. He rushed to Josie's side and placed the compress upon her neck. "This just has to work. Please, Josie, you have to be all right. I promise you in heart, I won't give up." He positioned a pillow beneath Josie to elevate her head. "Try not to force your breath. Relax, sweetheart, relax. Take it easy. Smooth breaths, dear. Smooth breaths. Jos? Jos, can you squeeze my hand yet? I know you can do it. Please try."

Tristan waited a few moments, then felt mild movement within his hand. Josie squeezed lightly as her eyes fluttered beneath their lids. "That's it, Jos. You're doing good, sweet pea." She briefly gasped for air as though she'd been delivered her life. Slowly Josie opened her eyes and looked toward her husband. "Oh, thank God. Josie, I thought I had lost you," Tristan cried.

Through delusional conception, Josie discerned her husband with a confused stare. "Who are you? Where am I?" she muttered.

"It's me, Jos. Tristan. Do you not remember?"

Josie peered to him with bewilderment as though she'd never seen him before. "How'd I get here?" she asked, glancing over the room. "I want to go home." She panicked. "How do I get home?"

Stupefied, Tristan shook his head. "Sweetheart, you are home."

Running to the corner of the room, Josie hunched down by the wall, terrified and afraid. "That can't be. I don't know you. Get off me. Don't touch me."

Backing abroad, Tristian nodded slowly. "Josie? Josie, do you not remember what happened?"

"Step away. Don't you come any closer. I'll ... I'll claw you."

"Josie? Josie, I'm your husband, for Christ sake."

"No," she screamed. "I haven't a husband."

"Sweetheart, I don't understand. Why can't you remember?"

"I. I was somewhere else. In a garden surrounded by others. I'm unsure how I got here. I just want to go home. Please let me go home."

"Josie, this is your home. You live here with me."

"Why do you keep calling me that?" she demanded.

"What do you wish me to say? Talk to me, please."

"Just you stay where you are. Guarantee my comfort, mister. You let me out of here safely."

"But where will you go?"

"I don't know, but you ensure me your word."

"Oh, please help me, God. I don't believe this. Can't you recall any part of the attack?"

"What attack? You fill me with lies."

"In the kitchen, Jos. Don't you remember?"

"Stop this, you're scaring me."

"He was choking you, you passed out. I brought you to the couch. I thought you were dead. Josie, you weren't moving."

Tristian's words burned within her mind. "You. You tried to kill me," she cried.

"No, no, Josie. It wasn't me."

"Liar! You lie."

"No, baby, no."

"Then what happened to your face? And that blood there. What happened to your arm? Why's it bleeding?" Josie reached for a letter opener. "Don't you come near me. I'm warning you. I'm not afraid to use this. Trust me, I will."

Aidan's sinister laughter filled the room, accompanied by a clapping applause. "Ye poor, depressed sap. Your sow doesn't even know the first likeness of you. Ye might as well give it up. If she wants to walk, ye let her."

Josie peered around in terror. "Who said that? Where is he? Why can't I see him?"

"Do you believe me now? I didn't hurt you, Jos. I promise, it weren't me. I'd never harm you."

"Then … then why do you bleed?"

"He attacked me. Trust me, Jos, I'm not telling lies."

"No! I don't believe that."

"Jos. Josie, just listen."

"You're pulling some kind of trick on me. I don't know how you've done it, but you have."

"Josie, I'd never lie to you. I'm not playing tricks."

"Answer me. How did you make that voice appear?"

"I didn't, I swear. Please, Josie, listen."

"No. I don't want to. I desire to go home."

Then, in unheeded occurrence, Aidan materialized on the couch. "I'll send ye back home. No problem," he relayed, getting up.

Josie's face drained of all color, turning her pale. Her eyes grew to the size of quarters while terror set in. Shaking uncontrollably, she whimpered in the corner.

"Don't you go near her. Leave her alone, you bastard. She isn't Ciara."

Aidan stopped, then turned around with his eyes glaring on Tristian. "Where are ye hiding that wench? Ye think you'll protect her from me?"

"If I could, yes. And I'd be more than willing to send you to hell."

"She'll never escape me wrath. I'll control her to the end. She's me property, ye hear?"

Outraged, Tristian ejected a forward demand. "Leave this room, you ungrateful spirit. Your presence is unwanted. To you, I command. Cast away, sling aside. I dismiss you."

Aidan turned to Josie. "Don't ye be hasty, little dastard. I'll be seeing you soon," he spoke, disappearing to mist.

Tristian walked over to Josie, reaching out. "I'm not going to hurt you," he assured her.

"Who was that awful man? He fills me with fright."

"He's a bad fellow. You don't need to think about him."

"Did he mean what he stated when he said he'd be back?"

"I would hope not, but then again I'd be wrong."

"How's that supposed to comfort me? You might as well hand me freely to him. It's me he wants."

"He won't harm you as long as I'm here."

"But this isn't my home. I don't belong here."

"Then where do you belong? Granted, you're my wife. It's you and me who've lived in this house." Tristian thought, then acknowledged Josie. "Something must have happened during the attack. That's why you can't remember."

"I'd remember if I knew you, but I don't."

A plan brewed within Tristian's mind. "I'm going to give someone a call. I think she could help." Walking over to the phone, Tristian dialed a number. "Hello? Yes, this is Tristian … I could be better … Well, thank you … I'm having some trouble … Not particularly. Listen, I'm sorry to bother you at this time. But I was wondering if you'd be able to come by? It's Jos … Yes. Something awful's happened. Oh, you could? Thank you. We'll see you shortly." Tristian returned to his wife, who was sitting among the couch.

"Are you planning something on me?"

"No, sweetheart. I'm just trying to get you some help."

"What sort of help do I need? If you wish to assist me, then let me go home."

Just then the doorbell rang. "I'll be right back, okay? Just sit here."

"What belief should I have to trust you?"

"You can sit across the room if you don't feel safe. I won't touch you or come near you."

"You promise?"

"I give you my word." Tristian trotted toward the door. "Mrs. O'Toole, I'm so grateful you came. I didn't know who else to call."

"It's no trouble, dear. No trouble. I came as soon as I could."

"Won't you come in?"

"Dear God, Tristian, what's happened to your face? Is everything all right? Where's Josette?"

"In the living room."

"Is she all right, son? Is she hurt?"

The Crying House

"She talked to you today? You told her about Aidan and Ciara?"

"That's right."

"Things have grown worse since she left your house."

"What sort of thing, dear? Do tell."

"Aidan strangled Josie in the kitchen. She passed out. When she finally awoke, she didn't know me. I'm afraid she's lost her memory or worse. Please, Mrs. O'Toole, I was hoping you could help her."

"Yes, dear, yes. I'll do whatever I can. You're also in need of aid, I see."

"I'll be fine. Just tend to Jos."

"I warned her about Aidan. He's so violent and angry. I just knew he'd lash out."

"Please, Mrs. O'Toole, this way to the living room."

"You get some tissue, Tristian, and pack your nose. Don't think I hadn't seen your arm. Put a compress on that, and I'll doctor you later." Agnus saw Josie upon the couch as she walked toward her. "It's okay, dear, don't be afraid."

Josie cocked her head sideways and stared upon Agnus. "Who are you?"

"Don't you remember? We spoke this afternoon."

"Do I know you?"

"You should, dear."

Josie nodded. "Mrs? Mrs?"

"Agnus, dear. Remember?"

"Agnus? Yes. Agnus. You live across the street, as I recall. Where are your husband and kids? Might they be coming?"

"Oh my, dear, child. What has Aidan done to you?" She saw the hand marks around Josie's neck and her swollen throat. "Josie, dear, do you remember anything that happened? Anything?"

"I ... I'm unsure how I got here. That man beside you claims he's my husband. But I know that he lies."

"Am I familiar to you?"

"For some strange reason I feel that you are. Your face. I somehow know your face."

"Good, dear. That's good. Do you know where you were before you came here?"

"I was in a garden. The most beautiful garden. I was home."

"Then what?"

"The next thing I knew I woke up here. But I'm unclear to how that's possible. Unless? Unless this man. This man here kidnapped me."

Agnus looked at Tristian. "She's had a near-death experience. Josie's had a glimpse into the gardens of heaven."

"Why doesn't she remember me? Is she possessed by someone else?"

"I don't believe so. I think Josette doesn't remember because the oxygenated blood to her brain was cut off. I believe she might be suffering from a short-term memory loss."

"Is there any way we could fix it?"

"There might be something I could do to speed up the process."

"What do you need? I'll get it."

"I'd need just the right herbs."

"I'll take you to the kitchen then. You can sift through the shelves."

Agnus laughed. "Bless you, dear. But the herbs I'll need are not for cooking. Let me return home and see what I find."

"Will you need anything else, Mrs. O'Toole?"

"Agnus. Please call me, Agnus, dear. You could lend me your help by boiling some water."

"In a pot?"

"A kettle shall work fine. I'll be back shortly."

"The door will be open. Just invite yourself in." Tristian walked toward Josie. "Do you mind if I sit?"

"Go on. It's your house after all." Josie paused for a moment. "Do you think that plan of Agnus's can help me?"

"I sure hope so."

Josie took a deep breath, then inched her hand into Tristian's. "I'm sorry if you are who you say. My husband, that is."

Tristian fought back his tears, though he wanted to cry. "You've been through a terrible ordeal. I just hope we can get you some help."

"For you, I know this has been hard and unfair. My attitude toward you's been unkind."

Tristian wiped his eyes and sniffled. "We can make it better. I just need my wife."

"It must be stressing to know the woman before you, yet she has no idea who you are."

"Never would I have believed something like this happening to us," Tristian spoke in sadness.
"Were we happy?"
"As content as any man and woman could be."
"Knock-knock, dears. It's me, Agnus."
"Any luck finding what you needed?"
"Oh yes, Tristian. I have them right here."
"What is all this stuff?"
"There's brahmi, a bit of sweet flag, a snatch of ginseng, a little rosemary, and some hawthorn berries."
"Is it safe?"
"As long as she's not allergic."
"Will she have to ingest these herbs and roots?"
"It'd be easier if I make a tea. It won't be the best tasting, but it should do the job. Do you have that water heating?"
"I was supposed to boil some, wasn't I?"
"That's all right. I'll heat some myself."
"I apologize, Agnus. I was sitting with Jos."
"Not a problem, child, as long as you have the available water."
"There's already some in the kettle. Josie keeps it filled. Right this way, Agnus. I'll take you to the kitchen."
"Do you have a mug on hand, dear?"
"Let me fetch one from the cabinet. Will this work?"
"Just fine. That'll do."
"Is there anything else I could get you? Sugar? Milk?"
"You wouldn't happen to have a strip of cheese cloth, would you? I just need a piece."
"Sure. Let me see what I find."
"You might happen upon some in the jelly cabinet. Won't you try there?"
"Right you were. Here you go. It's not too big, is it? I can find you another."
"That should do nicely."
"Do you need a hand?"
"Just the two I own."
"Okay. Well ... well..."
"I'm sorry, dear. I don't mean to offend you. I have what I need. I'm certain I'll get by."

"Then I'll be in the living room."

Laying out the cheese cloth, Agnus stretched it across the counter, then filled it with herbs. Tying a knot near the crest, she sealed off the opening. Within the ceramic mug Agnus drained steaming water. Then, dipping the pouch, she allowed it to soak. Agnus awaited the emergence of its rich tone, then removed the cloth. Steadily carrying the tea through the living room, she delivered it to Josie. "Now, dear, it's most important you drink this up. The elixir will help you get better."

Josie smelt the tea as her nose crinkled. "Must I drink all this?"

"I'm afraid so, dear. It's medicine."

Josie sipped a modest swallow. "It tastes funny."

"I know, dear. I know. Those herbs don't make the best tasting drink. But, deary, it had to be a straight infusion to account for its potency. There's no other way. Just pinch your nose and drink on up."

"It's terrible."

"Sweetheart, please," Tristian added.

"This won't make me sick? By no means do I wish to throw up."

"I should hope not. You'll get used to the taste over time."

"Over time?"

Tristian looked toward Mrs. O'Toole and gave question. "Agnus, how much does she have to drink before she's well?"

"It works gradually, my dears. It may take awhile, and it may not. It's determined by the body's ability to absorb the solution as well as the agency of the elixir's effect. We just need to be patient and hope for the best."

Tristian pondered, "How long might you think?"

"Well, with some I've seen elixirs like these work within a half hour's time. Others don't gain the full enforcement until two or three days. Possible results suggest an additional speculation. To be honest, it's somewhat a gamble. But, Tristian, dear, you mustn't give up on your faith."

"Then there's a possibility this won't work? Josie would be lost to me forever."

"I'm certain it will. At that, you may accept your own peace of mind. What I can't answer is when the effect will take notice by all parties involved."

The Crying House

Tristian was uncertain to her meaning. "Not just Josie?" he asked.

"Heavens no. Though she's the main obtainer. Once Josette regains her knowledge, she'll reclaim her memories. Following that, her defense against you shall weaken. She'll discern a found comfort to be at your side. As for you, the concept of her adjustment shall be viewed by your eyes and her familiar recounts released to your ears."

"Somehow I understand, but I don't fully interpret your saying."

"Then I'll try at a greater extent to make it more clear. Think of it as this. Josette suffered loss by losing her memories. You encountered deprivation from losing your wife. It's not just one person who's been afflicted, but all parties involved. Once Josette heals, then so shall Tristian. She'll regain what she's lost as will yourself."

"I've never thought of it in the sense you've said. Jos wasn't the only one effected by loss. It's completely making sense. That I see."

"You understood from the start, Tristian, dear. It was me, this short-sided, aging daft who wasn't clear." Agnus began to laugh. "What can I say? I'm an outdated and enfeebled lass whose speech is confusing. I babble in ways that are unknown to youths such as yourself."

"You're not outdated, Agnus. A little clear up had made me aware."

Agnus whispered in a low voice, "I'm angst to say Aidan's getting stronger by feeding off your fear of him. I'm afraid, Tristian, the next time he attacks could be to the death. I told Josette that you're both welcomed to stay at my house until this haunting subsides. It might be in your best interest."

"But isn't there anything we could do to keep him away from us?"

"You can use salt against him. It's pure and will protect you from harmful spirit's malicious as him."

"So pitch a handful when he appears?"

"Not quite the resolution, dear. Let's say you wanted a good night's rest without Aidan dropping in unaware. Before you go into your room, lay a line of salt at the threshold which separates the hall from your door. As much as he'll try, Aidan can't cross it. By no way will he get through."

"And that works?"

"Plain old kosher salt. But, Tristian, don't throw it, dear. You need a protective barrier completely sealed."

"Like a circle?"

"Oh yes. If you stood in a salted circle, you'd be safe from attack."

"What about the feather that Josie got from the raven? Should she keep it?"

"What feather, dear?"

"It plucked a quill from its back."

"It wasn't shed?"

"Not that Josie said. She keeps it with her at all times. I thought it might be a bad omen. What do you think?"

"Did Josie mention the raven attacking Aidan? If so, dear, was this before or after she received it?"

"I think it was after. I really can't recall, though. So much has gone on."

"Is he afraid of the bird?"

Tristian thought for a second. "I don't know if afraid's the right word. He just doesn't like it."

"The feather might be a charm against him. It may banish or ward him away temporarily. You said Josie has this feather at all times?"

"Right."

"Okay. Let me think here. Mmm ... whenever Aidan attacks either of you, does the raven always appear?"

"I believe so. But Aidan could dispose a damaged beating before its arrival."

"Okay, dear, my advice for you. Anytime Aidan makes his sighting, be sure to have that feather where he can see it. When in distress, this might be a way to communicate with the bird. A means of calling it forth; a conjuration, if you will."

"Then what?"

"If Aidan truly dislikes that raven as you say, he should disappear once spotting the feather."

"Why would he want to evade this bird? I don't understand. A malevolent entity cowering to a feathered creature doesn't make sense."

"It may have something to do with the past. Maybe the raven collected his soul after death? It could be a number of things which leave us to question. Why don't you strip off that shirt, dear? Let Agnus have a look at that wound."

"It's just a small hole."

"Still, they get infected. It's better I clean it." Agnus took a closer look at the wound. "Tristian, this nearly goes clear through. Thank goodness I brought a needle and thread. I must go back to the kitchen. My things are in there."

"Should I just follow you then?"

Agnus peered over toward Josie. "Finish your tea, dear. We'll return in minutes."

Tristian leaned into Agnus. "She won't try to leave, will she?"

"I should think not. The elixir she's drinking will force Josette into ease. I wouldn't suspect her going anywhere. Come now, follow me. Have a seat at the table while I unpack a few things."

"You certainly came prepared."

"I knew by looking at you, you'd need to be treated. Will you come to the sink? I'll need to pour this peroxide on there to bubble out impurities and filth trapped inside. Just count to three, and it'll be over."

Tristian took a deep breath. "Ready."

"That's an icky mess you have there. I'll just pour in a bit more."

"Agnus, this stuff really burns."

"It's nearly over, then I can swab you with whiskey."

"I think you want me to pass out."

"Here, take a nice gulp of this booze. It's better to have you tie one on before this stitching starts."

"In that case, can I drink the whole bottle?"

"Take what you need as long as you leave me enough for swabbing."

"One, maybe two gulps should do me."

"You ready now? Just give me the word."

"I'm feeling a wee bit warm in the head, and my body feels toasty. What say you give her a go?"

"You won't feel a thing. Maybe a dull prick to be experienced at most."

"Did you start?"

"Not yet, dear. I'm just getting you sterilized."

Tristian peered to his shoulder. "Hey, that there's a needle in my skin. I think you've pulled a fast one on me." He laughed.

"Are you feeling any pain?"

"I'm too stewed to know. This is great, Agnus. I should drink whiskey more commonly."

"Just you mind how much you drink. Okay now, we're through."

"Was that it?"

"Least for your shoulder it was. Time to align your nose."

"What's wrong with my nose?"

"Well, Tristian. It's crooked."

"I wasn't born that way."

"Not you, son, your nose."

"No, it wasn't born that way either."

Agnus laughed. "You're certainly bashed. Well, then, if you're ready I'll just pop you in place."

"Go on then. Do your magic."

"Hold still, dear. This will only be a moment."

"Say now, will this hurt?"

"I guess we'll find out. But, dear, let's hope it doesn't."

"I'm holding still."

"Just a little pop and…"

"Hey, now, I thought that wasn't supposed to hurt?" Tristian replied. "Oh no. My vision. I'm seeing black. I'm sinking, Agnus. I'm sinking here."

"I've got you, son. Don't you go passing out now."

"I've slipped into darkness. What if I don't survive?"

"I'm fairly sure you have. Take a deep breath, calm yourself down."

"Tell me you're done. I can't do that again. I almost felt sick."

"I just have to remove the tissue, unless you wish to do it."

"I think I've got it from here." Tristian cleared away the packing from his nose. "Am I still bleeding?"

"You look clean. No blood."

"How's my nose?"

"It seems straight. Don't worry, dear, you're not disfigured. Agnus cleared that up. You're good as new."

"Thanks for your handy work."

"Does everything feel all right?"

"Absolutely. I'm just going to grab a clean shirt."

"One more thing. I want to put some of this calendula ointment upon your shoulder."

"Cala-what?"

"Calendula, dear."

"Never heard of it."

"It's from marigold flowers which I steeped in petroleum. I boiled it down to make this salve."

"What's it do?"

"Helps aid in healing as well as minimize your scarring. You don't have to worry, it won't sting. This will sooth any discomforts from your stitching."

"Then my shoulder shouldn't feel stiff around the wound?"

"That's right. And now you're all set."

"Could I get my shirt now?"

"Certainly. I'll see you in the living room."

Josie was consuming her last swig of tea as Agnus came through. "As terrible as that was, I finished it all."

"Good, dear. You ready for more?" Agnus smiled.

Josie crinkled her face. "I couldn't force another swallow."

"Do you feel any effect?"

"More relaxed, I could say." Josie thought deeper. "My mind's discovered a prevalent state of peace. I feel free of smoldering tensions and restless anxieties."

Tristian was entering the room as Agnus gave further question. "You care to test that memory of yours?"

"We could try," Josie agreed as Tristian sat down.

"You remember our visit today? You brought over..."

"A cake, was it not?"

"Yes, dear, you did. We sat in my kitchen sipping tea and gorging sweets. Can you remember anything further on?"

Josie took a moment. "The baby. I'm to expect my first child."

"Well, congratulations, my dear. That I didn't know. And who's the father?"

"That's quite silly to ask." Josie giggled. "It's my husband's. Tristian's, of course."

"And where's Tristian now?"

"Sitting beside me. Agnus? Agnus, is something wrong? You seem, well, I don't know. Obscured in some way."

"I'm perfectly fine, dear."

"You began to worry me, that's all. The answers should have been recognized by you before the inquiry. You're sure you're okay?"

Agnus nodded and smiled. "Just cheery, dear. Now, back to you and Tristian. How long you been married?"

"Six years. Come a few months we'll be approaching our seventh."

"Good, dear. Now, do you have any objections to taking this further?"

"Further? Further how?"

"Are you willing to recall what happened in the kitchen?"

"The kitchen? I don't know. I can't seem to remember."

"Nothing?" Agnus pondered.

"It's all a fuzzy blur."

Agnus took Josie's hand. "Can you remember anything else?"

"I remember Tristian having blood on his face and shoulder. I thought he'd hurt me, but it was Aidan. He did it. He tried to kill me, I'm sure." Josie began to tremble and cry. "My throat. His hands are around my throat. I can't breathe. Tristian, help me. I can't breathe. Let me go. Please let me go." Josie wailed, grasping her neck. "Tristian. Tristian, help me."

"Jos, sweetheart, you're safe. I'm here at your side," her husband consoled her.

Agnus patted Josie lightly. "Aidan's not around to harm you. You're safe, like Tristian said."

"But, Agnus, he's hurt me, and he'll continue, too. That's his plan."

"Aidan believes this is still his home. He feels that you and Tristian are intruding his space. He wants you both out. He'll do anything in his power to make that possible. You shouldn't allow him to force you from your home if you're not willing to go. You have to fight him. The two of you have more power than he. You can't be afraid and show him fear. I know that sounds hard, dear, but you have to pass as the one in charge. Yell like you mean it. To be riled is the only semblance to showing him you're serious."

"He could become enraged. I don't know if I can."

"If you want this to work, you're going to have to hide your fears and let him have it. Remember, Aidan will only be here a short while. Afterward, he'll have to face death and the consequences he's inflicted himself. Sometimes a person's fate can produce terrible effects. As with Aidan's, his will tear him apart during death's consumption."

"He'll get what he's given?"

"He'll get his dues and nothing less. The harvesters of souls aren't the spirits one should mess with. They carry us into the afterlife that we belong. They'll transfer Aidan to the fiery pits of hell where he'll burn for eternity. If he tries to escape, his punishment will be that of ten fold."

"Agnus, who are these harvesters?" Tristian asked.

"We're all appointed to certain ones. They might be inhuman or human. Various shapes and different sizes. You'll meet yours come your time."

"And Ciara, Agnus? Will she find peace?" Tristian questioned again.

"Her vision of heaven, as it's been created, is Ciara's final venture. She'll be able to rest there where she belongs."

"Do you think they'll resurface come another fifty years?"

"A house blessing should probably be performed once they've made their departure. I could do this for you if you wish to assure no further rebound. To cleanse your home of all its negativity will additionally rid any imprints that might get left behind."

Tristian wondered aloud, "Is that similar to an exorcism?"

"The spirits themselves will be gone. The case is more of exercising residual energies which are absorbed within your home. You won't need to worry about a Catholic priest. And I tell you what, you sure don't have to wait for the church's approval. If not turned down, it could take awhile of evaluation and deliberation. If they see no reason for proceeding, you're out of luck."

"Agnus, I'd love for you to bless our home," stated Josie. "I'd be at peace with that."

"Then it would be my pleasure, dear."

"Could we pay for the supplies? Surely you'd need candles and whatever goods you can use."

"Nonsense, dear. I have the belongings at home."

"Well, then, if you ever need a thing, just you let us know," Tristian assured her.

Agnus smiled warmly. "That's very kind."

"Anything. Big or small. Just drop the word."

Agnus snickered. "Well, maybe a good million would be nice."

"Sure, we can work out a monthly payment for the rest of our lives."

"Would you like to arrange that the first of each month?"

"Shall I sign a contract?"

"Heavens no, dear. You save the money for that tiny life inside your wife's womb. Well, I'm afraid, kids, it's getting late for this old lass. I best be returning home. My door's open should either of you need it. You'd be of no bother. Might you find yourselves needing a place, I'll have you a room."

"We both really do appreciate what you've done for us," Josie remarked.

Tristian added, "Agnus, let me walk you home so I know you've gotten in safely."

"That's considerate." Agnus beamed. "What a fine gentleman."

Tristian turned to Josie. "Have a seat on the porch till I get back. I don't want you alone in this house while I'm gone. You'd be safer outside."

Tristian walked Agnus to her house, making sure she was safely inside. Sitting upon the swing, Josie awaited Tristian's return. The moon was a ripened shade of red. Ablaze, it glowed in the sky as it shined over houses.

Crickets sang throughout dark lawns while fireflies lit atop budding shrubs and towering grasses. With a lack of gleam, those lighted bugs had faded out, then soaring into visual sight, their entrancing lanterns returned their lights.

Josie yawned lightly as a warm breeze brushed her face. The mild wind wavered through trees and danced into bushes. In the near distance Josie heard the low, cushioned, hoos of an owl. The sounds of the night were indeed soothing, diminishing all stresses and leaving Josie's mind absent of afflictive thought. She watched Tristian from across the street as he trotted closer to their house.

Passing above each step, he sat beside her. "What a beautiful night, don't you think?" Tristian added.

"It's quite lovely, isn't it? These sounds are most calming, not to mention the conditions being fine for a light blanket. Tristian, wouldn't you like to sleep beneath the stars?"

"Mmm, it'd be the perfect night. I'm sure we agree. Toss out some sleeping bags, set out a few candles, and listen to nature as we stare to the cosmos."

"Indeed," Josie expressed as she gazed toward the sky.

"Jos, do you recall the name *Logan*?"

"The man in the nursing home?"

"You remember?"

"Why wouldn't I?"

"Did you still want to see him?"

"Wouldn't you? Wouldn't you like to know all we could about Ciara and Aidan?"

"I just wanted to ask."

"I'm sure there are things he could tell us. Like Agnus, he has his own stories. Aren't you curious, Tristian, to what Logan's are?"

"Of course I am. But I needed to know what you'd say."

"What for?"

"I wasn't sure you'd remember. But since you did, I've planned to call Mr. Ashford come morning."

"What's Mr. Ashford have to do with this?"

"I'd need to ask for a few days off. I'll arrange to be here till Aidan's gone. I won't have another incident taking place where I can't help you, Jos. Especially if I'm not home. Once he leaves, I'll return to work. Jos, understand, it only seems right to be here for you and our baby."

"When would you plan to see Logan?"

"Possibly tomorrow. Is that okay? It'll get you out of this house awhile."

Josie shook her head. "If we could find out anything that might help us, I say we go."

"I agree. We'll take our chances and see what happens."

Within the dark, the O'Briens sat quietly upon their swing listening to the melodic tunes offered by the nocturnal inhabitants. Then, stretching out alongside the house, Josie witnessed a faint glow. "Do you see that?" she asked her husband.

"What do you suppose it could be?"

Josie pondered the question. "It's not a lightning bug, I don't think."

The delicate light drew closer, and within that time Tristian and Josie recognized it as belonging to the shimmering flame atop a candle. Walking alongside the bobbing flare, Ciara carried a bundle of wild flowers. She stepped forth toward the face of the house where she proceeded before an old sturdy oak.

The O'Briens watched secretly as Ciara knelt down. And as though she were reciting a prayer, she bowed her head in silence. An instant later Ciara settled the flowers beneath the large oak where she cast them to rest. Sitting awhile, she accompanied the tree in quiet reserve. Then, feeling it was time to withdraw, Ciara got up and strolled on her way. The drifting candle bobbed along, alighting the path, all the while serving as guide. Gliding back alongside the house, Ciara disappeared through the dark.

Tristian wondered to his wife, "Why do you suppose she took flowers to that tree?"

"It makes me question rather something's buried."

Tristian shook his head mildly. "There must be an explanation. Maybe you're right."

"You ever notice anything?"

"Like what?"

"Whittling's, I guess."

"I don't believe so. Then again, I can't say for certain I've searched." Tristian took a moment. "Feel that? The air's turning cool."

"Perhaps it'll rain."

"How about I draw you a bath? You can soak for awhile."

"That would be nice."

Tristian took his wife's hand and helped Josie up. "Shall we?" he asked, opening the door.

"I see Agnus was right."

"About what?"

"You're a fine lad. A gentleman for sure."

Josie's response made Tristian smile. "I want to gather some salt right quick. Take it upstairs. I'll trace a line before our door. Maybe it'll keep Aidan out like she said."

"You think it'll work?"

The Crying House

"Agnus suggested it," Tristan explained. "She declared he'd be unable to cross through."

"Then how about salting the bathroom? I don't want any sudden encounters. With my ill luck, he'd try to drown me."

Tristan grabbed the shaker off the table, then led his wife up the stairs. Then, stopping Josie from entering their bedroom, Tristan acknowledged. "I need to salt this before we go in."

"Salt first?"

"If we hold back, Aidan would have an open invitation to come with. Surely we don't want that." Tristan unscrewed the top and poured a line down their doorway. "Easy enough. That ought to do it."

"Could we go in now? I need to gather my things," Josie stated.

"Yeah, go ahead. Just don't bust up this line. Keep an eye where you walk."

"I'll certainly be sure to."

"Get your gown then. I'll run your water."

Josie went into the room and looked around. Grabbing her nightie, she took a seat upon the bed. Proceeding to remove her shoes, she allowed her worn heels to gather air. Afterward, Josie guided her slippers upon her small feet just as Tristan responded her name.

"Jos. Jos, your water's ready."

"I'm here," she relayed. Then viewing the room, she suddenly exclaimed, "Oh, Tristan."

"I thought you might like it."

"Oh, I do. It looks so relaxing." She then laughed. "I may never come out."

"Then keep this door open if you want. I've laid the salt. Might you need me, just call. I'll be in the bedroom."

The space was alighted in candles that spread around the base of the tub. The room was aglow with the shine of warm flames which impressed one's suggestible fancy. Tristan kissed his wife's neck. "Relax awhile. Just lie back and enjoy this serenity."

Tristan exited the room as Josie slipped away her clothing. Then into the tub she sank through the water. The heated bath felt good against skin, upholding Josie within its comfort. Now laying her head upon the rim, she faded to solace. Unwinding quickly, Josie took a couple deep breaths before closing her eyes.

In the bedroom Tristan laid soundly. Then, yanking his sheets and blankets, he removed himself from the bunk. He paced toward a window with intensions of raising it several inches. The cool breeze swept through the screen inhabiting the air with its whirling draft. Tristian soon returned to the comforts of the bed and patiently awaited his wife's position.

"You suppose we'll make it through the night?" Josie gave question when entering the room.

"There's only one way to find out." Tristian smiled. "Did you have a good bath?"

"It was pure heaven." She glowed warmly.

"You deserved the pampering."

Josie held forth a container of salve. "Would you mind doctoring my back? I'm having trouble."

"Sure, sweetheart, come closer."

"Please be gentle."

"You know I will." Josie then exposed her injured spine. "Oh, baby, you look terrible. Your poor back, Jos. It's covered in bruises."

Josie sank her chin into her chest. "It'll heal come time."

"I can't believe he did this to you."

"Yes, you can, Tristian. You just don't want to accept it."

"How's that, sweetheart?"

"Did you cover them all?"

"Everything I see. God, Jos, this makes me want to cry."

"The worst has passed," Josie explained while jerking her gown. She turned to Tristian. "My wails were enough. Let's not weep tonight."

"Oh, Jos. Baby, what do I say to make you feel better?"

"You've already managed so much. No sight goes unseen. Tristian, all you've done means a lot to me."

"But there's so much more I might have done."

"Accept your doings, Tristian. You gave it a go. You did the best you could to help me. Don't batter yourself. It's not like you've failed on consistence."

"I just … I should have stayed home."

"I'm the one who urged you to go. If you want to be angry, direct it to me."

"Jos, no. I have no anger with you."

"Then how about us going to bed? We shouldn't argue before sleep. It's not healthy."

"No bitter reactions, dear. I'm fine with that. It's late, I see."

Josie turned off her lamp and retired while Tristian remained awake, gaining knowledge from a book. The room had been quiet the entire hour Tristian read. To his side, Josie somberly slept like a baby. Tristian soon found his eyes feeling heavy and sedated with sleep. No longer deciding to fight exhaust, Tristian accepted slumber, and turning off his lamp, finally sought rest.

CHAPTER TEN ◆

Day 4, the 9th of July, 1950.

Morning came as Tristian was the first up. He moseyed into the bathroom, then washed the sleep from his eyes. Returning to the bedroom, he found Josie awake. "Hey, sleepy head."

"Good morning." She yawned.

"You feeling well rested?"

"I should think that I am."

"Those are good words to hear."

"How about some breakfast?"

"What shall it be?"

Josie questioned, "Might eggs over easy and sausage suit you?"

"With some oatmeal pancakes?"

"If that's what you want."

"Sounds good to me."

"Are you coming downstairs now?"

"I believe so."

"Well, come on then. I'll get things going." They proceeded to the kitchen as Josie glanced toward the clock. "Don't you forget to call Mr. Ashford, Tristian."

"We've got enough time. I'll call after breakfast."

"Just as long as you do." Josie began cooking. "Any idea when we should see Logan?"

"Presumably after we've eaten."

"I figured that. You mind filling the kettle?"
"Halfway or full?"
"Full."
"You want me to turn on the fire?"
"I need some tea bags."
"Four?"
"Not too stout. Just three."
Tristian breathed deeply. "There's no better scent than those escaping the kitchen come sunup."
"Are you starved?"
Tristian laughed. "These smells are making me."
"They forcing your hunger?"
Tristian breathed again. "They're pleading to me."
"You'll have to deal with the tease furthermore. The tea's not quite ready. Probably a few minutes longer."
"Darn. That's not what I was set to hear." Tristian tried stealing some sausage.
"Hey, you. Now just a minute. Tame those sticky fingers."
"I couldn't help it. They're so golden delicious."
"You go. Shoo. Go on now, take a seat."
"One more?"
"I think not. You eat these, you won't have any with the rest of your meal."
Tristian kidded, "There'll still be yours."
"Then I'll brand my name."
"With what?"
Josie joked back, "I'll lick each one and claim ownership."
"You can't do that."
"The cook will do whatever she pleases."
"You win. I'm sitting."
"That's what I thought."
Her husband beamed. "Don't you skimp out on my sausage." Following breakfast, Tristian called Mr. Ashford. "Good morning, sir."
"Well, hello, Tristian. And how might you be this morning?"
"Fair to middling, sir."
"And your pretty wife? How is she? Much better, I hope."
"It's been a bit rough, I'm afraid."

"Well, I hate to hear that, son. Could I be of any service to you?"

"If it wouldn't be too much to ask for a couple days off, sir, I would greatly appreciate it. Josie really needs me now. I'm afraid to leave her."

"I see you're in a fix, son. You make sure Josie stays well. You come back whenever you can. Don't you be in no rush."

"Thank you for your understanding, sir."

"You give Josie my regards, and you both take care."

"Yes, sir, Mr. Ashford. You take care, too, sir. I'll see you in a few days." Tristian hung up the phone as he turned to his wife.

"You're lucky to have him. He's a wonderful man, Tristian."

"I sure couldn't ask for a better boss. That's a fact."

"Well, certainly. He has something others lack."

"Yeah, most don't have sincerity, compassion, and understanding."

"Bless Mr. Ashford for that."

"Jos, it's nearing nine. We should go on and get dressed."

"I'm going to wash these dishes, then I'll be right up."

Tristian carried on his way and got dressed while Josie attended dirty skillets and grimy plates. Then as she was drying tableware, the phone suddenly rang.

"O'Brien residence ... Oh, good morning, Agnus ... Just well, thanks ... Oh yes, for certain. We slept through the night ... Worked like a charm. Exactly like you said ... Oh yes. Due to you, I was finally able to sleep."

"Good, dear, I'm glad to hear that. Why don't you come by this afternoon? I'll fix you more tea."

"Like last night's?"

"At least another mug, dear. It'd be best for your health."

"Well, I don't like it much, but for you I will. It did help me, however, I give you that. I'll see you midday then. Take care."

Tristian approached the room. "Josie, you're still not ready?"

"I'm going up now. Have patience."

"I'd like to be out of here come fifteen minutes."

"I'll be down before ten."

Tristian footed to the fridge for a small glass of juice. Then, walking to the sink, he gulped it down. He proceeded to the front door and unlocked the hinges.

"All right, dear, I'm ready," Josie said as she surpassed the last stair.

Walking through the door, the O'Briens trotted to their car, but not before visiting the large oak.

"Hold on a minute, Jos. Let's take a look at this tree."

Standing before the hardwood, Josie soon spotted an engraving near the trunk when she pointed to Tristian. A whittled Celtic knot had been etched into bark along with a message. *May Nia rest in peace.*

"Of all the times, you know I've never seen this," Tristian stated.

"I wonder what's been buried?"

"Not sure, but we know it's Nia. Come along then, let's get to the car."

Tristian and Josie drove off into town. Coming upon the nursing home, they searched for a place to park. Once pulling along the curb, they journeyed toward the building and proceeded inside.

A lady sat poised from behind the desk. "Good day, folks. Might I help you?" she asked.

"Could you tell us where we'd find Logan?" Josie asked.

"Are you friends or family, miss?"

"Well," Tristian interrupted. "Thing is, we really don't know him. This would be our first visit."

"I'm sorry, sir. I'm afraid you have to be a family member or close friend to see him."

Josie responded, "We're friends of Mrs. O'Toole. Is that any help?"

"Mrs. O'Toole, you say?"

"Yes, Agnus."

"Poor lady's quite ailed. Her arthritis, I hear. Well, I'll be signing you in as friends. Wouldn't hurt, I'm sure. Logan's in room seventeen. Straight down this hall, then turn to your left. You won't miss it."

Josie smiled. "That's kind. We appreciate it."

They hunted down the hallway searching for Logan's room.

"Here it is, Jos."

She knocked lightly and awaited reply.

"Yes. Who's there?" a voice asked.

"We're looking for Logan," Josie said, opening the door slowly.

"That's me. And who might you be?"

"I'm Josie O'Brien, and this is Tristian, my husband. We're friends of Mrs. O'Toole."

"Oh, you are?"

"Yes, sir. She tells us she knows you."

"Please come in." He motioned. "Tell me, how might you know Agnus?"

"Well, sir, we live across the street."

"Is that so? And what brings you here?" Logan probed, getting out of his chair. He was about average height, faint eyed with strands of salt and peppered hair.

"Agnus said you knew the O'Neills. Is this correct?"

Tears came to Logan's eyes. "My lovely, sweet Ciara. She treated me like a son, you know? Of all the women, she was the sweetest in all Ireland."

"So I've heard."

"Excuse my hasty inquiry, but what be the meaning of this? Why have you come here?"

"We seek understanding on behalf of the O'Neills. Agnus thought you might be able to help."

Logan looked at Josie with an inquisitive stare. "Why do you stir the past?"

"My response to you isn't that simple."

"Go on, lady. Nothing surprises me. I've seen and heard it all."

Tristian interrupted, "What my wife means to say is they've come back."

"Are you foolish, son? You have the proof to bind that?" Logan suddenly stopped. Backing up slowly, he redirected his words. "You live in the crying house, don't you?"

"And it'd be far from a blissful home."

"So they're haunting you?"

"That would be it."

Josie commented, "The haunting started a few days ago. When talking to Agnus she said the anniversary…"

"The anniversary of their deaths is approaching. Yes, that I know."

"Then you remember?"

"How could I not? Ciara's death drove me on edge. I prayed to God, take my life. I was miserable. I had no one. My ole man was strung by his work. He never minded me. Ciara treated me like a parent should. Be it hard to fathom, at one time even Aidan had a tender heart."

"Do you have any personal tales circulating you and them?"

"By means I have many. Plenty were good, then situations turned bad. Aidan spoiled. He laid his hands upon Ciara constantly for petty reasons, even for no motive at that. Sadly, the Aidan we knew was lost. A foul and violating presence took form in his body."

"Did you ever see her get hurt?" Tristian asked.

"I saw him slap her a few times here and there. What I witnessed mostly were verbal arguments. Ciara would move me along so I'd not see. Her real beatings were within closed doors, meant to be absent of peeping eyes."

Josie shook her head. "All the folks knew what he did. Had Aidan actually thought he'd concealed his deeds by means of closure?"

"Who knows what he thought. The bastard probably wanted to avoid outside interference. Ciara was his business. That's how he kept it. He wanted no sort of deliberate meddlings inside his affairs."

"What about altercations outside his house? His pub, for example?" Josie questioned. "Agnus said he'd scuffle his clientele."

"Oh, yes. Yes, he did. Those fights he sought purposely. They had no association with his wife. If he was in the state to brawl, he'd instantly select an opponent. Bicker first, then rough them up was his measure of scrimmage. He loved insults and directed them fiercely."

Tristian probed, "Were you ever harmed?"

"Never physically, no. But the things he did to Ciara hurt me enough. One incident I particularly remember enraged me a lot."

"What was that?" Josie concerned.

"It was about a month or so before Aidan's change. I found a silver tabby running scared through an alley. I calmed the poor thing, then took her to Ciara." Logan smiled. "She had a way with animals unlike any other. She and Aidan became engrossedly attached and opened their home to the small cat. Honestly, I figured Nia had found a deserving family. Never had I suspected something foul to come later."

"The cat's buried beneath the oak," Tristian stated.

A tear passed from Logan's eye. "I aided Ciara with the burial. She'd chosen that spot to lay her to rest."

"What terrible thing had Aidan done?"

"Oh, it twas awful," Logan replied to Josie. "If I had only known, I'd have taken her for Ciara."

"I see this is upsetting you. Never mind it."

"No, girl. Nia's story deserves to be heard. That cat breathed air like all infant creations. I can at least honor her memory. Nia's entitled that. Like Ciara, that kitty was murdered."

"If he butchered her, I can't hear it." Josie frowned. "I'll walk out."

"She wasn't slaughtered, but she had a terrible death indeed. Nia was experiencing, well, heat, as folks call it. And so it had no setting with Aidan. Having a bellering cat in his house violently set him on edge. He and Ciara argued. When she didn't listen, Aidan took matters into his hands. He ended up tying a noose around Nia's neck, then, dropping her from the balcony, he let her hang. Nia strangled until breaking her small neck. Sickly enough, Aidan had also forced Ciara to watch what he'd done."

"Oh my God." Josie gasped.

"Ciara fought all she could to save Nia. In her desperate attempts Ciara viciously attacked her husband. Using nails, she scratched his face. A nasty welt raised beneath his eye and eventually scarred. After killing Nia, Aidan belted Ciara like a punished horse. She could barely move her limbs. Sometime thereafter that bastard-husband of hers retreated to his pub and threw down a few pints."

Josie dabbed the trickling tears from her eyes. "How did you learn of Nia's death?"

"It was that day. I saw Ciara outside crying. I could tell things were wrong from afar. There Nia's limp body rested atop Ciara's lap. Then, as I approached, I saw the bruises covering her body. I sat there alongside her, and we mourned over Nia." Logan paused briefly, then continued. "Aidan had a chunk of ice where his heart should have been. By far was he the coldest, cruelest person I knew to walk this earth."

Josie nodded. "Eventually you helped Ciara bury her cat?"

"As was stated. I dug the hole beneath the oak, and together we engraved a headstone in its trunk."

"A Celtic knot," Tristian replied.

"Of eternal life."

Josie pondered aloud, "Why didn't Ciara try to leave him?"

"In fact? Well, I knew she loved him, but come the end she feared him as well. Everyone in this town having knowledge of Aidan was afraid. He was as crazy as they came."

"We know how devilish he is," remarked Josie.

"I'm afraid to ask. Is he still harming her?"

"When has he not?" Josie cringed.

"In death I hoped she'd be free of him."

"They're continuing a cycle which now involves us. Aidan has Tristian and me retained in abuse."

"You must leave that house. His evils have befallen you."

"Agnus said they've only returned to reenact their deaths. Meeting that, they should be gone."

"And what if not? Are you two settled in risking your chances?"

"Agnus said she'd bless our home. Come that, they shouldn't return."

"Pardon my divert, but do you talk to Ciara?"

"I have."

"I wish you'd tell her how much I've missed her. My world fell apart when I found out what Aidan had done." A flow of tears rushed from Logan's eyes. "You should have seen him at her funeral."

"Agnus told me how shameful he was."

"Never had he shed a tear. Not even once. Ciara had been sick, for heaven's sake. We all knew she was dying, but he rushed her into an early grave, damn him. I remember that bastard telling me her death was an accident. She'd fallen and hit her head's what he said. I knew better. He either slammed or pushed her. That damned bastard thought his fabrication would trick all the town's folks. Yet I knew the truth as did Agnus. We knew he killed her. It was never no accident as he claimed. I think back on some of those folks who were too stupid to believe him. How shortsighted were they? Even if he tried, Aidan couldn't fool me, not for one second. That bastard got what he deserved following his wife's funeral."

Tristian interrupted, "His murder, you mean?"

"It was the best news I heard in my life. I felt he'd finally got what he deserved. Considering all the pain, torment, and misery he put Ciara through. Happily, I'd been elated to learn someone put him through hell. It was time Aidan felt what it was like to be the victim."

"Do you think Ciara had done it?" asked Tristian.

"Everyone came to believe she'd revenged her death," Logan remarked.

"And you? Do you believe that?" Josie wondered.

"It made a good ghost story."

"What do you mean? Is it something more?" Josie asked.

"There were a few people who could have done it."

Josie questioned, "Ciara's brother?"

"Being one. Kieran had good motive. So did their father and the small handful of folks enraged by Ciara's murder. There may not have been many, but that modest group perceived the correct knowledge. There were also those men from the pub. What's not to say some beaten sap had paid him a visit? After all, they sought vengeance, too."

"Do you believe you know who killed him?" Josie asked.

"Had it been Kieran? I'd say good for him. Might it been Ciara? That'd made a better story. If anyone had reason to kill Aidan, nobody's would been more proper than hers. Least I'd say. But you don't know."

"You'd like to think it could have been Ciara?"

"Yes, son, I would," Logan replied to Tristian. "Or at least someone doing it in her honor. Kieran could have been capable surely. He was roused. Ciara was his sister, after all. Blood is much thicker than water."

Josie relayed, "It seems Aidan's death will always remain in mystery. With no definite source to accuse, we're merely left to wonder who might have done it."

"If you remain in that house, you're liable to find out," Logan responded.

A short woman dressed in white entered the room just as Logan finished. "Excuse me. I'm sorry to interrupt you all. Logan, time for noontide lunch. All residence to the dining hall."

"Lunchtime already? I thought it was morning?"

"No, hon. Time's come for brunch. Shall I send for a wheelchair?"

"Now, Tullia, I still have enough pep in my stride. I can manage alone."

"Must you be hardheaded?"

"That's usually how you'd take me."

"We sure know I can't argue with that."

"Well, we'd better be going," said Josie. "We appreciate this visit, Logan. You've helped us a great deal."

"You're quite welcome, girl. I do hope you found what you'd been seeking."

"Quite certainly."

"Much applaud, sir. We respect you for seeing us," Tristian remarked.

The O'Briens shook Logan's hand upon leaving.

Josie whispered softly, "I promise if I ever talk to Ciara again, I'll relay her your message."

Logan smiled and nodded. "That'd make this old man happy."

"I owe you that." Josie smiled.

"Won't you two come back and visit? I honestly apologize for any fleeting speech that may have offended you or your husband. Please know I've enjoyed your company."

"We'd love to. You take care now," Josie remarked as she and Tristian exited the room.

The O'Briens made their way down the sidewalk as they paced toward their car.

"You happy we came?" Tristian queried his wife.

"I am," she relayed. "Learning more helps us possess further truth. How terrible about Ciara's cat, though. Poor thing had no chance. Quite upsetting it is. Just sickening she died in that fashion."

Tristian caressed his wife's hand. "Only monsters could do such things," he spoke, driving off.

Josie watched as they passed through the streets. "This isn't the way home. Sweetheart, where you going?"

"I've got a special plan. Just sit tight for the moment."

"But where are we going?"

"You'll see."

"Tristian? Tristian, what's this about? Why won't you tell me?"

"It's a surprise."

"Tristian?"

"Patience, dear. We're almost there." Tristian pulled in before a bakery.

"Oh, I see. I know what you're up to."

"You do?"

"Your weakness begs for a whiskey cake."

"Is that so?"

"I'm quite certain."

"You want anything?"

Um, she thought. "Would you mind picking up a half dozen buttermilk scones?"

"A half dozen?"

"I'll take some to Agnus."

"That all then?"

"I believe so."

Triatian traipsed into the pastry shop and trotted to the counter.

"Nice to see you, Tristian. Shall it be the usual?"

"No, not today, Keriana."

"Something else then?"

"Could you pack me a half dozen of these buttermilk scones?"

"Any certain ones for you?"

"Whatever you grab would be fine. I'm not picky."

"How's Ciara? I haven't seen her in lately."

"She's been a bit sickly."

"Oh, I'm sorry to hear. Do tell her to get better."

"Aye." Tristian nodded.

"Here you go, hon. They're on the house."

"Well, thank you. How kind. Say, is Zaira working the florist today, might you know?"

"She's working till five."

"Might I use your back door? I'd like to surprise Jos with some flowers. She's in the car."

"A tricky one, are you? Why, sure you can."

"Great. That helps me a lot."

"I'll phone Zaira, let her know you're coming round back."

Tristian raised his bag. "Hey, thanks again for these scones."

"My pleasure. Say hello to your wife."

Tristian snuck along the building's exterior until approaching Zaira's back door.

"You playing it low today?" she asked, peering behind the screen.

"Have to. Jos is waiting on me."

"Aren't you the romantic? My Eagan could learn a thing from you. Well, come on in. Let's get that bouquet assembled. Anything particular come to mind?"

"Well, these roses look nice."
"Which color you like?"
"How about a half dozen pink and a half dozen of these red?"
"You've got an eye for color. This makes a pleasureful combination. A becoming way to say I love you to your wife." Zaira smiled.
"I'd like to also get another bouquet when you've finished. I think some carnations."
"Might it be a mixture you'd like?"
"That'd work just nicely."
Several minutes later Tristian emerged from the shop. Opening the door, he presented Josie with the pink and red roses. "For you, my darling."
"Tristian, how thoughtful of you. Oh, aren't they exquisite?"
"They reminded me of you. Beautiful and sweet." Tristian passed the second bundle through the window. "Can you hold these till we're home?"
"Who're they for?"
Tristian got into the car. "Well, I thought they'd look admirable beneath the oak."
"Oh, sweetie, how touching. You got these for Ciara's cat?" Josie smiled warmly. "You really are thoughtful."
"Should she peer through the window, she'll see someone besides her remembered her kitty." Tristian pulled up to their house and helped Josie out of the car. Walking over to the oak, they stood silently before it.
Josie held the bundle of carnations in arm as she rubbed her fingertips over the engraving. "How sad I feel for your abducted breath, withdrawn so tragically." Tears came to her eyes as she remembered Nia's ill-fated life.
Tristian kneeled alongside his wife. "You may be gone, little kitty, but in our hearts you won't be forgotten."
"These flowers, to honor your remembrance. A token of our regard. May you be resting peacefully, away from these hardships, reproaching your keeper." Josie got up and walked with Tristian toward the house. Pulling out his key, he unlocked the door as they both walked in.
"Do you feel that cold chill? It blankets the air," Josie stated.
"It shouldn't be this cool in July."
A shadowy figure rushed pass Josie, then raced toward the stairs.

The heavy pound of footsteps could be heard clobbering the above floor. Suddenly a second pair emerged scampering and bustling about. It was after that the sounds of shattering glass soon filled the air. Tristian viewed several objects thrown to the walls, then shatter to pieces.

On the top step Ciara appeared, begging helplessly. "Please stop. You're drunk," her voice cried.

Aidan arose near side her as he yelled to her face, "I'm not drunk, ye pathetic wench. Come closer, ye slob, or I'll continue to break things."

"I'll clean the mess. Just let me be."

"I said get over here." Aidan spotted a capodimonte rose Ciara's mom had given her. "Ye cherish this, don't you?"

"Aidan, please, no."

"Then put a bloody step forth, wench."

"Put the rose down and I shall."

"You and your wishes. It won't bother me if I had to break this. One less thing to remind me of you." Aidan heaved the rose through the air as he watched his wife's face.

With a quick response Ciara recovered the object as she slid to the floor, then, uncupping her hands, found it unscathed and still whole.

"Damn thing must have slipped." Aidan laughed. Then popping away Ciara's hands, he laughed again. "Too bad it's now broken." He brought his foot down upon the porcelain rose with hefty appliance and stomped it to scrap.

Tears streamed from Ciara's eyes like that of a leaky faucet. "Whatever cause you find to hurt me, you act. When will this stop?"

"When I say," he raged.

"What, Aidan?" she cried at his feet. "What do you want? Hasn't the harm you've enforced been enough?"

"I've never hurt you intentionally, ye stupid sap."

"What do you call these bruises and cuts?"

"Accidents. All accidents. You did them yourself," he responded hatefully.

"No, never. I didn't do this, you know it."

"All right then. You want to know, ye stolid dolt? I do what I do because ye ask for it."

"What? No," Ciara cried.

"I've never beaten you because I wanted. If you were smart enough, you'd understand."

"Understand what?" she wailed.

"All the fights. You've brought them upon yourself."

"How, Aidan? How? I try to do right by you, and you cut me down."

"I have to keep you in line. Teach ye a thing or two till ye get it right. So ye better stop making me out as the bad man with that misconceived slander."

"I've kept my tongue to silence. A deed I see has led me to fault. All so I could protect you from an uproar. I had faith come one day you'd change. But now I see it not. Your curse will keep you."

"Mind what you say, wench. I can still take your tongue. Now get out of me face before I tear yours off," Aidan stated harshly as he pushed Ciara into the wall. Then, starting down the stairs, he buffeted pass Josie and Tristian, unknowing they were there. Upon the step, Ciara faded, but her cries had lingered far after her decampment.

Aidan's voice soon resurfaced. "Stop that infernal crying. Ye wish to whine? I'll give ye something to mourn about. Now hush it up. I'm in no mood to listen to your whimpers." Aidan walked to the kitchen, then returned to the living room with a bottle of bourbon in hand. Upon the stairs, Ciara's cries continued plaguing air. "I said hush it," he yelled. When she did not, Aidan started up. "Ye should have listened. That's your problem, wench. Ye never do as I say." Aidan swung his hand through air as his fist met the delicate bones in Ciara's face.

Her footsteps rushed against the stairs as she tried to evade him. A cool breeze brushed upon Josie and Tristian while Ciara made way for the door. Behind them Aidan rushed after.

"Get back here. I said get back here! Damn you, Ciara. You'll find yourself dead come one of these days." The front door had opened and allowed her escape. Then the barrier slammed, leaving Aidan behind raging with anger. He beat his hands upon the door, blaring loudly, "Don't ye think I won't be around when you come back. I'll get you. I'll get you, ye hear?"

Josie shook as she stood in place. "He's unable to go freely," she whispered to her husband.

"Maybe that's her only escape? She can leave the house when he can't."

Josie thought deeply. "He's left before, hasn't he? So why not now?"

"I wonder?" added Tristian while Josie walked toward the door. "What're you doing?"

"Testing something. Tristian, did you lock this door once we arrived?"

"We were hit by that cold when coming inside. I didn't think to."

"Ciara must have locked it from the outside. That's how she stopped him. She had the key."

"Why didn't he walk through the door like most spirits? I thought that's what they did?"

"It was their residual energy, as though they'd still been alive. It's an episode refrained in time. He wasn't able to leave then. Nonetheless, now he still can't."

Tristian responded, "It's better that way. Least then she's gotten away for awhile."

"We better get upstairs and tidy that broken glass."

"I'll tend to the cleaning, Jos. You go to the living room and have a seat." Tristian went to the second floor and peered around. He checked in all the rooms and throughout the hallway, but found the grounds clear. "That's rather odd," he relayed, scratching his head. "I saw those objects break. Where's all the glass?" Just then Tristian heard the sound of more shattering. This time it came from downstairs.

He rushed to the living room when seeing the roses he'd bought scattered about beside their broken holder. It was then he'd encountered his wife hunched fetal upon the floor. "Oh, God, Jos. Are you okay?"

"A searing pain, it struck my abdomen. It was so painful I lost my breath, and dropped the vase."

"Let me get you to the couch. I'll call Dr. Emerson. He'll come check you."

"No need, Tristian. I'm fine. It was just a wee-size pain."

"That little pain caused you to drop glass, Jos. I'm calling the doctor."

"Tristian, I'm fine. I assure you. Besides, Dr. Emerson said to call if the pain became persistent or I were bleeding. I'm not suffering either."

"You're so stubborn. Are you sure you're okay?"

"I'm fine. Really."

"I'll just gather another vase for these flowers and clean up this glass."

"What'd you find broken upstairs?"

"It's funny. I didn't find a thing."

"Did you search?"

"I checked everywhere. Whatever it'd been disappeared."

"That tends to happen in this house. Least to say it's self-cleaning."

"Maybe so, but not this." Tristian walked into the kitchen and grasped another jar from the pantry, then, filling it with water, returned to the living room to retrieve the fallen roses. Before Josie he set the vase at the table for her to admire.

While Tristian sat and talked to his wife he felt the sensation of something dripping onto his back. Looking up, he saw the phantom bloodstain upon the ceiling. "Oh, not this again."

"What is it? Is something wrong?"

"The blood's back."

"What are we going to do?"

"We'll just have to let it disappear like before. I can't go up there, Jos. I remember what I saw the last time this happened. It was everywhere."

Josie peered upward. "Aidan's trying to scare us out."

"Give it some time. It'll go away."

"Tristian, what about your shirt?"

"Just fetch me a towel or dirty rag."

Josie returned from the kitchen with a tainted linen in hand. "Use this," she remarked.

Tristian stretched the cloth upon the couch to soak the trill of dribbling blood. Then, stripping out of his soiled shirt, Tristian stated. "I need to throw this in the wash."

"Hurry back. I don't like being left alone here."

"Come to the kitchen then. I'll be a moment."

"Soak that shirt, Tristian, and pour in a little bleach."

Tristian gawked upon the shirt he had bled on the day before. "I guess this is ruined now."

"What's that, sweetheart?"

"Nothing, Jos. It's nothing." He allowed the washer to agitate a few seconds, then raised the lid.

Josie peered through the door. "You might as well let those steep overnight."

"That's what I've planned."

"Tristian, we'll buy you new shirts if those don't come clean."

"We don't have to do that. I could wear them when I'm in the yard."

"You're very simple, aren't you?"

"I have plenty enough, Jos. I can get by on that. Come, love, let's check that blot in the ceiling."

The O'Briens stood before their couch. "Look at that, will you? It's already starting to shrink," Josie relayed.

Tristian stood in awe. "Are you watching this? I can't believe my eyes. Jos, you're seeing this, right?"

From the sofa the blood pulled back to the ceiling. The experience was like watching a rewound clip. Instead of dripping downward, the dribble sucked back to the place it had fallen.

"This is the most abnormal sight I've ever laid eyes on," Josie mentioned. "I just want it to stop."

"That makes two of us."

"This house, Tristian, it's crazy."

"It's not the house, Jos, it's what's inside."

"Never had I thought these devastations could happen. It's like a nightmare's been granted life."

"It'll all be over in a couple days, then we'll return living a normal life."

"What's normal anymore?"

"Might I remind you, you asked for Agnus's help."

"I know I did. But I can't help wondering what we'll do if it doesn't work."

"Do you not have faith in her? If Agnus feels in her heart she could be of assistance, why question that?"

"I'm too doubting, I know."

"Ease up then. Have a little hope and trust in that. We'll make it through."

"She asked me by today. Did you want to come?"

"I don't think either of us should be alone in this house. If she doesn't mind my tagging alone, I'll be happy to go."

"Why would she mind? She told you, you're welcomed there."

Tristian peered around the room. "I don't know how you did it."

"What? What did I do?"

"All those times here alone. I'm as afraid of Aidan. He's unpredictable. How are we to know when he'll show?"

"You get by the best you can. If you feel a disaster's en route it's best to leave."

"Did you feel something any of those times?"

"I was always too late." Josie bowed her head. "Like the incident with the sink. I should have heeded the warning. If I had just left the faucet running and gone to the porch, maybe I would have avoided that dire situation."

Tristian patted his wife's hand when a mournful cry arose from the kitchen. Then, making its way to the living room, Ciara appeared most frightened and shaken. Freshened blood had dampened her face from the broken bones within her nose. Josie's jowl dropped when viewing her distressing sight. Ciara began to panic as she was additionally struck. Her eye swelled and quickly bruised. An affixed blow soon found way to her mouth, busting her fragile lips with splintering lines. Crying in anguish, Ciara was continuously beaten before the O'Briens.

"That's it! You let her be," Josie yelled from her lungs. "I demand you this instant. I will not watch as you batter your wife a second more."

Tristian lent a statement, "Let her go, Aidan. Step back and see what you've done."

An inhuman shriek echoed throughout the room carried on a powerful gust of cold wind. "She's me property. Mine, ye hear? I'll do as I see fit."

Josie raged, "I said unhand her."

"Ye think you can stop me, ye pathetic excuse for a mortal?" Aidan began to shake Ciara violently. Blood wavered from her face and splattered onto the floor. "Squall for me, ye gutless, little pig. I want to hear that squill."

Ciara found herself so frightened by Aidan she'd lost control of her bladder and urinated within her dress. Shoving her to the floor, Adain placed his overwhelming foot to her neck. "Tell me why I shouldn't stomp your throat?"

"Tristian, do something. He means it," Josie cried.

"Look at you. You're a disgrace." He laughed as an expansion of urine swelled atop the floor. "You've pissed yourself. How shameful ye be," he spoke in disgust.

"You're hurting me," Ciara wailed. "Please, Aidan, I beg you, stop. I can't breathe." She began to cough. "I said I can't breathe." A loud shriek broke the air.

"No, Jos, no," Tristian ejected as his wife ran to where Aidan was standing and fiercely tried to strike. Sadly, her hands passed through his body as he broke forth in laugher.

"Ye can't touch me, ye petty tyke. Why ye even try?" Aidan's laughter became more sinister than before.

Josie pulled forth the black quill and held it before his sight. "I may not be able, but I have an acquaintance who can."

Aidan raged, "Ye wish to engender harm? Ye hold a feather to me, ye blundering dolt. You're a deficient type. Senseless in mind and with absurdity ye speak. How I'd love to bleed the breath from your throat as I watch ye shudder." Aidan stretched forth his hands in an attempt to attack. It was then a loud squawk came above Josie's head. With it the raven soared upon air. Swooping down, it proceeded attack.

Aidan rapidly threw forth his hands, trying to defend his scalp. But the bird's beak dredged into flesh, sending stinging pains into his extremities. The moreover Aidan fought, the further distempered his opponent became. Shoveling its beak into Aidan's skin left deep bloody holes incised in his hands. The raven's contest further increased to bitter quarry, challenging its foe to full-fledged combat.

Weary and tired, Aidan temporarily removed his hands from sheltering his crown. In that time he learned his attempt was one of feeble mind. Aidan's undiscerning maneuver gave way to his cranium, grossly allowing the raven whole entry to his scalp. Through an inspired fit, the bird tunneled eight invading talons into the unprotected flesh of Aidan's dome. A seepage of blood surpassed his taupe strands, staining down to the ends of their growth.

Through fully developed clamor, Aidan yelped in surrendering pain while the raven progressed on tearing flesh. By way of uncalculated strive, Aidan grabbed the raven's body. Squeezing tightly, he hoped the raven would discharge him. But the bird became ever more violent as it set forth an unsettling shrill.

The creature's eyes then blazed like fieriest embers as its talons delved deeper into its prey. Surpassing layers of epidermis, its fissuring

The Crying House

hooks gouged into Aidan's skull. Hanging its beak before the face of its enemy, the raven launched a repetitive peck to his eyes. Aidan's defensible response was to squeeze them tightly to avoid having them transfixed from their holes. Bustling about frantically, he skittered the room until the feuding raven cast loose. Following his deliverance to escape, Aidan retreated to a wall where he'd eagerly vanished.

The raven reside in sight as it circled its territory, then sailing to the floor, settled near Ciara's body. Wobbling to where she laid, it nudged its head upon her face.

"Tristian, isn't there something we could do?" his wife relayed. "Can't we help her?" Josie asked as they kneeled beside her.

"I wish I could phone the doctor, Jos, but what help would that be?"

"She lies here busted and broken. What a terrible throe endured unattended. Might we do something?" Josie reached forth to Ciara.

"How are we to help if we can't touch her?"

The raven continued bumping Ciara until she slightly awoke. By her side the bird remained loyally as they both disappeared.

Tristian wondered, "Where do you think they go?"

"Surely they must be here, yet their vitality has faded."

"Is that why we can't see?"

"It takes energy to manifest. Might a spirit be weak, materialization will not form. It needs conductivity to do so."

"Why is it on occasions they appear for short times?"

"Every now and then they harness enough buoyancy to make themselves known. Depending on their effervescency, we might see them briefly or expansively."

Tristian stood dazed. "Where's all this knowledge emerging? I've never heard you speak this deeply."

"Thank Agnus. It was her wisdom that enlightened me."

"It's done something."

Josie smiled. "Don't be so surprised."

"I knew you were a fast learner, Jos, but never had I known you managed so quickly."

"It's my only virtue, if any."

"You have plenty worthies. That's one of many."

She peered to the floor. "I hope Ciara's all right. Not being able to help just kills me."

"Sweetheart, she's in care of the raven. I'm certain she's safe."

"I believe we're fully aware that devoted bird's her trustworthy guardian."

"Aye, and the Lord knows we're inefficient to interfere, so we must be thankful she has its protection."

"Tristian, what do you say we leave awhile? I've witnessed enough here for one day. Maybe we'll visit Agnus? It'd do us some good. What do you say?"

"Give her a call then. Make sure it's okay."

"Will you excuse me a moment as I use the phone?"

"Certainly, dear, go ahead." Tristian waited patiently as his wife left the room.

"We'll see you then shortly, Agnus … okay. Yes, that'd be good. Bye now. Tristian? Tristian?"

"Yes, sweetheart? I'm here."

"I'm about to turn this kitchen upside-down. Where on earth did you place that bag of scones?"

"They're not here?"

"I haven't found them."

"In the living room maybe? Did you check there?"

"I don't recall them on the table. Where'd you take them?"

Tristian thought back. "Did I bring them in?"

"They were in your hand. I remember."

"Well, this beats all. I'm not sure where I set them."

"Can't you think?"

"Trust me, I'm trying." Tristian gazed toward the steps. "Upstairs? Maybe I took them up there?"

"You mind taking a look? We planned to carry a fairing to Agnus."

"The table in the hallway," he exclaimed. "How could I forget?"

"You mind grabbing them then?"

"Yes, dear. I'm sorry. I'll be right back."

Josie walked to the bottom of the stairs. "Did you find it?"

"I have the bag in hand."

"Hurry then, she's waiting."

He stopped suddenly in his tracks. "Something's not right. This bag feels too light." Tristian opened the sack and peered through. "I ordered a half dozen of these. I saw her."

"What's the problem? You got some missing?"

"Two."

"You sure you ordered six?"

"I watched Keriana. Jos, I seen her bag them."

"Never mind it, Tristian. We'll get by on those."

"But this is ridiculous."

"Forget them. Most likely Aidan stole those two. There's nothing you could do. Anyway, it's not important."

"It ticks me off, Jos. Something this simple."

"Never mind your fuss. We've kept Agnus long enough."

CHAPTER ELEVEN ◆

Tristian and Josie traipsed toward Mrs. O'Toole's as she greeted them at the door. "How nice it is to see you both." She gave hugs and kisses. "Josette, dear, you on the mend? Improved, I might hope."

"Indeed." She smiled warmly. "I've made a splendid renewal."

"Impressive, child. I'm most proud to hear such news."

"You have no idea how grateful we were for your help," Tristian added.

"Might you know the two of you I hold dear. I love you like family in this drumming old heart of mine." She chuckled lightly.

Josie relayed, "I hope you know we love you, too, Agnus. And you're most welcomed to be a share in ours."

"How kind that is. You've warmed my heart and cheered my soul by saying that. Come along to the living room, dears. Might you be comfortable there?"

Josie handed forth the bag. "We've brought some fresh scones from the bakery."

"Buttermilk pastries, I presume?"

"Yes." Josie laughed. "That's quite amazing."

"I still acquire supersensitive predictions here and there. My duration with clairvoyance hasn't waned yet."

"Were you a fortune teller?" Tristian asked.

Agnus explained, "Visionary, I like to call it. Fortune tellers often acquired bad wraps. Those folks sought easy profit while consumers inherited an augur of lies."

"Lies?" Josie wondered. "But I thought they were reputable persons?"

"Not in the least, dear. Most fortune tellers are learned swindlers. They make better coaxers than prophets."

"And what about your visions, Agnus? Like now with these scones?"

"I acquired the gift early in life, and somewhere in my girlish growth I'd been taught to control it."

Josie thought deeply. "How could one control that?"

"You must understand that no soul aspires on being ruled by their ability. It's quite frustrating and nevertheless stressing for those whose visions are invariably persistent. Folks who're trained could tune it out for their peace of mind. That not only goes for seers, but empaths, well as those suited for telepathy and psychometry."

"Like shutting it off?" Tristian queried.

"In a sense, dear, but not completely. The gift will always be a part of the person. On behalf of the above mentioned who're impressionably susceptible, their gifts could easily prove maddening."

Tristian pondered, "Is that how things became for you?"

"Simply? Yes."

"What were your experiences like?" Josie polled.

"Much similar to an interminable radio, and my sight so perennial it'd even been effected as I closed my eyes."

"Sounds a bit nerve-racking," Tristian commented.

"Favorably enough, it's a wonderful gift to have. I've always enjoyed helping people, but it can take its toll mentally and physically. My grand-mumsy taught me how to harness what I had and use it with need, bless her soul."

Josie smiled. "You came from a close family?"

"We were very attached, I'm fair to say."

Josie leaned her head sideways as she gave thought. "I don't mean to pry, but your children? Don't they visit?"

Agnus became saddened. "I haven't received many visitors after my husband's passing. Only time my children come are near holidays. Once in awhile they'll call, yet it's nothing like seeing them before me."

Josie frowned. "That's quite depressing, Agnus. You're a personable type, plenty worthy of visitants."

"Sadly, dear, it gets lonely. I've been abandoned here in my old age."

Josie patted her hand. "They have no idea, Agnus, what they're missing not being here more."

"That's lovely of you to say."

Tristian pondered, "Do your children live aways?"

"Addie lives in Galway with her husband and sons, then Teagan lives in Dublin with his wife and three girls. I wish I could travel to them, but I'm afraid that's not so. As you see, I'm blessed to have you living so close. It lessens my lonesomeness."

"Oh, Agnus, I'm sorry you don't see your family. We know how terribly rough it must be," added Josie. "Seeing your pain hurts me here inside." She brushed her heart.

Tristian nodded in agreement. "We'll never replace them, but do know you'll always have us." Then hugging Agnus softly, he spoke again. "Jos and I enjoy your company very much. I couldn't imagine what we'd do without you."

Agnus's eyes swelled. "How blessed I am to hear that. It truly means a lot." She took a moment to wipe her tears. "Now how about those desserts, dears? Maybe a dollop of jam? Do you like strawberry?"

"That'd be most pleasant," Josie said anxiously.

"And you, Tristian, dear? Strawberry jam?"

"Certainly. Thank you, Agnus."

"I've brewed a fresh pot of tea. Oh, and Josette, I've made a much better elixir for you. Might you be ready?"

Josie made an angled face. "Only if I'm guaranteed not to gag."

"I think you'd be surprised. I've played with the recipe a wee bit, hoping to improve the taste. You should certainly find it pleasing."

Josie snickered. "You're pulling my leg, aren't you, Agnus?"

"Oh no, dear. I assure you. I sweetened the mixture with fruits and berries to make the flavor more sufficient. You'll still access the same results that helped you before. You'll find it goes down with less effort."

"I'll take your word then and have a cup accompanying my scone," added Josie.

"I'll be just a moment."

Tristian rose from his seat. "Might you need help?" he asked. "I don't mind."

The Crying House

"Oh no-no, dear. I'll cheat with my tray." She smiled. "You go on and relax here." Several minutes thereafter Agnus returned. "Pardon my delay. My shuffle's a bit slow, but here we go, dears. Tea's hot now, be careful. Josette, let me know what you think. Here're your scones, kids."

Josie collected the warm mug and held it between her hands. Steam rose to her nose while gaining an explosion of various scents. Slowly she pulled the vessel toward her lips and blew lightly upon the vapors, then acting cautiously, took her first sip. She relished the flavors coating her tongue, finding the experience as being a sweetly-lush mixture of fruit juices, with subtle notes of berries and a mellow undertone of fresh roots and herbs.

Josie exclaimed, "I can't believe how amazing this is. It all blends together nicely for that perfect cup of tea."

"See, dear? I told you it'd work. I'm glad you're indulged."

"This doesn't even come close to yesterday's. Why, I'd say you've perfected the recipe for sure. Agnus, your improvement's divine."

"Splendid, dear, just splendid. My concept proved pleasing, I see."

"I could certainly drink this every day." She laughed. "But remembering last night, I wouldn't have thought that."

"Well, I wasn't sure you'd even finish it, dear. But look at you today. You might as well be begging for more."

Tristian smiled at Agnus's comment. "Some change for her, huh?"

"I'd say. You care if I topped off your tea?"

"Oh, by all means. I'm running a bit low."

"You certainly are." Agnus smiled. "You care for more sweets? I've got a batch of shortbreads here."

"You make these yourself?"

"Bright and early this morning. They're great dredged in jam. Gives it something extra."

Tristian grinned with delight. "Would that be the strawberry jam we had with the scones?"

"If that's what you'd like."

"Indeed I do. Its flavor's most excellent."

"It's right on the tray, dear. Help yourself. More tea, Josette?"

She nodded. "You know, Agnus? I'd have to agree with Tristian. This jam's delish. Where might I buy some?"

Well, she thought. "I've never made sells. I've always handed these jars as gifts."

"You made this?" Josie queried.

"I make all my jams, preserves, and marmalades."

Josie beamed. "Could you teach me?"

"We'll make a day of it. It's simple really. When you make something, always do it with love." Agnus peered toward Tristian. "You all right, my dear? You seem a bit withdrawn. Might you have something on your mind?"

"I've just been thinking, Agnus."

"Maybe something I could answer?"

"Well, I don't mean to get off subject."

"Nonsense, child. I don't mind. What seems to be your trouble?"

"Well, earlier me and Jos were trying to figure out where spirits go when they disappear. She had a theory, and for some reason I find myself minding it."

"You're wondering about Ciara and Aidan?"

"I can't seem to help it. We share a home after all. It just frustrates me how they come and go. If I were a spirit, well, then I'd presumably understand it much clearer."

"Maybe I could help you understand a bit differently."

"I'm all ears, Agnus. Whatever you say."

"First know an earthbound soul is always around even when you don't see them. They're not necessarily in the same place or room as you, but they're about."

Tristian shook his head. "What causes an appearance?"

"Apparitions are formed from generated power."

"How's that so? Forgive me, but I've never given much thought into spirits or their activity until they infested our home."

"A person is contrived of electromagnetic energy. After death, depending on some folks and their circumstances, there's a possibility their energies remain. Despite the psychical body withering and dying, a soul for additional happenstance is forever. We are granted immortality in death. We continue to live forth rather that be in heaven or hell. But there are those poor souls who exist in limbo, and those who are earthbound."

Tristian questioned, "What's the difference with the two?"

"First you must know they're similar in ways, then dissimilar in others."

"Well, what are the similarities then?"

"Limbo and earthbound both mean to be stuck some place and forgotten."

"Okay, and the difference?"

"To be earthbound is to be an earthy spirit who haunts the land or foundations of a place. One in limbo, to my suggestion, is a never-ending world apart from ours. Much like a parallel universe. As a result, spirits wander alone, passing each other along their ways, but never seen. It could be a place refrained of light or maybe an endless desert they're left to roam. Personally, I'd much rather be earthbound than cast to a world of in between. But to speak justly, either way could prove disheartening."

"But there are those who aren't stuck?" Josie interrupted.

"Indeed. Most souls have a better place to go. My moto to folks is to believe that, when a loved one has passed, not to think it as eternal death. For they are very much alive, blessed with new life."

"What about floating objects, Agnus? Do they mount on their own?"

"Just like spirits need energy to appear, Tristian, the same goes for soaring objects. A spirit's strength relies on their ability to cast substances forth, slam doors, whatever their will. Because a person's not seen doesn't mean they're not there. A commodity doesn't move itself. Spirits do things at will."

"What makes the afterlife so…"

"Confusing? Well, people must take time to understand it. Knowledge leads to insight and awareness. The nature of spirits and how to conceive them is purely scientific. It's a category all its own called parapsychology. You'd be amazed by what you'd learn."

"Well, Agnus, I'm amazed by you and your teachings. You're quite brilliant. I'm not aware of any who know the things you do."

"It comes with curiosity and old age." She laughed. "There's so much more for people to know and understand if only they not be afraid. A portion of folks don't believe in such things. They think the idea of spirits is simply foolish thinking. Others are too afraid to grasp the unknown." Her eyes then twinkled brightly. "On the other hand, you have those special few who understand those things that others dare not venture. That's where people akin to me come into the picture."

"What got you into all this?" Tristian asked.

"I suppose it started as a child. I heard stories as a youth from my mother and grand-mumsy about wondrous things such as spirits and fairies. The first time I saw an apparition I was about three or so. Oddly, the older I got, the more aware I became to perceiving them. I always had a special knack for spotting fairies, too. The good as well as the bad. The nice ones are marvelous little people. When they don't feel threatened, they're wonderfully helpful friends."

Tristian wondered, then voiced a question. "Do you believe in other things besides spirits and fairies?"

"Oh yes, dear. I believe in many things. You don't always have to see something to believe in it."

"But what if you believe in something that doesn't exist? A one-eyed, zippered mouthed creature for example?"

"Then you've granted power and inspirited it. Belief and faith are your keys to effect and development. The more you believe, the more you encourage that thought."

"This is unbelievable. Then, well … well, where or how would it prosper and succeed?"

"An astral world more or less. It's not fit to live or survive in our reality. But that doesn't mean it couldn't coincide at some point. Like creatures of fairy lore, they cross into our dimension here and there. Simply, child, if you know in your heart something exists, then it does."

"Could you elaborate a bit further?" Tristian questioned her.

"Take God, for example, dear. You've never seen him, but in your heart you know He exists. The same goes for mystical creatures such as dragons and unicorns, even harpies and griffins."

"Do you believe in dragons and unicorns?"

"I do. Actually, I came up with a theory which I call the eight realms of existence. This deals strictly with all forms of astral realms and otherworldly levels of being, as well as this earthly planet we call home."

Tristian responded, "I see."

"Would you explain?" Josie asked.

"First, you must think with an open mind. That will enable you to understand my logic, my dears. In my theory you have the realms of good and evil. The first realm is an enchanting heaven. This kingdom belongs to the supreme creator, God, his angels, and all good souls who've ever crossed over. The second realm I actually label the range of in between, or limbo, if you will. In this case a spirit isn't in the existence of heaven nor is he or she in the company of hell. They are simply lost souls as stated before. The third realm is the final empire of glory and bane. This realm would be *Ifreann*. The realm of a lesser God, his demons and those who have fallen from grace. The forth realm is of magical existence. It's home to fairies, mermaids, unicorns, dragons, Gods, Goddesses, and etcetera. The fifth realm is a more scientific sphere of existence. Extraterrestrial beings of all forms. Then you have the inception realms of time and evolution. Realm six, the dominions of the past. Realm seven, the present region. Realm eight, the range of the future. So you see, dears, everything exists. It's just in different zones."

Tristian sat stunned. "Wow. That's really some intense thinking right there."

Agnus laughed. "I have nothing better to do with my time, so I think."

"You really came up with this?" he questioned her.

"I found myself thinking about coexistence one night and wanted to summarize it somehow. I figured if I composed a theory, surely I'd explain it. Dimensions are like having rips in the atmosphere. We don't see them, but if we're lucky enough to stumble upon one, it's for our awe and amazement. Unfortunately, it's like finding a leprechaun guarding his pot of gold at the end of a rainbow. Yet mysterious things do find their way into our world."

"Such as what?" Tristian pondered.

"Take a fairy, for example. A minor set of folks see them, but not all. Those wee ones are around, but mostly seen when they choose to be."

"I never thought about that, Agnus. It's like everything fits in a certain place and time."

"You know most people find it hard to understand. But if you're open to it, your perception will come effortlessly. As with you, Tristian, are you not more open now than you've ever been? The haunting within your home has made you further aware of the possibilities that there's much more out there than just physical matter. You've had a spiritual awakening, my child. Count that as a blessing."

"How did you know I've become more open? You're like the all-seeing owl. Your teachings are wise and your instincts advisable."

"Might you say I just sensed something, dear? A feeling that you were never a firm believer, but speculator instead. You'd been the type to look for logical explanations to reason rather than looking at the facts that were already before you."

"That's so right." He laughed. "It's like my thinking's been altered now, and I can finally see clearly. It's amazing you knew that."

"The first time you've witnessed the unusual, it's hard not denying it's there. It essentially seems tricky. Mostly as though your eyes had played games. But when your doubts subside, you accept what you've seen."

"Being in our home makes me uncomfortable and uptight. Since talking with you I feel more at peace. But rooted dread stalwartly instills my core, knowing we must return to that frightful place. Once me and Jos leave, that uncomfortable feeling will plague me full-fledged at our door."

"What is it you feel once you're inside?"

"The air feels heavy. I can barely breathe. Then a light emplacement of panic sets in, and it grows extreme. It's then I find my nerves uptight. I try to hide it, but I shake inside. I know I can't cower, but for some reason I twitch with a bolt of jitters. I tell myself shake it off, don't let it control you. Who in their right mind would stance gutless before their wife? It's I who's to be the solid chum. The brawny defender of my home and spouse, yet I'm … I'm disturbed out of my bloody mind." Tristian dropped his head in shame. "It'd be right to say I'm doused with affright," he spoke sadly.

"Don't feel shamed by your reactions, child. Everyone has a natural response to situations, including yourself."

Josie added, "You haven't disgraced yourself, Tristian. You're only saying the truth, and that's all right."

"But I thought in your eyes you'd see a coward."

"Why would I think that? You've been my brave knight in that house and have fought with your best. You stood up when activities roughened. If that's not bravery, then I don't know what is."

Agnus pondered briefly. "How were you when this first set afoot?"

"Not like this." He frowned. "I felt not afraid. I was the one to submit to what's going there. Now it's left me so terrified and beside myself. I feel like I have no strengths. How am I supposed to protect Jos when this entity's stronger? I'm at my breaking point, Agnus, I really am. I hate admitting it because I didn't want my wife knowing how truly afraid I've become." Tristian took a deep breath. "I'm a grown man who's terrified. There's no simpler way to put it."

"Dear, dear, child. No matter your age, it's okay to be afraid. You're only human, after all. Just because you're a man doesn't mean you can't be impacted by something. It's only natural to respond to the way things affect you. Tristian, it's all right to be afraid, just like it's all right to cry. That doesn't make you any less a man. In fact, it makes you more of one. It shows you're capable of feeling and that you allow yourself to respond to situations. So don't you ever be ashamed."

"Agnus is right, Tristian. You shouldn't feel cowered to say that. I'm proud you've admitted your thoughts not only to me, but Agnus as well. By relinquishing these feelings you'll make yourself feel better."

"But doesn't it anger you, Jos, to hear my truth? I'm scared, and I shouldn't be."

"Why shouldn't you be?" Agnus challenged.

"He's dead. Aidan's dead."

"That doesn't mean his soul no longer breathes, child. The only difference between you and he is you're composed of physical substance. Aidan's still capable of the things a living person can do. Regarding him being a destructive spirit grants your incentive for being afraid, but don't let him know it."

Tristian turned toward his wife. "You don't despise me for this?"

"Tristian, I married you because I love you. And that goes for every aspect. I'm not ashamed to speak of my fright, and neither should you. Our communication should be an open port and not some sealed channel." Josie put her hand upon her husband's shoulder. "I wish it'd all be over tomorrow, but I can't control that. With you at my side I don't feel alone. Knowing you're there's what makes me feel safe, and I'm content with that."

"I'm relieved to get this off my chest. Jos, thank you. Thank you both for understanding and reassuring me."

"Quite anytime, dear." Agnus smiled. "Now since that's settled, could I persuade you to accompanying me for dinner? The corned beef and cabbage will be ready shortly, and I have home-made soda bread to go with. Might you say you'll both stay?"

"Well." Josie thought. "Wouldn't we be intruding, Agnus? We've probably overstayed our welcome. Certainly you've grown sick of us," she joked.

"Sick of the two of you? Are you out of your mind? No pun intended, but at least with you and Tristian I can relive my youth. So come now, say you'll stay."

"Are you sure we're no bother?" Josie wondered.

"You kidding? Not at all. And if I get tired I can always kick you out. I like to wear a certain pair of shoes if I do that." She grinned.

Tristian laughed. "What if we get hurt?"

"I can always float you on my broom. Don't you worry, ole Dawn Redwood's a steady post. She'd comfortably fit the both of you."

"Do we sue if we fall off? Call it a brooming accident say?"

Agnus made a funny face. "Try telling that one to the judge."

"We'd need a lawyer first."

"Best to call it a simple transportation accident then. So does that mean you'll stay?"

Josie stopped laughing. "Thank you for the invitation. We'd love to. Anything you'd like us to do?"

"Might you be fit to set the table?"

"If those be the duties."

Agnus teased, "They're terribly hard, I know, but you can relax once it's over."

Tristian kidded, "Do your plates weigh fifty pounds?"

"Actually it's the silverware, dear. Don't ask where I got them," she joked back. "This way to the kitchen, please." They proceeded through the corridor. "Forks and knives are in that drawer there, Josette. Tristian, just open that cabinet, dear, and you'll find the plates. Does chilled tea suit you both?"

"Chilled?" Josie responded.

"Straight from the fridge or with ice?"

"Ice would be fine," spoke Josie.

Agnus opened her back door and allowed the breeze entrance. "Oh, me. You's feel that in the air?" she spoke softly.

"What's that?" Tristian pondered.

"My bones tell me it's going to rain come time."

Josie was perplexed. "Your bones?"

"I'm what you'd call a natural forecaster." She laughed aloud.

"I've heard that about people," Tristian added. "What's the cause to reason?"

"Arthritis, I'm shamed to say. Weather conditions make it worse. I love the rain, but, boy, I ache when it does."

"That's not fair. You can't enjoy it."

"Oh, it's all right, son. I've grown used to it. Well, kiddies, I believe dinner's ready. Go on and seat yourselves."

"Not before the host," Josie relayed.

"Don't mind my shuffle then. These old legs are slow."

Josie commented, "Take your time, Agnus, and whatever you do, please not fall."

She joked, "In my wise age I've yet to slip once. Just watch it be now."

"Tristian, be of some help," Josie directed.

"Oh, don't you worry, dear. I can manage. You'll see."

"Like it or not, I'm at your side."

"What a sweetheart you are. Would you be a dear and pull my chair?"

"Of course."

"All right. Here we are. Shall I say a few words?"

Josie relayed, "By all means."

Agnus bowed her head. "Thank you, Lords and Ladies, for blessing our table with this bountiful spread which lies before us. May it bless us to the use of our bodies. Amen."

"Amen," Tristian and Josie responded at once.

"Feel free to eat. Take as much as you want."

"You've overdone yourself, Agnus. It looks delicious."

"Why, thank you, Josette."

"It was most kind that you invited us as your guests."

"It's my honor. What's mine here is yours."

Agnus, Josie, and Tristian conversed while they chatted over dinner. Agnus relished in her husband's memories as she shared their fond stories.

Tristian thought awhile before summoning enough nerve to voice his question. "Mr. O'Toole? When did he pass?"

"It made nine years the fourth of July. And, oh, how I've missed him. Though physically Miles may no longer be here, I talk to him always, knowing he hears and watches over." Agnus caressed her hands. "My, how I've wished to touch him once more. It's the hardest part of losing the one you love. Never being able to see nor touch them again in this lifetime."

Josie's eyes glistened through tears. "Sounds like you were deeply in love."

Agnus shimmered with light. "I knew from the instant I saw him, Miles was my kindred soul. Never before had I felt that way. He was my soul mate, you see, and I was his. Even better, he knew it."

Josie urged, "Tell us more."

"Upon meeting Miles, I felt it instantly. I knew him. I spent the best years of my life with that man."

"How'd the two of you meet?"

"A small fair in town. He was there working a stand when I decided to approach."

Tristian expressed, "Way to go, Agnus,"

"Oh, but I was nervous at first, just as all young girls whose hearts pound fiercely. It wasn't until Miles and me started to talk that I felt ease. After that, we got along as best friends. It was two years later we were married."

"Were you a young bride?"

"Girl-like, Josette, but not too tenderfoot. I was nineteen and my Miles was twenty. His parents once owned the general store in town where Miles worked. When he was twenty-six, his parents gave us their small market. We worked side by side until he fell ill with what we thought was minor strep. At that time he began to get bad. We were later forced to sell the store so I could tend to him. Poor dear, he was sickly challenged eight years thereafter."

"What kind of ailment?"

"He had a bout with rheumatic fever. He fought long and hard until he miraculously pulled through it. Sadly, that damned disease scathed him, mind, body, and heart. His joints were so effected, he had no use. He was coherent most the time, but did babble. Several years after, he suffered a stroke. By that time apoplexy took his entire body.

The Crying House

If paralysis didn't fully get him that first period, it surely got him that second. He survived a little over a month after that."

Josie sighed. "How rough it must have been for you."

"It was, but the toughest of moments encountered him. Each day he got worse until there was nothing left. I hated it so, having to watch my Miles wither away like he did. Rest him now, my darlings, he's in a far better place, no longer hurting with his youth restored. I know we'll be together once more for I know true love never dies."

"I see you loved him dearly."

"And continue with every inch of my being. Miles was my life."

"You stayed strong till the end. You devoted your life to him, and he smiles upon you each day. You both share a bond that'll never be broken," added Josie.

"Such kind words. I appreciate your goodness, dear. I wish you both could have met him. Miles was such a joy to be around."

Tristian spoke softly with his reply. "I'm saddened we never met. What kind of person was he?"

"One of the most humble gents you'd ever meet. He'd do just about anything for anyone. Very sincere and kind." Agnus smiled with meaning. "Truly one in a million, he was. Quite funny, too. And, oh, what a wonderful father he was to our kids. He'd say the silliest things just to make you laugh. Miles had this gleaming sparkle in his eyes when he'd get a bit puckish. If I were ever down, all I needed was to look into those moonlit eyes, and I'd find myself better."

Josie glowed. "He had a special way of perking you."

"That was my Miles. I found happiness in that silly, loving soul. Best of all, he was a good man. I can speak with honesty when saying he'd have liked you both. You're good people. Miles always saw the kindheartedness in everyone. He was a friend to all, and I can say that in truth."

"The two of you had some good times together. Hopefully one day when our incessant lives run out, we can share them, too."

"How splendid that'd be," Agnus expressed as she gathered the dishes. "Won't you dears excuse me a moment while I tidy this table?"

Josie got up from her seat. "Please, Agnus, sit back down. I can tend to these." She took the dishes to the sink.

"Don't mind that. I'll wash them later."

"It's no trouble. Besides, it's the least I could do. You were kind enough to have us."

"Well, I appreciate it much, my dear."

Tristian spoke, "This was one of the best meals I've had in a long time."

"Quite anytime. I enjoy having you. My house doesn't seem so lonesome anymore. I've forgotten how wonderful it is to have someone here."

Josie returned to the table. "That was certainly tasteful, Agnus. The next meal's on me."

"Resting these ole hands for a day don't sound half bad. You've got yourself a deal, child. Tell me, have you eaten enough to feed the baby?"

Josie peered to her stomach. "My little button should be ready for a nap now." She rubbed her belly.

"What do you wish for?"

Josie thought for a moment. "I don't want to be greedy or selfish, so whatever the good Lord allows."

"May I?" Agnus questioned for permission.

"No need to ask. Go right ahead."

Agnus placed her hand upon Josie's stomach. "Hello in there, little button. Might I tell you what a wonderful set of parents you'll have. You'll have your mumsie's eyes and your pappie's toes."

Josie felt movement within her abdomen. "I think the baby likes you."

"I believe so. Isn't that right, little button? Rest now, wee angel, that you may grow into a healthy dumpling."

At a moment's impulse Josie clutched Mrs. O'Toole's hand.

"Agnus, would you come to the birthing?"

"What an honor that'd be. I'm so happy you've asked. Well, I'd be delighted."

"Excellent. Tristian, oh isn't this lovely?"

"Are you sure you can, Agnus?"

"You mean would my age interfere? Maybe suffer congestive heart failure?" She laughed. "Son, I delivered two healthy children sometime ago. As long as it's not me, I think we can do it."

Tristian blushed. "That's fair to say."

The Crying House

Agnus eyed Josie. "When's your delivery? Have you found out, dear?"

"Oh, I don't know. Doctor didn't say."

"Be expecting in January, around the first week to the morn of the eighth day."

"How do you know? Is it something you feel certain?"

"When the time comes, you'll see. You kids care for dessert? I have left over cobbler made yesterday."

"Sounds wonderful, but I'm about to burst. Thank you anyway," Tristian remarked.

"How about I cut some for your way home? You can eat tonight."

"If we're not robbing you, we'd enjoy that."

Agnus opened a cabinet and reached for a plate. Setting it upon the counter, she then removed the cobbler from the shelf in the fridge. Cutting two large sections, she placed them both in the center of the dish, then covered them to wait freshly. "Here we go. Just heat these and, if you want, put a spoonful of butter on top and let it melt."

"How could we ever thank you for all this? You fed us dinner and now you deliver us with dessert."

"It's just an act of kindness, dear. Josette, I'm sure you'd do the same."

"Quite certainly," she expressed. "Is there anything we could do before Tristian and I go?"

"I don't think so, dear. No. Thank you for asking."

"You certain?" Tristian polled.

"I believe so." She smiled at him. "Might I phone you if I have any?"

Tristian snickered. "That'd be just fine."

"All right then." Agnus pulled herself forth and walked Josie and Tristian to the door. Before they left, Agnus gave each of them a hug and wished them good night. "Now, should you need me, I'm here across the street."

"Bless you," said Josie. "We need more people like you in our lives."

Agnus blushed when she smiled. "Looks a wee-some foggy tonight. Better scat home before it rains."

"In that case, have a good one. Come morrow we'll see you."

"Same to you, dears," she stated before closing her door.

CHAPTER TWELVE ◆

The fog thickened, taking to the air like a blanket, while tiny drops of rain fell from the sky. Whirling gusts of wind blew through the night, carrying small leaves along the way.

In the distance Josie heard a sound that caused her to wonder. "You hear that?" she questioned Tristian, who stood still beside her. "Well, did you?"

He looked around. "Something out here, you mean?"

"Of course it was out here."

"Can't say I've heard a thing."

"Well, I don't know what to say. It came from above."

"Probably just the wind, Jos."

"Wait, Tristian. Just stand here and listen."

"Jos, sweetheart, it's late. Can't we go in?"

"Please? Just for a moment."

"Well, all right. What am I to hear?"

"I won't say. It's better you listen."

"I hear nothing, Jos. I'm going inside." Tristian dug into his pocket. "Blasted. I can't find the darn key."

"Try the other side, dear."

"Ah, right you are. I have it here." Within that instant he stopped fiddling with the lock. "Say, what's that? A voice in the sky? Surely not?" Tristian turned around, completely fazed by the sound. "Well, where is she? Do you see?"

Josie stood motionless. "I just hear a faint song."

Tristian ran to the bottom step. "I can't see anyone. Jos. Where is she?"

"Can't say. Maybe within the trees? Could be above."

"Must have climbed. I best help. She'll be hurt if she falls." Running out into the lawn, Tristian screamed. "Miss. Miss." He dashed to the oak. "I've come to get you. Please, ma'am, where are you?"

Josie stood below a branch. "The fog, Tristian. It's too dangerous for this sort of thing. Should I phone the fire department? Have them send help?"

"It'll be okay once I find her."

"She could be far up that tree. Least let me get help."

"Ma'am, I can't see you. Won't you just speak? One word. Say something."

"Tristian, please come down from there," Josie fussed. "We'll phone for help."

"She's quiet, Jos. Nor can I see where she's at."

"All more meaning for you to get down. Now won't you come on before you slip into an accident?"

Tristian inched his way back to the ground. "She must really be up there. I doubt I even came close."

"You can't even see. You had no business in trying."

"She's the one who climbed the tree. Why? I don't know, but it'd be our yard she'd fall in."

"Lower your tone. No need in entertaining the neighbors." Josie's statement was then overcast by the saddened strings of a violin while the singing once again emerged, this time through further projection.

"Josie. Jos, that's not in the tree. It's coming elsewhere along with that song."

"Then who's singing, and where?"

"Don't know, and maybe there's no need we find out. Let's rush on to the house." As Tristian made it toward their steps, he peered in the sky. "I have an eerie sense we're being followed."

"Damn it, Tristian, just open the door." Josie rushed pass her husband and hurried inside. "Did you lock it?"

"What do you suppose is going on out there? Whatever it is, it comes from the sky."

"Tristian, did you lock the door?"

"Aye." He breathed deeply. "But some safety we have inside here."

"Don't start," Josie snapped. "We're fine for now."

"For how long, though? Aidan decides to drop in, Jos, we're screwed. We can't stay in, and we can't go out. We don't know what's there." Tristian's eyes shot to the door. "Christ, those sounds are getting closer."

"Well, what do we do? I don't want to stand here like a scared chicken. Would you rather we hide?"

"There's no sense in hiding."

"But, Tristian, I'm scared."

"Calm down. Help me check the windows." Tristian rushed to the nearest and looked out. "Nothing here. Window's locked. You see anything?"

"Just ripples of lightning, and the rain's coming harder."

"Is the window locked?"

"Tightly."

"Move to the next."

As Josie checked the latch on another window, a developing sight took her by surprise. "My God, Tristian. Come here and look."

Tristian saw an object gliding through the sky. "There's something moving up there. Christ, Jos, is that what I think?"

"The carriage. You see it?"

"But how? How'd it get up there?" Tristian's eyes never blinked. "Unbelievable. How can that be?"

"Tristian, please close the curtains. I don't want to see."

"Move aside. I'm trying to keep my eyes on it."

"Good God, Tristian, what if you're seen?"

"By what?" He ogled through the glass.

"Whatever's up there. You don't want it coming to us."

"Josie, open your curtain. Jos, open your curtain."

She shook her head rapidly to his response.

"There's something there. There's something flickering through the rain."

Josie peeked from behind the curtain, then saw the same dancing lights. "Tristian, they're coming. They're coming here," she muttered. "Close the curtains. We've got to hide."

"This is too unbelievable, Jos. I can't." Stunned, Tristian watched as a row of ghostly candles drifted through the night air, approaching steadily toward the house. Flames skipped through the rain, but never burned out. Tristian attentively gazed forth as the candles then separated into pairs of mounting specters. Floating through fog and rain, they glided to the windows where they hovered before them in mid-air.

Finally taken with unease, Tristian backed away from the sight. "They're at the windows," he whispered softly.

"Why'd you wait the last minute to close these curtains? Why didn't you do it sooner? You should have closed them when I told you."

"Couldn't help it." He sighed. "Just curious, I guess."

"Well, won't you see what they're doing?"

Taking a deep breath, Tristian pulled the curtain back. "They're still here."

"What do you plan to do?"

"What do I plan to do?"

"You're the one who got them here, pulling the curtains and all."

"What do you want me to do? I can't say go away. They're candles, you know?"

"I don't think they plan on leaving, Tristian."

The violin played before their house just the moment his voice broke. "Sadly, I don't think there's anything we can do. They'll have to stay outside the windows."

Josie quivered. "Tristian, someone's here. They're waiting beyond the door."

"Suppose whatever's out there's come for us?"

"Let's not think that. Stay close to me, Tristian. By means this encounter's set me on edge."

Josie screamed as a loud crack of thunder broke the once somber sky, awakening it with a much violent rift. A fuse had suddenly shot, and the lights died to darkness. The house was now submerged in obscurity except for the faint waver of the candles which hovered near windows.

The playing of the violin grew evermore intense as it played its tune of sorrows. Tristian took Josie's hand, then leading her through the living room, quested the darkness for candles. He raised one to Josie as she clutched it tightly in hand. Soon she found her arms trembling, all the while fighting to keep still.

"Ouch," Tristian erupted. "You've spilt wax."

"I didn't mean to. I'm just so scared. I can't stop this shaking."

"You're not quite fit. Why don't you hand me that candle?"

"No. It's mine," she whined. "Please let me keep it."

"Don't you be spilling more wax. And stay clear of the floor. Seat yourself. I'm off to check the window."

"Tristan, no. You get back here. What if something hideous lurks? It'd pull you through."

"No room for worry. I'll be fine. Just a peek I'll spare." He walked carefully to the window and pulled back the curtains. The candles continued to bob as did the luster of their active flames. Tristian ogled all directions, but no signs of the carriage were pierced by his sight.

Josie questioned his inspecting stare. "Dear, is it clear? Are we safe?"

"Nothing but candles as far as I see."

"What?" She ran to the window. "But I saw a carriage. Tristian, I know you did, too. Those candles taking up residence were with it. You know as well as I what we saw. So where's it gone?"

"Jos, I'm not denying seeing it, but looking up now, you can see it's not there."

"I'm sorry to worry, Tristian, but what's there to do? Sit here all night and hope whatever's there doesn't get in?"

"Sweetheart, that's silly. I doubt these candles would hurt us. Jos, look. They're wax tapers. What harm might they bring? They wanted in, they'd be here."

"Fire, Tristian. They could burn our house."

"You suggest I snuff them?"

Josie shook her finger. "I don't want you back out there."

"Then allow them to linger. There's not much we can do."

Josie's anger interrupted her frustration. "Might we just stand here?"

"Sweetheart, calm yourself. You're upset and exhausted. It's best we put you to bed before you bring stress to the baby."

"Forgive me." She nodded, then took her husband's hand.

"Stay close behind." Tristian walked with Josie to the stairs. "Careful here. Watch your step."

Easing slowly, they passed a mirror hanging upon the stairwell wall. Within the corner of Josie's eye she took heed of the obscure image awaiting inside. Then, to make her perception most clear, Josie wavered her candle only to reveal the hideous reflection of Aidan's face. His eyes were jet black. And upon his mouth, his lips crinkled in a rigid grin. The encounter made Josie shrill from shock and horror. Forcing her hand upon Tristian's back, she hurried her husband along the stairs. "Faster. Move faster."

"What's the trouble?"

"Move, Tristian. Let me up these stairs." Josie returned her face to the mirror. "Christ, why won't you leave us?"

"Darling, you've allowed what he wants. Pay him no heed."

The candle which cast upon Aidan's reflection had emitted the sense of an alarming impression. Through her timidity, Josie discharged an enabled assertion. "Go along your way."

But Aidan sniggered at her comply. Then, leaning forth, he surpassed his head through cheval glass. "How bout I whip ye around?" He devilishly chuckled in bane. His foul breath gust upon the rushlight's wick, snuffing the taper of its flare. Josie then screamed in fright, dropping the candle upon the stair. Splatters of heated substance coated the walls and carpeted track. Upon her arms, hands, and wrists Josie felt the molten flush advance to the form of tempered wax. And it was the underside sting which caused the dewy generation to souse in her eyes.

"Jos, don't worry. I'll get you to the bathroom where we'll clean that off."

"Tristian, I can't see where I'm stepping."

"Just ease your pace, and you'll be fine."

"Please tell me you've come to the top." Thereafter, Josie felt the touch of a hand reaching forth and nuzzling her waist. "That's frigid as ice. Tristian, stop."

"What's that you say?"

"Your hand. Take it off. It's freezing my skin."

"What might you mean? My hands are with me."

Tristian's statement force upon Josie's realization that it wasn't her husband who grappled her waist. Aidan's menacing laughter rang within the stairwell, then straight into the darkened hall.

Josie screamed. "Tristian, he won't let go. He's got me."

Provoked by incense, Tristian turned down the stairs. "I don't know where you are. But you get your filthy hands off my wife." Tristian pressed himself against the wall. "Jos, move on up the stairs."

He led his wife into the bathroom and there, surrounding the tub, lit several candles.

"Tristian, I don't feel safe."

"Honey, you should. Sweetheart. Baby, don't you go on worrying. He won't get in. There's a line of salt before the door."

Josie took a seat in a chair while Tristian retrieved a cold rag. "Now this is nice and cool, Jos. It'll make you feel better." He wrapped it around her scraggy arm, then went about peeling the wax from her skin. "There now. How's that feeling?"

Josie peered upon the clumps of flaked wax. "It only hurt when it spilt."

"Well, be blessed you're not in no pain." Tristian returned the rag to cold water. "Here, let's see the other arm. Come now, Jos, give it up."

She sat there still as Tristian viewed the stress in her eyes.

"Sweetheart, what's wrong? Was I too rough on lefty?"

"He was there, Tristian. He was there waiting. He lingered in darkness for us to pass by him."

"Oh, honey, look around. You're okay now."

"But we won't always be." She frowned.

"Cheer up, darling. You'll see. We'll make this work." He snuffed the candles surrounding the tub as the thick cloud of smoke rose into air and encircled their heads. Tristian gazed upon his wife as he returned to her side. "How bout we get you to bed?"

Through the flame of her candle, Josie peered around the smokey room. "We're the safest here. There's no reason we leave."

Tristian cut his eyes to the bath. "I don't know about you, but I'm unsure how well a night in the tub might be."

Josie laughed lightly. "I'd suppose it'd be rough."

Tristian smiled. "Aye. Cold porcelain. A leaky faucet. Not to mention you smothering me. So yes, indeed. I believe that'd be rough."

"We always have the floor."

"If I slept there, by morning I'd be a crippled man."

"What'd I do without your humor? Tristian, you're certain we'd find our room safe?"

"It still stands salted, so that's on our side." Tristian reached forth. "May I take your hand?"

"Well, only since you're certain."

"Have a seat on the bed while I search for your gown." Afterward, he covered his wife with the sheets. "Now might you find that more comfortable than our cold porcelain bath?"

"A certainly welcomed relief." Josie patted the bed. "Won't you climb in?"

"Don't mind if I do."

Josie turned to her side. "Tristian, will you lie awake with me?"

"Of course, dear. We'll sprawl here stilly and be soothed by the rain."

Josie curled into her husband. "Ah." She sighed. "How calming the night."

Tristian spoke softly to her ear. "Just breathe in that air. It'll put you to sleep."

Lightning ignited the night, while gliding fog crept along windows. Time infinitely passed, withstanding the moon and nocturnal creations. Upon the quarter, sprinkling down, the sandman blew his mound of glitter. And from the heaven's receding fall, each gilded flake produced a shimmer.

Much like a snoop who prowls the night, the sandman slipped through an open trestle. Once within, he flurried the faint with sifted sands of sleep's suppression. Shushing minds of mixed reflections, and reposing bodies with calm suggestion. And enfolded in another's arms, the O'Briens imbued the sense of resting.

Two hours later Josie credited the impression of someone forcefully receding her sheets. Opening her eyes Josie viewed Ciara toward the foot of the bed. Before her the room had abruptly changed its discernment. Flowered paper spread over walls, while burgundy carpet raised from the floor. Against one enclosure stood a walnut tall chest in place of a dresser which had been furnished from oak. Upon the lectern set an embellished oil lamp risen to medium flame. Before the screened eyelets dangled opalescent drapes to shield outer sight. And aside from the windows, gracefully poised, was an old Victorian chaise draped with the delicate threads of an interlaced shawl.

With wonderment Josie watched as Ciara tidied the sheets and straightened the wrinkles. Then heedlessly, Ciara turned round, only to be startled by unwelcome shock.

Quietly erected, yet impatient within himself, Aidan stood fixed in his track. Within that moment, beholding the distended sight of Ciara's eyes, his commotion erupted like that of a deranged raver encouraging a brawl.

It was then Aidan's eyes glared as he raged forth in anger. "Ciara, ye never do anything right. Ye always mess things up. Look at the bed. I've told ye before. I want those sheets tucked in and me pillows fluffed. I don't know why I ever married you. Ye can't follow directions. You belong outside like a dog, ye stupid wench." His voice carried through the house.

Josie laid in awe, tapping lightly upon her husband's shoulder. "Tristian. Tristian, wake up," she whispered. "Please, won't you waken?"

"I'm sorry. Please, Aidan. Please stop your yelling," his frightened wife cried.

"Damn it, Tristian. Awaken. Awaken, will you?" Josie spoke lightly, while pinching his side. "Damn you. Wake up. Tristian, wake up. Wake up, I say."

"Aw, what, Jos? What is it?" he muddled.

"Open your eyes."

"Did I tell you to talk? You're pathetic. Look at you. If ye wanted to cry, I'd give ye something to cry about." Aidan put his hands upon Ciara's shoulders and began shaking her violently. Trying to look away, Ciara continued to squall.

Josie choked as she tried to whisper. "Tristian, are you seeing this?"

"Oh yeah. I see."

"Louder, you wench. I want to hear ye scream. Look at me. Damn it. I said look at me." The fear in her eyes excited him more. "Oh, what? Are ye frightened?"

Tears streamed down Ciara's face as she wailed uncontrollably. Aidan violently slammed his frightened wife against a wall, then leaned into her and began laughing. "You're good for nothing. You'd be better off dead, ye God damn bitch," he roared to her face.

"Please, Aidan, stop," she begged of him.

"What is it? Ye can't handle the truth?" He shoved her, and Ciara tumbled in sluggard motion. Catching her by the back of the head, he jerked her toward him.

"You're hurting me," she cried in pain.

Aidan snickered at her remark. "Oh, come now. Ye didn't feel a thing. But know best. I'll make you." Aidan slapped her forcefully upon the jaw, her cheek now stained within the print of his hand.

"Oh, God, Tristian, we have to help her."

"There's nothing we can do. It's all a part of the past."

An unpleasant squawk arose from outside the window, followed by a violent session of lengthened rappings, as though something impatiently awaited entrance.

"By the window," Josie whispered. "Something's there."

The squawking continued as it grew louder and louder.

"Damn raven," Aidan yelled in violent anger. He'd thrown Ciara into the corner of a dresser where she'd fallen limply to the floor. Walking over to the window, Aidan shouted at the bird, "Get out of here, damn you." Aidan threw his hands up to scare the bird away, but the raven just sat there tapping at the glass. Aidan continued to shout, "Go on, shoo." He raised the window as the raven flew to a nearby tree.

Its eyes glowed in the dark like burning flames. Looking in on Aidan, the raven continued to squawk. A heavy fog filled the air, accompanied by a rainy mist, and in the distance Aidan heard a woman singing a mournful song. The haunting melody came from the sky and seemed to float on air. Goosebumps covered Aidan's body as shivers ran down his spine, forcing his hairs to stand tall.

The raven squawked, then took off from the tree limb toward the house. Aidan hurried to close the window as the bird yet again began to rap. "Go away," he shouted. The raven beckoned him, but Aidan backed away. Looking down, Aidan saw Ciara unconscious on the floor. Turning her over, he saw the small scratch upon her forehead encased in a large bump. "Wake up. Damn it. Wake up," Aidan shouted, all the while shaking her repeatedly.

He gazed around the room quickly when spotting the small pearl of blood tainting their dresser. Looking back upon his wife, he saw her head continued to swell. At the window the raven still sat rapping. Fear overtook Aidan as he frightfully stared in its eyes. Alongside, a ghostly candle floated in air with its bright flame piercing in through the window.

Josie wept. "He's killed her."

"Jos, we need to move. He's carrying her here. Hurry, sweetheart. Get up."

Aidan laid Ciara upon the bed, then hurried to the window in desperation. In his promptness to close the curtains, Aidan became horrified by the lingering bird and eerie candle that awaited him. In the midst he heard the haunting melody of a ghostly tune refrained within the saddened aria of a lone violin. Sensing it, Aidan began to shake within his skin. Reaching forth his hands quickly, he tugged back the curtains. He then retreated to the bed where his injured wife reposed in sleep.

Josie and Tristian slid down the wall and sat in the floor, watching.

Ciara was still unconscious, but breathing. Shaken, Aidan balled up within a chair where he sat staring at Ciara until falling asleep.

Josie slid over to the bed to touch Ciara's face, but her hand passed through her. "How sad, seeing you like this." She frowned. "Lacking all nurture and the caress of a hand."

Tristian assured his saddened wife. "She'll soon be away and a part from all this."

"She looks so helpless, though, Tristian. The horror she felt." Josie slid toward the wall, then nestled into her husband's arms. "It was seen in her eyes. How terrible that was. I pray she'll soon find peace from this hell."

A few hours later Aidan awoke. Glancing at his pocket watch, he noticed it was two-twenty. The room seemed quiet and still. Rising from his seat, Aidan walked steadily toward the window. Peering out from behind the security of the curtains, Aidan no longer perceived the bird nor ghostly candle which had once hovered there. He'd taken a quick sigh of relief just before an unknown sighting would catch the full awareness of his wandering eye.

Drifting through the darkened sky, a strange object glided throughout the fog while shifting in and out of perception. As the unseen object grew closer, a rush of unyielding cries emanated through the air. Aidan looked on, horrified by what he was now seeing.

A creepy black carriage sailed through the night sky with its ghostly master, led loyally by a pair of shadowy horses. Two candles floated away from the carriage, lighting the way. Aidan realized it was a death omen, rightfully acknowledged in Irish lore as the banshee. As with all fatalities, she'd been called upon for collection. Her mournful singing sonorously increased as her carriage approached the dead house.

Floored with shock, Aidan fell to his knees in flabbergasted disbelief while attentively watching his wife's resurrection. Ciara's translucent soul pulled slowly from its quiescent body, detaching itself from Ciara's lifeless shell. Sitting poised within the bed, Ciara quietly floated away from the room and into an adjacent hallway. Guided by the banshee's tune, Ciara followed the haunting melody into the stairwell where she was hypnotically lured toward her home's fore door.

Racing to the bedroom window, Aidan rushed to peer out into fog and mist. There he beheld the banshee's carriage in full sight as it patiently awaited Ciara's arrival. Floating through the corridor, out into the dampened lawn, Ciara roamed the sunless night. Awaiting her entrance, the carriage door creaked open like a rusted gate. And from within its murky depths, a frail, aged, hag-like matron dismounted slowly as she descended disclosure.

Standing beneath the blowing rain, her grey cloak blustered against the swaggered winds, unveiling the gothic dress her body was fashioned within. Her clothes were seemingly tarnished like vintage rags through decades of wear while musty odors filled and escaped into the stagnant atmosphere. Her long hair was thick, straight, and silver. Her eyes captured the alabaster nakedness of a blanketed snow. And amongst her hands were elongated nails stretching afar from ossified fingers. Perched atop her left shoulder sat the raven in silent observation.

Extending her right hand, the banshee softly summoned Ciara. "Come, my child. We must go," the banshee had spoken.

Looking up through the window, Ciara grew concerned. "And what shall become of him?" she asked with sincerity.

"He is not your worry. Fate will handle him," the banshee then answered.

Knowing she had nothing to fear, Ciara trustingly took the old woman's hand and climbed through the carriage door.

Josie's eyes grew wide as she watched on. Poking Tristian's side, she softly ejected. "Look, Tristian, look."

Stalled beneath the oak sat Nia. Ciara called forth as she scampered the carriage. And jumping upon Ciara's lap, Nia purred happily, for in that instant she'd been united with her pleasant master.

With a light pull, the door creaked shut; then, rising into the fog, the carriage vanished. Candles that hovered before windows floated away into fog, disappearing along with the haunting melody of the lone violin. Clouded steam remained stagnant around the house, while sprinkling rain continued to shower the sky.

Behind them, within the room, the O'Briens acknowledged the incessant sound of Aidan's voice.

Heavily, Tristian's heart pounded with uncertainty. "Steady, Jos. Turn round with ease," he whispered breathlessly.

She choked, then grasped her husband's hand as they pivoted slowly. Angling toward the bed, they noticed Aidan's back affront to them.

While wailing into an old candlestick phone, Aidan deceitfully emphasized the affliction in his voice. "Dr. Collins? Oh, Dr. Collins. Ciara's had an accident. Ah, God, sir, I think she's dead. I can't bear it. Please, I beg, come quick," he mourn to the phone. Then, hanging the receiver, Aidan ceased from all sight.

CHAPTER THIRTEEN ◆

Day 5, the 10th of July, 1950.

The following morning came carrying forth anxious thoughts of the nightly occurrence. Josie's mind continuously hankered the alarming perceptions of its night-tide suspense. Churning within, simmered an eager announcement actively chasing discharge. Josie's unyielding want of release steered her to the phone, where she dialed Agnus.

"Yes, just last night. Oh, it was horrible. We saw it all ... Yes, you're right. Indeed, he's at fault. Just like you said. She was thrown to a dresser. How pitiful it was ... I certainly agree. He rushed her to an open grave. Ah, Agnus, if you could have been here. That scoundrel had the audacity of telling Ciara's doctor she'd had an accident. How deceitful he was, boasting forth with his lies."

"Josette, sweetness. He's a monstrous imp with immoral mind. Aidan had no longer adhered to that body. He'd been controlled by that rouge beast."

Josie sat in silence, milling over thoughts.

"Dear, are you there?"

"The phouka? Can it be expelled? Even though Aidan's passed. Has he any hope?"

"Well, I don't know, dear. Mmm?" Agnus gave thought. "I suppose it's possible."

"Did he really love her? Agnus, what amount of care had he toward his wife?"

"That's quite inane. No doubt he loved her. I'm sure before I'd made that clear."

"I just need your certainty."

"What's on your mind?" Agnus listened quietly.

"Together, might they ever find peace? Is there no way?"

Agnus sighed. "There is, but it'd be a dangerous matter."

"Is there nothing you could do? Don't you believe, Agnus, they have the right to be united? Aidan just needs a grant of release. To be pulled from the grasp of that creature's possession. If he and Ciara could be together once more, wouldn't you want that?"

"I'd need time to figure things out. It's not just the dealings of an entities grip. Banishing the phouka will be testy. But I'd also have to conjure Aidan from the depths of his casting. It's easy for another to cross in his track. That's where the danger awaits."

"Are you capable to meet the challenge?"

"Honestly, child. I've never embarked an attempt such as this."

"Would it scare you?"

"I'd feel bothered to some extent."

"So you wouldn't attack it?"

"I didn't say that. But I'd need time to master what's intended. I must read and learn before pursuing my encounter. Heed the intelligent. You don't mess with something if you're unsure what you're doing. Of many possibilities, the first potential is endangering yourself. The most imperative rule one should know. Never be in a vulnerable state. At all times the conjurer must be in control."

"Then you can do it?"

"The anniversary of his burial might be the time."

"Any idea how you'd go about this?"

"Well, presumably going to the cemetery where Aidan's been buried could be of some help."

"Do you have any objection?" Josie stressed. "I don't want to force you, Agnus. If you feel you're not in the state to tackle something like this, then I don't want you doing it. I consider your safety above all."

"It's like you've said, though, dear, and I must agree. If it'd bring him and Ciara together, it's worth the try. You were righteous with thought and sincere in your heart with your suggestion. After all the misery that's occupied you, my sweet dear, you have a want to help them. That's unselfish of you and very noble."

The Crying House

"My heart aches for Ciara. It's been my wish to help her. Might Tristian and I offer to take you? I promise you, Agnus, we'll do what we can. I don't want you alone."

"Watch yourself for now, dear. Once Aidan realizes Ciara's no longer there, he'll turn his wrath toward you. Knowing him, and forbearing your warning, he'll strike with full force."

It didn't take long for Josie's reply. "I already know his strengths."

"No, dear, you don't. His rage will empower. Aidan may think you've kept Ciara from him, and he'll resent you for that. His lashing will be ever more greater now that you're the only woman, and his violence will erupt into something you've never seen."

Josie began to worry. "How can I be protected?"

"Prayer, dear. That's the truest protection you'll have from him."

"What about religious paraphernalia?"

"If it comforts you, then by all means. Sweetheart, it doesn't matter if you're with or without. You're a strong woman, Josette. Prove that to Aidan."

Josie sniffled lightly. "I'm weaker than you think. I'll be destroyed."

Agnus assured her calmly, "God lives within the hearts of all good souls. Inside, you'll have his strength. There's your key, and with it, you'll not thwart. An inner light shall guide you. Trust that and rely on faith. Your power lies within."

"Your statement is powering, but will it prove worthy?"

"Only you can speak for that."

"Then keep me in your prayers." Josie sighed. "Tristian just came through the door. I better get breakfast."

"How's my beautiful wife?" Tristian rubbed her belly. "Good morning, button. How's my baby?"

"Sleeping soundly, I should think." Josie smiled. "Good morning, dear."

Tristian peered upon the sausage and eggs. "My stomach has spoken. Best to eat with your mouth and not your eyes."

Josie laughed. "Tell your hunger to polish this. When ready, you'll dine on seconds."

"I better get started," he expressed.

After breakfast Josie escaped to the tub for a refreshing bath. As she relaxed within the water's steamy warmth, an odd noise rose within her room. "I'm in the tub, dear. Tristian?" she called. The air stood silent of reply, so she roused again. "Tristian? Honey, did you hear me?" The noise grew louder. Josie abandoned her soothing waters to nimbly dry her stretch of skin. Opening the door, she peered through the hall. Within the transit stood a vacant pathway. When easing into the ingress, Josie regarded her husband as he outwardly stared through a window. Quietly, she stood within the corridor, studying the room. "Why's there a mess? Were you searching for something?" Leaning forth carefully she grasped the tossed garments that'd been cast to the floor. "Were you recovering your days of wild youth? This room's a sty."

Tristian continued his standpoint without speaking a word.

"Honey, are you ignoring me? I'm talking to you." She reached to touch his shoulder.

He turned his head slowly. Josie then realized the man before her wasn't Tristian. Her saucers widened when she became startled. Staring into her was Aidan's cold, dark eyes. He turned around, clutching Josie tightly, then heaved her toward a wall.

"Damn you, ye meddling wag. What be your right?" Aidan slid Josie down the blockade, swatting her face several times. "Where have ye hidden that wench? Spill it," he shouted. "Don't ye be testing me, lame skirt. I ain't got the patience. Open those scanty folds and speak, ye hapless sap."

Josie broke between tears. "She's moved on."

Angered, Aidan forced his hand upon her throat. "You're deluding the truth, weakling. I smell it in your breath. Ye fess up. Ye do it now."

Josie gasped for air. "It's the truth. I've told you the truth."

Aidan leaned into her. "Ye can't hide Ciara. I'll find that wench wherever she goes."

Josie struggled. "Your wife's gone. I swear. You can't hurt her."

The statement brought Aidan to his boiling point. Grasping Josie's shoulders, he cast her to the air. Across the room she towered in flight, then bottomed down near the door. The mighty impact squandered the breath in her lungs as she fought for an intake. Before her, outside the entry, Josie took notice of the broken salt line resting in disunion. Aidan rushed aside her standing tall, while Josie swiftly strived on scooting forward. Aidan brought his foot down in the crest of her back, weighing her to the floor beneath his burdening load of pressure.

"Ye ain't going nowhere. Lay down your rear," he demanded. Aidan loosened his belt, then removed it from the loops.

Josie stretched forth her arms, digging her nails within the floor. "Tristian," she muttered faintly. "Please help me." But her call went unheard. Reaching behind, she tried to knock Aidan back. "Get off me. Get off." Josie wiggled like an unearthed worm from the dirt. "Bastard. You bastard. Let me loose."

"I could collapse your lungs with the proper placement."

"Damn you. Get off."

"No one would hear your cries. It'd be too sudden and quick."

Much akin to a crock performing a death-roll, Josie endured her strength to flip herself round. She eased through Aidan's clasp and ran for the hall. Though her voice was weak, she attempted to shout.

Aidan sprung behind, catching Josie's hair as he retreated her toward him. "Where is she?" he demanded.

Josie erupted in faint screams.

"That's all ye women are good for. Wail and holler. Come on then. Drive it up a notch."

Josie began to shiver within his arms.

"Ah, what's this now? A frightened jejune? Ye want to quiver to papa? Well, I ain't gonna help you."

"She's dead."

"What's that ye say? Recount your claim a reach louder."

"Your wife."

"Ye think I'm naive? That I'm pure to believe you?"

"She died fifty years ago. So did you. You're dead, Aidan. Look around you."

"Stop this infernal lying." Aidan breached the edge of reserve as he once more broke into rage. As he strike Josie powerfully upon the mouth, her lip split as bright blood surpassed the rip. Aidan breathed deeply. "Then you'll do in her place."

Josie cringed with pain as Aidan clutched her hand. Then bending it back, it emit a loud pop. The rupture caused nausea to stir within the pit of her stomach. Quickly Josie's wrist inflated, following the painful rift of her fracture. Roused by his doings, Aidan expelled a barbaric shrill. And by way of his deeds, never once was his devilish conduct overwrought by her cries. Josie's anguish fostered impious thrill to further excite Aidan's twisted behavior. Pressing upon her ulna, Aidan caused Josie's discomfort to excessively elevate. His impulsive surge reached forth, grabbing hold of Josie's hair, then repeatedly he smashed her face and head to the wall. Blood ran from her nose, tainting that which was once clean and pure. The repetitive corruption continued as each defiled and burst the delicate bones in Josie's face.

A conglomeration of blood scattered the walls, spattered the ceiling and secreted the floor. Further seizing a mass of her hair, Aidan ran Josie's reduced face into the wall, expelling the final blow. Slowly she sank to the floor in defeat while Aidan applied his hands collectively, granting satisfaction to his work. Steadily, he spied upon her through glare. Josie's head was cast aside with her limp in despair and choking on a slew of cardinal spillage. Then, employing his foot upon her chin, he roughly raised Josie atop in perception. "Women, wenches, pigs, or dogs. Ye all be the same. Louts of lesser origin." While reviewing her battered face, Aidan offensively collected an array of phlegm, then discharged it upon her. Turning away, he trotted the hall, disappearing from sight through each step.

Josie laid against the wall in stillness. Her appearance had been disguised beneath bruised, swollen skin. Dried and dampened blood overlaid every inch of feature, concealing the true color of flesh. Within, Josie chuffed through congestion, battling each sigh of restricted breath.

Below, Tristian entered the fore door with an empty mug and folded paper. He proceeded to the staircase, then leaned against the banister. "Sweetheart, you out?" Tristian waited a moment. Door must be shut. He thought. Gathering himself, he paced toward the kitchen. Inside, he set his paper upon the table and the mug in the sink. Glancing at the clock, he noticed the time. "Surely she's not still soaking?" Tristian returned to the stairs and, stepping forth, kidded loudly, "I hope you haven't drowned yourself in that bath. I suppose you've been in…" Reaching the top, Tristian saw his wife slouched motionless at the end of the hallway. "My God." He feared. "Jos." He went rushing down the aisle. In his sight Josie's blood emit brightly. "Josie! Oh, Lord, dear, God. What's happened?" Tristian fell to his knees. "Don't you worry, dear. I'm here." He took her hand. "Sweetheart. Jos. Oh God, no. Josette. Please, sweetheart, come round."

The Crying House

Tristian raised her head only to expose her beaten, blooded face. His eyes were appalled by the amount of gore receding them. Barely was he able to recognize his wife beneath her pelted face. She'd been horribly swollen and deformed from the violent mar of her attack. "How could I have left you alone?" Tristian felt beside himself. Falling into her lap, he cried hysterically. "How shameful am I? How shameful? I knew better. I did. I know it."

Josie's voice broke as she fought to reply. "Tris…"

"Baby, shh. We must get you to the hospital. You stay with me." Tristian bundled her within his arms. "Jos, you stay with me. We'll get help."

Josie's breathing was raspy and shallow, then the uncertain transpired. She had fallen unconscious within the comfort of her husband's arms.

"Josie, no. Baby, no. Don't do this." Tristian's emotions brewed between frantic concern and ignited fury. "Damn you, Aidan. Damn you, I say," Tristian blasted through anger. "Why didn't you mess with someone your own size, you foul up? I would have taken that round, you aberrant devil. Me. Me, I say. You're a blanched coward, that be who you are." Tristian carried his unmindful wife down the stairs. "You're going to be all right, Jos, you hear?" The doorbell tolled as he approached the final step. Quickly giving way to the entrance, Tristian happened upon a fortunate chance. "Agnus, thank God. Please, I need your help."

"Goodness, Tristian. What's happened?"

"I must get her to emergency."

"Josette? Oh, honey, your wife. Twas Aidan, weren't it?"

"Agnus, please, will you come?"

"Dear, of course. No need you ask. Hurry now. Hurry on."

CHAPTER FOURTEEN ◆

Tristian rushed through the emergency doors with Josie lifelessly cradled in arm. "Somebody. Somebody help! My wife. She needs a doctor. She needs someone now," he yelled. "Bloody hell. Don't you fools listen? Fetch her some help."

Agnus rushed to a nurse and called her attention.

"Sir, calm down. Can you tell me what happened?" the attendant questioned.

"She's been beaten. I beg you, do something. Do something, please. I'm urging you."

"I need an open room, girls. Clear me a room."

Another nurse responded, "All rooms are occupied."

"Then get me a gurney stat."

Tristian cried. "Nurse, please, I ask that you help her. She's inattentive, you see?"

"Is this lady your girlfriend?"

"No, she's my wife. Damn it, she needs help now. She's pregnant."

A tall, round man eased aside Tristian. "What's going on here?"

The nurse replied, "We have an emergency, doctor."

"Looks like she's hemorrhaging. Find her a room."

"All rooms are settled."

The doctor checked Josie's vitals. "What's the cause of this woman's condition?"

"Sir, she'd been beaten."

"I've got a second heartbeat. How far along is she?"

Tristian was unglued with fraught. "God, I don't know. Several weeks at most."

"Nurse, take this gurney and get her to x-ray. Here're the orders. Start her on one-thousand milliliters of sodium chloride. I'll be along shortly." The doctor turned to Tristian. "You're her husband, I take?"

"Yes, sir, I am."

"What's your name, son?"

"Tristian. Tristian O'Brien."

"And your wife's?"

"Josie. Josette O'Brien."

"I'm Dr. Kentworth. I'll oversee your wife this morning."

"Sir, will she be all right?"

"I'll let you know shortly, son. Why don't the two of you take a seat for now?"

"I can't be with her? I want to be with my wife."

"I understand that. But right now we're running tests. We don't know the severity of her injuries just yet. I promise, you'll be with her. Just give us time."

"I acknowledge your job. But I'm a mess with worry, doctor. I'm sure you understand."

"Of course, son. Of course. Now I apologize for asking, Mr. O'Brien. But were you present at the time of your wife's beating?"

"No, sir. I was outside our home."

"An intruder then?"

"That'd be best to call him."

"Would you like to file a report? I could set you up with someone."

Tristian turned to Agnus, unknown what to say.

"I believe Mr. O'Brien would like his rest now," she interfered.

Dr. Kentworth was shocked by the reply. "Surely you'd want a report?"

Tristian bowed his head. "I didn't see the attack, sir. I'm vague to what happened." He wiped away tears. "I found Jos lying in blood, and I rushed her here. Never had I seen anyone, in house or on grounds. Yet when I found her, I was certain what happened."

"Had there been an instrument involved?"

"From what I saw? Definitely it'd been the wall." Tristian's face took to more tears. "I don't know how I'll go back there. Smelling that blood and knowing it's hers knots my innards. I'm at shame to go home."

"I could imagine how hard the situation is, son. But I'm sure you'll pull through when ready. As I've said, I'm going to run some tests on your wife. I'll return once I have knowledge. It'll be a few hours, so make sure you both eat."

"Aye. Thank you, doctor."

Agnus gently rubbed upon Tristian's back. "She'll be fine, dear. Josie's strong. She'll pull through this. You'll see," she assured him.

"God, I hope you're right. If you could have seen all her blood, Agnus. I worry. I worry. What if she and our button not make it?"

"Don't speak like that, dear. Look at the brighter side, child. She's in good hands and taken care of."

Tristian peered upon the waiting room. "I couldn't bear being seated here alone, Agnus. I thank you for coming."

"Don't you worry that faint heart. I'm at your side all the way."

Tristian sat alongside Agnus, waiting and wondering on Josie's condition. After an hour and a half, Tristian's nerves became increasingly flustered. He looked upon his watch every five minutes which induced Tristian's troublesome worry. Finally, getting up, he embarked upon pacing the hallway.

"Why hasn't the doctor come? I want to know how she is."

"They're doing their jobs, dear. Have patience. Hospitals are never greased in motion. They're run rather remiss for a reason."

"But I need to know. I need to know Jos and our button appear all right. This standing here, knowing nothing, it ignites my concern. How much longer must we wait?" Tristian returned to his seat aside Agnus. "Surely you'd have thought they'd send someone. Just a word could have eased my tension."

"Soon, dear. We'll know soon."

"This is nonsense. I'm about to go ask."

"You heard the doctor. He said it'd take awhile. Now won't you calm down a bit? Stressing yourself just makes matters worse."

"Awhile or not. I need to know."

"Tristian, they must find everything that's wrong. That's a chore which can't be rushed. Why don't we get you a sandwich? A little food in your belly might be of some help."

"I can't. What if they come while we're gone?"

"We'll tell that good nurse there who you are. That you're waiting for word on your wife. We'll let her know you're taking a moment to go eat. Even the doctor said you'd need food."

"I think his imply was for the both of us."

"I believe you're right. Come along, dear. You need some fuel for your engine."

"Then just something light. We shouldn't be wasting time with this."

"That's rubbish, child. You know you need food. Now tighten your brim and follow old Agnus."

Tristian's hesitance set him back. "I don't feel right leaving."

"Dr. Kentworth won't be here till we're back. Trust my word. Now up, child, up."

"You're quite persistent, aren't you?"

"I could always get a nurse to dope you, set you in one of those speedy chairs, then race you through the halls."

Tristian blushed with laughter. "All right, you've won. But I'd rather walk."

"See? A little humor has brought you round."

CHAPTER FIFTEEN ♦

"So, dear, have you made up your mind?"

"I think I'm ready to order."

"Go on then. I'm still eyeing the smorgasbord. This old hen still can't decide."

Tristian stood in line awaiting Agnus.

The food slinger called out. "Good afternoon, sir, and what might I get you?"

"Could you tell me, how's your pork?"

"Pretty outstanding for a hospital cafeteria, I might add. We have a few bragging rights to suit your ease."

"Fair enough. I'll have the roast pork sandwich on an oven roll, a couple pickle spears, and some fries."

"Excellent choice, sir. Coming right up."

Tristian smiled. "If that gets any larger, it'll have to feed two."

"Oh yes. We make sure our customers get plenty. Here you go. See Fallyn to my left. She'll help you with your beverage."

"I appreciate it, sir. Enjoy your day."

Fallyn smiled. "Good afternoon there. Could I get you a drink?"

"Aye. An iced tea and a wedge of lemon."

"Here you are, sir. You'll find sugar at the end of this line."

"Straws?"

"That, too. You won't miss them."

"Aye. Good to know." Tristian turned round to Agnus. "I'll hunt us a table and be back for your tray."

"Then I wait here, I take it?"

"Only for the being. I won't be long."

Fallyn stood behind the counter. "A drink for you, ma'am?"

"Um, a club soda, dear."

"Here you are. The cashier there will ring you up."

Agnus slid her tray down the aisle. "Excuse me, clerk? Where might I find napkins?"

"Come down a bit farther, ma'am. I'll have you some here."

"Well, isn't that swell? Thank you, young lass."

"You're quite welcome, ma'am. Your fare's been paid. No need for charge."

"Paid?"

"Yes, ma'am. The gentlemen ahead of you covered the expenses."

"Agnus, I found a table."

"Tristian, you little sneak."

He blushed lightly. "I've got your tray. Tag alongside."

"Might I repay you?"

"Repay me for what?" Tristian cackled.

"Well, this lunch, child. It didn't come freely."

"Of course it did. Now tighten your brim and enjoy."

"What you did was quite generous. Thank you, my dear."

"You're most welcome, Agnus. You're helping me out through an awful time. It's the least I could do. Thank you for being here."

"How's that sandwich?"

"Actually, pretty good. The fries are a bit cold, though. What's that you've got?"

"A chicken salad melt. Bacon's a little crispy for my frail ole teeth, but I like it."

"Why don't you take some of that out to be safe?"

"I believe I will. Don't need no sudden accidents befalling me."

"You think Jos is okay, Agnus?"

"I'm quite certain she is. And I believe your little button is, too. Rest assure you."

"I've been a nervous wreck over this."

"I know you have. It's not an easy toll, but you're doing some better."

"I've got to stay strong for them, if not myself."

"It takes time. With traumatic encounters, one shouldn't expect to be of sound mind that instant. It's a gradual process to regain your accord."

"But you think I'm better?"

"You're more at ease, aren't you?"

"I'm not as rattled as I'd been."

"See then? You're more collected now. Let's keep you this way."

"You ready to get back?"

"Once I've finished this bite."

"Would you like another drink, Agnus?"

"I think not. One was enough."

"I'll carry these trays to return, get another tea, then I'll be back."

"In that case I'll meet you outside the cafeteria. That way you won't have to wait."

"Well, all right then. I'll be just a minute."

CHAPTER SIXTEEN ♦

"Well, child, any word?"

"No one's been out. Least that's what the nurse said."

"Well, we'll wait a bit longer then. Won't you sit?"

"This is what frustrates me, Agnus."

"I know, child. I know. Surely we'll know soon."

"I would hope so. It's been two hours." Ten more minutes elapsed. "This is entirely pathetic. Do they not think we worry?"

Dr. Kentworth finally passed through the doors, creeping upon Tristian without warning. "Mr. O'Brien."

"Oh, finally. Thank God," he expressed.

"I apologize for your wait."

"How is she, doctor?"

"Established through review, it's apparent your wife's suffering benightedness resulting in connection to a grade three concussion. Her brain has been irritated by way of repeated vibrations which had caused the cerebrum incessant shaking within the skull. That initiated an interruption in the brain's function. We did a bisected neurological exam to check her eyes for opening and movement. No speech exam was contributed. Your wife has no voice response, and she's aloof to vocal command. Further exam affirmed a depressed skull fracture along the frontal bone. We collected samples of discharged extract from her nostrils and ran tests. Our lab concluded the detection of blood and cerebrospinal fluid."

"Wait a minute, doctor. This is a lot to take." Tristian breathed deeply. "Let me make sure I understand what's been said. You confirmed

Josie having a concussion, and following your take, she's still not alert?" Tristan tried to remain sane as possible.

"I'm sorry, son."

"What of this fracture? You mentioned a fluid leak? Is this something you could control or correct?"

"The flow of cerebrospinal fluid could be based on two things. The amount of trauma to her brain, along with the depressed fracture, may have caused it. There's a chance I believe she's ailing from what's known as a subdural hematoma."

"A subral hetoma?"

"Subdural hematoma. It's a broken blood vessel within the brain. The result is a collection of clotted blood upon the tissue. With this type of hematoma, blood gathers between an area of the cerebrum known as the dura and the arachnoid. The accumulation of blood is generated from tears in the veins which crosses that which is referred to as the subdural space."

"What can be done to correct this?" Tristian choked. "Will this dilemma result in death?"

"Because of the amount of swelling, we've made a small cranio incision upon her head. Placing a small tube within the dissection, we've been able to reduce an extent of her pressure. As for treatment of the subdural hematoma, our only qualification would be further surgery."

"Do whatever you can. I just want her well."

"There's also a significant amount of bruising upon her brain. After Josie's surgery, for her best interest, that is, I attest she be induced to a coma. We don't want the possibility of your wife waking shortly after her operation. Do I have your agreement?"

"What about our baby? For Christ's sake, you've been refrained to its condition."

"I apologize for my delay, but I calmly guarantee, your child's in good health. We'll keep its condition closely monitored should any developments arise. We won't give Josie any medications that might affect the well being of your child. To that I assure you."

"And what be the involvement to this procedure?"

"It'd be a craniotomy we'd perform. The engagement would be the opening of her skull, then coursing into the dura to suction the clot."

"You're certain it'll work, doctor?"

"I'm sure the operation will be of success. We have a professionally trained staff capable of adequate conduct. After surgery, Josie might experience additional swelling. That's why it's best she be placed into an induced coma. The lack of motion on her behalf would prove just to her recovery. And she'd not need to worry about pain."

"Well, if that's the most humane way, I say we ought to do it."

"Some minor injuries also inflicted your wife as well, Mr. O'Brien. We found a fracture upon her wrist and were able to set that. In addition, Josie acquired a nasal fracture during her struggle. We've packed her with gauze to control the bleeding. She received several sutures upon her lip to correct the breach. Other than that, she appears to be in stable condition." Dr. Kentworth patted Tristian's arm. "I know it's been long on you, son, so I hope those final words find you well."

"She's really all right?"

"As a husband like you, I give you my word."

Tristian breathed with further ease. "That's the best thing I've heard all day."

Agnus emerged through silence as Tristian took a moment to collect. "When might this operation take place, Dr. Kentworth?"

"Soon as I get Mr. O'Brien to sign these papers. After that I'll proceed to OR, talk to the anesthesiologist, then prep the supplies."

"Will it just be you overseeing this procedure?"

"No, ma'am. Myself and another doctor." Dr. Kentworth turned to Tristian. "Here're the papers. I just need you to sign here, then here."

Tristian jotted his name. "How long will this take?"

"I can only give you an idea. Operation time will be based on the severity of her affliction. General cases could take to two hours. Further circumstances can lead up to twelve."

"So anywhere from two to twelve hours?"

"It's a fair estimate."

"And you're sure our child will be safe?"

"You have no need to worry. We'll send someone out to keep you aware of your wife's physical wellness."

"Okay."

"Do you have any questions?"

"Not on hand."

"All right then. The two of you follow me. I'll take you to another waiting room where you'll stay for the remaining time."

CHAPTER SEVENTEEN ◆

Two hours passed as Tristian and Agnus sat waiting.
"How about another coffee, child?"
"I've had two already. Maybe another after while," Tristian responded.
"Well, I'm going to get another. Might you like some juice?"
"No, I don't believe so."
"Suit yourself." Agnus walked to the beverage station and poured another cup.
An older man stood alongside her. "Here, ma'am. I'll get that for you."
"Well, thank you, sir."
"My pleasure." He smiled. "Where would we be without coffee? It keeps us awake during these long hours."
"I'll be taking in my third. How bout yourself?"
"I'll be starting my fifth. Come these hours, that's all I do."
"Waiting rooms are rather long for sitting."
"That's the part I hate most. I'm Coyle, by the way."
"Nice to meet you. I'm Agnus."
"Ah, the pure and holy one."
Agnus smiled. "Only by name."
"Well, I believe it suits you. I'd seen you sitting with your son there. You must be waiting on your husband?"
"Oh, that young lad's my neighbor. His wife's in surgery."
"I'm terribly sorry. I hope she'll do well. I'm waiting on my wife,

The Crying House

too, so I know how he feels. Watch these hours transpire as we pray for good news."

"I don't mean to be meddling. Do you mind I ask what's your wife's having done?"

"Doctor's repairing a leaky valve. Said she'd do fine, but, of course, I worry."

"You poor, dear. You here alone?"

"For the moment. My daughter should be here shortly."

Agnus patted his shoulder. "I know these waits are hard. Tristian and I are the same with you. Continuing this pause."

"And long ones they are."

"That's why there's coffee."

Coyle pointed toward Tristian. "What's the boy's wife in for?"

"Brain surgery. The sweet youngster has a clot."

Coyle gazed upon Tristian with sorrow. "So young they are. It's terrible for a fledgling of that age."

"Josette's a strong one, though. I'm sure she'll be well."

"Please know she'll be in my prayers."

"Bless you, deary."

"Well, ma'am, I see my daughter coming in."

"And I should be returning to Tristian."

Coyle smiled. "I've enjoyed our chat, Agnus."

"I as well, dear. I wish you the best for your wife." Agnus meandered back to her seat. "You dozing there, child?"

"Just a little." He yawned. "One of the doctors was here. Jos and the baby are doing fine. Said she should be in recovery by another half hour."

"Splendid news. I knew she'd be fine." Agnus gave Tristian a hug. "Your wait's almost over, then you can see her."

CHAPTER EIGHTEEN ◆

"I have good news, Mr. O'Brien. Your wife's made it through surgery. The clot was cleanly removed by suction. She still has a small cranio tube inserted to release any pressure built upon her brain. She's now in recovery. We've given her an anti-seizure medication and something for swelling. She's sleeping soundly. We'll be giving her some barbiturate sometime within the hour to induce her coma. We'll keep her monitored closely for an hour after, then you'll be received to come see her."

"Will she be all right with the medications?"

"That's why we're going to monitor her for this while to make sure everything remains under control."

"What about food, Dr. Kentworth? If my wife's in a coma, then how might she eat?"

"I'm glad you asked. Tomorrow we're going to start her on total parenteral nutrition, or TPN. This will be added as an intravenous drip. This solution will ensure your wife and child receive sustenance to maintain physical nourishment."

"That'll take care of the both of them?"

"Sounds strange, I know. But the medical field has come a long way since the twenties. The TPN will allow a suppliance of nutrition into your wife's blood. And your child will receive that same nutrition through the umbilical cord."

"Well, that brings me more ease knowing so."

"I hoped it might. I'll be returning to her side now. Myself or another doctor will acquire you when ready."

"Thank you, doctor."

CHAPTER NINETEEN ◆

Agnus and Tristian stood round Josie's bed as Tristian whispered, "I don't feel grateful seeing her like this. She looks disabled and helpless there. Those wrappings upon Jos make her resemble a partly swathed mummy. I can't bear it." He frowned.

"I know this image you see's a disheartening sight. But be thankful she rests peacefully, child, and unknown to her strife." Agnus patted Tristian's face. "Have relief she extends breath, and be appreciative of her life. For those two things you should find praise and be grateful."

"I am, Agnus. I just don't like viewing this aftermath of her trial. It brings my heart to pain." Tristian stood away from the bed. "Josie's always been in good health. How quickly Aidan changed it." He sighed. "This has been the hardest day in all my life." Tristian peered up as he saw Dr. Kentworth. "How long must she stay like this, sir?"

"About five to seven days, depending on improvement."

"You're certain she'll come round?"

"Most of them do."

"How is she now?"

"In stable condition. We're monitoring your wife on a constant basis. Vitals seem good, and her oxygen intake's ninety-two percent. We'll transfer Josie to ICU soon as we have an available space."

"How much longer might she remain here?"

"Probably another hour or two."

Tristian peered at his watch and noticed it was late evening. "We haven't had much to eat since lunch. I guess Agnus and I could grab something quickly."

"Certainly, son. No need to worry about anything here. As her doctor I'll be examining Josie in quarter spans to maintain updates."

"We shouldn't be long. We'll hurry back shortly."

CHAPTER TWENTY ◆

Tristian stood before the counter in the cafeteria. "Everything looks like it's been picked over. There's not much to go on."

"Dagda's is a pub grub a little ways. It's not far from here. Maybe a five-minute stride."

"You fit to walk?"

"As long as these ole legs still work, I'm fit to try."

"All right then. Let's find this place."

Agnus paced slowly beside Tristian as they exited the hospital. "Turn right here and continue straight along the path."

"You been to this place?"

"It's been awhile. Once a week Miles and I would go for a meal and a pint of crisp ale."

Tristian expressed with daunted amazement, "You drink?"

"I may be an old gal, but I still like my brew of suds and spirits."

"You're such a etiquette type, it seems. Befitting and proper. I wouldn't have figured you had the likes for such places."

She laughed lightly. "As you've learned, my secrecy reveals."

"I'm impressed to agree."

"Here we are, dear. This is the place. Good ole Dagda's."

Trisitan held the door. "After you."

Agnus traipsed through the aisle. "Just as I remembered. Happy faces, pints of beer, and that praiseworthy whiff of pub grubbing food." Agnus stopped in her tracks and pointed out. "That was our table there. Miles and I had a many great meals at that booth. And we'd dance away as the night grew longer. I can almost see us. My how lovely it is to be here once more."

"Your face is aglow and beaming with light." Tristian smiled. "It's a nice thing to see. These memories you have of you and Miles. How quickly you've revived that knowledge."

"We enjoyed our time here. The fondest of moments were shared in this place."

"Limber limbs?" a man shouted. "Well, spot me a shot and tell me I'm lying! I don't believe me bloody eyes. Is it true?"

Agnus cackled. "Digby, you ole coot. You still running strong?"

He came out from behind the counter. "Come along here and let me see you! It's been ages, I bet."

"Several years, for sure."

"And you're just as pretty as the last time I saw you. I be darn, Agnus. Cuddle to ole Digby and give him a hug! Where've you been? You stopped coming to see me."

"I'm at home most the time. Stiff joints and old bones became my pity."

"Let me have another look at you." Digby smiled. "I still can't believe it. Wait on here a minute." He quickly paced to the counter, shouting, "Ashlynn. Ashlynn, pull yourself from that sweltry cook's room and come here."

"What be with your shouting, Dig? I'm trying to run a kitchen."

"Woman, pull yourself away and come here."

"I'm coming. I'm coming." Ashlynn came into the bar wiping her hands upon her apron. "This better be important, Dig. I've got several orders to fix with little time."

"Look who's come see us. It's ole limber limbs herself."

"Well, I be. Is that really you, Agnus?"

"How's my favorite cook? Still governing the kitchen, I see?"

Ashlynn joked, "Best I be the chief to that griddle and stove. I think you might know ole Digby's not fit to master my kitchen. My, oh, my, how have you been, old friend?"

"Fair to aging."

"Well, you look good. Then again, I can't say you never did. How are things at home? You managing all right?"

"I've come along. Took time to settle, though, and adapt to lone living."

"Digby and I always wondered why you stopped coming. Thought maybe my food had decreased to your taste."

"Hardly. I've missed coming here, and that be the fact."

"So who's this young lad tagging alongside you?"

"Goodness, I'm sorry," Agnus apologized. "Ashlynn, Digby, this is my neighbor, Tristian. I'm sorry, child, I should have introduced you sooner."

"I hope you've both come hungry, because I won't let either of you leave till you eat," Ashlynn responded.

Agnus blushed. "Well, you best get to cooking."

"In that case, what can I get you and Tristian?"

"Well, you know I've always fancied that sheppard's pie you fix."

"Then that's what I'll make you. How about you, dear? Have you eyed anything on the menu you might like?"

Tristian replied, "I'm thinking the Celtic stew possibly."

"I'll whip you up a hearty bowl. Might you both care for an appetizer? Maybe a hummus platter with fresh vegetables to get you started?"

"That'd be good."

"All right. I'll have that up shortly."

"We'll have a seat now," Agnus mentioned.

"A pint of ale for each of you?" Digby questioned.

"Certainly, dear. If that's fine with Tristian."

He easily nodded. "You care to lounge in your old booth?"

Agnus smiled. "I'd be honored you joining me."

Tristian took Agnus's arm in his as they walked to the table. "Ladies first."

"My, this brings back memories. Such a wonderful feeling to be here again, and in this booth, mind you."

Digby came with drinks. "Two pints of cold ale right from the tap. Here you are. I see I've got customers, but I'll be back."

"Take your time, Digby. We've still got to eat."

"Well, in that case you're glued to your seat. I'll be back shortly, folks."

Tristian teased, "I think that Digby's sweet on you, Agnus."

"He's a good person, that man. Used to lend a hand at the store stocking shelves. After locking up, Miles and he would sit at the stoop eating pickles they fished from the barrel."

"You've known him quite awhile?"

"A long time indeed."

"Ashlynn? Is she his wife?"

"She sure is. That good dear always said they were wed for her cooking."

"She's something, huh?"

"You'll be in for a treat."

"Okay, I've got to ask."

"I'm sure I'll have an answer."

"Limber limbs? Is that a byname?"

"Here it was more a stage name." She cackled. "My famous pub sweeps had led to a title," she explained. "Limber limbs they called me for my elastic legs and nimble stir." Agnus patted her knees. "Who'd have figured walking the way I do? Seems like centuries ago."

"Sounds like you really knew how to entertain a crowd."

"It was just for fun, but yes, it pulled in attention."

"Could your husband dance?"

"Oh yes. Miles was snappy feet. You put the two of us together, and we were a dancing plague. Boy, did we spread the spell like a fevered disease."

Ashlynn stretched forth to the table. "I've got your platter here. All these vegetables were picked from my garden. Nice and crunchy and bursting with flavor. I hope you enjoy. Your meals should be up in a bit. Oh, nearly forgot. Here are some plates for you two."

"This will be a nice snack." Agnus beamed.

"She loaded us up here, didn't she?"

"Just you wait. Would you mind passing the salt?"

"Of course. So you were saying Digby had been of some help to you and your husband? Did he have this pub at the time?"

"He sure did. Ran the night shifts here after leaving the store. I'm surprised he and Ashlynn still run it. Then again, Dagda's always been a popular place for food and drink."

"Sounds like they've had this place a long time."

"This pub's seen a few decades come and go under their ownership. They must still be in good health to keep up with this place."

"How old's your friend Digby?"

"Surely he must be in his mid seventies by now. But evermore he's going strong. Any good eye could see that."

The Crying House

"It's a nice pub he has here. Not one of those rowdy places for drunkards and such."

"Dagda's is a jollity stead. Not meant for tumults or brawls. Everyone pretty much knows another. You'd get broods together, and they'd play a collection of folk tunes. I've seen a lot of talent come through these doors."

"You've had some joyous times here, haven't you?"

"The best. It's a good place to be whether you're young or old."

"Aye. I'm glad you mentioned this place. I'm certainly liking it."

Agnus patted his hand. "I hoped that you would."

Across the way, a group of men broke into song.

Ole Calder was an Irishmen who lived upon the sea, he had a clash with a feuding crab he lost inside the deep. Scarce fury spread to storming rage, of course he felt the heat. So damn that crab, he dubbed Strachan, one day you won't go free. Time had passed and the sun had raised along the beryl sheet, ole Calder cast his crabbing net into the ocean deep. When he pulled mesh upon his boat he saw his enemy, and with blissful roar he cheered his glee, to the pot ye steep and cease.

One man screamed lively, "All right, men, let's say it!"

The group sprightly diffused while slushing their pints. "Now Strachan's ours to eat!"

Agnus and Tristian applauded as Agnus raved with homage. "I give a big hand to you, gents. That was sheer excellence."

"Thank you, ma'am." They all ejected.

"We're glad to have thrilled you," one claimed.

"Oh yes. I enjoyed every bit."

"Then we'll ravage our food and break you another!"

"Please do, men. I'd adore to hear more."

"Aye," Tristian divulged. "You have my plaudit."

"Make headway, men. Make headway. Ole Ashlynn's coming through. Hot food. Hot food."

"How bout you bring that to me, Lynn? Ole Caleb here could use that feed." The man laughed.

Ashlynn quickly responded, "Why don't you tuck in that belly? That pregnant plump's had plenty to eat."

"Aye, but one more round should kill the plead."

"One more fare and you'd find yourself sick."

He joked, "Then I'll make my way to the comfort station carrying me plate in hand."

"You're a daft one for sure, Cal. Settle yourself, and I'll be alongside you." She approached the booth seating Agnus and Tristian. "Sorry bout the wait, dears. That ole Caleb and his restless trap. Well, that loon could scoff and jabber more than any man."

Agnus joked innocently, "Well, he's your brother, dear. Maybe it runs in the family?"

"Heavens, don't you get me started with that."

"How old's he now?"

Ashlynn turned round. "Cal, what are you? Fifty-six?"

"Aye. But I'd rather be thirty-six. Least then I'd have me looks and vigor. Say, who's that you're serving up?"

"Just an old friend, Cal. Get back to your drink." Ashlynn bent over the table. "He's a bit sloshed. Didn't figure you'd want him over. I better fix some feed to sober him up. The ole nitwit's been conked at the counter."

"No wonder I hadn't seen him," Agnus mentioned.

"Well, you ain't missing much." She raised her brow. "Enjoy your meals."

"Quite certainly. This looks exceptional."

Ashlynn turned to Tristian. "Careful with that stew, dear. It's festered with heat."

"Aye, ma'am. That's plenty steam. I'll let it cool."

"Dig," Ashlynn shouted. "Digby, get over here and top their drinks. They're running low."

"Another round coming up."

Agnus looked upon Tristian. "My, how I've missed her sheppard's pie. To savor that first bite just melts in your mouth."

"I can definitely tell by your eyes that it's good."

"Dig in if you'd care for a try. I don't mind it, dear."

"Here we are, folks. Two more pints of ale for you both. Enjoy your food now."

"Oh, we will, Digby. Thank you."

"I'll let you alone to eat. Might you need anything, best you let me know. Don't fret to holler."

Tristian's stew finally cooled enough. He ladled his spoon to a

The Crying House

hearty portion of mutton, carrots, onions, potatoes, and parsley while Agnus watched.

"Tell me what you think," she added. "I'm sure to believe you'd like it."

The first bite surpassed his mouth, soaring Tristian into the splendid tastes of savory pleasure. "This is incredible." His face alighted. "Simply agreeable to every flavor. It's rich, hearty, and well seasoned. I must add, Ashlynn's achieved further success than any. She's won me over," he gratefully expressed.

Agnus snickered. "I told you she could cook. She's the best of any, she is. Always knew how to assemble her kitchen. Why, she could even turn any scrap to a meal. She's got a knack, that girl."

"The secret's out. I'll start coming routinely. Had I known this place existed, I'd have frequented sooner."

"Sounds like ole Agnus's unsung taproom has rubbed off."

"That be a fact."

"I'm pleased. I see nothing's holding you back on that stew. It's good to see a man enjoy his food."

Tristian confessed, "Candidly, I'd eat anything. But when it's something superb as this, I take pleasure."

"Indeed you do." Agnus cackled. "Indeed you do." She acquired the last bites of her pie, then leaned back to her seat. "That certainly has me swelling. If I wasn't so old, I'd believe I were pregnant."

Agnus's humorous utterance caused Tristian to rattle in laughter. "That was quite curving of you. I didn't expect you'd say that. All in all, you're a gaiety delight. You don't care your age. You just say what you want."

"Bless me the freedom. I've surpassed eight decades, you know?"

"And you're lively at that."

Ashlynn weaseled to the booth. "And how're we doing here?"

Tristian was the first to announce, "That was the best stew I ever offered my mouth."

"I'm happy to hear that. Come again, and I'll make you more."

"The child couldn't quit rattling on about your flair." Agnus hailed. "You should have heard him."

"I welcome the praise of any new patron." Ashlynn smiled at Agnus. "And the followers as well. How was that pie?"

"I think you know."

"Could I take your plates now?"
Tristian piled them together. "Absolutely."
"You two in the mood for dessert?"
"We might have to come back later for that."
"Of course, Agnus. There's plenty of time. You both come when you're ready." Ashlynn heard the bell upon the bar's door clangor. "Will you look there, Agnus? Look who's come in."
She took a second. "That isn't who I think?"
Tristian turned round in his seat and peered upon the lone man who was shuffling the aisle.
Ashlynn acknowledged, "It's been more than a decade since he's passed through those doors."
"It is who I think!"
"Kieran Kirkaldy, of course. Your eyes don't lack truth."
"Well, I be. Never had I thought of encountering him again."
Tristian pondered, "Has that man caused you trouble?"
Agnus leaned forth and whispered lightly, "That man you see's Ciara Ann O'Neill's brother."
Tristian was floored with awe. "You're joking me?"
"I kid you not. He's right there in flesh."
"This is incredible. I must talk to him."
"The time, dear. We're running behind."
"But I must. Damn it."
"We've been here come near an hour, child."
Ashlynn interrupted, "Must you be off?"
"I'm afraid so. We have business at the hospital."
Ashlynn set each hand at a hip. "Agnus, why didn't you tell me? You're ill and not saying?"
"Not me, dear. Tristian's wife."
"Oh, sweetheart, I'm so sorry. And here I thought you've both come for a visit."
Agnus assured her, "We did, dear, but we had to eat."
"Don't you worry. I understand." Ashlynn turned to Tristian. "I hope your wife gets well, dear. I'm sorry to hear your news."
"Aye." He nodded. "I honor your concern."
Within that time Kieran hiked to the table. He patted Ashlynn's shoulder as she turned around. "How you been, Lynn? Digby said I'd find you here."

"Well, it's been a long time since I've seen your face. It's good to see you."

"Same here. Still making business, I see."

"Same steady crew." She smiled. "We're open as long as there's customers, come rain or shine."

"How generous of you. Well, I just dropped here to say hi. Don't want to interrupt you and these folks. I'll be heading to the bar now."

"Surely you remember the face at this table?"

"Who? This young lad?" Kieran studied Tristian. "Can't say I've ever seen him."

"Not him."

"Then that lady there?"

Ashlyn nodded. "You should know."

"Is that right? Let me have a good look at her." Kieran peered upon Agnus. "A pretty lass, isn't she? Only one woman could age with beauty like hers. That must be Agnus."

"How've you been, Kieran?"

"My God," he expressed. "Come here you and give me a hug."

"You've grown old. But my, how handsome you've become."

"I can't believe I recognized you. After all these years."

"Twenty-one at most. That's a long enough time."

"I say it is. You still living in town?"

"As always. Yourself?"

"I stay two cities over. Been there since my last move. Hadn't come to Roscrea for some years. Figured today I'd give it a drive."

"You hitting up the old haunts?"

"I'm making my way. Thought maybe I'd pass that old house of Ciara's. Take in a glimpse, then say goodbye. You and Miles still across the street?"

"Just myself."

Kieran's face drooped. "He in a nursing home?"

"No, dear. He rests not far from your sister."

"I'm terribly sorry. Your husband was a good man, I recall."

"As good as any."

"I'd like to catch up. Maybe over tea, if you wouldn't mind a visit?"

"I'd be accosted to your company. It'd certainly be a pleasure."

"I agree. I'm glad you accepted. I know there's much to talk about."

"Kieran, I'd like you to meet someone. This here's Tristian."

"Hi there." Kieran extended his hand. "It's a cheer to meet you."

"Likewise, sir. Actually, it's a miracle you've come in today. I believe this encounter was chance."

Baffled with speculation, Kieran tweaked his head to the side. "Have we met?"

"No, sir. But I'm familiar with you and your family."

"That can't be, son. Most of them are gone from this world. I'm the only survivor."

Agnus interrupted, "Keiran, might you have a seat a moment? I have something to tell you."

"What's going on? I'm afraid I don't apprehend." He peered up to Tristian. "How is it you know me?"

"It's not personal. But I know who you are."

"Tristian occupies Ciara and Aidan's house," Agnus straightforwardly stated.

"That so? Well, I hope you're a better man than that Aidan."

"Tristian's heard of you through me," Agnus claimed.

"Why's that? Am I of some importance?"

"Kieran, you were Ciara's brother. From living in that house, Tristian knows of the stories. He'd like to talk to you when we have more time."

"What happened there was long ago. I'd like to forget Aidan. I keep my sister's memories, but his I could do without."

Tristian nodded. "If you'd consider, I'd really like to speak with you. Think about it, please."

Kieran took heed. "You sound desperate."

Breathing deeply, Tristian replied. "If you regard my plea, you'll find out why I am."

"I'd like to say, what happened in that house, I've made attempts to forget. Figured it was best to stray from the pain and hate of that place. I've been consumed for so long. Though he's dead, my eternal despise was burying me. My hate burdened my life. Twas then I knew to forget about him. I haven't heard his name mentioned in a mere forty years. But now I've met you."

"All I'm asking for's consideration. Just think about what I've said. If not, I won't taunt you. Either way, you have my respect, sir. I apologize, but we must be going."

"You're leaving, too, Agnus?"

"You know where I live. I uphold you to that visit, Mr. Kirkaldy, so I'm expecting you by."

"One day soon. I promise."

"I'll be seeing you, I hope. Take care of yourself till then."

Tristian peered around the table. "Ashlynn never gave us the bill."

"Then we'll take a trip to the counter."

Tristian stood. "It was nice meeting you, Mr. Kirkaldy."

"Mind you, get Agnus home safely."

"Digby, we're missing our bill."

"What's that, Agnus?"

"Our bill, dear. We don't have it."

"Well, it's on the house, that's why."

"Digby, you sure? I have some money here."

"Put it away. You know that's no good. All I hope's that you enjoyed your feast, and we'll leave it at that."

"At least take this tip."

"For you, I'll do that. But it's really not necessary."

"Oh, just take it, you ole coot."

"Never could I argue with you. Okay, give it here."

Agnus smiled. "That's much better, dear."

"Well, I don't want to upset you."

"What's going on?" Tristian pondered.

"Digby wavered our fee."

"He did? Well, thank you."

"No problem. Come back and see us. We'd enjoy you again."

"With a spread like that, I guarantee I'll be. My hat's off to the cook."

"Agnus, you, too. Come back and see us. None of that wait between years. I won't have it. So you best give me your word, ole limber limbs."

"Might you be driving a bargain there, Digby?"

"We could launch a full pledge. A little spit to the hand, a gentle shake, and say it's on."

"That be the pub way, but rather than that, I give you my word."

"Fair enough." He laughed. "You folks take care."

CHAPTER TWENTY-ONE ◆

"Come along, Mr. O'Brien. Your wife's being wheeled to the preserve," Dr. Kentworth had stated.
"She's still going to ICU?"
"Correct. We merely had to wait for an opening. The ward tends to stay full. Luckily for her, a patient was moved."
"Are we both allowed in to see her?"
"Yes, of course. But admittance allows only two visitors a time. Here we are. Visitation ends at eight, so you'll only have fifteen minutes."
Tristian shook his head. "I can't stay all night?"
"You'll have to return come morning. My last review concluded Josie's still stable. I won't lie to you, Mr. O'Brien. Cases like this are delicate. At times, situations change even if there's no warning. It could go either way. I just want to prepare you for that, should it happen."
"Should I be worried?"
"Well, her condition's fair as of this moment. You can rest to that. But you'll be acknowledged should her status shift."
"I understand. Thank you, doctor."
"Josie's in bed six. I'll be on call if there's any change in her condition."
"I appreciate it, doctor."
"If I don't see either of you again, for sure I'll see you come morrow. You folks get some rest and have a good night."
Tristian and Agnus stood aside Josie's bed. Her diminutive stature made her petite beneath covers. Tears filled Tristian's eyes as he looked upon his beloved wife. Holding her limp hand, he began to pray. "I

hate she can't talk to us," he stated to Agnus as she came behind him, placing her hand at his shoulder.

"You know now this is for the best, dear."

"I do. It's just so hard, though," he explained. "What was wrong with me? I left her alone. I thought she'd be safe. How'd it go wrong?"

"It was something that happened. Sweetheart, you didn't know it would. Unexpected events are apart of life. We can't change that."

"I feel at fault. The time she needed me most, I wasn't there. This was the second time I've failed her, Agnus. What's wrong with me?"

"Absolutely nothing. You're forcing the blame upon yourself."

"I am. It's the only truth I accept."

"Then we need to work on that."

"It won't change me."

"Give yourself time."

Tristian brushed upon his wife's arm. "Agnus and I are here, sweetheart. Every day we'll watch over you till you wake."

Agnus whispered softly, "The good angels will attend you and bring comfort as you sleep. When you awake, Tristian and I will be right here. Know we love you and retain you in prayers."

A nurse traipsed to Josie's bed. "How're you folks tonight?"

Tristian responded, "I'm sure we've seen better days."

"I need to check her temperature and pulse."

Tristian and Agnus stepped aside of her way.

"I know this is a hard time for you both. But if it comforts you, I see she's doing well. Might I add her doctors supplied remarkable care."

"Thank you, miss. That means a lot."

She smiled at Tristian, then went about with her work.

Agnus checked the time. "Tristian, why don't you stay at my house till your wife's well enough? There's no need for you to be alone in yours."

"That's very nice, Agnus."

"I take it you'll stay?"

"Yes. Yes, I will. And if there's anything I can do in turn, don't hesitate on asking."

Agnus patted his face. "You'll be my guest, dear. I'll make sure you're taken care of."

"That's polite of you. Well, I see our time's about up. I guess we need to be going." Tristian walked to Josie's bed. Kissing her atop the head, he whispered, "We'll be back tomorrow, love. I'll call later to check on you. Stay well through the night." Tristian then turned to her nurse. "We'll be going now. You mind if I call in later? I'd like to check on my wife."

"That's no problem, sir. My shift ends at eleven, if you'd wish to speak with me."

"By means I'd appreciate that. I'm sorry," he regretted. "I don't believe I caught your name."

"Kylee," she revealed. "Just ask for me when you call."

"I sure will. Well, we better be off."

CHAPTER TWENTY-TWO ◆

Tristian remained with Mrs. O'Toole an hour at her house. "My, it's been a long day," he stated. "I guess I'll have to get used to this."

"You'll learn to with time. The first few days are the worst. After three, your body adjusts."

"I'm sure we'll see how it goes. Roughly, how long do you suppose she'll be there?"

"The least? Probably a week. Maybe two, but who knows?"

"Two weeks of this would be an overloaded drain. I'd be a walking zombie."

"Yes, you'd be tired, but you'd push yourself on."

"You're head-on saying that."

Agnus caught on to a grumbling roar. "Have mercy. Was that your stomach?"

Tristian lightly ejected. "You heard that?"

"I know a hungry gut when I hear it. Come to the kitchen. I'll fix us some feed."

"Aye. It has been a few hours since we've had anything. I know it's getting late. You're sure you feel like doing this?"

"I can whip up some sandwiches. That shouldn't take long."

"Well, all right then. But I don't want you cooking. It's too late to be dirtying your pots and pans."

"Let me see what I've got in the fridge." Agnus rummaged through her dishes, removing several plates and bowls from their shelves. "I've found some creamed grouse."

"That'd work fine."

Jillian Osborn

"I'll just heat this in the stove, then grill us some bread. There's tea in the fridge. Help yourself."

"Will you be having some?"

"Just a small glass. Now, while you're here, Tristian, I want you to make yourself at home. Don't feel like a stranger. The only way to get used to a place is getting to know it."

"I'll do my best then."

"You can search for some plates and get those to the table. Tomatoes are on the counter if you'd like one."

Tristian looked around the tabletop. "Ah, you're out of napkins."

"Check the pantry then. You'll find some there."

"Okay."

Agnus carried her skillet to the table and placed a few pieces of bread to each plate. Returning to the stove, she removed the grouse. "This is ready. Go on and take a seat."

Tristian spoke poignantly, "Agnus, if I haven't told you, I want you to know I appreciate you having me. I really do."

"Frankly, I'm glad you accepted my offer. To be honest, Tristian, I feared you staying home. We don't need another O'Brien in sick bay."

With no hesitance, he stated, "No, we certainly don't."

"You made a wise choice staying here. Had you argued with me, I'd have hit you in the head."

"Agnus, could I ask a question and you completely be honest?"

"Have I not always been honest?"

"You have. But I'm wondering if you had bad feelings about something you'd tell me, wouldn't you?"

"Of course, Tristian. Of course I would."

"Like Jos, for example?"

"I've told you plenty times, dear. Josette will be fine. Had I felt apprehensive or distressed, I'd tell you. There's no fluster plaguing my mind. Now, if you decided to go home, well, then, I'd feel otherwise."

Tristian shook his head. "I know you've talked to Josie, but if you wouldn't mind, could you tell me more about the O'Neills?"

"What might you like to know?"

"I'm aware they'd been your neighbors, but how did you get to know them? Had you just been acquainted that way, or did you share friendship?"

The Crying House

"We became good friends soon as they'd moved in. Actually, thinking back now, we met at the general store. Probably two or three days after they'd settled was when they came. Miles and I were both working that day. Ciara and Aidan had gathered their stock and were about to concert wages. As I totaled them up, it came to me. The pair looked familiar. It was then Ciara divulged they'd bought the house across the street. From that day forth we all shared a friendship as it came to be with most folks in town. The O'Neills were the type couple one could easily accept. They were polite and respectful. Any good eye could tell those two were in love. They regarded each other highly and were affectionate when out. There was never a time they weren't holding hands. Between us, in confidence, Ciara boasted about the perfectly, wonderful life that they shared. He was her shooting star, as it seemed. After his change, Ciara never talked much about Aidan, nor what went on in their house. We weren't fools. The people knew. Ciara couldn't hide the facts. Her face and body revealed the truth, not to mention the fighting heard inside the home. Ciara loved him too much despite their misfortune, and that's why she stood aside him. She'd been mindful her Aidan was ill. Because those two facts, I think they'd been the reason she'd never left. It'd been the turn of the century. Back in those days loyalty meant everything, and twenty-eight-year-old Ciara was proof."

"She was a strong woman, wasn't she?"

"Indeed, the strongest I'd ever met. To put up with that extent of abuse, she continued to love that person who hurt her. It was true she honored her vows. To have and to hold from this day forward, for better or for worse, for richer, for poorer, in sickness and in health, to love and to cherish; from this day forward until death do us part. Now, Tristian, I'm not saying she wasn't afraid of her husband, because she was. You could see in her eyes, that display of fear. In matters like hers, no one should stay with a person who harms them, but it was Ciara's choice to. As I've said, Aidan was possessed with an illness. Those with good hearts won't turn their backs to that victim. But unfortunately, as you know, Aidan never received the proper help he needed. As an entity in torment, his rightful self is stuck somewhere in limbo. His remains need to be exorcized of that *diabhal* so his soul could be cleansed. It is then his true form may emerge and move on."

"Is this something you've planned?"

"Well, during a conversation, I told your wife it'd be something I'd do."

"Have you considered the danger?"

"I have, but my faith won't fail me."

"How do you know for sure?"

"As long as I'm focused, prepared, and delivered my strengths, I'm certain to beat it."

Tristian sat in silence till another question began picking his mind. "Going further in time. Did Ciara ever tell you how she and Aidan met?"

"Oh yes. As I recall, her father had been the president of a bank. Ciara worked as a teller. Aidan had gone in one day to get a loan for his pub. Then, I guess, you could call it love at first sight. He was smitten with Ciara as she was with him. They soon became an item. One thing led to another, then by a year's time they were happily married. After that, well, it wasn't long before they moved in your house."

"Agnus, how are you planning on performing this exorcism? Wouldn't you need a bible to know the exact words?"

Agnus said simply, "I'm writing my own."

"Aye. But do you think this incantation will work?"

Agnus thought deeply and disclosed, "I've learned to have faith in my abilities. I never think negative, and I assure to the positive. Should one position unfavorable thought into something, well, inadvertently they're empowering it to happen. So always think with good intentions. I call that Agnus's words of wisdom. The powers of the mind have extraordinary abilities. Make sure you use them sensibly. More tea?"

"It's already nine-thirty. I haven't even made it to the house. I'll have to go to gather my things."

"The later you wait, the more trouble you'll see."

"I figure I'll go soon then. I just want to go in and get out."

"You be careful there, Tristian. Try not to be vulnerable to Aidan should he appear. Remember your strengths, child. They're what get you through, then you can return here."

"Well, if I plan to do this, it should be done now."

"Mind you, don't walk in afraid. Aidan will sense your fear and manipulate it to his advantage. He'll do whatever he can to terrorize you. Don't let him benefit from that. I warn you."

"I'll hurry on and see you shortly."

CHAPTER TWENTY-THREE ◆

Tristian stood before the door of his house where, taking a few breaths, he had stopped before entering. Walking slowly within, he regarded each visible location, discreetly confirming the advancement was safe. With further aim he wandered toward the staircase in pursuit of his mission.

As he accessed mid-flight, a profusion of flashbacks compiled his mind. The retention of Josie disrupted his sight as Tristian retained the harrowing vision. Recalled within his spectacle was the display of her prompt sluggish to the wall. Passing through the hallway, the spray of blood raised his remark. "Oh God." He then stopped. "I can't do this. It's a bad idea. Maybe I should turn around?" Do what you need and go, his conscience told him.

Heavy inhalation lapsed from his lungs as Tristian then paced the bathroom. Inside, he retrieved a tattered cloth along with a bottle of dissolvent. Returning to the hall, Tristian began scrubbing the stained walls. After finishing, he'd cast the disgraced material to a trash, then proceed to the bedroom.

Tristian mount in shock. The once tidied room was anything but straightened. The place had been shambled to a chaotic mess. Through a raging tantrum, Aidan had disrupted everything in grasp. Covers were violently snatched from the bed. Curtains were ripped from their placements and clawed into shreds. Drawers had been pulled and tossed in disposal. Hurled upon the floor were piles of clothing thrown to the room. Shards of glass covered the carpet from broken trinkets and keepsakes. Above the bed Tristian ogled a rigid poem purposely scribed in blood. *A fray to she who dare cross me now brinks to plucks depart, like a hapless sap alighting bout that duffer challenged thee, that simple lass who's fair to pass, to the collector's keep she'll be, now brush along ye urchin one to the ground for boundless sleep.*

Tristian erupted with anger. "You haven't won this yet, Aidan. Josie's not going anywhere, you hear?" Going to the closet, Tristian grabbed several shirts in addition to other attire. He packed his belongings and was ready to leave.

Within the hall he found himself taken by distraction. The blood he so gruelingly cleansed had curiously returned and claimed its place. Before his eyes, Tristian watched as it bled through the wall. Then thicker it became as it further expanded toward the floor. Violent rappings then took to the surface, vibrating the hall, then through Tristian's feet. It was then words began to arrange in blood, *What have ye done with me wench?* Stunned by the rising commotion, Tristian skittered down the hallway. Approaching the top landing, he confronted his adversary. At the bottom of the stairs Aidan laid in wait. Abiding his step, he presented an ambush.

His blue-white eyes glowed fiercely as he started upon the stairs. A foul, filthy scent rose forth, dominating each breath of clean air. The vile essence was so repulsing it immediately made Tristian weak with revulsion. Detained in place, he discouragingly found himself unlikely to progress. In his moment of conceding dread, Tristian regarded the throaty growls of glottal sonancy looming forth from Aidan.

"Shit," Tristian affirmed. How do I get away from this? he thought.

Upon the stairs, Aidan's movements became mechanical. His head contorted in fixed motion, while his body wrenched with submission.

Tristian stood frozen in stance as he gazed forth in fear. Aidan's growls grew deeper while white foam dripped from his mouth. Tristian peered round to a crystal ewer filled with marbles and took his chances. Casting the amassment to the stairs, he watched them scatter in clattered racket.

Aidan continued his pace, unharmed by the onrush forthcoming him. Anger oversaw his temperament while rousing the phooka's awareness. It was that time Tristian witnessed the impulsive flashes surrendering its beastly appearance. Though it wasn't more than three feet in height, its feral impression was enough to cause fright as its

The Crying House

semblance closely guised the most hideous of goblins. Baring its snaggy set of angular teeth, the monstrous spectral alighted the landing.

"You're a bloody disgusting sight," Tristian wailed.

"Not more disturbing than you."

"I wouldn't count that."

"I know of your kind, human. Ye think you're the most beautiful species. I can make you superior. Give ye powers and virtue beyond your ambitions. Your skills would be stupendous."

"What is it, devilkin? You tired of your form?"

"Incurred to fifty years. I want a new soul."

"Well, you can't cling to mine."

The phooka raged forth in anger. "You're right where I want you. There's no slipping away. The only exits are below this ground."

"And so be them."

The phooka presented a challenge. "Try passing me then. It'd only be seconds till you'd see what I'd do."

Tristian eased toward the balcony, alerting his eyes to every corner.

"Don't be stupid, human. You'd break your back. I'll be fair and edge along. I'll guarantee you'll have first go."

Grabbing the banister, Tristian steadily heeded his exit. "Why should I accept a word you say?"

The phooka lingered in wait. "It's your assumption to believe or not."

Tristian's credence made him reckon the truth. Never credit a liar, whether they're human or not. In his withholding, he ceased to elude the tense situation. As he mused in applicable thought to escape, the incredible once again ensued in reflection.

Horrified, Tristian watched flesh tear away from the phooka's appendages. And stretching forth were a pair of bristly, black paws. In wailing throe, the goblin blared as its body prepared to contort and disfigure. Bones then snapped and cracked as they disjoined from relation. The repositioning of its skeletal structure soon followed, reorganizing each breach of osseous matter.

Black hairs arrived through skin covering the entire span of its body. And ranging from the beast's face was a downy snout spanning exposure. When the transformation was complete, staring back at Tristian was a sizeable slate hound.

"Bloody hell." Tristian then panicked.

The mongrel snarled. "It will be."

Tristian edged against the wall, looking for anything to fend his safety. "Go on, you miscreant shuck, shoo."

In throaty laugher, the canine detonated bluster. "Don't badger your God. He can't help you, human. Holiness doesn't dwell in this place. It is I that do. And I'm going to maul your throat as I have ye for fare." The dog then stalked its prey, inching closer and closer.

In desperation Tristian gawked around anxiously. Gripes. He thought, I have to do something. Thinking quickly, he grabbed the railing, and with no apprehension, exceeded the banister.

In mid-flight he departed to safety. While sustaining solid landing, a singe of pain burned in his foot. "Shit! Oh shit," he cried. The impact exhausted Tristian's ankle from further walking. He shrieked. "Bloody hell. The pang."

The feral canine lowered its head to the stairs, all the while displaying its rigid jowls toward Tristian. In gnarrs of anger it snarled. "Ye think ye can outwit me, peasant one?"

Tristian yelled to his troubled leg. "Damn it, move. Come on, you whacked limb. No gain without pain."

Leaping into the air, the misborn crossbreed crashed to the floor. In frenzied hysteria Tristian staggered near the door with the beleaguer to his back. The slate hound suddenly stopped and looked in, upset.

Catching his breath, Tristian then yelled, "What is it? Can't you come for me? Just pass those confines."

Growling from conniption, the displeased stray paced before the door. "Come on back, and we'll even this score."

"Don't have the time," Tristian said. "Seeing and all I have an injury to mend." He turned his back and tottered aimlessly.

"Get back here. Damn you, human. I'll just lie in wait while I know I have time." Aidan laughed.

The door slammed as Tristian nevermore turned back.

CHAPTER TWENTY-FOUR ◆

Agnus held a bag of ice to Tristian's ankle. "It's merely a sprang, child. Be happy there's no break."

"God, I was terrified."

"But you made it out, didn't you?"

"With the Lord at my side. If I'd known I'd see what I did, I hadn't have gone back."

"The phooka's guise is a nasty sight."

Tristian agreed. "An ugly thing it twas."

"You're lucky that rowdy bugger didn't tear you apart. Be thankful you escaped with your life."

"I'll have to go back sometime, though, Agnus. Things need to be done."

"What's so important to demand your return?" she questioned.

"Me and Jos's room. It needs straightening before she arrives."

"When do you suppose you'll have time?"

"This week, I'd imagine. If possible, I'd like to try tomorrow. I hate to ask, but you think you could help?"

"I certainly don't mind, dear. An extra hand's always in need."

"You sure I'm not bothering you with this?"

"How would you be bothering me? If you're in need, I'm there to help. I hope I've made that clear."

"I just don't want to inconvenience you. I worry about that."

"Heavens, child, you're too galling. Rest yourself and lighten up."

Tristian blushed. "I'm trying to learn."

Agnus peered over his body. "You didn't get bit while at home, did you? Answer up."

He sighed. "No, thank God."

"Had you been bitten your blood would have been tainted."

"He aimed to, I won't lie. Being honest, Agnus, I was afraid he would. He was set on taking me down. That's a fact I know." Tristian glanced to his watch. "Oh shoot. Agnus, you mind if I use your phone?"

"Go to the living room, dear. It's on the table."

Tristian picked up the phone and dialed the operator. "Yes, could you connect me to the hospital? The ICU ward please."

The phone began to ring, then a nurse picked up. "Intensive care."

"Oh, I hope I'm not late. Is Kylee still there?"

"Yes, one moment, sir. She's with a patient. Who's speaking?"

"This is Tristian O'Brien."

"Sir, she'll be with you in a few moments if you care to hold."

"Yes, ma'am, thank you."

"Intensive care, this is Kylee."

"Yes, hi. This is Tristian O'Brien."

"Oh, yes. Mr. O'Brien, how are you?"

"Could you tell me, how's my wife?"

"Very well, sir. She did have a slight fever earlier, but we were able to bring it down. We've given her more medication for her swelling. She seems to be tolerating well. Visitation starts at nine each day if you wish to drop in come morning."

"Yes, certainly."

"If there's any change in her condition, either the doctor or a nurse will give you a call."

"I'll need to relay the number where I'm staying."

"Yes, sir, go on…" She spoke kindly, "Hopefully no one will need to call."

"It'd be a blessing."

"You have a good night, Mr. O'Brien."

Tristian returned to the kitchen. "Josie's doing well. Had a slight temperature, but it's under control."

"That should make you relieved. Maybe now you'll rest through the night?"

"We'll see how it goes. Kylee said visitation starts at nine. Would you like to come?"

"You should know that answer, dear. I wouldn't make you traipse alone."

Tristian smiled. "I appreciate it, Agnus. So does Josie."

"You care to join me in the living room for a drink?"

"Thanks, Agnus, but no whiskey tonight."

"How bout a bottle of ale then? Usually I'll have one before bed."

"Oh, well, why not?"

"It'll give you good reason to repose," Agnus stated as she handed it over.

"To the living room then?" Tristian took a seat on the couch. "I've never felt comfort so grand in my life." He relaxed into the sofa. "Sitting here diminishes my blatant mind."

"You sound exhausted."

"Aye. I'm used up for the day. Come morrow, I'll be feeling the same."

"Then you make sure you rest up tonight. This first day fostered the beginning."

Tristian raised his head to the ceiling. "I hate hospitals. I hate going to them. I hate sitting in them. I hate waiting in them. I hate worrying in them."

"I agree. It ain't much to like. But if it makes you better, or the one whom you love. Be thankful for them."

He looked toward Agnus. "You always have a positive comeback for everything. How's that so?"

"Because I don't want to live my life with bitterness." Agnus picked up a gold box. Opening it, she extracted a slender cigar.

Tristian's eyes raised with surprise. "Is that a stogie you've got there?"

"Does smoke bother you, dear? I'll put it out."

"Not at all."

"You're probably wondering when I took up the habit?"

"Well, yeah. I've never seen you toke. I'm dumbfounded, I'll say."

Agnus laughed. "It's just my nightly routine. I'm sorry to shock you."

"Each moment I spend with you, the more I become amazed and

aware. I think I know you, then something up and does over. Is there anything else I don't know?" He cackled.

"I think you'll find that out in time."

"Then there's more?"

"If so, you'll let me know."

"Tell me at least. You didn't counter dance at the taproom, did you?"

"When I was agile and energetic. But don't suppose the wrong idea. I certainly wasn't a bar wench. Miles was always with me. We were a couple young folks having fun."

"A life should be lived in fondness."

"It was innocent fun, dear. That's what we had. No crude behavior or offensive conduction. Just plain, simple, fun."

"You should have become a dignitary. You know, one of those starlets who sings and dances. You could have been brushing shoulders with all the big stars."

"Funny you say that." Her eyes beamed. "There was no one more I wanted to dance with than Fred Astaire. My, how that man could dazzle a stage."

"Why didn't you get into show biz?"

"Simple, I guess. I never sought it. Miles and I enjoyed what we had. After the children's births, our focus went there. For most, they fantasize and dream a delusion. But when they're those who want it, easily you'll see they drove on ambition."

"So you were an impressionist who inhabited their musing?"

She smiled. "It made a better reality for me."

"And you were happy?"

"It was my choice to be."

"Well, then cheers to you." They tapped bottles. "I've breached the last of my hoist. My vessel's dry."

"I take you'll be turning in for the night?"

Tristian rubbed his sore neck and eased his tense muscles. "Got to go sometime while the hours be dark."

"That brings me to thought." Agnus leaned forth in her chair. "I'm afraid I don't have a clock in your room. Shall I wake you come morning?"

"That'd be excellent."

"Is there any certain time then?"

"Probably around eight, then we could get to the hospital on time."

"All right, dear. Eight it is. I hope you get rest."

"Well, I guess I'm off. TTFN."

"Ta-ta for now, dear."

CHAPTER TWENTY-FIVE ◆

Tristian awoke during the night with an irritated throat. Seeking a glass of water, he roamed toward the kitchen. While passing the living room, Tristian noticed Agnus sprawled asleep in her chair. The chimes of the grandfather clock rose sonancy as he quietly shuffled the range.

Walking to Agnus, Tristian noted a framed picture resting at her chest. Carefully handling it, he regarded the image of Agnus and Miles merrily posed within their wedding print. Tristian set the frame aside to a nearby table, then gingerly patted her hand. "Agnus," he whispered tenderly. "Agnus, let me get you to your room."

Awaking to his voice, she declaimed. "Oh, goodness me. I must have fallen asleep," she whispered.

Tristian held forth his hands. "I'll help you upstairs."

"Bless you, dear. Let me just glide on my slippers."

Tristian helped her from the chair, steadying himself aside her. "Are you fair to walk?"

"Once these ole legs get moving." Her eyes darted toward the clock. "Will you look at that? Already two o'clock."

"Aye, it is."

"And I thought you'd be sleeping."

"Well, I was before I had this hankering thirst. I wouldn't have found you had I not awoken."

Agnus smile quiescently. "I'd have been just fine in my chair."

Helping her to the stairs, he ejected, "I couldn't leave you like that. You deserve a restful bed. Now where should I take you?"

"First door to the left." She staggered.

"Careful now. You all right?"
"I'm fine, dear. Just a little sway."
"You'll need to lift your feet."
"Oh. Oh yes."
"Just take it slow. I won't rush you."
"You're a darling for keeping your patience."
"I don't want you getting hurt. We're almost there." Tristian guided Agnus into her room, then helped her in bed. "See now, isn't this more suitable for sleeping?"
"By certain it is."
"All right. I'll see you in the morning." Turning off the lamp, he removed himself from the room. Once more Tristian journeyed to lower grounds in search of water. While approaching the final step, an unusual display stole his sight through a window. Peering out, he spied upon his house. The lights committed to ridiculous behavior absurdly flashing on and off. "What's become of that place?" He shook with disbelief. Recoiling his view, he gathered water. Then, satisfying his request, Tristian contentedly returned to his bed.

CHAPTER TWENTY-SIX ◆

Day 6, the 11th of July, 1950.

The sun broke through the window alighting the first rays of day. Wrapped within sheets, Tristian slept soundly in peace. The scent of breakfast crept upon the stairs, then beneath the crevice of his door. Hearing a light knock, he then opened his eyes.

"Top of the mornin', sunshine. Breakfast is ready. Rise and shine," said Agnus as she traipsed through the room. "Let me raise your window and get you some air. You slept well, I hope?"

"Like a still baby. This bed's so comfortable. I want to lie here forever."

"It's a good bed, it is. Well, rise up. I'll be down filling your plate."

"I'll be there in a moment. Just have to pull myself from this bed."

"Don't let your food get cold, dear. You'll have a short while before it lessens heat."

Tristian stretched as he climbed out of bed. Then, inclining his drift, he joined Agnus for breakfast. "Something smells good."

"In that case, I sure hope you're hungry."

"You've caught my attention."

"I've made a big breakfast. So go on, take a seat. I have everything tended to."

Following their morning meal, Tristian and Agnus journeyed to the hospital.

"Good morning, Dr. Kentworth."

"And a bright morning to you, Tristian. Come on in, son. Hello, Mrs. O'Toole. Nice to see you again."

"How's my wife today, sir?"

"She seems to be doing quite well actually. As a noteworthy matter, undoubtably much of her swelling's subsided. It's an enigmatic miracle, I'll have to say. Honestly, I've never seen protuberance diminish at this pace. I'm quite stunned."

"You suppose it was the medication that did it?"

"It'd have to be, son. There's no other logic to prove it. Her body's ability to adjust to the drug has proved highly impressive. Her metabolic rate must have an accelerated absorption enhance. It's incredibly remarkable."

"How do you know this exactly? Had you run tests?"

"I had changed her dressings about an hour ago. And from visual observation, I encountered the change. The drug itself has common effect on most patients. A ten to fifteen percent decrease in amassment. But your wife has clearly surpassed that reduction. Because of this measurable tread, I've downsized the immensity of her injection."

"Would you still be keeping her in catatonia to the time you intended?"

"Well, I wasn't planning on this extraordinary change so soon. I've had to reevaluate my plan and purpose. If she continues the way she's going, then it's likely she'll be conscious sooner than expected."

"Oh, that'd just be wonderful, doctor."

"We don't want to move too promptly with this. There's a possibility the swelling might return. We'll give her two or three days, then go from there."

"I see." Tristian and Agnus inched over to Josie's bed. Kissing her on top the head, Tristian told her good morning. "Sweetheart, it's me. Agnus and I've made it in. We've been told how substantial your incidence's become. Seems you're improving at an incredible rate. I'm so thankful for that," he proudly whispered to her ear.

Agnus pulled a chair toward the bed and held Josie's hand. Taking a seat beside her, Tristian settled upon his perch.

"Looks like you've had some answered prayers, child. I'm pleased she's doing this well. Hopefully soon she'll be well enough to go home."

"Not while Aidan's there. I'd rather have her return when it's safe. I don't want her encountering another inch of his crap. She's seen and felt enough."

"Dear, I agree. It's not wise. Wait till he's gone, as you've said."

"That bastard's given her a bellyful. He's caused a great deal of affliction. Jos doesn't need an ounce more."

Agnus immediately conveyed, "Something's wrong, dear. Rush on. Get a nurse." Josie's hand quivered within Agnus's. From peaceful somnolence, her body began convulsing under sheets. An array of moans frequented her throat as she slept.

A nurse ran to Josie's bed in fleeted steps. Opening her eyes, she shined a light upon Josie's pupils.

Tristian panicked. "Please tell me, is she okay?"

"I'll have to ask you and your mum to step out, sir."

"Please just tell me."

"I'll be with you in a moment, sir. Please exit to the hall."

"Tristian, come on, dear. I'm sure she'll be okay. Just let the nurse do her job."

"But what's going on? That lady wouldn't say."

"Josette's seizuring. There's no reason you should be in fear. Convulsions look scary, but there's no need to worry."

The nurse finished administering a dose of carbamazepine into Josie's IV. Afterward, she checked her pulse. Josie's rhythm was at one-hundred-seventeen beats per minute. Soon after, Josie's convulsions started to wind in severity. Again the nurse checked her pulse. "You're getting there, miss. Just a teensy more." The nurse waited three additional minutes. "Seventy-three beats. That's what we want. I'll get your husband now, and he'll return to your side."

"What caused it, Agnus? All this time she's been fine," Tristian wondered.

"Mr. O'Brien. Sir, you could come back now."

"Is she all right?"

"Don't you worry, sir. Your wife's fine. She's resting soundly."

"What might have caused this?"

"It could have been a number of things, sir. Her brain injury, an immune disorder, a bodily infection, low potassium. The possibilities

The Crying House

go on, so I can't be precise. I'll phone in her doctor. He may wish to do tests."

"Nurse, pardon me. But could she have encountered a seizure due to an accelerated heartbeat?"

"It's likely. Some experience an increase prior to onset; others, it's during an episode. If you could excuse me now. I need to call her doctor."

Tristian turned to Agnus. "Do you suppose it was our conversation that caused it? Evidently she'd heard us. That may have served as a trigger."

"Noting the fact she still hears, I don't doubt it. Seems maybe our words provoked a response. A brewing of images probably played in her mind, repeatedly disclosing the happenings of yesterday."

"I feel awful now we even mentioned anything in front of her," Tristian whispered back.

"Listen here, child. It was purely an accident. Don't beat yourself up."

Half an hour later Dr. Kentworth returned to ICU. "I'm going to run several tests to make sure nothing outside of Josie's brain injury caused the seizure."

"What are you looking for, might I ask?"

"I'll be screening her levels of glucose and sodium. A liver function test will also apply as well as a creatinine test to check her kidney's function."

"Why all this?"

Dr. Kentworth responded, "Should any problems be detected, we'd have an understanding on why she had the seizure. From there, I'll be able to treat the problem to prevent further attacks."

"Any idea how long these results should take?"

"I'm going to run this stat. As her doctor, I'm in the position where we need to know any likely issues straightaway. You might wish to step aside momentarily. I see a lab technician coming now. Won't you give me a moment, Mr. O'Brien, and I'll be with you in the hallway." Dr. Kentworth waited for the tech's approach. "Run a CBC while you're at it. I'm working in urgency, so have someone report to me soon as the results are in."

"Yes, sir, Dr. Kentworth."

"I apologize for your wait, Mr. O'Brien. I'll acquire the results once they've been given, then I'll get back to you and let you know how things look."

"I appreciate it, doctor." Tristian and Agnus returned to Josie's bed. "Things were going so good. I'd dread to hear anything bad."

"There you go with that worrying. Why don't you hold back and take things as they come?"

"I'm not accustomed, nor am I resilient. It's just a part of who I am."

"Hadn't you ever thought if you had less tension in your life, your days would go better?"

"How do I correct it?"

"Maybe you should learn to meditate and release the stresses inside you."

"But my mind's never quiet."

"You'd train it to learn."

"I'm certain doubt to that."

Agnus shook slowly. "Not everyone succeeds at first try. That's why there's other chances to learn and improve."

"I don't know if I'd have the patience. My luck, I'd be frustrating myself evermore."

"Those niggling worries you could do without. Trust me when I say that."

"I've been in trust to all you say. Your directions never proven doubt. You've been head-on with Josie all those times. Maybe I should learn these things you've personally denoted. Lessening my fretful load. I'd tell you now would be a miracle."

"The best lesson for you, just aim to be simple. Your life's less hectic that way."

"Now I know how you've done it." He smiled.

"In too many cases we get ruled by our heads. Take the time to feel with your gut. You'll see your instincts are better."

"I'm ruled by my mind, like you said."

"Then let's try an easy test. I want you to clear your mind. I'll say one word. I want you to listen to your mind, then your instincts. Following that, I'll be asking two questions."

"Sounds simple enough. Go ahead."

"Listen to yourself. Now tell me what you feel when I say Josette?"

The Crying House

"I hear my mind. Things will be bad, I'm listening over and over. Something's wrong. The doctor's encountered problems. It's not good, I just know it isn't."

"Pull yourself from that and feel with your gut. What are you saying? What do you sense?"

Tristian took a steady breath. "I feel calm. Jos will be fine. I shouldn't worry. There's nothing defective with the tests."

"Do you still feel we're at fault for causing that seizure?"

"My gut says she overheard the conversation. Agnus, it was our stupidity which signaled the occurrence. The nightmare of him. It was nothing more. I feel almost certain this is right."

"Remember what you've said as we wait for the doctor. Come on now. We'll take our seats."

"Is this supposed to prove something?"

"We'll see, child. You'll find out in time."

"That seems to be all we have. An hour here feels like three. The silence is deafening. The coldness brings chills. And that stench of bleach mixed with ammonia, well, a whiff of that could get you queasy."

"Don't breathe so deeply."

"If only I couldn't."

"We'll stuff your nostrils then."

Tristian smirked. "I'd like to see you try."

"Don't tempt me, dear. I'm one of those who follows through."

Tristian shook modestly. "I have good reason to believe that."

"So when shall I start? Left nostril first?" Agnus kidded.

"Ain't nothing going in these holes. I broke my nose that day, and having that packing pulled, nearly had me sick stomached."

"Thank God you don't box."

"I tried. Wasn't till my first fight I tethered away. I'd like to say I was smart enough to find my limit. At that point I figured I'd be a better banker."

"How's that working for you?"

"You know, I really do love it. I work with great folks, and my boss is simply an amazing lad. I must say I feel blessed for that."

"You work for Mr. Ashford?"

"Aye."

"He's a wonderfully, sincere man. Has the heart of an ally. You're lucky to have him."

Tristian retracted in thought. "He's never given hassle. He's polite in his demands and involved with his workers. I don't know of any other who's more pleasant than he."

"I'm sure he'd be gracious to hear that."

"He's a likeable man indeed."

Agnus ogled the room. "What do you know? There's Dr. Kentworth."

"Already?"

"Let's pray for good news."

"Well, Mr. O'Brien, I bear a good announcement."

"No more sitting on pins and needles?"

"Not at this point, son. I think you'd be glad to know the blood work's come back normal. There were no elevations or decreases."

"Positively? You've found nothing wrong?"

"Her levels are all stable. So I imagine it twas the injury that bought about her seizure. In cases, but not all, seizures may develop following head trauma. As result, the crisis disrupts the pathways in the brain, setting forth a reaction."

"Will she continue to have more?"

"The possibility always lingers."

"Then chances are she will?"

"I can't say for fact. However, it is likely. I'll reassign her medication and hopefully control any outbreaks."

"You mean to tell me she wasn't on anything?"

"Son, we had to know if she'd tolerate without the medication. There's no reason to treat seizures if she's not having them."

Tristian took to upset. "Don't you think you're at fault if you theorized its ability to happen?"

"I didn't mean to distress you, Mr. O'Brien. But it's hospital regulation. We have to set apart facts from uncertainties."

"Excuse me, sir, for getting carried away. But I'm sure you understand my concerns."

"I'd probably have been the same way. I don't blame you for being involved. With incidences like this, one must."

"Aye. But pardon me if I at all appeared cross. It's not my nature."

Dr. Kentworth reassured him, "It's a natural response to be on edge. Stress can bolt to increased levels as anxieties become unquiet.

But in hope to relieve doubts or regards, I insure you now your wife is fine. If everything stays at a positive pace, she'll be relocated to a private room in one of our regular wards. Confidently, a few days at most."

"That'd be a big liking."

"We'll see how things go. If in two or three days her healing progresses, we'll have no requirements on further maintaining her in ICU."

"You're confident on this?"

"Time will be our adviser."

"I'd like to thank you for personally coming to report the results, doctor."

"I said that I would." He smiled. "Well, I have one more round to be making, then it's off to home. I suppose I'll be seeing you both sometime tomorrow?"

"Of course, Dr. Kentworth. May you have a good evening."

"I unquestionably hope to."

CHAPTER TWENTY-SEVEN ◆

Tristian commented as he drove to the house, "I tell you, those six hours have me wanting to nap."

"Well, sitting a length of time can simply drain the life from your stir."

"It's always puzzled me. Why do hospitals do that?"

"Rooms tend to stay quiet. That quickly gets to a person when all he does is sit and wait."

"I don't like it much, being drained so early in the decline of day. I wanted to get over to the house before nightfall. Now I doubt I'll do that."

"You have further days ahead, dear. You'll get there when you can."

"You've got a point there."

"Feel free to nap if you'd like. I won't disturb you."

Tristian pulled up to Agnus's. "I'll help you from your side."

Across the way, a man traipsed through the street. Tristian helped Agnus from the car as he lonely approached.

"I thought I might find you at home."

Agnus turned round. "Isn't this a surprise? Kieran, how are you?"

"Came by earlier, but never got an answer. Figured I'd try back later. Lucky I am to be seeing you now."

"Well, you've made perfect timing. Come on in, I'll make us some tea." Agnus laid forth her hand. "You remember Tristian?"

"Yes, ma'am, I do. I had intentions to see you, Mr. O'Brien. I stopped, supposing you were there. And by my attempt, I knocked at the entry, but it wasn't your face I'd seen through the door."

"Sir?"

"He was there waiting. That damned, foul thing."

"You saw him?"

"I attest he was there. I left your place and headed here. Surely I figured Agnus was home."

"Kieran, have you been waiting in your car all this time?"

He answered to Agnus, "I paid a visit to Logan. Ashlynn said he'd been placed in a home. I didn't want to believe till I saw him. The man's younger than I, and already he's dying. It was a hard reality going there."

"He did look a bit pasty and worn at the edges," Tristian responded.

"I don't give him long, the poor man."

"You, boys, have a seat at the table. I'm warming our tea," Agnus relayed.

Kieran continued his claim, "He confessed to heart pains, but won't be honest to those nurses. I asked calmly if he was waiting to die? Sad what he said."

"You're sure he wasn't jesting?" Agnus wondered.

"Not with his tone. Logan said literally I've lived all I can. It broke me, it did. I'm seventy-nine years old. Figured ten years ago I'd be in my grave. I've hardly ever been ill for a day, along with the fact these extremities still work. I've come to think I'll be living forever. I can't give up, Agnus. I've got nothing to lose."

"You still have things here you must do. Live your time while you can."

"My life's all I have, and for me it's grown boring, maybe even meaningless. Returning to Roscrea, I see all that I've missed. I've lost so much because that has house kept me astray. I've wandered from place to place over these years, and they've never much seemed like a house to call home. Sometimes I thought I should have stayed here, but within me I knew I just couldn't face it."

"One of the things I learned from my time on this earth is we can't run away from our trials and torment. They'll always be a part of us, Kieran. Memories remain where ever we go. If you can't build your peace, you'll harrow eternally."

"What I wish to bring my ease I'll never have. It'd be an impossible gain."

"What is it you seek?"

"I want his apology for what he did to my sister. But that's something I'll never get. He died a bastard and, as I sensed it, that's what he still is. The filth beneath my soles."

"Exactly how did you see him?" Tristian wondered.

"He literally opened your door, lad. Going there, I wasn't prepared for that shock. Believe me when I say how startled I was seeing that man looking back. Last time I'd seen him, that bastard was running late for my sister's funeral. His own wife. Well, let me say, I was ready to tear his bloody limbs apart."

"You didn't see him later that night?"

"Every nerve in my being ached to kill him."

"How long did you lie in wait?"

"Lie in wait, young lad? I wasn't the one who took his life."

"You were with someone else then?"

"If I were there, I'd done it myself."

"So wait a minute. Who'd have killed him if it wasn't you?"

"If I knew, I'd congratulated that gutsy chum. It took a lot to do what that individual did."

"You suppose it might have been your father?"

"No doubt ever crossed my mind. Ciara was his baby. When he learned of the abuse, he asked her to leave him. Pop begged her to come home. When she didn't, he went after Aidan and, violently yelling, tore into him."

"What'd your father say?"

"Well, pops said what any father would. Told Aidan if he wanted to beat someone, he'd be ready for the round. He made his attempt, but his request failed. Aidan didn't mind what it was pop had said. It never stopped him from beating my sister. After her death my dad was a toppled wreck. He told me he wanted to do away with that no-good son of a bitch. Said he'd club him if he could. I saw the anger in his veins. When he said that, I knew pop was for real."

"Was it your father? Surely you must know."

"He never spoke of it. But my reasoning led me to suspect him."

"Do you remember at all where he was the night your brother-in-law was killed?"

"I hadn't seen him till the following day when he walked through our door. His clothes were soiled with dirt, and he looked a mess. At that time word already spread of Aidan's death. I confronted pop, asking him where he'd been. He seemed secluded in a sense. Had a remote gaze when he spoke."

"He say if he did it?" Agnus queried.

"Pop claimed he slept at the cemetery all night. Said he couldn't leave his baby alone in that place. He was overwrought more than I'd ever seen him. Then on he never talked much."

"Had you not asked about Aidan?" Agnus questioned.

"When I relayed his death, pop just stood there. I don't know if he even comprehended what I'd said. It took a moment for his answer. He'd turned around, leaving the room and mumbled, I hope he rots quickly."

Tristian polled, "Had that been it?"

"That's all he said. Nothing more. After that day there'd been no further talk of Aidan."

"Staying in the cemetery sounds a bit suspicious. I've never known a living soul to do such that."

"Either have I, Mr. O'Brien. I was frayed to believe him and torn to have not."

Tristian acknowledged, "Seems to me it's possible he could have done it."

"All this time I've wondered it being you," Agnus told Kieran.

"Hadn't everyone? Folks here came to believe what they'd wanted. Even a preposterous story of my sister's return. In life, she wasn't a killer. I doubt she would have been in death. I honestly think it was my pops who killed him."

"Had he any blood upon him?"

"I just remember him being a mess. It was possible he could have, Mr. O'Brien. He trashed those clothes, but I never went looking."

"Had he not said anything upon his death?"

"That was twenty-six years ago, lad. Only thing I recall pop saying was, they'd both been in the cemetery that night. That'd been his last words."

"Leaves you room to wonder. Had he meant your sister?"

"Had to be. That's why he stayed there. Maybe he was telling the truth, but I just couldn't grasp it."

"It could have been a part of the truth," Agnus responded. "Maybe he'd stayed alongside her grave awhile. There his anger boiled into rage before the murderous insist fell upon him."

"Funny. That's what I'd thought."

"Kieran, why hadn't you ever said anything of this before?"

"It was my father's secret, Agnus. As not to betray him, I kept it in heart."

"I understand you were trying to protect him."

"He's all I had. Both my mum and sister were gone. I had no further family but him."

"I'm relieved to know this truth now," Tristian interjected. "I'd been left to wonder what might had happened. I saw that bloody mess, and I've heard all the possible stories from Agnus. It's delivering to know we can finally set aside facts from fiction."

Kieran patted his hand to the table. "Well, between us, let's just keep it our secret. There's no reason for others to know of this truth."

Agnus affirmed, "The validity remains in this room with us. What's been spoken will abide to untold silence. To that, you have my word."

"Aye," Tristian agreed. "But I think my wife should have a right to know at some point."

"Then confirm it upon her, but no more."

"I concur, sir. It'd be her and no other."

"Well, folks, I guess the time's about come. I've enjoyed my visit. Hopefully we'll do this again sometime."

"Does that mean you'll be drawing upon Roscrea more often?"

"As long as you'll have me, Agnus. I'll be willing to come."

"I hope then you'll be keeping your word."

"Most certainly." He smiled.

CHAPTER TWENTY-EIGHT ♦

Day 7, the 12th of July, 1950. Roscrea hospital.

"I must tell you again, Mr. O'Brien, I'm amazed. Never in all my years of doctoring had I ever seen a patient recover this quickly. Her swelling has continued to decline in rapid pace. She's had no further convulsions. Vitals are strong. Josie definitely has someone watching over her."

"How much longer then, doctor, before she's awakened from this coma?"

"Her changes have unquestionably been drastic. I have no reason to worry about bleeding within her crown. Had she had that, Josie's condition would be in crisis. From attestation there's absolutely no evidence indicating hemorrhaging upon either half of her brain. From the instant you brought her in, that's what worried me. I was afraid her blood vessels might rupture, causing a stroke. But again, she seems to be doing remarkably well as I've noted. Regarding an early rise from her state of catatonia, it's seems likely. If Josie can manage through tonight with a cessation of problems, I'm hopeful to draw her out come morrow."

"What about the tube, doctor? Is that something you'd be taking out?"

"That'll be left in, Mr. O'Brien, until I'm completely positive she can do without. I don't want to make a wrong move by rushing along."

"Will she have any type of brain damage? An inability for speech? Concentration difficulty? Inattention?"

"We'll only be able to tell come time. At this point I can't really speak for that. Possibilities abound, sometimes they don't."

"Aye. I understand, sir."

CHAPTER TWENTY-NINE ◆

Further on that day.

Tristian and Agnus returned to the house at three pm. Lounging upon the porch, they enjoyed the mild breeze.

"If you'd like to go to your house later, I'll help you there, dear."

"Well, sure, if you're up to it."

"That's why I asked. Seems Josette might be home in a few days."

"I don't know who's been floored more by her recovery, myself or the doctor."

"Continual prayers make everything better," Agnus responded.

"Some reason has me thinking you've been a part of her getting well."

"I've just talked to Miles every night and prayed him to heal her."

"I seen you were asleep with his picture my first night here."

"That's when my prayers began."

"It wasn't but that following day we heard she was better."

"I trust Miles. And when he hears me, I assure his response."

"Agnus, I thank you for that. My wife wouldn't be where's she is if it weren't for prayers."

"You should credit yourself, too, dear. It wasn't all me."

"It was the both of us." He smiled. Tristian then peered upon the lawn. "Looks like your grass could use a trimming. What'd you say, you let me do it?"

"If that includes the back."

"More problems there?"

"It could use some weeding." She laughed. "Those grasses are tall."

"Where might I find your mower?"

"Round back in the shed. I'll show you."

Tristian traipsed through the grasses behind Agnus, then taking in the sight of the back yard, he spoke in awe. "My, I didn't know you had all this. Just look at that garden. It's a magical land you have here. I bet you spend a lot of time in this place?"

"Indeed, I try. I find it most soothing. Go on, Tristian, and have a closer look. You'll find the colors of these flowers are uplifting. And with those different scents, makes it intoxicating to stand here."

"Look at all these birds and butterflies," he exclaimed.

"Oh, yes. All types and different shades soar about."

"What are these tall clusters of flowers you have?"

"Those are foxglove."

"I see stalks all throughout your garden."

"They come in such vivid shades of color. Amazing and bright. I must say the fairies love it. They've made their home here."

"You have fairies?"

"Of course I do."

"But I don't see any."

"They come out and about when they please. Best time to catch them's at dusk. Come out at night, and you'll find the wee ones celebrating their little parties throughout my garden."

"Are you serious?"

"We'll come out one night, and you'll see. They're spirited little sprites. They love to dance and shimmy. They request me, but my fact springs forth. I'm far too old for that sort of pleasure. Instead, I watch them and enjoy the time," Agnus explained. "Besides my pixie folks, I'll glance little elves and suited gnomes frolicking within the yard, gathering their bushels of fruits and berries. Over there I have my pond where fairies drift on little boats of leaves and twine. For me, this is an enchanting place of magical retreat."

Tristian relayed thought, "I guess places like this don't only exist in fairy tales."

"I promise one day you'll see."

"Well, you're quite lucky to have this dreamy escape by your home."

"I'll have to bring Josette here to frolic with the fairies. I'm sure she'd enjoy every moment."

"That'd be a fabulous idea, Agnus."

"It'd be something in the making. Soon as she's here and on her feet, we'll set the plans," Agnus pointed out. "Go yonder and you'll find the shed. But don't be mistaken. It's been taken by Hardenbergia vines."

Tristian removed the mower from the shed and shaved the grasses. Following that, he sheared the shrubs, then pruned an array of flourishing trees. Later he found himself weeding the garden and combing the dirt. Soon after, he tended to a fragrant bed, misting the flowers and drizzling some herbs. Returning to the front, Tristian gathered the rake and trowel.

Agnus walked through the door with a glass in hand. "You've done a magnificent job here and at back. With all this heat I thought you might like some refreshment. Come upon and have a seat on the porch. I've got some fresh lemonade. It's cold as ice with a punching kick."

"You couldn't have made better timing. I was just wrapping up."

"The wise always know." She modestly laughed.

"I figure we'd be able to swing by the house in an hour."

"That's fine, dear. Just say when you're ready."

"You suppose I could take a quick bath?" he asked, tugging at his shirt. "I'd like to tidy up and get rid of this stench."

"Well, certainly. You don't have to ask."

Tristian blushed. "Force of habit. What can I say?"

"It's who you are."

Tristian checked his watch. "I shouldn't be long. I'll let you know when I'm out."

"I'll be here."

CHAPTER THIRTY ◆

Tristian stood before his door, searching his pocket. He grasped for his key. Agnus followed into the house as they'd each perceived the shavings upon the floor.

Agnus remarked, "Oh, my dear."

"What's all this?"

"Looks like Aidan's clawed your floor."

"What a mess." Tristian pulled to his knees and examined the damage. "I don't have a moment's time to be fixing this."

"That's not the only thing he got." Agnus showed Tristian the back of his doorway. "Had any of this been here before?"

"The house was a mess, but he hadn't clawed it to shreds. Seems I'll have more work than I thought." He took a breath. "I dread to walk farther."

"I hate to tell you, dear, but if you plan to get anything done here, you best ease forth."

"Then we'll make our way upstairs."

They passed deeper into the house. Along the walls pictures had been smashed. Paper had been ripped and tattered. And upon the ceiling a strange, chalk-like substance oozed through the housetop, lingering steadily overhead.

"What's he done to my home? Repairs alone will take forever."

"Mind this later. We'll do what we came for."

"I'm sorry, Agnus. This just sickens me. I'd put so much work into this place already. I guess that money's been washed down the drain." Tristian toddled toward the stairs when he saw the engravings upon each step. "This is just going from bad to worse. Look at this chaos. Why didn't he just burn the place while he was at it?" Tristian shook his head, then backed away. "Agnus, had you read these words here?"

"It's a sentence, mind you. And I don't like what it says."

Tristian quoted the condemnation, "Innocense is slain while the wicked roam? What's he mean? Us?"

"Tristian, I know it's hard, but do try to disregard it. Aidan has a morbid mind. He'll do what he can to unglue you. They're just words, mind you. Nothing more."

"Let's move along. There's something I want to show you." Tristian led Agnus through the hallway, then stopped.

"Oh mercy," she spoke sadly. "This from Josette?"

"I cleaned it last time I was here, but the blood came back. I don't know what else to do, Agnus. My wife shouldn't have to see this. Think what it'd do."

"Jar memories and cause nightmares. She can't have it. Why don't you round me up a bowl of saltwater? I'll clean with that."

"Saltwater? What's that supposed to do? I need these stains cleared away."

"Do you trust me or not, dear?"

"Is that warm water you'll be needing?"

Agnus nodded. "It's best I come with you. I'd prefer you not be alone."

Tristian gathered a large bowl from the cabinet, then handed it to Agnus. Walking toward the table, he retrieved the saltshaker. "It's all yours now. Do as you want."

Agnus poured a mound of salt into the bowl, then ran in water. Stirring gradually, she recited words. "Water to cleanse and salt to purify. I consecrate and empower this solution to work for my aid." Following that, Agnus stirred the water three times, then tapped the bowl. "Let's go."

"That's it?"

"Pretty simple."

"No cleansing solution?"

"Don't need it. By the time I'm through, that wall shouldn't bleed. Whatever impurities Aidan's contributed will be cleansed away."

"I'll wait for that proof."

Agnus raised her brow. "It'll be proof you see."

Tristian gave a reassuring nod. "I'll be off in the bedroom then. Give a holler when you're through with that wall."

"Best you take this. Salt that door before you enter."

Tristian did as she advised, then, getting on his hands and knees, scoured the carpet for slivers of glass. It was a tedious procedure that took several minutes and owl trained eyes. Once finished, Tristian vacuumed the smaller shards, ridding the floor from unseen flukes. He pushed the vacuum to the closet before minding the bed.

Agnus peeked into the room. "Anything, dear, I could help you with here?"

"Is that hall cleared?"

"Just as said."

"You mind tackling that poem?" He pointed to the wall. Tristian gathered sheets and blankets, then tossed them aside to a corner. Within a chest he pulled forth fresh covers.

Agnus relayed, "I'm just about done, then you do what you need."

"No rush. I'm gonna run to the laundry room to get a hamper."

Agnus finished scrubbing the wall once he returned. "Does that look clean?"

He eyed in amazement. "I hardly tell it was there."

Agnus left the room to pour the tainted water down the sink, then rejoined Tristian seconds later. "Are all those clothes dirty?"

"I think some of these have fragments of glass."

"What of this pile?"

"Those get hung in the closet."

"And these?"

"Drawer."

"I'll hang these for you."

"There's some pillow cases to your right. Could you hand me two?"

"Green, yellow, or white?"

"Yellow's fine."

"There you are, dear. Would you like me to fold these clothes when I'm through?"

"You mind putting them in drawers?"

"Any order?"

"However you'd want. I appreciate all your help, Agnus. Seeing that, we're just about through." Tristian removed the damaged curtains from their placement, reinstating them with unmarred textiles. "Finally," he commented. "It's back to normal."

Agnus beamed warmly. "We've made a good team, you and I."

"Well, guess I'll carry this hamper down then." He placed the basket in the laundry room against the wall. "You in a hurry to get back?"

"Was there something else you had to mind?"

"Thought maybe I'd sweep this floor right quick. Get these shavings out of the way."

"You have an extra broom? I'll tidy your stairs."

"Check the porch. Should be one there." Tristian swept the grains into a pile, then scooped them into a dustpan.

"Where might I find the trash?" Agnus wondered aloud.

"Cabinet, below the sink."

"I'll empty your pan while I'm at it."

Tristian put away the sweepers. "Guess that's it for now."

"What will you do to these boards?"

"Pull them up, replace them one day. Same for the stairs. It's a lot of damage here."

"You should get along just sanding them. The scratches are deep, but not far from repair. You can restain when you're through. Mind you, it'd lessen your load."

"And the mess I'd be making. It's a job I'd tackle once things settle down." Tristian peered to the ceiling. "I'm in doubt to fix that. Hell, Agnus, I'm not even sure what it is. A film of some sort?"

"It's spiritual energy, though I've never seen it like this."

"It's what?"

"Plasma that transmits through the body of a medium, materializing into substance. But I don't know how'd that be here without a host. It doesn't make a bit of sense. If indeed it is ectoplasm, it should dissipate, given time."

Tristian questioned, "Could it be something else?"

"Possibly a smog of some sort. I wouldn't touch it if I were you. Let it go away on its own."

"But what if…" A thunderous roar breached Tristian's speech, echoing throughout the house. "Bloody hell. What was that?" He looked around.

A thick smoke encircled the staircase as a body took form.

"That's our cue to leave," Agnus calmly remarked.

"Ye come to finish what was started?" Aidan spoke, harshly. "It's about time ye showed."

"Crap," Tristian expressed. "He's got a score to settle, and I see he'd want it soon."

"Ye owe me," Aidan yelled. "We relieve this now."

"I have no debt to you. This house is yours till you're gone."

"I want more than just that. I think ye know."

Tristian raged, "You can't claim it."

"Ye watch me," he argued. "A simple bite, and I'd stretch through your blood."

Agnus interrupted, "You're still the same, Aidan. Demanding and cold."

"Who're you to talk to me, ye old fool?"

"An old acquaintance."

"Shut that sweet talk, ye old hag."

"Does it ache you to know you once had a friend?"

"I don't want that crap in me house. I'll bend ye like a twig and make your bones snap one after the other."

Agnus began laughing as she walked toward him.

"Get away. What are you doing?" Tristian worried.

Aidan shouted, "This is my space. Ye back off."

"You fearful of me?"

"I'm warning you, hag." His eyes glared.

Agnus circled round him. "You know, Aidan, it's been near fifty years."

He tried walking alongside her.

"Hold your place," she demanded.

"Your magic's no force upon me."

"It's more than you think. You battle a crone, you'll get burnt."

"In that case, I'll stand in me place," he sarcastically responded.

"Your time here's about up, Aidan. I think we know what happens from there."

"Ye can't send me back." He growled in low tone.

"It won't be me taking you. When that time comes, you'll be fighting a desperate battle."

"This house is a part of me as I'm a part of it. I won't be driven off. I'm much too strong."

"Is that so? And who holds who in place?"

"Watch yourself, witch. I still have me tricks."

"I don't have time to stand here and bicker with the dead." Agnus turned to Tristian. "I need to make dinner, dear. You ready to go?"

"Don't ye turn away from me," Aidan shouted. "I'm not finished with you, ye fumbling hag."

"But I am with you." Agnus dismissed him. "Come along, Tristian, dear. We'll leave him to dwell among his hatred."

Aidan set forth a violent roar which shook the foundation. A swarm of flies emitted from his mouth and buzzed toward Tristian and Agnus. Around their heads the pesterous hoard quickly consumed the air. "None of this is through. Damn ye both. I'll get ye when you least expect it. Remember that, for one day you'll crumble."

CHAPTER THIRTY-ONE ◆

Agnus and Tristian were finishing their meal when Tristian proposed to wash dishes. "You see, I don't mind it. It's not always the ladies' job."

"Shameful more men don't think like you."

"You done with your glass?"

"I consider I am."

Tristian sudsed his rag. "I'm quite impressed how you handled yourself at the house today. I had no idea you possessed such a force. You had Aidan stunned. I doubtfully imagine he bargained for that."

"He thought he might have had me, he did. But then you saw that shock in his face when he couldn't move?"

Tristian pondered, "How'd you do such a thing?"

"Power intensifies force whether it be a physical or mental aspect. To use mind effect, one must dedicate themselves to the principles of training. Projection and assuredness are key to mastering its access. Once harnessed, it's within the individual's potential to do as he'd please."

"That's how you overcame him?"

"Precisely."

"What else can you do?"

"Plenty. But I don't like relying on my strengths. To me, it's an easy way out. Better yet, lazy."

"Might you show me one thing? I'm curiously intrigued by all this."

"I suppose."

Tristian's fascination advanced. "I don't mean to seem like a delighted child, but this is exciting."

Agnus chuckled. "Parlor tricks have a way of absorbing all ages. But hence, mine are kosher. If you truly wish to see, step aside from the sink." She minded the remaining pile of unlaundered dishes, then using her will, projected ambition. Into the air a plate floated steadily beneath an outflow of water, and rising along, a lathered rag buffed about its surface.

"Amazing," Tristian disclosed.

The plate nestled onto the drain rack as a knife then took to a cleansing shower.

"Absolutely amazing." Tristian perceived forth in awe. "I had no idea you were capable of this."

"Keep watching," Agnus advised. A lingering towel dried the washed dishes. Soon after, drawers and cabinets unshut themselves, each awaiting their proper inductions. "Does that satisfy your curiosities, dear?"

"By all means, Agnus. I say, you really are something."

"It'll be our little secret. We'll keep that between us."

CHAPTER THIRTY-TWO ◆

Day 8, the 13th of July, 1950. Following afternoon.

Dr. Kentworth stood aside Tristian. "We've had a discharge in 248. Once it's cleared, your wife should be transferred to that room. Why don't you and Mrs. O'Toole come along?"

"Any idea how long a wait?"

"I'll talk to the nurse and see what I can find out."

Tristian and Agnus followed Dr. Kentworth into ICU.

"I'll be right with you, folks."

Tristian took a seat beside his wife. "I'm so pleased, Agnus. We've patiently awaited this day, and finally it's come."

"I'm happy to see you're no longer depressed. I tell you, child, you had me worried there awhile."

"Aye, but you've helped me much. Honestly, I wouldn't have gotten through this alone. You were a reassuring voice in my head."

"Dear, you needed that boost to push you along. Had you not had it, you'd be in a mess."

"That's an undoubted fact. I can't disagree," Tristian complied. "But now with Jos advancing to a general room, it's lifted the tension from my chest."

Agnus disclosed from her heart. "You've found yourself blessed in more ways than one. Consider yourself lucky, dear. Situations have worked in your favor."

Tristian patted her hand. "It was an alliance of prayers. And your contributions mean a lot."

Dr. Kentworth walked up to Tristian. "I've got some good news, son. Josie's room's all ready for her. We just got word."

"That's sooner than expected, sir. Will you be moving her now?"

"There's no reason I shouldn't. I know you're eager to stray from this room. Everything's set, so I think we could go."

"Will she be on a different floor?"

"Yes, son, she'll be on second. We'll take this elevator here. You mind holding that door?"

"I've got it for you, doctor," Agnus responded. "Everyone in?"

"Follow me through the hall. It's just down this way." Dr. Kentworth rolled Josie along the path. "Here we are, folks. This is a private room she's been given. If you'd like to request a cot, you can stay overnight."

Tristian nodded. "Sir, will you be bringing her out soon, or might you give her more time?"

"I think it's safe to bring her around. I'll check her vitals once more. If all's well, I'll administer the medication." Dr. Kentworth took a moment to check things over. Once confirming satisfaction, he declared an announcement. "We can advance forth with treatment."

Tristian pondered, "You're positive it's safe?"

"I'd need to first prepare you for the effects of this regimen, Mr. O'Brien. Conclusively, she'll temporarily be groggy for a period, but that'll wear off, passing time. When she initially awakes, I'll aware you, she'll be confused. Don't be alarmed. There's a possibility she may not know you upon sight. You might find her slow in responding to you. It's a normal process. I'd advise you not to panic or worry. In addition, it'll take a day or so to wean her off the sedatives, so she'll remain a bit dopy. Having said that, might you have any questions?"

"No, sir, not at the moment."

"Then I'll proceed." Dr. Kentworth swabbed the connected access devise along the IV. Then, inserting the syringe, slowly injected the solution. "She may not fully wake right away, and that's okay. Things like this take time. Any slight movements are significant, even a sparse shift of her hand." Dr. Kentworth patiently awaited the medication's effect. Within a few moments he noticed Josie's toes astir. The medication persisted to disperse in her system when an attempt to moisten her lips ensued.

"Josette? Josette, sweetie, this is Dr. Kentworth. Can you hear me? Squeeze my hand if you do." Dr. Kentworth awaited response. Slowly he felt a mild clasp surpass from her clutch. "Very good, sweetheart. Are you awake enough to understand me?"

"Josie?" Tristian relayed.

"Hold on a second, son. Give her some time. Josie, this is Dr. Kentworth again. Could you give me a sign you understand?" He waited a moment more when she tapped upon his hand. "Your husband brought you to the hospital several days ago. Since then you've been in a coma. I've just awoken you, so if you're feeling groggy, that's why. Do you follow so far?" She squeezed at his hand. "We had to do surgery, dear. Thankfully, it was a success. I'm proud to report you've done well over these last few days. Your husband's here, and so's Agnus. They've been waiting for your revival. You think you can open your eyes?" Dr. Kentworth waited an instant further. "How bout giving it a try?"

Josie's lids flickered as she fought to release them. Finally her eyes were open enough to see Dr. Kentworth.

"It's nice to finally see you. How bout a smile?"

Tristian and Agnus edged closer to the bed. Josie steered her eyes toward her husband, then rising her finger, tried to wave briefly.

"Hi, honey," he said as a small tear ran from his face. "It's a blessing to see you. I've missed you like crazy." Tristian kissed her hand, then rubbed Josie's arm. "Look who's here. She's come every day."

Woozily, Josie gleamed upon Agnus, who was patting her leg. "It's good to see you're up. I'll tell you, deary, our lives haven't been as bright without you in them. I'm glad you're okay. Seeing you pull through the way you have; you're a tough little lassy."

Dr. Kentworth delivered, "Could you make some way? I'm going to check her vitals again. Make sure everything's still fine."

"Yes, doctor," Agnus responded. "I don't mean to be in your way. I'll move for you now."

"If you'd just back a tad, dear, you'll be fine." He leaned over the bed with his stethoscope. "All right, Josie, deep breaths ... okay, can you bend forward? Good, I've got you. Deep breaths ... excellent. Your heart and lungs sound normal. Okay, now, Josie, I'm going to hold up my finger. I want you to watch it." Josie moved her eyes back and forth as she followed his motion. "That's good. You're doing fine. Are you experiencing any problems? Blurred vision? Anything of that sort?" Josie shook no. "I'm going to shine this light over your pupils. Okay ... good. Now the next. And ... we're done. That wasn't so bad. You suppose you could eat something? I'm going to get an attendant to gather your meal."

Several instances later a nurse returned with a tray in hand. Setting it on top of a table, she rolled it to Josie's bed. "Here's you some soup and a sandwich, Mrs. O'Brien. Eat what you can." She turned to Tristian. "Sir, do you wish to feed your wife, or would you rather have me?"

"I'll do it. It's no problem." Tristian got up from his chair. "Let's start you off with this nice, warm, soup." He put the spoon into the bowl, then blew away the steam.

Josie opened her mouth while Tristian fed her. But the first few attempts fumbled as broth drizzled down her chin. With a napkin in hand, Agnus dabbed Josie's face to wipe away the excess fluid. Tristian continued to feed his wife until she withheld any further. Taking a seat beside her, she soon fell to slumber. She woke an hour later rested and restored.

"Tris..."

"It's all right, sweetheart. I'm here. You feeling okay? You need me to get your nurse?"

"Head aches."

"Agnus will stay with you while I get a nurse."

"I'm right here, dear. I'm not going anywhere. You just lie back and relax."

"Agnus," she declared feebly. "I have something to tell you."

Agnus leaned forth. "What's that, dear?"

"Miles. Your husband. I've seen him, Agnus. He's been in my dreams." She rose her hand toward her head. "He talks to me in here."

"I know, dear. I sent him to you through prayers."

Tears streamed down Josie's face. "He told me who he was, Agnus, and he stayed with me every second."

"You needed someone to ease your adversity, so I petitioned Miles' aid. I knew he wouldn't fail you, dear. You mean a lot to me, and you would have meant a lot to Miles had he known you."

"How do I thank you for what you've done? Simple words aren't enough."

"But they are, dear." Agnus held Josie's hand. "Save your strength, child. We'll talk when you're able."

A nurse approached the bed. "Mrs. O'Brien, your husband says you're experiencing pain?"

She replied weakly, "Yes." Josie put her hand upon her head when she felt the tube. "What? What's this thing in me?" She broke into tears.

"It's a cranio tube, sweetheart. Doctor put it there to remove any pressure," the nurse responded.

"My God. How long must I have this?" she asked with depression.

"Most likely you'll be losing it within the next couple days. Dr. Kentworth will talk with you tomorrow and let you know then. I've got you something for pain. This will help ease you."

Tristian reclined in his seat as Josie relaxed to her pillow.

"Tristian? Tristian, when do I get out of here?"

"That's up to the doctor, sweetheart."

"How long have I been in this place?"

"Well, it's about three days now."

Josie breathed deeply several times. "Where're you staying?"

Agnus commented, "With me, dear. Tristian's been at the house. Once you're out, you'll be coming, too. I've got you a nice bed awaiting."

"Do we still have our home?"

Tristian relayed, "We'll always have it. Ain't nothing going to take that away."

Josie patted her eyes. "I've been afraid to ask, but I must."

"Sweetheart? Sweetheart, why're you crying?"

"Tristian, answer me truthfully now."

"Sweetheart, what is it?"

She looked to him through swollen eyes. "I lost the baby, didn't I?"

"Sweetheart, no. Button's guarded, growing inside you. The baby's fine."

"Oh," she spoke with relief. "I was just sure of it. I want our baby to be safe."

"I know, Jos, but you have nothing to worry about. I promise. Dr. Kentworth ran tests to make sure."

"Tristian, that medicine's putting me to sleep. I'll be out before I know it. It's late, you see? You and Agnus should be getting home. I'll see you both tomorrow."

"I'd planned to come back after dropping her off."

"There's no need you stay all night. Go on home, dear, and get your rest."

"Well, Jos, are you sure?"

"I'm positive." She yawned.

"Can we do anything or get anything before we leave? Jos? Are you awake?"

Agnus confirmed, "That medicine's knocked her out. She'll be sleeping till morning. It's best we just go."

"Let me gather my coat." Tristian kissed his wife on top of the head. "Sleep well, my darling. I love you," he whispered.

CHAPTER THIRTY-THREE ◆

Agnus and Tristian stopped by Dagda's for a quick bite.

"I'm glad you both decided to stop in again," Ashlynn remarked. "Here're your meals. Agnus, your sheppard's pie. Careful, dear, it's hot. And your pot roast, Tristian. Is there anything else?"

Tristian looked at his plate. "Would you happen to have any bread?"

"Oh, good grief. I forgot that, didn't I? How bout I get you a full loaf?"

"One fourth would be fine."

Ashlynn joked, "Don't you argue with me. You'll get the full round. Take home what you don't eat. Be right back. Digby! Digby," she yelled. "Attend to their drinks, ye ole coot. They're running dry."

"Sorry, folks. I get a bit caught up here and there. Well, with those ole gents aside me, we just sing all the time. Limber limbs, I'd like to see you hit the floor for a spin."

"Oh, these frail ole bones would break, Dig. I'm much too old."

"Well, if you change your mind, come out for a dance."

"We'll see, dear. But if I do, it'd have to be a granny dance. Don't have the elasticity no more for that fancy stuff."

"Oh now, I bet you can."

"I think Ashlynn's right. You are an ole coot."

"That's why she married me. She knew."

"Oh, get out of here, you."

"Well, the both of you enjoy your meals. You need another round, you give a holler."

The Crying House

"Is that ole Digby at it again?" Ashlynn wondered. "I tell you, that man's a load of crazy. Since last you were in, all he's talked about is seeing you shimmy. You want to get out of it, Ag? Tell him your bones have dried up."

"He might take me for a puppet."

"You know, you're probably right. There's no sense in romping with him. Hell, there's none in declaring truth either. You've known Dig to drive his bargains. I've told him time on. You should have been a door salesmen."

Agnus cackled. "He still has some time."

"You're true on that. I just don't think I'd ever get him in a suit."

Tristian raised his brow. "Maybe a starched shirt and a tie?"

Ashlynn shook her head. "God, no. Not Digby."

"He wouldn't even try," added Agnus. "He likes the comforts of simplicity."

Ashlynn giggled. "You've said that spot on."

"Say, has Kieran been in anymore?"

"Just the other day. Said he was going to see you. Had he made it?"

"As a fact he did. Seemed sad after seeing Logan."

"He did go, did he? Wasn't sure if he would."

Agnus commented, "I think he was torn between going and not. But, yeah, he did. Said Logan wasn't looking too good. Come a day soon I'll have to go see him."

Ashlynn agreed. "I should make some time, too. After all, he was a child to each of us. So sad if he goes."

"What I heard from Kieran, he says he's given up. Compared to us, that man's still a baby."

"Well, you know Ciara's death killed him. He wasn't the same since. You know he's waiting to see her."

"What can we do? He has no fight. He gave up on life far long ago."

"And a sad thing it is." Ashlynn hung her head. "Well, folks, you all done with your plates?"

"I reckon so, dear. It was as good as always."

Digby peered from behind the bar. "I see you're finished there." He came round. "How bout that dance?"

"Oh, all right."

"Have fun," Tristian ejected.

"All right, men. Get to singing," Digby yelled.

Ashlynn returned to the table. "I see she crumbled upon request?"

"She's pretty good out there, isn't she?"

"You should have seen Ag in her day. She was one of the best performers I've had the pleasure of knowing."

"I know that'd make her day. She's talked to me about how much she loved it."

"She had stars in her eyes that'd just glisten and shine. Had you been mistaken, you'd think they were diamonds. It's a shame she never pursued something further. But I know she had fun here, so I guess that's what matters."

CHAPTER THIRTY-FOUR ◆

Day 9, the 14th of July, 1950. Mid-morning.

Dr. Kentworth stood outside the room with Tristian and Agnus. "Following last night's removal of the cranio tube, Josie seems to be in good spirits. She hasn't had any problems following the operation." He reviewed her chart. "The swelling in her brain has completely diminished. There's no signs of bleeding. Her sight's crisp. Equilibrium's stable. Furthermore, she seems of good health. I don't have any reason to keep her here longer."

"You're releasing her today?"

"That'd be the plan. I'll have a quick talk with her and see what she thinks." Dr. Kentworth traipsed into the room. "So, how're you feeling today?"

"Like I need to get out of this bed."

Dr. Kentworth smiled. "You're an eager one, aren't you?"

"Seems it's time to be."

"Are you experiencing any pains? Numbness? Tingles?"

"No, but if I stay on my back I'm liable to get bedsores. Doctor, shouldn't I be walking around? Get used to standing?"

"You feel that you're ready?"

"Quite certainly, sir. I keep this up, I'll be a potato."

"You ready to go home?"

Josie smiled. "Just hand me the papers."

Dr. Kentworth presented her with release forms. "Just sign these then."

"You serious? I get to go home?"

"You have to sign those x's first."

"I thought you were joking. I'm really being released?" She looked up to Agnus. "Is it true?"

"Yes, dear."

"Oh, blessed God, thank you. Here you are, doctor. Can I change now?"

"I'll need someone to remove your IV. I know you don't want that going with you."

"Of course not."

"Good. Hold still, and I'll be back." Dr. Kentworth returned with a nurse.

"Okay, I'll be taking your IV, Mrs. O'Brien."

"She's ready for that." Agnus chuckled.

Dr. Kentworth turned to Tristian. "Mr. O'Brien, couple things here. Make sure she doesn't use that broke wrist. I want her activities limited. Absolutely no heavy lifting. If she gets tired, let her rest. She starts complaining of any severe headaches, get in touch with me at once. I wrote a number down on this paper if you'd need to reach me. Here are her medications. Make sure she takes them as directed."

"Thank you, Dr. Kentworth. We appreciate all you've done."

"Well, that about covers it. Mr. O'Brien, you get that little lady home and make sure she gets pampered."

Tristian shook Dr. Kentworth's hand. "I will, sir. Thank you."

"Good day to you all," he said, walking from the room.

CHAPTER THIRTY-FIVE ♦

Josie lounged on the couch. "Thank you so much for having us here, Agnus. You've been a blessing."

"Well, I enjoy having you with me. Would you like a blanket, dear?"

"I'll be fine for the moment."

"Let me know if you change your mind. I'll warm us some tea, dear. Would you like that?"

"I'll take mine with cream."

Agnus went to the kitchen and heated her kettle. Once the water boiled, she made three cups of black tea. Setting them upon a server, she carried the tray to the living room. "Here you go, dear. A nice cup of hot tea." Agnus took a seat in her chair. "Now, come morrow marks the anniversary of Aidan's death," she told the O'Briens. "I've prepared myself for the challenge you've asked. By tomorrow, the essence you know there will change."

"Tomorrow?" Josie quizzed.

"Your house should be rid of him soon, then you and Tristian can go on with your lives."

"You're sure it's the anniversary?" Tristian wondered.

"Ninety-nine percent certain, but I'll check the obituary." Agnus opened an old wooden chest and dug through her things. She came across an aging scrapbook with worn pages and began to sift through each leaf. Opening the book to the third page, she found the ethereal death notice. It had yellowed and fawned at the edges, with hairline rips tainting the sheet. "Ah-huh, Aidan passed away the fifteenth of July. He was buried the twenty-first."

"It is tomorrow. You were right," Tristian responded.

"I'll need to go to the cemetery the day of his burial to perform his release. I know that's still another six days. But Josette, dear, with you just getting out of the hospital, I'd prefer you stay here alongside your husband."

"Agnus, you'd need someone with you. You can't go alone. I urge you, take Tristian," she pleaded.

"For your sake then, maybe I will."

Josie smiled. "Could you still bless our home?"

"I'll do that tomorrow, dear." Agnus took a second. "Aidan was murdered not long after Ciara's funeral." She peered at Mrs. O'Neill's obituary. "Says her services were at noon here. So, I'd believe sometime before six Aidan was killed."

Tristian asked, "Is that when you'll be going?"

"Thought maybe I'd get there by five; set things up."

"It doesn't matter what time it's done," stated Josie. "I just want my house back. I don't want the fear anymore."

"Sweet, dear, don't you worry. I'll have it tended to. Now, why don't you take some time to relax? Settle in and take a nap. You look tired."

"I am."

"I'll put her to bed," Tristian added.

Agnus stood from her chair. "It's about time I fix dinner. I better go off and do that."

Tristian helped Josie into the bedroom and laid her down. "This bed's comfortable. You should fall asleep fast. You'll find good rest here. I promise." Tristian smiled to his wife. "I'll check back later."

"Tristian, don't go. Stay aside me awhile."

"Oh, honey, I won't leave you."

"Please stay till I fall asleep."

"You know I will. Come close, sweetheart." He held Josie within his arms, caressing her softly. Twenty minutes would pass before Tristian joined Agnus.

"Your wife sleeping, child?"

"Peacefully asleep."

"Good. She needs that rest. Her body must heal."

"You're making soup, I see."

"Some hearty chicken noodle."

"Smells good."

"I thought if Josette feels up to it later, we'd show her the garden. My fairy folks would bring her some smiles."

"Aye," he agreed. "I have some errands to run right quick, Agnus. Would that be okay?"

"What's taking you off?"

"Thought I'd run by the hardware store. Get some things to sand those boards at the house and pick up some stain."

"I'll keep an eye on Josette while you're gone."

"I shouldn't be long."

"Well, be ready to eat when you get back."

CHAPTER THIRTY-SIX ◆

Tristian scoured the aisles of the plenty shop searching for appropriate materials to fix his house.

A clerk stood aside him. "You look a bit lost there, son. Is there something I can help you with?"

"Sir, I'm trying to find something to sand boards."

"You'll be needing glass paper. Come this way, and I'll show you our selection. We have everything from extra coarse to ultra fine."

"I'd need something for rapid removal."

"If you're not working with bare wood, I'd suggest either coarse or extra."

"I think several sheets of this coarse shall do."

"And how many for you?"

"Oh, I don't know." Tristian relayed, "Maybe ten for now."

"A wood plane might also interest you if you'd need to level things."

Tristian looked at the tool. "I'll take one of those, too."

"Any certain one for you, son?"

"That one you've got's fine. What about stain? Do you carry that here?"

"Absolutely. I have darks, mediums, and lights."

"I'm looking for a medium taint."

"I have several colors here."

Tristian peered them over. "I think this one should do."

"One can?"

"I've got a lot of work. We better make that three."

"All right. Does this round things up for you?"
"As of now. Should I need further supplies I'll come back."
"I'll ring you up here."
"Oh, I forgot," Tritian told the man. "I'll need a brush."
"Right behind you there. You can't miss them."
"This should work. I'm sorry, sir. I'm ready now."
"Three cans of stain, a brush, ten glass papers and one plane. Okay, your total comes to $7.25, son."
Tristian counted his money. "There you go, sir."
"Thank you very much. You have a good day."

CHAPTER THIRTY-SEVEN ◆

Tristian came through the front door. "It's just me, Agnus."
"In the kitchen, dear."
"Still cooking?"
"No, soup's all done. You getting hungry?"
"I reckon I am." He looked around. "Jos still sleeping?"
"Last time I checked."
"Should probably wake her." Tristian set his bag upon the couch, then went to the guest room. Rubbing his wife's shoulder lightly, he roused her from sleep. "Dinner time, love. How bout you wake up?"
"How long have I been sleeping?"
"Just over an hour. Come on. Rise up. You need food in your system."
"Could you give me five minutes?"
"Sure. I'll be in the kitchen. Holler if you need me."
Tristian joined aside Agnus. "She'll be down in a few."
"You mind helping me with something, dear?"
"Of course. What do you need?"
"I set candles in the back yard and around the garden. Would you help me light them?"
"You having a party?"
"Thought it'd be magical for Josette. It'll be enchanting having flames dancing beneath the moonlight."
"What a wonderful idea."
"They're all over the place now. On the ground and in the trees. Let's make sure we get them all."

After finishing, they stood in the mid-section of the garden.

Tristian poised in captivation. "This is breathtaking; those candles lit up a glow. The beauty's trancing."

"Just wait till it's dark."

"I can only imagine."

They returned to the house just as Josie made her way to the kitchen.

"You nap well, dear?"

"Haven't slept good as that in a long time."

Agnus put her arm around her. "You feel rested enough to see something later?"

"I won't go to that house if that's what it is."

"No, dear, no. It's something marvelous."

Josie peered with wonder. "What is it?"

"You'll have to wait and find out."

Josie then giggled. "It's like that, is it?"

Tristian added, "Trust me, Jos. It's a good surprise you're really going to like."

"Oh, you two. Now I'm curious."

"You're eager now, aren't you?" Agnus patted her hand.

"Can we hurry and eat?"

"Give me a moment to ladle your bowls."

Following dinner, Tristian removed a hand towel from a drawer, then stood behind his wife.

"What's this?" she asked.

"For your security. We can't have you peeking."

"I'll shut my eyes, Tristian. There's no need for this blindfold."

"Not good enough. I don't trust you."

"Ah," she expressed.

"Let me tie this around your head. Not too tight, is it?"

"No."

"Okay, take my hand and stand. Carefully follow me."

"You bought me a cake, didn't you?"

"No questions now." Tristian told Josie while Agnus held the back door. "Watch your step."

"Where're we going?"

"Ah-ah, no questions, remember?"

"Agnus? Agnus, what's going on?"

"It's a surprise, dear. You'll see."

"Oh, this taunting abounds."

"Soon, sweetheart." Tristian led Josie out to the middle of the yard.

"We're outside, aren't we?"

Agnus walked before Tristian, handing forth a velvet red rose she had cut from her garden.

"I can't take this suspense any longer. Would someone give me a hint please?"

"You ready, Jos?"

"Yes, yes, I'm ready."

Tristian untied the knot, loosening the blindfold from Josie's eyes. "Here it is, sweetheart. Surprise."

Josie opened her eyes with amazement as Tristian was holding the rose before her. "Oh, honey, it's lovely."

"Now look around you." He said, stepping aside.

Josie beheld the yard through first glimpse. Her mouth dropped as she was taken by its entrancing allure. Turning around, she spoke in marvel. "It's a beautiful dream."

Agnus came aside her. "Welcome to enchantment."

The sun slowly set below the sky, splashing upon casts of radiant pink, purple and golden undertones. Large shrubs filled the yard, intermixed with sparkling lights. Flowers surfaced the ground in every stain imaginable, while innumerable candles gleamed about. The fragrance of wild flowers winded through air as each scent carried toward Josie. Breathing in, she inhaled their ambrosial honey. Beneath the darkening sky, taper flames lit the green earth upon mounds of white wax.

Josie ejected, "I've never seen anything so amazing in all my life."

"Come over here, dear." Agnus pulled apart the petals of a rose. "Look closely inside."

Nestled within the secluded cradle slept a baby fairy no more the size of a dime. She laid upon her tummy, sucking her thumb tightly.

Josie smiled. "How precious she is. I'm amazed. Amazed to see something this magical resting here."

"You like to see more?" Agnus led Josie to another part the garden where fairies soared in the air, dancing atop flower petals, they spun

The Crying House

round. Two thimble-sized sprites flew toward Josie, kissing her upon the cheeks. Another fluttered onto her shoulder, then took a seat.

"We're having a wing-ding," said a tiny voice. "Come join."

"Why, I'd love to," said Josie, happily, while a few flew around, sprinkling her with dust.

A young fairy child whisked toward Josie and smooched the tip of her nose. "I'm Elora Elderberry," she spoke softly. "I picked this for you."

"How sweet. Thank you, kind sprite."

Elora exclaimed, "It's a bush berry. I'll pick you another."

Agnus took Josie by the pond where fairies waded in crystal waters. Some had small boats of twigs and twine, while others sat upon lily pads and stared at the stars. Others drifted below to the wrinkled lagoon on leaflets that passed from unbinding trees. Dragonflies soared across the rippling current, while fireflies blazed their tiny bodies like alighted lanterns.

Elves and pixies ran freely through the yard gathering fruits, nuts, and herbs.

"It's a whole new world here," Tristian commented. "One would be blessed to see."

Agnus gathered chairs for herself and the O'Briens. Then, sitting, they watched the wondrous things before them.

Elora drifted back to Josie and showered her with berries.

"Another thing I love about this place besides its beauty and mystique is, if you want something, the wee ones will get it." Agnus waved forth her hand. "Elora, my little dear. Would you and Arianna gather gramsy Aggie some berries?"

"We'd be delighted. What shall we bring?"

"Gooseberries, dear. You know I like those. Make sure they're ripe."

Elora gathered Arianna as they hovered to the bush.

"Mind those thorns, dears. Don't want either of you getting pricked."

Arianna responded to Agnus, "We're okay." Her tiny voice lingered. "Here you are, gramsy. The biggest we could carry."

"You babies are the best."

"It was our pleasure," Elora responded.

"Tristian, dear, why don't you try? What might you like?"

"I do adore cherry plums."

"I've got those here. Arinana, you mind?"

"She can't get that big thing alone," Elora declared. "It'd have to be three of us, gramsy. Maybe four."

"Gather some friends to help you."

"I'll race you," Arianna challenged Elora as they fluttered off.

Elora laughed. "You won't win. Your wings don't race as fast as mine."

Tristian smiled. "They're no different than humans."

"In some aspects," Agnus agreed.

Josie questioned, "How long have you had them here?"

"Since Miles and I moved in. My garden grew along with them. This place is their home. I'll do everything to keep them safe."

"That you must. A world that lacks magic is a world without bliss."

"But only those who believe can speak of that truth."

"I'm an upholder to that, Agnus. Not only do I believe with my eyes, but I believe in my heart."

"That's why I showed you this place, dear. Only those who are deserving to see are allowed the sight."

Elora and Arianna returned with a company of friends. Each supported the singular plum with their teensy hands, while their tiny wings buzzed like a roundup of bees. "It's a heavy one," their stunted voices shouted. "Hurry. Oh, hurry. It's slipping. It's slipping."

Elora ejected, "We can't hold on. It's going to plummet."

"I've got it." Tristian opened his hand as the plum plunged to his palm.

"Nice save," Arianna declared.

"Aye, it was. And a stout thing it is. I applaud your might."

"I work out," said a friendly male sprite. "If it wasn't for me, they'd have dropped it for sure."

Arianna flew up to him. "Oh, stop your boasting, Finn. We all helped."

"You needed me, Ari. Go on, say it."

She crossed her little arms. "I won't say a thing."

"Can I at least fly you back to your berry bush?"

"Fine then. We'll make it a race."

Finn responded, "In that case, no cheating."

The Crying House

Arianna shimmied her little body. "Come on now. I'm ready, you slow poke."

Agnus yawned lightly. "It's getting late for these ole eyes. Best for me to get back inside."

"I'll blow out these candles." Tristian then told Agnus and Josie, "Go on, you go. Off with you both."

Josie rubbed lightly upon his shoulder. "I'll meet you in bed."

Agnus walked alongside her as they talked for a moment. "I hope you've enjoyed yourself tonight. I think being out has done you some good."

Josie smiled. "You've given me a wondrous surprise. I've had the time of my life here."

"It's yours when you want it. You come on out when you please."

Josie went on up to the bedroom and awaited her husband.

Agnus was sitting in the living room drinking a bottle of ale when Tristian appeared.

"Candles are all out."

"Even those in the trees?"

"Every last one's been blown."

"And a good dear you are. I might have to start hiring you to tend to my garden."

"I'd be more than happy to do what you'd need."

"You have a good night, dear, and I'll see you come morning."

"Same to you, Agnus. Sleep well." Tristian went upstairs to the bedroom.

"Sweetheart, I put your pajama bottoms on the chair. Hurry, change, then come to bed," Josie told him.

"You take your medicine like the doctor said?"

She nodded to him. "Yes, I made sure. Now come on, climb in." Josie turned aside and looked in his eyes. "You know, Tristian, how thankful I am to have you as my husband?"

"And I'm ever the more grateful, having you." He smiled.

"Through all of this, you've stood beside me." She tasseled his hair lightly with her hand. "I know just how much you care, and it means a lot. Having yours and Agnus's dedication was an honor. You're both dear to my heart, Tristian. I'm blessed to have the two of you in my life, I really am."

"We're as much as lucky having you." Tristian pulled himself from the bed. "Sweetheart, you've always been my life. You've kept me going each day. Without you, Jos, I'd literally crumble. My entire world would perish had you not been here."

Josie caressed his face. "I'd do the same and waste without you. You've brought so much to my life, Tristian. Not only are you my husband, you're also my greatest friend."

He kissed her softly. "We're blessed to have each other." He then held his wife as they descended to sleep.

Josie slipped away into a dream while it vividly played forth in her mind. She'd been out in her back yard gathering wildflowers as butterflies lit upon her, kissing the rounds of her shoulders. Then, taking the arrangement into the house, she settled them into a vase upon the kitchen table.

Proceeding to her room, she stripped the bed sheets, relining the mattress with fresh covers. Then, unfolding clean blankets and a comforter, stretched them to straightness. She removed old pillowcases, reinstating them with speckless shrouds. Then, fluffing the pillows, she puffed them to life. Josie took the dirtied laundry down to the wash before gathering the still moistened clothing from their bath. Grabbing a basket, she trotted outside and hung the dampened threads on the line.

Birds passed through the yard singing their merry tunes. And it wasn't long before a familiar squawk pierced air. Josie turned in search of the lone bird responsible. It was then, upon a tree, Josie spotted the perched raven ogling down. Abandoning the clothes line, Josie eyed the bird.

The raven took off from its limb, then alighting the house, sat in bluster, persisting its squawk. Josie shook away regard as she recollected her thoughts and carried forth with the clothes.

Turning toward the house, she'd noticed a shadow near one of the windows. It was that time the raven cawed louder. But to Josie its strident inform was of worthless regard. Discounting the spectacle which had now gone astray, Josie carried ahead, inching closer toward the door.

Once inside, she removed a dusting rag from beneath the kitchen sink. Then, proceeding upstairs, made way to her room. From the exterior window she once again heeded the persistent request of the raven's call. Becoming agitated the feathered ascender began to tap glass.

"How goes it, pretty bird? You looking for seed?" she asked. "Just you wait there while I gather you some."

The raven pecked the glass even harder. Now flaring its wings, it shifted them back and forth.

"Calm your excitement. I'm going, you see?" It was then, in glass, she'd noticed a man's reflection. An unsettling feeling crept over her body as she frantically collected breaths. Slowly turning round, Josie encountered a long, silver, blade stretched to her face. With fright, her eyes widened, while strain imbibed her nerves.

"You've taken from me, wench. While me wife was my business, ye thought she was yours to attend. What gave ye the right?" Aidan leaned into her. "Ye better start talking, or I jam this shiv right into your pretty little throat."

Josie quivered with fear as Aidan threatened her. And pecking the glass ever harder, the raven tried to break in.

"What's wrong, wench? Cat got your tongue?" Aidan held the blade upon her throat. "Answer me, damn you," he violently expelled.

Josie squeezed her eyes as tears emerged from pressure. "I've tried telling you. I've done nothing." She released her hold. "Ciara's where she's at, not because of me," she cried. "I can't help you, Aidan."

"Don't ye ever, ever, speak me name."

Josie peered toward the ceiling. "God, tell him. She isn't coming back."

"You're bringing your God into this? I'm upon me last nerve with you. You've got one final chance, wench. Ye tell me now, and I'll let ye alone."

Hysteria settled in on Josie as she pondered an escape. Taking her chances, she vigorously kneed Aidan's groin. While doubled in pain, Josie passed by, allowing enough time around him. But her battle was far from over as Aidan at once caught the back of her ankle, dragging her to the ground.

Screaming, she fought to get away, but Aidan was much too strong. Pulling her across the floor, he crawled her body like a giant spider. Then, proceeding to settle upon her legs, held her down. "Ye had to go mess things up, didn't you? Be it the innocence within you that pays."

Aidan raised the knife above him as Josie began blaring forth grieving shrieks.

Trying to shield her belly, she wailed. "Not my baby! I beg you, please. Don't hurt my child. Don't hurt my child."

Aidan dismissed Josie's pleas, plunging the knife deep into her abdomen and striking the fetus. Blood oozed from the wound, pouring to the floor. It was the first of many elongated sticks. Soon after, Aidan cleaved her twelve more times, twisting the blade with each blow. Back and forth within Josie, the slicing swept across her organs.

As Aidan commenced on stabbing again, she reached forth to scratch him. The session would pass until there was no fight left within her. By the time he'd finished, Aidan had carved her like a butchered turkey.

Inside her chest, Josie felt her heartbeats lessen. A sudden sequence of past memories flashed before her. Gargling through blood, Josie's breath had thereupon shallowed, as her life began to fade. "Save me," she cried in bed. Seconds later would mark the instant when her breathtaking approached its conclusive halt.

Discerning her delusional trial, Tristian awoke. "Jos. Josie. Sweetheart, wake up."

She screamed in clamorous dread. "Tristian!"

"Honey. Honey, it's okay. It's just a nightmare." He tried to console her. Her breathing transcended into hyperventilation. Sitting forth, Tristian rubbed upon her. It was then he'd noticed she'd still been asleep. "Jos, honey, wake up."

She flew from bed, screaming. "My baby! He's killed my baby! That bloody bromide. How dare he. How dare he, that filth." She rocked back and forth, sobbing uncontrollably, then fell backward, rubbing her stomach. Barely able to breathe, she whimpered. "That caitiff. God, damn, him. That caitiff took button. Damn him. God, damn, him. I need help, Tristian. I bloody need help."

"Sweetheart. Sweetheart, calm down. It was nothing more than a dream. You're all right."

She continued screaming. "He stabbed me, though, Tristian. I felt the knife."

"Jos, look." He pulled back the covers. "Look here. You're all right. You see? Your stomach's fine. Not a scratch on you."

"I don't understand?" She breathed heavily. "I felt that knife. It tore me apart."

A light knock then tapped at the door. "Everything all right, dears? I heard shouting."

"All's fine. Jos just had a bad dream."

"You mind I come in?"

Josie hollered, "Aidan killed my baby! He killed it, I say."

"She won't stop saying that," Tristian ejected.

"Bloody hell. Won't you listen?"

"Josette. Child, you have to calm down. You're not doing yourself good by this."

"Why don't either of you listen?"

"Ease yourself, dear. You must catch your breath."

"Just listen to me, damn it. I know what you'll say, and it wasn't a dream either!"

Tristian tried holding her hand. "Sweetheart, it was only a nightmare. It can't hurt you."

"Stop saying that."

"Jos, honey, folks get them all the time."

"But something doesn't feel right." She cried to her hands. "Please just call the doctor and have him come check me."

"Baby, I've showed you already. Your belly's fine."

"I want an exam, Tristian. You don't know what to do. You're not a doctor." She wiped her head. "Shit. All this damn sweat's pouring from me. I need some cold water."

"I'll get it for you," Agnus responded.

"Tristian, get me out of this sopping gown. The thing's clinging stuck." Josie pulled the covers beneath her waist and stood from the bed. "Oh my God, no. No, no, no. Tristian. Tristian, you said it didn't happen." She exposed a stain upon the sheet. "That's blood there, you see? That's blood, Tristian, blood." She began shaking hysterically.

"Lord, no. It can't be," he uttered.

Agnus returned to Josie's screaming as she wailed to her husband. "You said it couldn't happen. You said. You said." Josie's panic heightened as she felt the rear of her guise. "It's all on me. All this blood. Make it stop. It won't cease," she cried. "Aidan killed my baby, Agnus. He killed my baby. My baby. My baby. No, God. My baby."

Agnus turned her away. "Shh, honey, shh. I don't want you looking." Agnus peered upon Tristian. "Call Dr. Kentworth, dear. Do it now."

"Why'd he take button? Agnus, why?" Tears ran down Josie's face in streamlets. "How am I here? After all that he's done? I want my baby, Agnus. I want my baby button." She began gasping without a breath of ease.

"Josette. Josette, no, no, no. I can't hold you, dear. I'm not steady."

Josie's winded pants made her to turn dizzy.

"Tristian!" Agnus yelled. "Get here quick. I need help."

He ran behind his wife. Barely catching her, she passed backwards in his arms and blacked out.

"You've called the doctor I hope?"

"Be here shortly. I'll get the door opened." Tristian raced to the first floor while Agnus stayed with Josie.

Before her window, Agnus spied a washstand. Atop it a floral pitcher sat upon the trestle. Pulling forth its grandiose bowl, she soddened the base. Agnus arrived at the bed, setting aside the sink. Then, submerging a towel, Agnus hydrated its thirsting implore.

Tristian returned to the room. "How's she doing?"

"Resting for now. I'll need to gather more cloths."

Tristian secured the towelette and patted his wife's face. "Oh, sweetheart. Sweetheart, what do I say?" He sniffled lightly. "I thought you and button were safe. How could he have been so merciless? We didn't deserve this pang."

"Hello? Mr. O'Brien?" a voice called from below. "Anyone home? It's Dr. Kentworth."

"Sir, upstairs," Tristian responded.

Dr. Kentworth met Agnus as she exited the bathroom. "This way, doctor."

"I came as quickly as I could."

"Here we are, sir."

"How is she?"

Tristian peered upon him. "She passed out just a bit ago."

"Oh mercy." Dr. Kentworth walked the room where Josie laid. He put his black bag upon the floor, then reached for his stethoscope. Placing it upon her stomach, he listened for any indications of the baby's heartbeat. Soon after, he cast his auscultator aside while Tristian and

Agnus stood in distress. "I'm very sorry, son. I'm afraid I didn't hear a heartbeat."

Tristian crumbled with ache. "That was to be our first child." He cried.

"I'm most grieved for your loss. These experiences are most unfavorable for patients. I'm mournful for bestowing the news, son. I know how cheerful you were."

"There's no chance it survived?"

Dr. Kentworth shook slowly. "Even with this amount of bleeding, there's no way."

Tristian dropped his head to his hands and cried harder. Agnus traipsed alongside, caressing his back. "I hate that this happened, dear. I'm terribly sorrowed." She held him tightly. "She'd been doing so well."

"I don't understand." He mourned to her shoulder. "I thought we were safe?"

"Tristian, if there's anything, child. Anything I can do, please, you let me know."

Dr. Kentworth spoke forth, "I'm going to give Josie a sedative. I'll be performing a minor procedure to remove the fetus. In all it should be about thirty to forty-five minutes."

Tristian questioned, "Will you be taking her to the hospital for this?"

"I can do the operation here. Would that be a problem?"

"What type thing will you do?"

"A simple dilation of her cervix, then scrape the uterus."

"She'll be okay?"

"She's under anaesthesia, son. She'll be sleeping soundly."

Agnus added, "Go on. Do it here. I'll get whatever necessities you may need."

Dr. Kentworth reached into his bag and began setting out instruments. He placed a metal clamp upon the dresser, along with a speculum and a long metal rod known as a curette. Then, into a deposit bowl he set his gloves and a stack of square gauze.

Dr. Kentworth looked upon Tristian. "You may want to leave the room awhile, son. I'll get you when surgery's over."

"Sir, I hate asking, but I'm a nervous wreck. You have anything you might give me? I'm hardly able to deal with this."

Jillian Osborn

"Of course. Of course." Dr. Kentworth fished through his bag. "Try this."

"I appreciate it, sir. Thank you."

"Mrs. O'Toole, do you have any medical experience?"

"Some."

"Good enough."

"But, sir, I'm not a doctor."

"I'd only need an assistant. You think you'd manage?"

"Well, I don't mind. I suppose. Tristian, would you be okay with that?"

"Josie would like that you helped."

"What about you, dear?"

"I'll be fine."

"You're sure?"

"She couldn't be in better hands. Do what you must."

"Take my bed for now, dear. Find you some rest. We'll let you know when it's over."

Dr. Kentworth prepped Josie for surgery as Tristian left. "Mrs. O'Toole, could..."

"Agnus, dear. Just Agnus."

"Okay, Agnus. I'll need a wet towel."

"Here you are."

"All right, let me wipe away this blood. Very good. I'm ready for the speculum."

"Speculum."

"Could you get the clamp ready while I put this in place?" He dilated Josie's cervix enough to see the uterus. "I need that ampoule there and those two syringes." After clamping the cervix, Dr. Kentworth put a local anesthetic into both sides of Josie's cervical wall. "Yes. Yes, I see the head. I'll need that curette now." He inserted the sharp loop into Josie's uterus and began scraping. "Scalpel, please." Dr. Kentworth cut a thin line into the placenta as a flow of blood rushed forth. Scouring away excrements, he further exposed the fetus. Then, slowly he pulled the remains of the fetal sac. "Scissors." Cutting the umbilical cord, Dr. Kentworth severed the embryo's nutritional connection. Then, with further braying, removed the rest of the endometrium and was now finished with surgery.

Agnus wondered, "Might you be able to tell what caused the miscarriage?"

"I'll need to take a look. You have somewhere I can set this tray?"

"Let me clear a place on the dresser."

"That's fine there. That'll do. Let me excise the fetus and we'll see what we've got." Dr. Kentworth examined the placenta closely. "This incision I've made was too small. I'll need to cut farther." He lengthened the split, then withdrew the infant child. "What might we have here?" It was then Dr. Kentworth's eyes had widened. "My, I've never before seen anything like this. Won't you come look?"

Agnus eased beside him. "Oh, dear God. That poor little soul." She stood in dreaded regard. "A mutation, you think?"

"Not this, no. Definitely not. Look closer here. See the way her stomach's incised? It's as though this child's belly had been deliberately perforated to the point of disembowelment. In natural cases, the intestines shouldn't be exposed. For this, there's no plausible means. Only feasible fact would be murder. Even at that, Agnus, it's beyond rational belief. Her physical conditions make no sense." Dr. Kentworth was highly perplexed by his findings. "I don't understand. I really don't."

Agnus peered upon the child once more. "That's the most distressing sight my eyes have ever seen." She soon thought back to Josie's words. "The poor dear was right."

"What's that, Agnus?"

"I know what's happened."

"Did Josie somehow do this?"

"No, not her."

"Then there's no way to explain this."

"Yes, sir, there is. You may find it weird, even hard to believe."

"Can't be any stranger than what I've just seen. If you have a way to resolve this, then please go ahead."

"Earlier tonight Josette claimed to have been stabbed in a dream. That would account for the wounds on her daughter."

Dr. Kentworth looked at Agnus in disbelief. "You really think a dream killed this child?"

"Wasn't her dream that did it. It twas the person inside."

"I ... I don't know what to say. You really want me believing this?"

"Ever heard of the crying house?"

"It's a local legend. Of course, I know it."

"Then you know where it's at?"

"I just know of tales passed down by my father."

"That house, it's across the street, Dr. Kentworth. The O'Briens live there."

"What's this have to do with the legend?"

"If you know the legend, surely you've been told of Aidan?"

"Aidan O'Neill. He was the wretched bastard who killed his wife."

"Well, that wretched bastard's been haunting his former grounds."

"That, I follow. But, Agnus, I don't get the full picture. What's this have to do with the O'Briens?"

"Josette was in the hospital because of him."

"Clearly you're saying his spirit has harmed her?"

"More times than once."

Dr. Kentworth peered down at the child. "And you're declaring he'd done this?"

"Josie would argue. There's no doubt in her mind."

Dr. Kentworth took a deep breath, then divulged. "My father once knew him. Said Aidan was the meanest person he'd ever met. Told me all he ever saw were flames in his eyes and a vacant heart."

"I only acknowledge what I know, Dr. Kentworth. Much like Josette, I don't distrust it was him."

"You seem to stand confident in your belief."

"You're a man of high intelligence and reasonable judgment, doctor. Do you accredit spiritual beings or diabolic possession?"

"Well," he spoke aloud. "I consider myself fairly open to the ideas of supernatural possibilities and occurrences. I've seen things I can't explain, but I know exist."

"Do you understand the circumstances that have been plaguing the O'Briens?"

"You think this child was murdered?"

"I most certainly do."

"As hard as it might be to conceive, I think you're on to something. I'd like to additionally examine this child's body; see if I can't conclude further reason." Dr. Kentworth looked over Josie. "There's one thing I still can't understand. Why there's no visible wounds anywhere upon her?"

"Shall I gather Tristian?"

"We'll see what he says." Dr. Kentworth wrapped the infant in a towel.

Tristian peered innocently toward the bed.

"Come in, son. Come in. Agnus, I need water."

"I'll rinse this bowl and get more."

Tristian slowly entered the room. "She do okay?"

"Have a seat on the chair. How're you doing? You feeling all right?"

"Sort of numb, I guess."

"You think you could tell me about the dream your wife had tonight?"

"It was a nightmare. What about it?"

"Could you disclose what happened?"

Agnus whispered softly, "Your water, doctor."

"She'd been moaning and screaming. By the time she awoke, Jos was yelling she'd been stabbed." Tristian shook in confusion. "Pardon me, but I thought you'd go over her surgery?"

"Well, I had a question of concern before I got to that."

"She didn't miscarry the baby from natural reasons, did she?"

"No, son. I'm afraid not."

"What caused the trouble?"

"I'm not sure we should get into that."

"I'm the father. I should know."

Dr. Kentworth reluctantly told, "She'd been disemboweled."

"You're telling me my daughter was gutted?"

Dr. Kentworth stood silent. "I know it's a horrible reality to hear. I'm extremely sorry, son. I didn't want to tell you. I was at loss when I revealed the discovery. Agnus told me what happened. I didn't want to believe. I didn't. But after realizing it made sense, I had to accept it."

"This is all Aidan's fault. Everything's been because of him. Here I thought we'd be safe. But that bloody devil still finds ways of achieving hell."

"Why don't I take you back to my room so you can settle down?" Agnus told him.

"How was I so blind? He said he'd get us when we least expected it.

I never imagined he'd go after our baby. Why didn't I pay more heed? Innocence is slain while the wicked roam. It was right in my face. The bastard wanted our child."

"Son, why don't you let Agnus help you to her room?"

"I don't care to lie down."

Dr. Kentworth pondered. "Had you ever thought about moving? You know the farther you are, the better you'd be."

"It was I who didn't want to be forced from our home. I pushed Jos into putting up with its frightful terror."

"I understand sometimes you need to stand your ground. But what if he doesn't leave you? You willing to risk your life?"

"Seems already we are," Tristian divulged.

Dr. Kentworth looked upon Josie. "What might you tell your wife? Wasn't just a coincidence she had that horrific dream. May be best to keep things straight."

"How much time before she awakens?"

"Should be shortly. We need to get another gown."

Agnus responded, "I'll fetch one from the drawer, then gather fresh sheets."

Tristian helped Dr. Kentworth pull the blooded gown from his wife. Holding her steadily, they bathed her swiftly. Agnus returned to the bed, then handed forth the sleeper.

Tristian held Josie within his arms while Agnus pulled aside the sopped sheets. Dr. Kentworth then aided in scrubbing the mattress. After finishing, they capped the bed with laundered covers.

"I better throw these in water." Agnus took the soiled linens to the wash.

Tristian lounged into a chair while Dr. Kentworth planted his instruments within his bag.

Tristian rose from his seat. "Agnus forgot a towel. I better go catch her."

"No, no. Not that, son. It comes with me."

"It's a blooded towel, sir."

"I'll need it."

"Is there something in this?"

"Don't touch that, please."

"It's our baby, isn't it?"

Dr. Kentworth drooped his head in shame. "I tried warning you."

"Oh, God."

"Please, son, just let it be. I'll tend to it."

Agnus reentered the room with a piece of plastic in hand. "Doctor, I thought you might use this." She leaned forth to whisper, "It'll stop the blood from ruining your bag. Cape the towel in that."

"That's a gifted idea you've got."

"I figured you'd need to protect your stuff." From the corner of her eye, Agnus spotted movement. "I think your patient's waking, sir."

"Yes, I see. She's coming round." He edged aside the bed. "Josie, you hear? It's Dr. Kentworth."

"I'm ... I'm cold."

"We'll get you more blankets."

"Where am I?"

"Home. In bed."

"No. No, you must get me out."

"You're safe. Agnus has you in a room."

"Oh."

"Are you feeling all right?"

"I want to sleep," she muttered.

Dr. Kentworth turned to Agnus and Tristian. "We'll give her a bit longer."

"Wait." Josie fluttered her eyes. "My baby. Did you save my baby?"

"We'll talk when you're up, dear. Just rest for now," responded Dr. Kentworth.

"I must know. How's my baby?"

"I promise you, dear. We'll talk later."

"Tristian? Tristian, are you here?"

"Right aside you, hon."

"Please, Tristian. Tell me."

"Josie, it's Dr. Kentworth. Frankly, sweetheart, it'd be best we talked once you're absolutely aware."

"I'm awake. I can talk."

Dr. Kentworth stared upon Agnus as she conferred her suggestion. "We can't evade this forever. At some point we'll have to give."

Dr. Kentworth agreed as he took a belabored breath. "Josette.

Josette, there's nothing I could do, dear. I'm afraid she was already gone."

Josie howled nonstop, grievously mourning the death of her daughter. "My baby girl. My baby girl. God, no. No. No. No. My little button. No. I want her with me. Bring her back."

Dr. Kentworth morosely acknowledged, "I don't have that power. I would if I could, dear. I truly mean it. But I can't. There's just no way."

"Never will I see her. That makes me ache."

Tristian's eyes filled with tears as he shared in her pain. Agnus held Josie and tried to calm her, but it wasn't any use. She was suffering a complete breakdown.

"Where is she? Where's my button? I want but one glance before she's gone," Josie demanded.

"I don't think that'd be a fair idea," Dr. Kentworth commented.

"I want to see my daughter. I have a right."

"Josie, you really shouldn't. Please listen to me."

"It's my choice, doctor. If I want to see her, you should abide by my wishes," she shouted.

Dr. Kentworth looked at Tristian and awaited a response. Tears flowed down his eyes as he nodded.

Agnus asked, "You sure you want to see her, child?"

"I want to be at peace. Knowing I at least got to see her would apply my content. Even if it's just a few seconds." She then pled to Dr. Kentworth, "Please, I beg you, grant me the time."

He patted her hand. "I really don't see this as wise, but again, you insist. It's my respect to listen." Dr. Kentworth opened his bag.

Josie broke down when he'd exposed the plastic-bound towel. Panting hard, she began to shake violently. Tears showered her face as her eyes swelled and ripened red.

"I hate for you to see this," he added. "Is there no way to change your mind?"

"Please, just hand her to me." Josie cradled her tiny baby as she pulled away the plastic. Slowly she peeled the towel astern and unveiled her daughter's face. She then gasped. "How helpless, my button. So fragile is she." Waiting a moment, Josie gazed upon her child's face, soaking in her image. Then, rubbing her hand across the baby's head, she tasseled its hair softly. "She'd have been perfect." Josie brushed her fingertips across her tiny little cheeks. "I would have been tender had I been a mother."

Agnus stood before her. "You'll always be tender, dear. It's best now, child, you hand her forth."

Josie disregarded the plea. Pulling the towel away from her daughter's body, she unclad her stripped organs. Stricken with fright, she began to bawl louder. "Why's her tummy apart like this?" Josie continued to cry. Not able to take the sight any longer, she folded the towel over the baby and shadowed her wounds. "It isn't fair. He stabbed me to get to her. It isn't fair. Why is it I breathe?"

Agnus took the child from Josie and released her to Dr. Kentworth.

Tristian walked to his sobbing wife, then took her in his arms. "I know, Jos. I know. It's not fair."

"How do we move on from this, Tristian? When I breathe, it's despair."

"You're important to me, Jos. Just as much as our daughter. Though she's not here, I still need you. We can deal with this together. Sweetheart, we've experienced the same loss. More than that, we'll never forget her. We can have more children, Jos. There's always time. God granted the gift of you being here. Let's not give that up. We'll shoot to keep trying."

Josie cried in his arms. "If only I'd escaped, Tristian. She'd still be alive. It's my fault. My fault I couldn't get away."

"It's not your fault. Don't you go on blaming yourself, Jos. I'll not hear of it."

Dr. Kentworth queried, "How bout I give her a little something to aid her with ease? It's best now she rest."

"Jos, I think you should take the shot. You heard Dr. Kentworth."

Soon as it entered her veins, Josie commenced peacefully. The injection tired her rapidly, and before long she went to sleep.

"She should be sound till morning. Here are some pills. Make sure she takes one every four hours for pain. I'll check in tomorrow and see how things are."

"You've been a great help, doctor. Thank you," said Tristian, as he and Agnus escorted him downstairs.

"I hope you'll both get some rest. Good night to you, Tristian.

Nighty-night to you, Agnus." Dr. Kentworth paced to his hardtop as Mrs. O'Toole shut her door.

Within his car, he placed his key in ignition. It was then a strange, sudden, chill crept over as he progressed to the old crying house. Catching his attention, an unexpected forced curved his head.

Peering through the shelter of his window, Dr. Kentworth took heed of the O'Briens' front door, and it was in plain view that he saw the hatchway stood opened.

Fixed between the wooden frame, a single man stared into darkness. Firmly grasped within his palm was a long, shiny knife, notably ascribed as a butcher. Upon him soaked a bloody mess, covering his pants, hands, arms, and shirt. With steady restrain he faced the blade en route of the floor. A single blooded pearl managed to descend the stone mat. Dr. Kentworth could hear the splatter not far away as it emphatically struck a top pavement.

Goosebumps crept over every inch of Dr. Kentworth as he peered in dismay. In an abrupt act Aidan heaved the knife forth, intentionally directing it toward the doctor's car. Trying to avoid the sinister point, Dr. Kentworth willfully swerved in hope of averting collision. But his window shattered, sending forth rigid shards of fractured glass. Exiting the passenger window, the butcher became scarce as it dropped out of sight.

Upon him, the doctor endured smithereens of glass which discomfortingly gouged his hands, arms, and face. Shaken by what had just happened, the doctor pulled aside promptly, stopping his car. Looking upon his review mirror, he gawked in sight of his disfigured face. Through unwavering approach, he pulled the fragments from the skin of his guise. It was then his anguish spread quickly. Dr. Kentworth realized he was in much worse condition than he thought. The competent doctor knew he'd need to get to the hospital.

CHAPTER THIRTY-EIGHT ◆

Day 10, the 15 of July, 1950.

Tristian watched the sun rise as the first ray of light illuminated the room. Confronted by conscious wake, he decided to arrange breakfast. Searching Agnus's kitchen, he scouted cabinets for a frying pan. Within the fridge he found some pork sausages and a basket of eggs. He set the links into the skillet on low fire as he began to cook.

Recovering a bowl, he broke in his eggs, then fished the rooster from around the yolks. He gave a pinching dash of salt and pepper, then quickly gave his eggs a scramble.

Upon the counter he eyed a loaf of bread. Then, abducting several slices, he tossed them to a toaster.

Agnus snuck in. "You're up early. And cooking, too, Tristian? What a marvelous favor."

"I suspected you weren't up. Figured I'd try this myself and award you a break."

"That's most sweet of you, dear."

"Please have a seat. It's time I pamper you." Tristian picked up a plate and assigned a few links along with some eggs, then topped it with toast.

She whiffed deeply. "My, doesn't this smell great?"

"I gave it my best."

"And a fine job you've done."

"Milk or orange juice?"

"Juice please."

"Go on and eat, Agnus. Don't let it get cold."

"I won't take a bite until you've joined me."

"In that case just give me a minute."

"Won't Josette be joining us?"

"I didn't want to wake her. She was still sleeping." Tristian sat beside Agnus. "Well, I hope it's edible."

"I'm sure it is."

"Don't be so definite until you've taken your first bite." He laughed.

"You're a silly one, you are. You know it'll be good." Agnus grabbed a napkin. "Was your wife okay the rest of the night?"

"Never woke once. But we're going to have a heck of a time keeping her in bed. I don't want her up until the doctor says."

"We'll prepare a tray later, then you can take some breakfast up."

"She'd think that's fancy."

"Dear, I don't mean to meddle, but how're you holding up? I know it was a tough night for you."

"A rough one it was. Didn't get much sleep. My mind was overworked."

"Nightmares?"

"Aye. I'd fall asleep and get bad visions."

"I wish you'd have come to me, dear. I have tea to dispel bad dreams. Wouldn't have taken long to heat."

"It was late, Agnus. I wasn't going to wake you. I wandered the house most of the night. I'm surprised you weren't roused by my pacing."

"You must have been light as a mouse, dear. I never heard a thing."

"I tried to stay quiet." He smiled.

"I know it's quite lonely, child, when you're strolling alone. Next time you get me."

After breakfast Tristian gathered honeysuckle from Mrs. O'Toole's garden while Agnus stayed in to attend Josie's tray. Near the plate she staged a crystal vase and awaited the flowers.

Tristian returned through the back door. "The bees are swarming this morning. I thought I'd be stung."

"Mind you, you've stolen their honeysuckle. They're attracted to that heavenly sweet fragrance."

"It was too good to pass."

"It is a wonderful contribution to this tray. Just smell that splendor. It awakens the senses."

"You want to follow me up? I'm about to take this." Tristian crept the stairs with Agnus behind.

Josie was wrapped within covers, sleeping soundly.

"It's nice to see she looks peaceful," whispered Agnus. "I'll give you both some time. Call me in when you're ready."

The aroma of food and flowers swirled beneath Josie's nose and awakened her abruptly.

"Hey, resting beauty. I brought up some breakfast."

"Breakfast in bed? Tristian, that's so thoughtful. What a waking surprise. Mmm ... looks so good."

"Hope so. I made it."

"You did all this?"

"Agnus sure seemed to like it."

"You even got honeysuckle."

"Aye, well, you know. Nothing but the best, sweetheart." Tristian helped Josie up, then rested the tray on a pillow.

Josie leaned forward to kiss her husband.

"Careful there. I don't want you hurting your tummy."

"The pain's made me numb, Tristian. I've endured all I can take."

"How're you doing with all this? Is there nothing I can do to make you better?" he asked.

"I'm trying to deal the best I can. You know it's not easy."

"I don't mean to upset you. But I need to know you're all right. Seems you slept well."

"Thanks to Dr. Kentworth. I probably wouldn't have slept if he hadn't given me that shot."

"He's supposed to call later. I'd like to give him good news. You know he's worried?"

"The man has a heart. You can tell him I'm fine."

"What about pain, Jos? Are you hurting at all?"

"Of course there's discomfort. But I'll learn to get along. It's not like it'll last forever. Well, not that at least. How might you be? Are you dealing at all?"

"Well, Jos, I'm like you. Trying to cope's the only resolve. I do know your devastation is more experienced than mine. Without you, she wouldn't have had a place to form and grow. She's our angel now, love. The tiniest cherub to protect us above."

"She's earned her wings." Josie cried. "Her feathered white wings. Maybe she'll sleep in a rose like the fairies."

"One day we'll know. But let's not rush it just yet."

"Tristan, there's something I want to talk to you about. I wouldn't feel right if I didn't."

"What about, dear?"

"I can't bear to not appoint her a name. It wouldn't be right. She deserves something pure."

"Have you even had time to think?"

"My mind's been settled. Her name's Annalise."

"Annalise O'Brien," he pondered. "That has a nice ring." He cocked his head to the side. "You've identified our angel."

Tears filled Josie's eyes. "I think she would have liked it."

"I know she would, Jos. It's a remarkably, beautiful name you've bestowed."

"You've done a wonderful job on breakfast. I must thank you."

"I better get your medication. Save you a swig of that juice."

"Tristan, where's Agnus? I thought maybe she'd come through."

"She's outside the door. Would you like me to get her?"

"Well, of course. Call her in. Tristan, I need to talk to you both."

Tristan gathered Mrs. O'Toole. "She's requesting you now."

"Hi there, dear. You've eaten all your breakfast. That's a good thing. Tristan's worked hard. I tell you, that boy would do anything to please you."

"He has. It was a wonderful thing he's done by this."

"He loves you very much."

"I'm fortunate to have him."

Tristan gave forth his hand. "Here, sweetheart. Swallow this pill."

Josie spoke, "Would the two of you have a seat? I have something of importance to say. I don't want any bickering brought on about this. I ask that you respect what I say, the both of you. I'm going to divulge

The Crying House

this plain and simple." Josie peered upon both her husband and Agnus. "Danger or not, I'm going to the house come later."

Tristian sat floored. "Absolutely not."

"I want to be a part of the blessing when Agnus does it. Neither of you can say anything about it. It's my personal choice to do this. My mind's been made."

Tristian became highly upset. "You've been through terrible calamities, Jos. You have no business there. I won't let you go."

"Why worry, Tristian? Aidan should be gone by that time. I'm going."

"You don't have the strength," he argued.

"All I do's lie in bed. How do you ever expect me to strengthen if you don't let me out?"

"You just had surgery. Are you that naive?"

"Tristian, don't quarrel with me."

"Despite last night, you're just getting over a major operation, Jos. You're not even healed."

"I'm not listening to you, Tristian."

"Agnus, will you help me? She won't try to understand."

"Your body needs rest, dear. This bed's the best thing for you. Don't surrender yourself to further pangs."

"The only thing left for me's death. I won't let Aidan take that. I'm tired of running away. And no more shall I display him my fear. I've wised up and learned my lesson."

Her husband declared, "I'll strap you to this bed, Jos. You battle me all you want. I can't let you go."

"Tristian, it's time Aidan gets pushed around. If I have to fight your restraints, I will."

"You feel that strongly?"

"Aidan's torn our lives apart. He's like a disease, Tristian. We have an opportunity to regain our lives. Why not do it together?"

He sighed deeply. "I'd still worry about you being there. Especially if he isn't gone. He's far too strong for me to fight. Myself alone, I couldn't protect you. I'll admit that."

"Agnus will be with us. She has ways of dealing with him. You know that, Tristian."

"What if something happens to her? We'd blame ourselves."

Agnus responded to Josie's earlier reply. "I can only stall him so long, dear. Reserved power is only meant to last an approximate time, then it'll dwindle. Energy drains when being used. I have no way to recharge myself. I can give all I've got, then again, it may not be enough."

Josie quickly responded, "Put me in a salted circle. By that I'll be protected."

"I could. But if he's still there, dear, would I have time?"

"Your magic's of pure goodness, Agnus. I have belief in you. I know you could help. There's no reason we be afraid of him."

Tristian replied, "He's not as you remember, Jos. His strengths have somehow evolved to more sinister means."

"How's he stronger, Tristian? What makes him different than before?"

"I don't know what's caused his change, but he's more violent. His abilities have surpassed what we've known. We've never dealt with him in the form he is now."

"How would you know?"

"I've been in the house."

"You what? But why, Tristian?"

"I needed clothes while you were in the hospital."

Josie narrowed her brows. "What'd you encounter while there?"

"I've seen him shift guises. I saw the phouka, Jos, and even the dog. That thing's not Aidan. It only took his form."

"It's more than that, Tristian. I think you know. Why won't you tell me?"

"You want the truth?"

"Yes, I'd particularly like it if you told."

Tristian looked upon Agnus as he clinched his lips. He then redirected his eyes toward his wife. "Okay, Jos, you want to know, then I'll tell you. It wishes to possess a second soul. It's tired of Aidan's form. It wants a new face."

"It lied to you," Agnus told him. "I sensed its truth. I just didn't tell you."

"And what truth is that? Because I had good understanding to believe what it said."

"Let me explain from the beginning, and I'll work my way on. At the dawning of your dilemma, dear, you were dealing with a residual haunting. Harmless imprints from the past making their way into our world and time. Residual spirits can't interfere with the living; however, they can be seen along with their actions in progress. At some point your encounters altered, manifesting into what's known as an intelligent haunting, meaning the spirit knows you're there and can interplay however it chooses. What I don't understand's how Ciara and Aidan were capable of assigning themselves to two completely separate forms of haunts. A parapsychologist might deem that impossible. They'd say you either have one or the other. But there are also exceptions. In some cases folks might experience both, but each haunting would retain its own spirits."

"Retaining separate spirits?" Tristian remarked.

Agnus spoke forth, "Ah, an example. Let's use the O'Neills as our residual and a child for the intelligent. Now you're seeing the O'Neills on occasion. They're stuck in a frame of time, doing what they were, but never interacting with you. On the other hand, you have this child in your home. But in his case the child can see you and has the ability to connect when desired. You understand?"

"Aye. So how were Aidan and Ciara able to do both? Scientifically it wouldn't seem possible."

"I'd like to know myself, child, but I don't have that answer."

"What's this have to do with a supposed lie, Agnus?"

"Taking consideration, Tristian, and pondering effectively, what I'd thought was in residual form neither of the O'Neills knew they'd passed. It was simply living their time as they knew it, without knowledge of their perished lives. Now the big reveal, dear. In intelligent form, Aidan's aware of his demise. He realizes he is what he is, expired. Don't let him fool you, child, he's quite alert to his position. Having that knowledge of his prior casualty, the phouka will do anything to escape the soul harvester's second coming. It's been in hell once, but was momentarily granted time of return. It knows the sequences subjecting its death will yet again arise. The reason it's searching for a new soul is so it can cheat death to remain on this earth. That there's your truth."

"It won't happen, Agnus? Will it?" Josie worried.

"Not by my guard. I won't let it."

Tristian confessed, "The reason I worry, Jos, is this thing's faster now, even more swift."

His wife relayed, "I thank you for worrying, Tristian, but that doesn't change my decision."

"I see I've spoken no words to shift your mind?"

"Sorry, sweetie, but my determination's set."

"Very well."

Josie pulled herself from bed. "Hold this a second." She referred to the tray.

"Ah-huh, Jos. Where do you think you're going?"

"To wash these dishes."

Agnus interfered, "Nonsense, child. You rest."

"Please, Agnus, let me get them."

"Josette, dear, you're most determined. Don't you mind these. I'll do them myself."

"But I feel it's my place to be helping."

"Oh, child. Child, you listen to me. You're in no condition for work. Worry about your rest. You can stir around later. Right now you take it easy."

Josie became frustrated. "I have too much free time. I'm not use to this lounging. For me it's not normal. I have to do something."

"You are, dear. You're resting."

"That's just it. I need to be up, Agnus."

An idea sparked her mind. "Sit tight." Agnus had gone downstairs and retrieved a small bowl from her cabinet. Thereafter she'd proceeded the back porch. Leaning against the wall propped a large bag. Inside a mound of seed settled the brim with a small scoop resting atop. Agnus shoveled a batch into the bowl, then returned to the bedroom. "Here, dear. We'll find you something to do with this."

Josie spied the bowl and saw seed. "What am I supposed to do with that?"

"This is my special blend. Sunflower seeds with dried fruits and berries."

"I hope you're not intending me to eat that." Josie laughed.

Agnus joked, "You could if you want, but our little winged friends need feeding."

"You let birds in your house?"

"Usually I'll open this window. I'd like to ask that you do it today. Have a seat here and keep them company. I assure you, you'll get more than birds."

Josie wondered innocently with confusion. "Should I worry?"

The Crying House

Agnus chuckled lightly. "About the wee ones? Dear, are you kidding? They're just wanting to eat."

"They come for breakfast?"

Agnus smiled. "Why shouldn't they?"

"And you feed them there?"

"But of course, dear. Of course."

"Oh, I'm excited." She became tickled. "When do they come?"

"Well, pull yourself here. Have patience while you give them a moment."

"I've always wanted to see a fairy, Agnus. Then last night you showed me their world."

Agnus raised the window, then set the bowl on the frame while Tristian helped his wife across the room. A few birds had already flown to the dish and began pecking at seed. Moments later a third bird flew toward the window, accompanying two fairy children riding its back. Soon as the finch landed on top of the windowsill, the two tiny fairies bounced off.

"Good morning, my children," Agnus expressed cheerfully.

"Good day, gramsy Aggie."

"Have we come on time?"

"Yes, sweet things, you have. Josette will accompany you today."

"Lovely." They smiled.

"Come on up here, kids. Introduce your sweet little selves to Josette."

The first little sprite flew up. "I'm Loxy."

"And I'm Rhoswen."

"Now, you dears, gramsy has things to attend. I'm entrusting you both to keeping Josette company while I'm gone."

Rhoswen twirled round. "She can watch us dance."

Loxy got on her tiptoes. "We've learned ballet. We'll show our recital."

"I'd love nothing more." Josie smiled. "I'd be happy to watch."

"All right, dear, I'll leave you to your visit. Tristian or I will check on you later," noted Agnus. "Oh, I think I hear the phone." Agnus paced toward her bedroom to answer it.

"A good morning to you, Agnus. This here's Dr. Kentworth. I was wondering if Tristian might be home?"

"He's right here, dear. Let me put him on."

Tristian took the telephone from Agnus's hand. "Sir? Sir, hello?"

"Morning, son. Thought I'd put my call in for now. Everything go all right last night? Is the missus okay?"

"She stayed sound, sir, like you said. I got her up about a half hour ago. She seems to be managing fairly well."

"Oh good. Good. I'm glad to hear that. Listen, Tristian, there's something I must tell you. Something happened last night. It was a God dreadful thing, and I can't help but be in fear for your life."

"Doctor? Doctor, what is it?"

"The bechances that proceeded last night frightened the life out of me. Things happened on my way home, Tristian. Bad things. Please, son, I urge you, find another home. That house is sour. Agree you'll stay out."

"Dr. Kentworth, what happened? Sir, are you all right? Dr. Kentworth? Dr. Kentworth?"

The line remained silent, then Tristian heard him once more. Barely able to talk, the doctor divulged, "I saw him. It was Aidan, I'm sure. He'd been waiting."

"Where, sir? Where had he been?"

"He'd been there at the door. Almost like he knew I'd come out. He was waiting. Just standing there. That sight, so awful. My, the look of him. It was a horrid perception. I couldn't help but peer on as I was passing him by. Didn't take long cause it was then when he'd done it."

"What, Dr. Kentworth? He did what?"

"He threw a knife at my car. Son, I tried to swerve, hoping I'd miss it. But it broke through my window."

"Oh, my God. Oh heavens, doctor. Doctor, were you all right? Were you hurt?"

"I suffered some injuries, but I'm fine, son. Had some stitches at the hospital."

"You're sure it was him?"

"I couldn't be mistaken. He's bad, Tristian. That man's bad. I worry about you going back. That house isn't safe."

"I can't believe this has happened. I'm sorry, I am."

"Oh now, it's not your place to apologize."

"You could have been killed, sir. Are you sure you're all right?"

"Son, don't you worry. I tell you, I'm fine. I just wanted to know how your night was. Be sure you're all safe. We'll talk more when I have time."

Tristian hung up the phone. "Dr. Kentworth's had some trouble," he told Agnus.

"Well, is everything all right? Does the man need some help?" she asked in concern.

Tristian turned toward her. "Aidan attacked him last night as he left."

"Oh, goodness. Tristian, what's happened? Was he hurt?"

"I don't know how bad. He wouldn't say. This has me upset, Agnus. Aidan's ready to have us pushing daisies. I'm at the point of second guessing. Maybe Jos and I shouldn't go back. We'll just abandon the place and find a new house."

"He'll leave, dear. I'll make certain he never comes back. You won't be plagued by him ever again in that house. I give you my honest word."

"I want to be sure, Agnus. I need to know that in my heart."

"Don't lose your faith, dear. That's the most valuable possession you've got. I tell you, something's coming for Aidan. Whatever it is will take him to hell."

"That's what I pray."

Agnus and Tristian returned to the guest room where Josie sat at the window still minding the fairies. Upon the ledge, colorful butterflies and bright red ladybugs had taken residence. Josie had been fixed with content as she looked after her recently found friends.

"You enjoying yourself?"

"Oh, Agnus, how amazing it is. Watching them simply fills me with joy."

Agnus smiled warmly. "Your eyes look brighter than they were."

"Was that Dr. Kentworth who called?"

"It was," added Tristian. "He'd been nice enough to ask how you were."

The phone began to ring again as Agnus left the room. She came back awhile later and got Tristian. "It's Dr. Kentworth again. He's asked for you, dear."

Agnus remained aside Josie as he left the room.

"Oh, doctor, please don't say more badness has befallen."

"Son, I've found something I'd like to show you. Would it be a bother to come by sometime later?"

"Not at all, sir. No. What have you found?"

"Papers that might be of interest to you. I came across them in my father's things. I'll be a few hours before I can come. Would it be all right if I see you in two?"

"That'll be fine. We'll be waiting for you then." Tristian relayed the message as he entered Josie's room.

"What kind of papers?" Agnus questioned.

"Now that, I'm unsure. He said he'd be here later. I guess we'll know then."

"Tristian, I want to go downstairs awhile," Josie begged. "I enjoy this room, but the place is getting old."

"Fine, Jos, I'll help you." Tristian aided his wife from the chair. "Now you take it slow. I don't want you rushing. You be careful, and no falling." He held onto her arm as they walked from the room. "Do you need to rest? You all right?"

"I can make it. Keep going."

"Agnus, stay behind in case she stumbles."

"Tristian, I'm not going to stumble," Josie relayed.

"We don't know that. Anyway, I wouldn't want either you nor Agnus trailing down these stairs."

They made it to the bottom as Tristian helped Josie to the living room. "I'll put you at the couch. You can sprawl there."

"Would anyone like tea?" Agnus wondered aloud.

"Please, Agnus. I'll take a cup."

"You, Tristian? Would you care for any?"

"I wouldn't mind a cup. Sure."

"What do you suppose it is Dr. Kentworth's bringing?"

"I'm not sure, Jos. All he said was he'd found some papers in his father's things and asked to come by."

"He didn't say what they were?"

"We'll have to wait till he gets here. I haven't got much clue."

"I wish he'd said something. This wondering gets on my nerves."

Agnus returned with tea, handing a cup to Josie, then one to Tristian. "I want to gather my things in a bit for the ritual tonight. I'd like to beforehand prepare and know I'll have everything."

"How will this work exactly?" Tristian questioned.

"What I'll be doing is driving out any negative imprints absorbed in that house. You can think of it as starting a clean slate. Your house will be purified and blessed with the goodness of spirit."

"How do you prepare for this? Are there special tools involved?"

"All I need, Tristian, dear, is kept upstairs. I'll gather some candles and herbs, and another few things."

Josie had wondered, "Where will Tristian and I be when this happens?"

"Having you both there will charge the ritual. You'll experience the powers of the blessing. It's not only meant for the house, but yourselves. After it's over, you'll be revived your sense of accord."

"Is it dangerous what you'll be doing tonight?"

"The only way we'd be in danger, Tristian, is if Aidan hasn't left."

"Are you prepared to fight?"

"Are you?"

"As long as you're certain, Agnus, we'll win. I'm prepared for the round."

"One thing to keep in mind, always expect the unexpected. There can always be a wildcard messing things up and steering you sideways."

"What do you mean?" pondered Josie.

"Don't think he's gone, don't think he's not. You won't know till you're there. If the air's calm, he's left. And if not, it'll anchor."

"Should we have a cross just in case?"

"It'll be your faith in that cross which casts him astray. If your belief is with it, it'll grant you some comfort."

"I have faith in the cross. I do."

"If it's your will, child, you take it."

Josie mulled. "But having it with? Is that okay with you? You come from a line of old religion, Agnus. Would that affect you by the merging of faiths?"

"Belief in the almighty creator is greatly accepted. If your approbation's with him, then so is your sanction. I have no arguments with that, dear."

"Being what you are, I didn't know how you'd feel."

"The rule in my world is to harm none. We only mingle with the good side of things, never darkness. Aside the few anomalies, we're no different than you. It's our aim to help, not destroy."

Tristian dwelled in thought. "Then why is it most folks always seem to think witches are bad?"

"Because they only see the one form. Those doing evil deeds and harming others. Thing is, dear, we're not all that way. But society has claimed us as foul. Folks like me don't pray to the devil. In fact, there are those who don't believe he exists."

"Believing in the devil's only Christian belief?"

"And those of similar accord. Benevolent magic, just like monovalent is pre-Christian. For benevolent practitioners like me, we have a central deity, the Willendorf; our great mother Goddess as well as mother earth. Much like Catholics have the virgin Mary, dear, we have the mother goddess who is prime in our worship."

"What about monovalent practitioners then? Were they not involved with Satanism."

"Christianity wasn't around at that time. And because of that, neither was the devil."

Tristian comfortably admitted, "I don't get it then. Who or what did they worship?"

"Various dark Gods. Those of war and disease. Any type of malignant spirits such as baneful sprites and maleficent fairies. Some called upon loathsome goblins and archfiend beasts. To inform this correctly, they'd call upon the proper entity for the task."

"What about Satanists?"

"Well, they came with Christianity. Instead of following God, they became supporters of Lucifer, minding his ways, and praising his stand. Just like pagans, you either access the darkness, child, or you advance toward the light."

"Then the difference between a Satanist and the ole day wizards of black arts is that the main worship of Satanists is, in fact, the devil?"

"You've learned your history lesson for the day, dear. Now you know how to distinguish the facts."

"I didn't think it'd be that deeply involved."

"Folks suppose things too often, child. The only way they learn truth is digging for it. Books are the best way to go. Their pages are filled with much knowledge. I'm not saying convert to the ways of another, child. But instead of supposing how separate religions outside your own really work, I suggest you become aware of the truth behind their practice. In cases, folks have found their professed thoughts were, in fact, misleading. It's indeed religion which makes this world go round. Respect other folks for their approach to beliefs. As long as goodness resides inside them, there's no need for any fear." The doorbell rang just as she finished.

Tristian relayed, "That must be the doctor now. Keep your seat, Agnus. I'll get it." He saw Dr. Kentworth through the window as he unlocked the door. Pushing lightly, the barrier door gave way and opened. It was then Tristian became overwhelmed with startling shock. His mouth dropped, once focusing upon the doctor's mangled face.

A profusion of jagged disfigurements and tailored stitch work made the man hardly recognizable. Tristian choked upon speech when relaying his words. "God almighty," he delivered. "I, I - I apologize. I don't mean to be rude, sir, but I can barely tell that's you."

"Only trouble seems to be when I open my mouth. My face pulls. Feels at times these stitches might burst. To be honest, son, I'm quite surprised I've decided to come back. I fear Aidan is watching."

"Well, hurry yourself in. I've told Agnus what's happened, but didn't say anything to Jos. I didn't want to upset her more than she is. Forgive me if I've offended you by not telling."

"No, no, son. It's best that you didn't."

Tristian gave a bothered expression. "We've a problem on hand, sir. Jos is in the living room. She'll wonder what's happened."

Dr. Kentworth acknowledged, "Then I'll try to be brief should she ask."

Tristian walked alongside the doctor as they roamed toward the room. Agnus stood herself from her seat when she ogled his face. "Lordy, me. You poor dear. You should be at home getting rest."

"I'm quite all right. There's no urgency I be in bed."

Josie frowned. "What on earth's happened to you? Had you been in an accident?"

"Just a minor engagement with glass, dear. There's no need to be worried."

Agnus queried, "Would you like something for those wounds?"

"I'm using ointment to keep them moist, but thank you for the offer. Hopefully they don't scar too badly." Dr. Kentworth then joked. "I'm already monstrous as is."

"Give yourself time to heal, dear. I'm sure you'll recover just fine. Won't you have a seat?"

"Well, certainly. I don't mind if I do."

"You care for some tea or juice?"

"Oh, I'm much too full. The missus fed me a hearty breakfast. But thanks, though, for asking."

"Let me know if you'd like something later then. I'll be happy to get it."

"I believe that's kind. You're a much humble host, Agnus." He then turned to Josie. "Tristian says you've been doing fairly well? Still feeling okay?"

"Well, I've noticed the medicine you've given seems to keep my mood soothed and settled."

"I'm surprised to see you from bed soon as this. Merely considering the following day, I wasn't expecting you to be doing so well. But I'm grateful you are."

Josie affirmed, "It was a nice thing you did by calling. I know we're all indebted to your sincerity, especially myself. I've never seen a doctor so concerned as you've been. That means a lot to a patient." Josie smiled.

"Well, I know when I'm rickety I'd like to be treated the same way," he confessed. "Anyway, the reason I've come was to show you these papers. My father kept a bunch of articles in a box. I remembered there'd been something of interest inside. It was when I dug around that I came across these." Dr. Kentworth handed the folded papers to Tristian. "I thought you'd might like to see them."

"These are newspaper clippings. Is there something important to these?"

"If you read on, you'll find that apparently your house had been abandoned for years following the deaths of both the O'Neills. It was in 1913 that a man by the name of Drake O'Maley bought the place and began renovations. He and his wife Riana had moved here from Dublin to start a new life. During repairs, Drake found what he'd thought to have been the remains of a baby buried beneath the fireplace ashes. His wife was beside herself with his findings and begged they move to another house. After much deliberation, reports came back that the bones were that of a horribly deformed being. It'd been thought the skeleton belonged to some type of fairy creature. Possibly a phouka, the scientist debated. It was said the beastie's eye sockets were fairly large, and its jowls sheltered rather sharp fang-like teeth. The rest of its body had been keenly similar to that of a toddler. Another difference to show was the fact that the legs had three toes to each foot, and the arms had four fingers to each hand. Point of fact, Mr. O'Maley came to believe that creature was indeed a phouka. He figured it'd taken residence within the last thirteen years. Might that have been the absolute truth? If so, my curiosity arises. Why would a phouka have taken refuge in that place? Is it likely Aidan could have been living there all this time? Agnus, you've remained here several decades. Do you recall this allegory?"

"As a matter, I do. But I believed those bones found were that of another phouka. For various reasons it happened upon that house and decidedly lodged there."

"But how? It'd seem a wandering spirit might be more inclined to attaching itself to a deserted location. Why would a phouka inhabit itself to a populated street? I'd figure it'd been more dedicated to staying hidden within nature."

"You have a good assumption, as it would seem most valid. But considering the evident truth, doctor, phoukas are foul creatures by nature. They have a distinct odor that others of their kind sense. The probable account for it having occupied that house is, it may have detected that recognizable scent of dirty-soiled stench soaking into the walls. By that, it regarded the dwelling as making a perfect den. I honestly wouldn't be surprised, dear, if other phoukas in actuality lived there as well."

Josie interrupted the discussion. "How can we be sure once the blessing's been done that no others will come? I don't want to banish one creature, then contribute a welcoming for more."

"Except for the one, dear, they're all gone. Once it's driven from that house, there'll be no more. They'll only reside in musty places, which they'll claim home. Such as small caverns, caves, even graveyards."

"But if one phouka were to inhabit an area, like my house, what's not to say others won't dwell there? If they sense their kind like you've said, wouldn't that give them incentive?"

"Like Dr. Kentworth said, my dear, Josette. That house had been abandoned awhile. No one was around to tend to the place, and it took to shambles. Disgustful odors adhered, dust picked up, and wood rotted. In all, your home permitted the perfect place for such vile creatures. Following the success of the ritual, all odors will be sanitized, then removed entirely. No other phouka will ever know its kind was there."

Dr. Kentworth added, "Since that's straightened, I'd like to talk to you folks. I have some notifications about the baby. Mr. and Mrs. O'Brien, the decision's up to the two of you. I don't want to force this if you're not ready."

"I can't wait a day longer," Josie answered. "Knowing this now is a better time than any."

"Mr. O'Brien, do I have your blessing to proceed?"

"Aye, sir," he agreed.

"I returned to the hospital early this morning to conduct an autopsy. Myself and another doctor preformed the exam. It was my wish to have him present for a second opinion. In review, it'd been clearly apparent your daughter was stabbed in her upper belly, abdominal midriff, and pelvic cavity. From the measurement of derma lacerations, we concluded the instrument involved had, in fact, been a butcher. At this time I'm still perplexed on how she acquired these wounds, while you, Josette, had none on yourself."

"It'd been the dream that'd done it, doctor. Even I've asked myself, how'd I escape without, when knowing I had many? Upon my chest, onto my breast, atop my stomach, then trailing into my lower anatomy. Why was it his intention to take her away only?"

Agnus spoke forth with knowledge. "The dreamworld's a peculiar place, child. Domains concede however inspired. A realm could be complex and transcending, concrete and defining, or psychically inclined as it had been for yours. Aidan dominated you, dear, pulling a reluctant Josette into his reality. Not having the capability for leaving his house, he sought separate ways, then found that with dream. There he had power to do as he pleased, however he'd want. It was then you'd been placed in his slot and controlled by his strength."

"He's bound there, yes."

"I know, dear. I witnessed the mysterial restraint that retained him. He had no power to cross the threshold of the outside world," Agnus told her.

Dr. Kentworth looked toward the O'Briens. "I could only imagine how troubled you've been. You've encountered both physical violence and unnecessary loss from this. I can only pray you both find peace and put your restrictions behind you. When that time comes, I wish you both the best."

Josie politely remarked, "We appreciate your kind words."

"It's your faithful belief, doctor, that'll help us conquer this feud," Tristian admitted.

"I'll plead to God everything goes as it should. You may keep those papers if you wish. Truly stating, I have no use for them."

"It's a part of our house's history. We can look upon them someday and remember the tragic story that manufactured its legend," Tristian settled.

"There's also papers reporting the O'Neill's murders. One on Ciara, the other's for Aidan. If you quest through, you'll find their obituaries."

"You've done an awful lot to help, sir. The information. The stories. Even the prompt inspection of our daughter," Tristian remarked. "And you've saved my wife's life. I couldn't be more grateful."

"I have one thing to ask before saying goodbye."

"Some money, of course?"

"I wouldn't ask it."

"Then what can we do?"

"Oh no, son. I'm not asking of anything. What it is regards the baby. I don't mean to sound barbaric or ruthless, but usually we'd incinerate discarded bodies. Your case, it's different. I thought yourself and the missus might both find peace with laying her to rest."

"She did have a life at one point. Unfortunately it'd been viciously taken." Josie frowned. "I'd appreciate a burial. She deserves that respect," she added.

"I'll get some arrangements set. In a couple days I'll have her ready. Father McKinney, I'm unsure you're familiar with, is a personal friend. If you don't have a pontiff, I can see if he'd be interested in directing her funeral."

"That would be favorably accepted, sir. You've gone beyond your means to help us. That's significant of you. Like us, I feel Annalise would be pleased," Josie noted.

"Forgive me. I hadn't known you named her. It's quite beautiful."

Josie expressed, "I considered it so." She then peered to her husband. "I deemed it'd be an appealing name for our radiant angel."

"Well, folks, I'll be calling in another day or so and let you know how all goes."

Agnus thought quickly. "Doctor? Oh, Dr. Kentworth, there's something I'd like to give you before leaving," she mentioned. "If you'll excuse me, I'll be back."

"Certainly, ma'am. I can wait."

Leaving, she went upstairs to a back room. Inside, Agnus traipsed to an altar she'd established along the wall. Sitting on top of the table was a small, brown leather bag filled with such things as burdock root, John the Conqueror root, vervain, and periwinkle herbs and finally a polished stone of tiger eye.

She held the bag over the flame of a white candle where she'd blessed it with protection oil. Then, within a small salted circle, she laid the pouch inside. "May protection encircle the wearer of this bag. Blessed be." Now walking to an armoire, she opened its doors. Upon the shelves were all sorts of books, jars, and candles. Agnus dug through her things, then pulled forth a small jar of calendula ointment. Walking back to the altar, she blew out the candle, then seizing the small bag, left the room. "Thank you for your wait, doctor. This here's for you."

"A jar of…"

"Calendula ointment. To help heal your wounds."

His eyes became expressive. "Marigold salve, isn't it?"

"You've done your research." She smiled. "It's completely homemade. I've strained it myself."

"An actual folk medicine here in my hand. How generous of you."

"Best time to use it's at night just before bed. You could treat your arms throughout the day, then veil them with gauze. Then on, you should see they'll heal quickly."

"I'll heed your advice. And I thank you for this." Dr. Kentworth glanced at his watch. "I apologize for my rush, but I'll need to be rejoining the hospital. We've had a nice visit."

"Most certainly. We'll talk soon," spoke Agnus.

Dr. Kentworth shook Josie's hand. "You take it easy, dear. I'll see you before long."

Agnus and Tristian then walked him to the door. Waiting until she was out of Josie's sight, Agnus pulled forth the small pouch. "Dr.

Kentworth, I didn't want to hand this to you in front of Josette," she spoke softly.

"What'd we have here?" He examined the bag.

"It's a protection pouch. I know how you feel in regard to passing that house. You'll stay safe from Aidan long as you have it. Keep it for the extent you'd like, then bury it in your yard."

Dr. Kentworth took a breath and confessed, "It'd taken all my nerve to come here again. After that encounter I had here last night, well, I wasn't sure I'd ever feel safe again while coasting this street."

"You have no reason to fear now, dear. I'll be taking care of business come soon. Everyone will be fine, including yourself."

"I honestly feel good having this. And if I might add, I'd like you to know I genuinely trust you, Agnus. It's my belief you'll undoubtedly succeed and not fail tonight. May the good Lord be with you, keeping each of you safe. Good day," Dr. Kentworth relayed upon exiting the house.

CHAPTER THIRTY-NINE ◆

Just before 5:00 pm that evening.

"It's about that time, dears. You feel you're both ready?"

Tristian confirmed, "I'll admit, Agnus, I'm a wee bit afraid."

"I promise you, child, you'll be fine. It's just your nerves being uptight."

"How can I calm them?"

"Take slow, steady breaths while telling yourself you have nothing to fear."

"And that'll work?"

"Give it a try and see how you feel. Reassurance is key to this affair. If you haven't yet got it, it's best you strengthen up."

"Okay. I'm taking it easy."

"Positive affirmation. Shake your worries aside. Find your sense of peace."

Tristian closed his eyes, then waited several breaths before speaking aloud. "I embrace only goodness. I have not one fear in my mind. God will enable me. From him I have strength, and his strengths power me."

"Release your breath. Now open your eyes. How do you feel?"

"I feel a sense of renewal. A feeling of enlivenment. And the collection of spirit inside of my soul."

"And you, Josette? You're sure, dear, you'd want to go?"

"I've calmly awaited this moment. And by no means shall I thwart. It's within my will that I be going."

"Then I tell you this now, child. If you're weak and cannot manage, you have no reason there. If your response be a lie, I'll sense it."

"My mental strength's there along with my physical."

"Then be it soon we leave."

Agnus gathered her things from upstairs. Within a small crate she tossed several white candles. Following that, a meager cauldron made of cast iron.

She'd hunted her shelves for smoke blends and smudge sticks, then amulets and stones. Thenceforward, she searched for a taper of red, some soil from earth, a ceremonial athame, and a jar of brook water.

She returned to the kitchen with her materials in hand. It was then Tristian resoundingly voiced. "I guess now you're ready?"

"Not until I've affixed my cloak, dear."

"May I do the honor?" he asked.

"Absolutely. Closet there, purple cape."

"The velvet one?" Tristian pulled it forth. "Well, the thing's a beauty. You make it yourself?"

"Many moons ago."

"Its condition's superb."

Agnus held forth her arms while Tristian shrouded her shoulders. She'd then turned around so the O'Briens could behold.

"My God," Josie declared. "You look ever most stunning."

Agnus stood surrounded by the impressive majesty of the heliotrope cloak. Her pale skin bloomed forth by its color, just as her cheeks had flushed to coral hue. And it was her pallid eyes of resplendent light that cast forth each glint of shimmer. It'd been then, upon a moment, she untwisted her bun of snowy hair, unraveling each silken strand to loosely tumble down her back. For uncharted reason, at that instant, she magically recaptured her youth.

Tristian eased forth to her face. "That really you, Agnus?"

"Impressive, isn't it?"

"How's this so? You've … you've cast away at least thirty years. Well, I'm … I'm…"

"Speechless, dear?"

"Wow. I mean, yes. Amazed. Quite amazed." He then laughed lightly. "You're looking so radiant. I think I'm spellbound."

"Come join hands, kids. Let's all be surrounded by light. Feel it within you. Embrace its protection."

"I feel my palms pulsating." Josie gleamed. "It's like a thrumming surge is twirling round. Does anyone feel that?"

"I'm feeling something," Tristian confirmed. "Like mustered warmth upon me." He looked into Agnus's eyes. "I actually sense it. Wow. Incredible."

"It's now time. I must bless you. Stand before me, child." Agnus then took a small bundle of sage from her crate and lit it with fire. Onto Tristian she swept the smoke upon his face, then round his body. "Gracious keeper, fair and strong, defend this man from wicked harm. Safe within your guarded care, he now repels the soured air. No harm to he who's cleansed and pure because the spirit of sage is near. Wrapped within protective drapes, I now decree, this man is safe. So mote it be. You may step aside now. Josette, dear, your turn."

"Just stand before you like Tristian?"

She then nodded. "Come forth, child." Sweeping round Josie's body, she recited the chant once more. "Gracious keeper, fair and strong, defend this woman from wicked harm. Safe within your guarded care, she now repels the soured air. No harm to she who's cleansed and pure because the spirit of sage is near. Wrapped within protective drapes, I now decree, this woman's safe. So mote it be."

"Well, Agnus. Shall we do this?" Tristian asked.

Interrupting her response, the phone then rang. "Blasted. Well, I'd been ready," she'd expressed.

"Go on. We'll wait."

Tristian stood with his wife beside the door where they lingered patiently.

Agnus returned a short while later, shaking her head. "We have a problem."

"A problem? What sort?" Tristian queried.

"That was Logan."

"Logan? From the nursing home?"

"He demands I come see I him." Agnus's face drooped. "He doesn't sound well. I believe this is it."

"If you need to go, you should. We can do our work later."

"Tristian, this needs to be done now, child. I told Logan I had business to attend, then I'd meet him."

"You're absolutely sure?"

"This was a promise I've kept to you. We need to go."

CHAPTER FORTY ◆

A light breeze spread among the air. It was then, when they approached the house, the wind picked up, blowing them along their way. Above, the sky turned gray as the sun had hidden behind the clouds. During that moment a deviant feeling crept upon Agnus as she knew they were about to witness something unholy.

Tristian placed his key into the hole and unlocked the door. With a light twist he turned the knob. "Gracious. It's cold as ice," he remarked. "Jesus, I'm stuck." Tristian tugged. "I can't get myself loose." He then fought further, yanking and straining himself much more. Upon the final jerk, flesh tore from Tristian's hands where it remained amid the knob. Viewing his palms, he saw the surprising feature of frostbite upon him. They were blistered and worn with blotches of red patches that covered the skin. Tristian freaked. "I wasn't banking on this."

"You'll be fine, child. All wounds can heal," mentioned Agnus.

They walked into the darkened house one by one. Reaching farther inside, Tristian discovered the flames of lanterns take to light. "Whoa, wait. Where are we?"

"The lay before you is how Aidan once identified this dwelling."

"Do we proceed?"

"This place is his dimension. We've taken a step back in time. Proceed with caution."

"Aye," he agreed.

"Carry on."

Agnus and the O'Briens preceded the hall, then prowled toward the stairs.

Josie breathed deeply. "What if we encounter him?"

"Just you stay calm, dear. Keep yourself aside me."

While in the act of accessing the first step, Aidan appeared midway, his back toward them and slouch in slant motion.

Tristian and Josie looked to another in fright.

Agnus then whispered, "No need for fear, my dears. Aidan has no discernment of us."

Watching him, he drunkenly staggered upon each step. Making his way toward the top, he stumbled to the bathroom. Agnus and the O'Briens silently paused near the balcony where they secluded their view.

"Are we to wait?" wondered Tristian.

"Child, we'll have to. Situations aren't over. Until they are, we'll rest right here."

"Might you know that stretch of time?" Josie pondered.

"That I can't say. It'll be over when it is."

"I'm uneasy with this. What if something goes wrong?"

"Josette, sweetheart, you have to be calm. We can't rush anything. It's not our right to interfere with the past. We just settle and wait."

Tristian interfered, "Should we inch closer or mind our stay here?"

As they'd been talking, Josie heard a noise stir from within the guest room. She rested her head against the door and listened sharply. When the donation became louder, she drew back and began poking her husband. "Come listen. Quick, Tristian, quick. Put your head here."

He then heard the rustling patter behind the closed door. A perplexed look crossed his face as he drew his head away.

"You heard that in there?"

Tristian listened quietly as he channeled Agnus's attention. "Do you hear this?" he voiced lightly.

Agnus cast her eyes to the door. "You heard something there?"

Tristian stated, "Have yourself a listen."

Her saucers then widened when realizing the doorknob had turned. "Dears, back yourselves."

Josie watched the door open quietly. "Something's emerging."

"Come back to the stairs," Agnus told the O'Briens. "Hurry, kids, hurry," she whispered.

Transpiring through the illumined room, a sickle crept forth to one side. A few inches away had been the exposure of an unblunted knife. Both objects steadily floated from the doorway by unseen hands, then passing through the hall, drifted toward the privy.

It was then Agnus and the O'Briens watched on at the events to unfold.

Aidan had been staged before the bathroom mirror while the whetted objects drifted in his direction. "You're a bloody genius, ye flushed bastard." He'd laughed to himself. "Ye finally dried that wench from your life." He sloshed with praise, "Gone ye be forevermore." He stared to the ceiling. "Ye hear that, ye bitch? It's just how I wanted. I tell you, ye hear? Ye hear thee?" He chuckled. "That bloody life of yours meant not a thing. Well, I'd been so clever, see? I've buried you and got away."

Within the corner of his eye Aidan met the sickle's blade upon the air. "What the bloody..."

"Shut it, ye lousy sap," a youthful voice blasted.

Aidan then felt the icy blade against his throat. And upon a slice, Aidan's neck had been swiftly cut, scything his voice box from ear to ear.

Blood sprayed from his wound, covering the mirror, walls, and floor. Aidan gasped for breath while grabbing his gushing throat. A consumption of panic completely steered within his thought. Scaling backward, Aidan hit the wall where he'd regressed instantaneously. Air rushed within his throat while the bastard choked upon his blood. It was then he'd known through horror, it'd been the intimacy of death upon him, and so he peered upon his killer. Aidan looked in dismay. Reflected in his eyes was the figure of a butcher's knife.

The youthful voice rang forward. "This one's for Ciara, ye bastard."

It was then the blade was driven deeply into his chest, keenly piercing his frigid heart. A projection of spray dispersed from the laceration, covering the room with even more blood than before. Sinking along the wall, he hunched to the floor. Not caring whether Aidan had been dead or not, the intruder continued his fit of bloodstained rebellion. Striking Aidan's heart time after time, the youth yelped in howl. Toward the end, the room appeared a place of slaughter, with the revolting smell of sanguine fluid embracing air.

Josie was horrified by the images witnessed before her. Turning aside, she nestled her head firmly into her husband's chest as she sheltered her sight.

Tristian and Agnus watched on as bloody footprints rushed pass them and raced to the stairs.

It'd been soon after the lanterns made popping clamor, then their flames extinguished.

"Uh-oh," Agnus expressed.

"Uh-oh? Uh-oh what, Agnus? What's going on?" Tristian asked.

Josie became alarmed. "Why can't I see? Where be the lights? Someone answer. Answer me please."

"It's possible we're moving ahead through time. Give it a moment," Agnus remarked. "I imagined we'd return shortly."

"I want to see. I don't like this."

"Josette, dear, it's all right. Just stay together, child."

"But something's coming. I have that feeling. Please, let's get out," Josie pled.

"I'm afraid we can't see, my dear. We'll have to wait for the lights."

"They aren't coming back on. It's best we leave."

"Nothing's going to harm you. The worst is over. Trust me, child."

Tristian tried adding, "Sweetheart, Aidan's dead. We'll do as Agnus says. She wants us to stand here, we do."

Down the hall Josie noticed the flicker of a light, soon followed by another. "Something's coming this way. I see it."

Agnus and the O'Briens watched as a row of candles drifted through the hallway. Approaching the privy, they then made an outline before the door, using the resplendence of each widowed flame.

A crack of thunder abruptly broke, echoing throughout the house. Down along the mid-section of the foyer, a bolt of lightning rippled, alighting the room in a blue-white aurora.

Racing from within the firebolt, the raven aviated, its head outstretched from its body. It's amberous eyes blazed like hot embers while it rushed through the air.

It came upon the bathroom, then fixedly hovered between the exit. The argent light of the candle flames were enough to glimpse within the door. Upon notice, the vital fluids covering the walls and floor appeared black beneath lighting.

A second ripple of lightning concisely bolted through air as the raven then took the form of a woman. Blue-black hairs spanned toward her shoulders with onyx feathers intertwined among strands. Her skin was pale white like the most delicate of porcelains. Her eyes captured fierce flames of russet copper which danced among darkness. Upon her rested a cloak extensively capped in sable plumage. Beneath her mantle the woman wore a velvety long dress of aubergine fabric that dust across the floor when she'd bustle. Her head motioned like a bird with set eyes boring steadily upon prey.

Hanging below, upon her thigh clung a leather pouch. Dangling her hand within the bag, she retrieved a palm of sterling dust. Wielding forth her appendage, she blew the sands atop Aidan. "I influence life upon this perished form. I resurrect ye breathless soul. It is now I call ye forth. Rise up."

Thunder cracked through the house as a bright flash filled the room. Beneath the flash the discernment of blood all vanished.

The woman abided between the frame where she'd unabatingly waited. Then before her, in a flicker, Aidan stood.

Looking at the woman with confusion, he ejected, "Who the hell are you, ye feathered patsy? Ye know where ye are? My house, that's where you be, and ye better get out," he spoke harshly.

"It is I, the Morrigan," she spoke. "Goddess of strife and battle. I'm the Queen of phantoms and reaper of souls. I've come to collect."

"What? Ye think you can take me? Well, ye got another thing coming. I belong here, collector," he shouted in her face.

"Correction. You belong to me."

He raged, "I belong to this house. The bricks and the mortar."

"Your soul is mine for taking. It is your destiny."

"Poppycock." He laughed. "I believe not in the word."

"Then be it your doom."

"My conclusion is changeless, wench. It's hence where I stay."

"The karma ye carelessly endued has come back. It brought me to you. You're held liable for your actions that befall in your lifetime, and now's the time you must answer to them. Ye must pay your dues."

"What actions do ye speak of?" he demanded.

"Killing your wife."

"Don't tag me with that, ye featherbrain. Her death was an accident."

"Ye only claimed it as so. You knew what you'd done. You'd always had the intention. Ye lived in a life of battles. Ye take life, ye lose life. You're no different than warriors on battlefields. Unfortunately, in your case, your soul's not of honor." Below her cloak, the Morrigan reached forth to a stretching sword obscured within a scabbard. Raising its blade high in air, she spontaneously transported it upon Aidan's neck, quickly beheading him with that one disgorged blow.

Bending forward, she obtained his head and hoisted it in hand. Turning round languidly, the Morrigan decamped and tramped outside the room. She walked the hall with Aidan's head, spilling his blood amongst the floor.

A crack of lightning burst mid-air as the Morrigan escaped into blue-white radiance. The candles drifted afar from the doorway, vanishing down the hall as they went. Soon after, a strange buzzing occurred, then slowly the room alighted. Within the privy the place had cleared of Aidan's torso.

Agnus moved away from the balcony and motioned for the O'Briens to follow. "Looks like Aidan finally got what he'd been due."

"It's over?" Josie catechized. "It's really over?"

"The woman, Agnus. Who was she?"

"She was the Morrigan, Tristian. In Celtic mythology, she's a war deity."

"But why her to collect him?"

"In life, Aidan set loose an assaulting force derived from the phouka. Once taking over, dear, there'd always been combat. Mostly his wife, of course, but also those brawls inside his pub. He may not have contest in battlefield warfare. But, child, he was, to the core, warlike with those around him. His violence was equal to the sum of scrimmage found on any ground. It'd been that storming aggression overseen by his actions which summoned her forth."

"What if he escapes her?"

"No, Josette, dear. Not even if he dreamed. There's just no way. Her powers are beyond his own. Defiled as he is, she has the strengths to control him."

"That wasn't Aidan's soul, though? Am I correct?"

"That'd been the phouka's. The *diabhal* resembled him in almost every sense."

"Then it's as you've said? He's stuck someplace else?"

"I'll have to pull him from the world he resides, Josette. But that'll come a later time. For now let's worry about the blessing." Agnus reached into her crate and pulled out a bunch of blanched candles. "Here, take these. Put them in all your windows downstairs. I'll get the altar set."

The O'Briens followed Agnus down to the living room, then began setting out tapers. Agnus posed her crate upon the boards, then taking a bottle of salt, made a pentagram within the floor's center, followed by a circle upon its outside.

Agnus positioned candles within the triangles of each element, air, fire, water, and earth. Reaching into her crate, she pulled forth her cauldron and settled it within the core of her pentagram. Inside the earth's element, she placed a small bowl of dirt. Amid air, the athame. Among water, an obtained bit of brook. And inland to fire, a spirited red taper. She then surrounded her cauldron with amulets and stones. And off to the side, she laid her smudge sticks and smoke blend, then her whittled shag pipe. She then kneeled with her protective barrier.

"Josette, dear, come stand within water. The western space there." She pointed. "Tristian, I want you within fire. The southern space here."

Agnus kneeled within the protective barrier, alighting a charcoal. Sprinkled atop the fervid graphite, she flaked rose, fern, and crushed clove. Speaking loudly, she then cast a circle. Staged before Agnus mount a milk colored candle she dressed with repellant oil. Crouched toward the ground, she centered her thoughts and empowered herself. Holding her athame forth in her right hand, she recited an incantation. "Wraiths of hate, distemper and harm, I banish your tenancy apart from this home. Driving afar afflictions and fear, may it only be good which dwells within here. Upon the windows, sills, and walls protective forces provide their guard, casting abroad all evils and sin, this house, be it blessed with protection within. As I say, so mote it be."

Agnus stood before the fifth point of spirit and began closing her circle. Then, turning to the south, she recited, "Go in peace, ye powers of fire. To you, I give thanks and blessing." Turning to the east she continued. "Go in peace, ye powers of air. To you, I give thanks and blessing." Next she faced west. "Go in peace, ye powers of water. To you, I give thanks and blessing." Finally Agnus reached the fourth corner. "Go in peace, ye powers of earth. To you, I give thanks and blessing."

After things settled and the tapers were cooled, Agnus asked Tristian to bury the ceremonial candle in the front lawn and cast the ashes of herbs toward the street. He'd done as she'd said while his wife helped clean the remains of the altar.

Josie smiled warmly toward Agnus. "I actually feel lighter breaths as I breathe."

"That's just the start, dear. You'll see more good things will follow."

Josie came round and gave her a hug. "Thank you. Thank you so much for what you've done. You've set me at ease, Agnus. Nevermore shall I be scared."

"Why don't we sit here and enjoy the newly restored peace this house has just found?"

Josie continued expressing, "You did it, Agnus. You really did. What a wonderful relief. You've returned this house to Tristian and me."

"This place is now protected from all evil. Nothing shall ever bother you again, child."

"Might it be all right if Tristian and I stayed here?"

Agnus embraced her. "Oh, my child. As long as you're ready." She withdrew and held her hand upon Josie's head. "Those visions. The ones you have here. They're past reflections, child. Allow them not to linger no more. You let them die. Get on with your life. Be merry. You and Tristian have many happy days ahead."

"You've given our lives back to us, Agnus. For that, we're greatly indebted."

"But, dear, you've already done enough."

"I haven't done a thing." She laughed. "I'd been lazy."

"It was you, voicing appreciation that returned my pay."

Josie sat quiet awhile, then spoke. "On the day we visit the cemetery, I'd like to take flowers as a part of respect. It's my regard, Ciara deserves them."

Agnus beamed. "In that case. She loved the scent of lilac."

"Then I'll take her that. I'd like her to know she wasn't forgotten."

Tristian returned to the room, then taking a seat aside his wife, spoke. "Everything's been done as said."

"Our house, Tristian. It's been absolved of its evils. I'm feeling confident and not afraid to ask." She then radiated. "You think you're ready?"

"I know I'd be happy to return."

Agnus cheered. "Then it's settled. You come back tonight."

CHAPTER FORTY-ONE ◆

As Agnus crept upon her stairs, she heeded a letter beneath her mat. "Tristian, dear, you mind handing me that?"

"Seems someone's been by." He handed it forth. "Here you are."

"You and Josette come on into the house."

"We'll just gather our things right quick, then go."

"Nonsense. You'll both stay for dinner."

"That's awfully sweet, Agnus," Josie responded.

"Well, I can't let either of you go on empty stomachs." She then unfolded the note and began reading. "Oh Lord," she expressed sadly.

"Agnus, what is it?" Tristian became worried.

"A letter from Ashlynn." She continued to read. "She and Digby went to see Logan. Says he kept calling for me. She urges I go see him."

"If he's dying, Agnus, you really should go."

"We don't have much time come later. If we go now, we can make it."

"Jos and I will give you a ride. We'll leave now."

"Let me return my cloak to the closet and gather a jacket."

"I'll get Jos to the car."

"I'll meet you out there."

Tristian walked Josie to the vehicle and helped her inside. "Here, put the key in ignition. I'm gonna get Agnus."

"I'll drive."

"Oh no, you're not. You stay where you are." He raced to the steps of Agnus's house as she locked the door. "Grab my arm. I'll help you on these stairs."

CHAPTER FORTY-TWO ◆

The O'Briens and Agnus stopped at the front desk.

"Mrs. O'Toole, what a pleasure to see you, ma'am," the attendant conversed.

"Good evening, Clodagh. I've come to see Logan."

"I wondered when you'd come. Heard he's been putting in calls. Are those folks there with you?"

"They are, dear."

"Go on. I'll sign you all in."

The O'Briens inched behind Agnus as they sauntered along the hall.

"Here we are, dears."

"Would you like us to wait?" Josie quizzed.

"You folks aren't strangers. Come on in."

"He might not want us," she responded.

"If he doesn't, child, he'll let you know."

Tristian queried, "You're sure this is the right thing?"

"We'll find out." Agnus took a breath, then opened the door. "Hello? Logan? You mind we come in?"

It took a moment before his response. "Agnus?" He coughed. "That you?"

She spied him upon the bed. "Oh, sweetheart. What kind of mess have you gotten yourself into?"

"My end comes near." He wheezed. "Agnus, I'm holding by a thread."

"I say so. You look awful. They not feeding you?"

"I don't care about that mush no more. All these years eating it. I'd rather do without."

"Don't you say that."

"I just did."

Agnus drug herself toward the bed. "I don't remember you looking this bad last time I saw you. Has something happened?"

"A blasted mini stroke a few days ago. Damn thing left me retarded before waning. You know, doctor tells me I'm likely to have the real thing come soon. It's going to kill me, Agnus, if not another heart attack."

"Logan, now, you don't know that. You look malnourished, though. You keep not eating, then that's what will do it. We need to fatten you up. You've lost too much weight."

"Forget me damn weight. I didn't call you here to argue about me health. I know what's going on. I haven't had a bit of care. I'm ready, Agnus. This chapter needs closing."

"Is that why you called everyone?"

"You, Kieran, Digby, and Ashlynn. I just wanted to say goodbye while I could. I don't see none of you. So I thought it'd be fair you coming now before you read some notice."

"Logan, you know I'd been here more often hadn't my health deterred. I ask you not be mad."

"I don't blame you, Agnus. How could I ever?"

"You'd been alone, Logan. I know that, and I'm terribly sorry no one made further attempts to see you."

"Kieran started coming. Seems he's trying to shake his past. You know, I never thought he'd come back. Just last week I had a nice couple come in. Said they were living in the O'Neills' place. Happy folks, they were. Young and lively. Claimed they knew you."

"Josette and Tristian. They hadn't lied. They live there and are neighbors."

His face drooped. "Well, I lied to them, I'm afraid to say. If they were here, I'd speak now the truth."

"They're standing aside the door, dear."

"Is that so? Well, let them in."

Agnus motioned the O'Briens. "Come on in, dears. Come on. This here's Tristian and Josette, you remember?"

Logan acknowledged, "I'm glad you've all come."

The Crying House

"It's nice to see you again, sir." Josie smiled.

He studied her a moment, then asked, "Have you done something new to your hair?"

Josie clouded up and confessed, "I lost most for surgery."

"Well, you're still beautiful, girl. Come have a seat, you and your husband."

Tristian respectfully acknowledged, "If we're taking up your time with Agnus, we'll step aside and let you talk."

"No, son. You and the missus will be involved."

"Involved? In what business?"

"What needs clearing."

Agnus interrupted, "Logan, whatever you're talking about, dear, it's over our heads."

"I don't want to die taking lies to me grave. I'm ashamed. I haven't been completely honest with a soul to this room. Especially you, Agnus. I've known you decades on end, yet I've never been truthful."

"What on earth are you talking about?" she queried.

"All of you. You've believed a lie made up from me mouth."

"What lie?" she insisted.

"Close that door."

Tristian got up and did as he'd said. Logan declared, upon his return, "The words spoken within this room shall not leave here. Do I receive your vows, each of you?" He awaited nods. Looking among the O'Briens, he confided, "Last week you asked if I'd known who killed Aidan. And in my persuasive bribe I'd made you suppose Kieran."

"That's all been cleared, sir. We've spoken to Mr. Kirkauldy. Kieran told us about his father and his return the next day. We know it'd been him who'd done it."

"Then I challenge your thoughts, son, and say it was not."

Agnus's mouth dropped. "To learn it'd been Ciara all this time. Her thirst for revenge enraged her to do it? Such a mild soul was she. I hardly believe it."

"Don't accredit the legend. It's not true."

"Do you know what actually happened?" Tristian questioned.

"I know the facts, the person who did it, and from whom he got help."

Agnus inquired, "Are you saying two were involved?"

"One had been the murderer, the other, accessory."

Josie begged, "Please, sir, if you know, just say it."

"The one who slain Aidan had been a heartbroken boy. His age was thirteen."

Agnus's face took complete impact. "Why hadn't I figured that?" she whispered.

"A boy?" Tristian doubted, not yet heeding the truth.

"A boy waited that night after the funeral. He'd known Aidan had been at the pub, so he broke into the house. He then snuck to an upstairs room. There he moseyed with a sickle in hand and a knife in his other. During his hour remission, he prepped himself. He'd come with extra clothing. And beneath a chair he set his shoes, so his feet would retain only socks. He waited his hourly period before Aidan drunkenly staggered upon the stairs. In the lavatory he praised his freedom like the heartless scum he was. The boy snuck upon him, then yelled. He cut Aidan's throat, never minding his blood. As he stood dying, the child stabbed him upon his heart several times. Out of amusement, the child poised above him and watched Aidan die. When reality hit of what he'd just done, the boy ran to the kitchen and washed his blades, face and arms. It took several moments before he returned upstairs. He smeared his footprints around to show no detection he was there. Still standing near the privy, he removed his stained socks. He changed his clothes and put the defiled ones within the cover of a burlap bag. In his thoughts he tried to figure where he'd do away with the spattered baggage. His concern led him to the cemetery. It'd been there he'd accost the desponding cries of Ciara's father. The child told him what he'd done. The two had then buried the saturated clothing within the graveyard near some overgrown shrubs. Afterward, the boy collapsed upon Ciara's headstone and cried upon it. I've killed him for you, I said. All that I've done, I did in your honor. Sprawled upon the cold stone, I caterwauled as though she were there. May you rest in peace, my loving mother. That'd been fifty years to this day."

Josie sat in pegged stare. "The boy had been you?"

"I'd never suspected it," Agnus admitted. "You isolated yourself after Ciara's death. No soul would have concluded a child."

"She'd been like a mother. Inside, my sadness leveled revenge. It'd been the brutish of ways he'd taken her from me. My God, she was sick, and for him to have known. Then again, he didn't care. He just wanted her out of his way. If Ciara didn't deserve life, neither did

Aidan. No one's known of this truth until now. Folks believed a myth they'd inspired. It was the perfect murder, bound by a ghost story. So I left it that way. As you've said, Agnus. No one would have suspected a thirteen-year-old boy to have done the deed."

"Why didn't you say something? Dear, you know I wouldn't have told."

"It's been my secret, Agnus. A dirty discredit done by me hand. It was my pledge to not tell. Times come. Decades have past. And in this age I'm dying. I didn't want to take this to me grave. I wanted resolve."

"Then you've freed yourself, dear. Accept your peace."

"I've been waiting a long time to rid that from me. Over these years it's been chewing my mind." Logan expired breath. "You all vow to not speak this truth to outsiders? Some mysteries need to stay hushed in their own right. The truth about the crying house is one of those secrets. Folks knew what went on inside those walls, but they didn't know the validity of Aidan's fate. It's the people who'd once lived there which made a story. And it's the myths behind it that emit curiosity. A slight twist where the spirit of a murdered spouse comes back to kill her deranged husband. What could have made a better story? I wanted folks to believe Ciara came back and achieved her repayment."

"I won't tell a soul," Josie confirmed. "I respect you with my honor."

"That's all I ask, girl. That the three of you keep it to heart. Talk about it among yourselves if you like, but involve no outsiders."

CHAPTER FORTY-THREE ◆

That night Josie and Tristian stayed in their home for the first time in over a week. Days passed as their hearth finally returned to normal. Except for those usual settling sounds the dwelling made, the place had been peaceful.

Tristian returned to work while Josie, once more, got used to the life of a housewife.

One day they received a pleasant call from Dr. Kentworth pertaining news that Annalise would receive proper burying. The day of her funeral happen to mark the fiftieth anniversary of Aidan's burial.

Agnus and Dr. Kentworth showed up to support the O'Briens through that time of depressing sadness. Josie carried with her two bouquets of lilacs in arm, one for Annalise and the other for Ciara. The first she laid atop her daughter's headstone as it began to shower.

Agnus stated as she stared to the sky, "Those are her tears falling from heaven. They're weeps of joy she cries for you. It's Annalise's way of thanking you for putting her to rest."

Teardrops surpassed Josie's eyes. "We all have heaven's infant angel to guard us."

"And we're lucky to have such a keeper watching us the rest of our days." Agnus smiled.

Following the funeral everyone remained, but Father McKinney. Agnus led the O'Briens and Dr. Kentworth over to the O'Neills' graves. As they made way toward the headstones, they felt a frigid air encircling Aidan's mound. The unsettling freeze had brought an icy chill to their backs as they each shivered.

Tristian grilled, "Why's it so cold?"

"This soil Aidan's buried beneath is as gelid as he," explained Agnus. "If you notice, nothing grows here either. Unlike Ciara's resting place, this ground is soured. Her's is productive and brings life to the flowers."

"Has it always been this way?"

"Since he was put here. The ground seems to absorb his cold essence. Alike his bones beneath this space, it caused this soil to become frigid."

"Might it leave ever?" Dr. Kentworth raised question.

"Hopefully, dear. That's why I'm here."

Tristian made comment, "I presume this must be your most challenged intention?"

"Well, it's certainly something no amateur should aspire."

"It's no small engagement, Agnus. You ready for this?" Dr. Kentworth speculated.

"Conjuring a spirit can be dangerous. It opens a gateway that might allow other entities to crossover that aren't invited. One must be professional for magic such as this."

"You believe you harbor the authority to do this correctly?"

"It'll lie within my efficacy, doctor. In that, I believe I'm capable. I ask you all stand round now. Josette, behind the headstone. Dr. Kentworth, to my left. Tristian, to the right. Forming a circle, I'll stand before the grave. I'll sage each of you before I begin."

Agnus placed her cauldron atop Aidan's stone just as the sun embarked to set. She handed a lit candle to each person, then before them held a bundle of sage and repeated these words. "May you be cleansed, purified, and protected as you stand before this circle. Amen." Agnus lit a candle for herself, then acknowledged. "Is everyone ready?"

"I believe so," added Tristian.

"Everyone, stay within the circle. Do not my any means stride away. If you do, it'll cause us trouble." Agnus tossed the bundle of sage into her cauldron as it filled with smoke, then rose through air. Hovering above, it encircled their heads. "You're in a place of protection. Know nothing will harm you."

Agnus set a large white candle within the center of the grave, then proceeded to light it. She cast a handful of quartz to the ground, then threw a fistful of salt to purify the soil. Upon the dirt she carefully positioned an uncooked egg. "We gather within this sacred place to extract the expired from empty space. We knock upon the doors of naught to consult Aidan O'Neill, our only instruct. Be him now upon this site as he's cast from woeful plight."

The wind began to blow lightly, carrying afar the swirling smoke. Beyond the graveyard a distinctive squawk was heard abided by the arriving raven. She'd flown into the cemetery with the wafting air upon her back, swiftly approaching Aidan's grave. Her wings outstretched as she forward soared, bringing behind a veiling of fog.

The rain continued to pass softly upon the ground as it dismounted the heavens above.

Sailing down, the raven alighted Aidan's stone. Upon his marker she tapped the tomb in hope of waking him.

Agnus looked to the sky, watching crackles of lightning spread throughout the celestial sphere. Before all of them gathered a swirling haze within the center of Aidan's grave. Onward, a body took form and a person stepped forth.

With an inspection of bewilderment upon him, Aidan regarded each face that befell him. It was moments later when his eyes scoped upon Agnus that he peered even more through confusion. "Agnus? Agnus, is that you there?" he wondered aloud.

"Yes, dear, it's me."

"But you've aged."

"Time's come and gone. And, dear, as you see, it is I who's grown old."

"I don't understand this." He looked around. "Where's Ciara? How's been my loving wife?"

Agnus looked upon her grave with sadness and bowed her head. Aidan followed with his eyes. It was then he read the name among the tomb. Ciara Ann O'Neill. Beloved wife and friend to all. "No. That can't be." Aidan walked to his wife's grave and fell to his knees. From his mouth surpassed a wrenching cry as he laid his hand upon her stone. "My fairest of love," he wailed. "Gone now from me. Two souls divided by realms, alone. A jewel so delicate lying apart my embrace. It is here which I stand bearing loss and ache." Aidan wiped tears from his eyes as he looked to the headstone adjacent his wife's. With disbelief he read his name and began to sob harder. "What occurred to us?" He turned to Agnus and begged her to tell. "What tragedies befell and drove us to this?"

"It'd been the night you passed the cemetery near Kinley's hill. It'd been the happenings thereafter which led you to this."

Aidan thought deeply. "I'd been attacked. The monster had been a beast."

"And possessing you, it then drove you to madness."

"I don't recall a thing beyond the next day."

Agnus explained, "It'd been because it'd taken over. Your body served as host. Once within, it'd shunned you aside. You died and not known it. It'd been the phouka which lived your life thereon, changing you into something horrible. It'd battered Ciara on many occasions."

"No," Aidan cried. "I'd never have harmed her. Why did this thing?"

"Seems it might have been ruled by its evil. But I couldn't really say for certain, dear."

"Had that foul thing killed my wife?"

"Ciara had been diagnosed with a brain tumor not long after the change."

Aidan broke. "And I wasn't there to help her."

"Her head hit a dresser during a fight. The impact caused its rupture and spread. Eventually she passed later that night. It'd been the ninth of July 1900."

Aidan fought his tears, then asked, "And what became of me in that time?"

"You'd been murdered the day of Ciara's funeral."

"Murdered?" Aidan phrased. "Someone killed me?"

"Not you, in fact, but your form," Agnus made clear.

"Why can't I remember anything beyond the next night?"

"You've been in limbo. Caught in a place between life and death. I've brought you forth that you may move on with your life and be free from the old."

"I do remember. I'd been in a place cold and dark. Within the middle of nowhere. I was lost and alone to myself. Confused with no direction. I searched endlessly to find my wife. And after a probing eternity, I've come upon her above cold soil."

"It's my intention, Aidan, to reunite you and your wife. To cross you over to where Ciara's waiting."

"Then please, Agnus, send me to where I belong."

The raven began to squawk, then took off through the air where it had flown in distance. It was then the fog became thicker, rolling astir amongst headstones. Within the purview the reverberation of a violin began to play.

Within the boneyard had been the faint image of a woman strolling the cemetery. She sauntered unaidedly with the mist astride her back while toting a small bundle within her arms. Gaining closer converge, she'd approached Mrs. O'Toole and the others.

Agnus soon recognized the woman as being Ciara. Her gown waft upon wind as though she'd been carried forth. Accessing closer she seemingly loomed atop air. And down by her blustering dress Nia strut beside her.

She glided toward Aidan where he'd taken her in hand, culling her readily into him. It was then they engaged their first kiss in a gangling fifty years.

Ciara peered to Tristian and Josie with a congenial smile, then spoke. "You don't need to worry. I'll take care of Annalise," she vowed, drawing back the blanket upon her arm. "I promise to love her as though she'd been my own."

Streams of tears showered Josie's face as she looked upon her daughter, alive and within the arms of her gentle guardian.

"She'll be safe with me." Ciara bowed her head. "I give you my oath. I'll commit to look after her until it's your time."

Tristian held his wife as they walked to Ciara and admired their child. Annalise opened her eyes, revealing her bright blue saucers as her parents approached. Josie stared into them as long as she could, knowing that it'd be the last time she'd see her button's face. "Hi, my baby. It's mummy, and beside me's your daddy."

Annalise beamed and cooed happily as she peered upon them.

"What a beautiful little angel you are. Yes, you. You're just so pretty."

Tristian wept. "We've done a good job." He smiled. "She looks just like you, Jos."

"Can I hold her?" she mildly asked as tears brimmed over.

"She's yours. You may cradle her. But I'm afraid, Josie, she'll have to venture home with us. You understand, she doesn't belong here?"

"I just want to say goodbye. It'll be an eternity again till I hold her."

Josie cherished Annalise in her arms while she and Tristian spent their last moments with her.

Agnus patted Josie's back. "She's a perfect little doll. Sweeter than sugar and finer than gold. With Ciara, she'll have a good suitor."

"I know. It's just so hard to let her go."

"At last you'll have these memories, child."

"And the most pleasant of ones they are."

Aside, Dr. Kentworth stood amazed to see the drastic changes in Aidan as was everyone else. He wasn't the malevolent entity all had come to know. He was sincere; a kind man with love in his heart and warmth in his soul.

Ciara gazed upon Agnus and spoke gently. "You've done a sincere gesture bringing my love back to me. And on better note, we may finally start our lives. I just had to thank you."

"Oh, you, sweet dear. I'm glad it's happened."

"I'm afraid we must go. Our time here is up. Aidan, Annalise, and I must journey home." Ciara took the O'Briens' daughter. "Until your time, we'll both be waiting."

Josie kissed Annalise's forehead and told her she loved her as did Tristian.

Everyone stood in a circle as the raven made its way back into the graveyard. Following, the ghostly carriage transporting the banshee proceeded. Flying aloft, it glided through misting rain with crackles of lightning firing the sky. Ahead of the carriage had been its loyal horses and servant candles mounting ground.

The rusted door creaked open, and from within a voice had spoken. "Come, my children. I must take you, for your greatest journey awaits."

Aidan looked upon his wife as he took her hand. "Let's go home, my love," he gently delivered while holding Nia within his arm.

"We have but one added voyage before our journey is final," Ciara told him.

"What be it, my darling?"

"It's Logan. Aidan, his time's about to expire. We must gather him so he may take his fare with us."

CHAPTER FORTY-FOUR ◆

The carriage soared through the darkened sky, then made one final trip to the nursing home in Roscrea. The banshee stopped her loyal horses outside the window of Logan's room where Ciara floated into the showering rain. She approached the building's side, then disappeared through the wall.

Logan had been resting soundly within his bed when a sudden attack of pain struck his heart. He awoke to the anguish consuming his chest and fought to catch his breath.

As his vision became clear, he could see Ciara sitting near him. She took his hand in hers and gently caressed his face. "I've come to free you of this pain."

"Ciara? Ciara?" he muttered lightly.

"Shh. Rest now, for I shall ease your pain." She cascaded her view upon Logan while consuming him with warmth. "Easy. Easy. Easy," she whispered like an angel. "No more pangs. No more. Breathe softly. Softly. Ever so softly."

Logan gazed into Ciara's eyes lovingly, then whispered to her lightly, "My heart has stopped hurting," he said with last breath through a smile.

"A better place awaits you, for I've come to take you home."

Within moments Logan stood before Ciara. He'd been restored of his youth, and not one ounce of pain riddled his body. A single tear ran from his eye as he looked upon his surrogate mother's face. "I've longed for this moment for what seemed an eternity. I've waited through endless years for your return, my mother, and now you've come."

"Circumstances have altered to the way it once was. You're now free from this worn, old body," Ciara said, looking upon the bed. "That empty vessel no longer needs your inhabitance. Take my hand and journey with me."

Logan took Ciara, and together they drifted through the wall, then out into the falling rain.

They floated steadily toward the carriage when Logan made a sudden refrain. Ciara gazed into his eyes and gently brushed upon his hand. "It's okay. You need not fear it," she softly spoke, while easing his doubt. Ciara motioned her head lightly, then she and Logan emerged through the door as it creaked shut behind them.

The horses pranced their hooves against the pavement, then took off through mist, carrying away the carriage as they flew into the sky.

The banshee sailed away with her coach, disappearing into the night and taking with her the phantom travelers to a place they'd belong.

THE END